Praise for the novels of Sherryl Woods

"Sherryl Woods writes emotionally satisfying novels about family, friendship and home. Truly feel-great reads!"
—#1 *New York Times* bestselling author Debbie Macomber

"During the course of this gripping, emotionally wrenching but satisfying tale, Woods deftly and realistically handles such issues as survival guilt, drug abuse as adolescent rebellion, and family dynamics when a vital member is suddenly gone."
—*Booklist* on *Flamingo Diner*

"Woods is a master heartstring puller."
—*Publishers Weekly* on *Seaview Inn*

"Once again, Woods, with such authenticity, weaves a tale of true love and the challenges that can knock up against that love."
—*RT Book Reviews* on *Beach Lane*

"Woods…is noted for appealing character-driven stories that are often infused with the flavor and fragrance of the South."
—*Library Journal*

"A reunion story punctuated by family drama, Woods's first novel in her new Ocean Breeze series is touching, tense and tantalizing."
—*RT Book Reviews* on *Sand Castle Bay*

"A whimsical, sweet scenario… The digressions have their own charm, and Woods never fails to come back to the romantic point."
—*Publishers Weekly* on *Sweet Tea at Sunrise*

SHERRYL WOODS

Wildflower Ridge

mira

Recycling programs for this product may not exist in your area.

ISBN-13: 978-0-7783-8806-7

Wildflower Ridge

Copyright © 2020 by Harlequin Books S.A.

Natural Born Lawman
First published in 1998. This edition published in 2020.
Copyright © 1998 by Sherryl Woods

The Unclaimed Baby
First published in 1999. This edition published in 2020.
Copyright © 1999 by Sherryl Woods

This edition published by arrangement with Harlequin Books S.A.

For questions and comments about the quality of this book, please contact us at CustomerService@Harlequin.com.

Mira
22 Adelaide St. West, 40th Floor
Toronto, Ontario M5H 4E3, Canada
www.Harlequin.com

Printed in Lithuania

MIX
Paper from responsible sources
FSC® C021394

This one is for all the readers who've embraced
my characters and stories through the years.
You've been such a blessing in my life
and I treasure the friendship you've offered.

CONTENTS

NATURAL BORN
LAWMAN

Chapter One

Patsy Longhorn held her fussy two-year-old son in her arms and tried to soothe him back to sleep. He was exhausted, feverish and hungry, had been for most of the day, and she was getting desperate. Driving nonstop with a cranky toddler was beginning to take its toll.

She hadn't intended to take another break yet. She'd wanted to put as much distance between herself and Oklahoma as she possibly could today, but she hadn't been able to ignore Billy's whimpers a second longer. She'd pulled into a rest stop and taken him out of his car seat, praying that holding him and rocking him a bit would accomplish what her pitiful repertoire of lullabies hadn't.

So far it wasn't working. Worse, he felt warmer, as if his fever had gone up a little more.

"Come on, sweetie, go to sleep. You'll feel better after you've had a little rest."

At least she prayed that was all it would take. She didn't have money left for medicine and a doctor at this point. Even juice was stretching her tight budget. She'd been giving him sips of cool water and praying that would do the trick.

Billy shifted restlessly, still whimpering, his dark, dark

eyes staring back at her, accusing her. Guilt, never far away, washed over her again.

Had she made a mistake leaving Will? Was she crazy to have walked out on her marriage? Walked out with only clothes for the baby and herself and a few hundred dollars from the checking account she had opened several months earlier and had kept secret from her husband?

Though she'd had every right, she hadn't touched a dime in their joint account for fear Will would accuse her of theft. With her name on the account the wild charge wouldn't stick, of course, but she hadn't wanted to give the police any excuses at all to chase after her. It was terrifying enough that Will was likely to go ballistic.

That, she reminded herself staunchly, was exactly the reason she had left. She'd had no choice. Will's temper was out of control. He never talked anymore. He shouted, he threw things. A vase had whizzed past her head, just a few nights ago, only inches from making contact. The violence in his eyes had terrified her. He hadn't hit her or their son yet, but she'd heard enough about abuse to know that it was coming. She wasn't going to stick around and wait for it, not when each scene was already escalating to a more dangerous level.

Nor was she going to waste time trying to convince Will to seek counseling. His pride and his very visible career would never allow him to admit he needed help. For once in her life, she was doing the smart thing. She was going to cut her losses before tragedy struck.

She hadn't been so smart when she'd impetuously moved to Oklahoma City and almost immediately begun an affair with Will Longhorn. Barely nineteen, she'd been so anxious to get away from home and her overly protective parents, to be on her own. The irony was that she'd spent hardly a minute truly on her own before becoming entangled with Will.

He had been her first boss, a twenty-six-year-old attorney in the town's top law firm with a dazzling career ahead of him. Everyone had said so. He was a Native American with the whole world spread out before him. There'd even been talk of a run for political office, first in Oklahoma, then for Congress. Will Longhorn had charisma. He was smart. He had unblemished integrity, as well, a rarity in politics.

And before too terribly long, he had a beautiful, blond-haired, all-American wife at his side and a baby on the way. The image had been set, the campaign posters all but printed.

At first Patsy had been thrilled to be a part of it all. She'd been caught up in every girl's dream. She had been so proud of her handsome husband, so in love with him.

But all too soon, behind the public displays of affection, behind the jovial smiles for the camera, there had been the private dissension. Even as he showcased his trophy wife and beautiful baby boy, privately Will seemed to resent both Patsy and their son. And because she had given up her job to be a stay-at-home wife and mom, she was totally dependent on Will for everything. It was what he'd wanted, but he'd thrown that back in her face a time or two, as well.

In general the abuse was subtle and mostly verbal, but it was signal enough to her that it was time to go. She might have married in haste, but she had no intention of paying for it for the rest of her life. And no one was going to harm her son. No one.

Protecting Billy became her first priority. Already in his young life, he had heard too much fighting, witnessed too many vicious arguments. If she and Will couldn't live together peacefully, if not lovingly, then it was time to go.

She had fled first to her parents, but Will had followed and the scene he'd caused had terrified all of them. He'd bashed the headlights on her car, dented the hood with a blow of his fists. He'd threatened her, accused her of trying to ruin his career, their future. He'd threatened her parents, blamed them for harboring his wife when she belonged at home with him. Her parents were just old-fashioned enough to agree that a wife's place was at her husband's side, no matter the circumstances. She had seen the unspoken agreement in their eyes, but still she had balked at leaving.

And then Will had sealed her fate. He had calmly vowed to take Billy away from her if she didn't agree to come home with him.

"You won't even get weekend visitations by the time I'm through. I can do it," he'd said with cool cruelty in his eyes. "You know I can."

She hadn't doubted it for an instant. She had gone with him simply to keep her baby and to get Will away from her frightened family.

Satisfied that he'd gotten his way, Will had promptly gone back on the campaign trail in the mayoral race that was to be the stepping-stone to his entire political future. And the low-key pattern of denigration had begun again—the sarcastic barbs, the ruthless demands, the never-ending criticism. She had taken it for six more humiliating months while she secretly made her plans. And all the while she watched Will, waiting for an explosion of temper that always came.

This time when she'd left, she had known that wherever she went, she was on her own. A local shelter had provided a safe harbor for a day or two. Then she had turned the car toward Texas, hoping that simply crossing the line into another state might offer her some protection. Too many cops, too many judges, too many politicians in Oklahoma owed favors to Will or to the partners in his law firm. Even though she'd worked there, if it came to a choice between her and Will, she had no doubt which of them would receive the partners' backing.

The memory of that violent explosion in front of her parents' home in full view of the neighbors had kept her on the run for a week now, trying to decide where it would be safe to settle down and begin an anonymous life. While in Oklahoma, she hadn't dared to stay even in a cheap motel for more than a good night's sleep.

As of today, her options were running out. Her pitiful savings were pretty much wiped out and she didn't dare phone her parents for help. For all she knew Will would have bugged their phone. It wasn't beyond him to use the law to his own advantage, especially when her second disappearance at the height of his first campaign for office was no doubt causing him a great deal of public embarrassment.

This time she was truly on her own, for the first time in her life, and the decisions she made were critical not only to her own future, but to the baby's. This was the ultimate test any woman could face. How she handled it would prove what she was made of. So far, she feared, she was falling pitifully short, but she was determined to pull it together. She might be almost out of money and be running low on ideas, but the one thing Patsy Gresham Longhorn had was gumption.

Billy whimpered, reminding her that she was going to have to come to a decision in a hurry. He needed food and, quite possibly, medical attention, though she was pretty sure the fever was little more than a summer cold.

With the two-year-old still cuddled in her arms, she tried awkwardly to unfold the road map she'd picked up at an earlier highway rest stop. Dallas was close, but was a big city the best choice? Wouldn't the police there be on the lookout for her, if Will had spread the word that she was missing?

A small town with more casual, less experienced law enforcement seemed a safer bet. If her logic was faulty, so be it. She felt more at ease with the thought of trying to make a home for herself and Billy someplace quiet and peaceful, someplace where they'd never heard of Will Longhorn. Her gut instincts had gotten her this far. She might as well trust them a little longer.

Staring at the choices on the map, all of them unfamiliar, she finally zeroed in on a tiny speck in the southwestern part of the state.

Los Piños. It was only a couple of hundred miles away. The name suggested forests of pine trees, which appealed to her. She craved the serenity such a setting suggested. It reminded her of the town where she'd grown up, the town she'd been in too much of a hurry to leave. Funny, what a difference a few agonizing years could make. She would have given almost anything to be able to go back there now. Since she couldn't, it would have to be Los Piños.

The decision made, she got back on the highway, then took the next exit and stopped at a minimart to buy milk and some cereal for the baby and a ready-made sandwich and soft drink for her. After filling the car with gas, she had ten dollars left, that and whatever change might be buried in the bottom of her purse and in Billy's diaper bag.

Despite the dire circumstances, Patsy felt almost upbeat as she drove into Los Piños a few hours later. She gazed around at the small downtown area with its quaint shops and family-owned restaurants. Though the buildings were old, everything was freshly painted and brightly lit. There was no mistaking that this was a town that took pride in itself. For a second she allowed herself to envision being a part of it, to imagine belonging. For a moment anyway, despair vanished. A feeling of contentment, mixed with a rare smidgen of hope, stole over her.

"We're here, Billy," she whispered to the now-sleeping boy. "We're home." Whatever it took, she would find a way to make that true.

She reached into the back seat and touched his cheek to seal the vow, then drew back in shock. He was burning up with fever. Hope gave way to panic and desperation.

"It'll be okay, baby," she promised. Whatever she had to do, it would be okay.

"Dadgumit, Justin, if you'd been the law around here when we were kids, I'd have spent my entire teens in jail," Harlan Patrick Adams grumbled, standing on a corner in downtown Los Piños just before dinnertime.

Justin grinned at his cousin. "Probably should have," he said.

"You were no better than me," Harlan Patrick reminded him. "If I belonged in a cell, you surely belonged right there next to me. What happened to you? When did you turn into a saint?"

"Hardly that," Justin said. "It's just that there's right and wrong. Somebody's got to see to it that folks remember the difference."

"Yeah, but that kid you just threatened with jail time threw a gum wrapper on the street. He didn't rob the savings and loan."

"Stop the little crime and you'll have less trouble with

the big stuff," Justin retorted. "That's what that mayor up in New York says and it's worked."

"It makes my blood run cold hearing you talk like that," Harlan Patrick taunted. "Guess that means you won't be playing poker with the rest of us out at White Pines later tonight, seeing as how gambling's illegal. Or were you thinking of coming along and arresting Grandpa Harlan when he rakes in his first pot?"

Justin scowled at him. "Very amusing. I'll be there and I intend to take every dime you lay on the table, cowboy."

Harlan Patrick didn't appear unduly worried. "Just as long as you leave that gun locked up at home," he said. "It makes me very nervous to know that you're carrying a weapon. You never could shoot worth a damn."

Justin grinned and fingered his holster. "I'm better now. Want to see?"

Harlan Patrick shuddered. "I think I'll pass, thanks." He gave Justin a mock salute. "Later, cousin."

"Yeah, later."

After all their years of troublemaking, Justin got a kick out of watching Harlan Patrick squirm at the sight of his uniform. No one in the family, least of all his own father, quite understood what had motivated him to become a sheriff's deputy. Jordan Adams had saved a spot in his oil company for Justin and he was mad as hell that his son had turned it down. Justin figured his brother-in-law would settle into the position just fine and sooner or later everyone would get over his defection.

Ironically, it was the family's very own values that had taken root in Justin's heart and made him long to keep the whole community of Los Piños as safe and secure as his family was on their various ranches. In the cutthroat oil business, his father had a straight-arrow reputation for honesty and never cutting corners. Grandpa Harlan's instinctive decency and tough-love brand of justice were as ingrained in Justin as breathing. Even as a kid, when he and Harlan Patrick had played cops and robbers, he'd always, *always* wanted to be the good guy. To him, becoming a cop was less a surprise than a destiny.

He stood on the sidewalk in the middle of town after his cousin had gone and surveyed his domain. Not a bit of trouble in sight. Not even a gum wrapper on the sidewalk, he observed, smiling at the memory of that kid's expression as he'd snatched up the offending piece of paper and thrown it into the litter basket on the corner. His actions had been accompanied by a stern lecture meant to put the fear of God into the boy.

Yep, Justin thought, all was right in his world. Maybe he could actually get fifteen minutes to himself to grab a burger at Dolan's before it closed for the night. He radioed Becky at the station.

"I'll be at Dolan's, if you need me. Want me to bring you anything back?"

"A hamburger, double fries and a milk shake," the very pregnant receptionist said with heartfelt longing.

Coached on her dietary restraints by her worried husband, Justin asked, "How about a tuna on rye and a diet soda?"

Becky sighed. "It'll do."

"Ten-four."

As he walked down the block, he spotted the dusty, expensive car with the out-of-state tags. Los Piños didn't get a lot of tourists. He glanced around for some sign of strangers, but everyone out in the heat of the day was familiar. He shrugged and walked on after making a mental note of the tag number.

Inside the drugstore, he glanced at the counter, expecting to see Harlan Patrick's sister, Sharon Lynn. His cousin had taken over a job once held by her mother and now was thinking of buying out Doc Dolan so he could finally retire. If she actually went through with it, she would hire a new pharmacist and continue running the rest of the store as she had been for the past couple of years, anyway.

"Hey, Sharon Lynn, you in here?" he called out, even as he dragged a notebook from his pocket and wrote down the Oklahoma tag number.

"Back here, Justin," she replied from the back of the drugstore. "I'll be with you in a sec."

He'd barely settled on a stool at the counter, when he heard what sounded like a whispered argument. His cop's instincts, already alerted by the out-of-state car, kicked in. Drawing his gun, he moved silently down the aisle in the direction of the voices.

At the end of the row of shelves, he spotted Sharon Lynn and another woman, her blond hair scooped up into a careless ponytail, damp tendrils curling and clinging to her neck. The desperate expression on the stranger's face spelled trouble.

She was talking so fast he couldn't make heads or tails of what she was saying, but he didn't waste time trying to figure it out. While she was distracted, he moved in beside her and laid a restraining hand on her shoulder. Though she was dressed in expensive, tasteful clothes, she was so thin he could feel her bones. At his touch, she jolted as if she'd been shot, her panicked eyes clashing with his. It all added up to the kind of vulnerability that could make a man lose sight of the job he was being paid to do.

Keeping her firmly in his grip, he glanced at Sharon Lynn. "Everything okay?"

The stranger's eyes pleaded with his cousin. Sharon Lynn touched her hand gently.

"It's okay. Justin's my cousin. He's not going to hurt you."

"That all depends," Justin said, contradicting her. "What happened?"

"I needed some children's Tylenol," the woman said in a voice barely above a whisper. "My son's sick."

Sharon Lynn sighed. "I caught her trying to slip them into her purse," she admitted with obvious reluctance.

Justin tried not to react to the tears that were welling up in the woman's eyes, turning them into huge pools of green light, like sunshine reflected in a pond surrounded by tall pines. She was little more than twenty, it seemed to him, and fragile as a bird. He had a feeling if she was shoplifting Tylenol, then she hadn't had much to spend on food lately, either. Just because her clothes were pricey didn't mean she wasn't truly down on her luck. At the thought of the sick child, his rock-solid value system shifted ever so slightly. He felt justice clashing with compassion. Because he had a sudden, uncharacteristic instinct to bend some rules, his next words came out more harshly than he'd intended.

"Where's the boy?" he demanded gruffly.

"In the car."

He fought to hold his temper in check. "You left the baby in the car by himself? As hot as it is out there today?" And why, he wondered, hadn't he spotted the kid if he'd been securely strapped into a car seat as he should have been? He hadn't even checked inside the car. Obviously he was slipping.

"He's okay. I left the windows open a little. He's sound asleep. Besides, I knew I'd only be gone a minute." She stared at him defiantly. "You don't have to tell me all the terrible things that could happen. Believe me, I know. I weighed every one of them and decided he'd be safer there than with me. I didn't want him to cry and draw attention to me." Her shoulders sagged. "It didn't matter. I really am no good at this."

"Get him," Justin said tightly. "Now."

The instant he released her, the woman scooted past him and out the door.

"She'll run," Sharon Lynn said, staring at him in astonishment.

"No, she won't," Justin said.

"How can you be so sure?"

He held up the package. "Not without medicine." He handed his cousin a ten-dollar bill. "Pay for them out of this, okay?"

Sharon Lynn gaped. "Are you all right?"

"Just take the damned money."

She grinned. "Yes, sir."

"And then fix a couple of milk shakes. I'll grab some juice for the baby."

"Uh-oh," Sharon Lynn said. "What did it, Justin? Those big green eyes or the tears?"

"Go to hell."

"You ought to be nicer to me," she taunted. "I can tell this story far and wide by morning. Grandpa Harlan will know every touching detail by the time you get there tonight for the poker game. Your life won't be worth living by the time they finish teasing you about letting a nasty, evil shoplifter off the hook just because she was beautiful."

"You know, Sharon Lynn, there are things about you that old Kyle Mason doesn't know about," he said grimly, referring to her fiancé. "That man's been dangling on the hook for the past fifty million years, it seems like, waiting for you to marry him. Could be I know just the way to cut him loose before the latest wedding date next month."

"You wouldn't dare," she breathed.

He could see her calculating the risks and twisted the knife a little more. "Wouldn't dare tell him that you were the party girl of your senior class at ole Los Piños High? Wouldn't dare mention that you landed in jail on your senior trip?" he taunted. "Try me."

"Kyle knows all that," she said airily. "He loves me, anyway. Besides, you know perfectly well what kind of party girl I was, all talk."

"So you say."

Her gaze shifted toward the front window. "If you ask me you'd do a whole lot better to be worrying about why your suspect appears to be about to pull out of the space in front and hightail it out of town." She shot him a smug look. "Just the way I predicted she would."

Justin looked up in time to see a car shoot backward into traffic amid a squeal of tires. As he'd expected, it was the fancy car with the out-of-state tags.

"Well, hell," he muttered, and took off running, the carton of juice he'd just grabbed still clutched in his hand.

"If you catch her, tell her I'm not pressing charges," Sharon Lynn shouted after him, laughing.

"If I catch her, I'm throwing her in jail," he vowed. "You give me a reason, even an itsy-bitsy reason, and you'll be in the cell right next to her."

Chapter Two

Patsy wasn't sure why she'd run. Obviously she hadn't wanted to be hauled off to jail, something that the sheriff's deputy had seemed perfectly capable of doing. But it was more than that. Fleeing had been instinctive, which told her quite a lot about the damage even a few days on the run had done to her normally assertive personality.

Seeing the judgment in the deputy's eyes, the disdain, ordinarily would have infuriated her enough to make her stand her ground. She was capable of holding her own in an argument, or at least she had been until living with Will had taught her that silence was often the only way to escape from escalating tensions.

One look at the deputy had told her that arguments would be wasted on him, too. There was an unyielding air about him, the kind of steadfast determination that would be great if he were on your side, not so terrific if he weren't.

She had been startled when he'd released her and sent her after Billy. Grateful for the unexpected opportunity to escape, she had seized it, not pausing to consider just how incensed the deputy might be by her actions.

Maybe the woman in the store could calm him down and

keep him from chasing after her, she thought hopefully. Patsy had seen the compassion in the woman's eyes, had known that she was only a hairsbreadth from getting both the medicine and her freedom when the man had turned up. Though she hated taking advantage of anyone's kindness, she had been relieved that Billy would have the medicine he needed. That was all that really mattered.

Now, not only did she not have anything to bring her son's fever down, but she was a criminal, with an attempted shoplifting charge pending if that deputy decided to pursue matters.

For all she knew there were kidnapping charges on file back in Oklahoma, too. Will was perfectly capable of doing something so despicable just to make a point to her, to prove that he was the one with all the power. What would turn up if the deputy happened to catch her tag number and run it through his computer? There was no telling.

She couldn't take any chances that he might find something damaging. She would just have to drive faster and more cleverly than she ever had before. Suiting her actions to her thoughts, she skidded onto the highway and headed north, back toward Dallas, after all. She would exit a few miles ahead, then take back roads to elude any pursuit.

Though her plight was increasingly desperate, she reminded herself that she still had a bank card with her. Though there was a risk that Will would use any transactions with it to track her, she would use it to get cash if there were no options left to her. She could get enough money to last a few more days, until she could find another town, maybe get a job and find a safe place for herself and Billy. It might even be smarter to abandon the car and fly to another state. If she used cash for the tickets, it would make

the job of tracking her more difficult. It was a huge country
and Will's reach surely couldn't extend to every corner of it.

When the car sputtered then chugged to a stop barely ten
miles outside of Los Piños, she realized that in her rush to
get away from the deputy, she'd made a terrible miscalcu-
lation. The blasted car was out of gas. It hardly mattered
that she had the credit card or a few dollars left in her purse.
She hadn't passed a gas station heading out of town. It was
impossible to know how far ahead the next one might be.

That was the only reason, she assured herself, that Justin whoever-he-was-lawman caught up with her. He found
her on the side of the road, cursing a blue streak about the
gas-guzzling car Will had insisted she have, and rocking
the fussy toddler in her arms. His reflective sunglasses
prevented her from getting a good look at his eyes, but his
I-told-you-so smile said it all. He'd never doubted for a moment that he'd catch up with her and haul her into custody.

"Get in," he ordered, gesturing toward the patrol car.

"You're arresting me?" she asked, as if it were the most
ridiculous notion she'd ever heard. Will had been a master
of haughty indignation and she had learned by example.

Their gazes clashed, hers defiant, his unreadable.

"No," he said finally with a heavy sigh. "I'm taking you
back into town. Unless you'd prefer to stand around here
and wait for someone else to come along and offer you a
lift. I'll tell you right now, though, that it's a very long way
to the next town and hardly anybody uses this particular
stretch of road."

Patsy had guessed as much. Not a single car had passed
by while she'd been standing beside the car, cursing her
lousy luck.

"Sooner or later…" she began, thinking anything would be
better than going someplace with this hard, no-nonsense man.

"Are you willing to take that chance? If your son's sick, this heat won't help."

Her resolve wavered. "But the car..."

"Isn't going anywhere," he said. "I'll have someone bring out some gas and drive it back into town."

"I could wait," she suggested hopefully.

"I don't think so."

"Then you are arresting me."

"Dammit, no. Like I said, I am just trying to get you and the baby out of this blazing heat."

"Oh."

He opened the door to the front seat, which reassured her slightly. If he were arresting her, surely she'd be locked securely in the back. He tossed the bottle of Tylenol over to her, then indicated the carton of juice on the seat. "I brought those along for your boy."

So he did have a heart, after all. Patsy swallowed hard against the tears that threatened. It was enough lure to get her inside. "Thank you."

He closed the door, then went around to the driver's side. When he was behind the wheel, he said, "There's a milk shake in the holder there. You look as if you could use it."

Patsy shook her head, unwilling to be too indebted to this man who so clearly—and justifiably—disapproved of her. "No, thanks."

He rolled his eyes at her deliberate contrariness. "Suit yourself."

The drive into town was made in uncomfortable silence. She waited for another explosion of temper or a stern lecture, but instead he glanced over at Billy, who was belted into the seat with her, no doubt a bending of the rules he was so fond of enforcing. He hadn't argued with her, though, or insisted she get his car seat and put him in the back.

"Is he okay? Are you sure you don't want to get him to a doctor?" he asked. "There's a hospital in Garden City. I could run you over to the emergency room there."

"No," she said in a rush. When he shot a sharp-eyed look at her, she explained, "He'll be fine, once his fever goes down. He's just tired and fussy. I think he's getting a bit of a cold."

"Okay, if you're sure."

"I am."

The same uneasy silence fell again. Billy squirmed in her lap. "Mama?"

"Yes, baby."

Billy stared back at her with fever-bright eyes, then looked over at the man behind the wheel. "Who's that?"

"He's a policeman. He's helping us."

"Nice 'liceman," Billy murmured approvingly and fell back asleep.

Patsy glanced up just in time to catch a fleeting smile at the corners of Justin's mouth.

"At least the boy knows when someone's on his side," he commented.

She regarded him doubtfully. "Are you on my side, Deputy…?"

"Adams," he supplied. "Justin Adams. And as long as you don't break any laws, yes." He gave her a sharp look. "So far you haven't, at least not technically."

"Just because I got caught."

"Be grateful that my cousin has a forgiving nature. She won't press charges."

"Is that the only reason you're letting me off so easy?"

"Yes," he said curtly.

Patsy studied him intently, then shook her head. Her opinion of the man had undergone several drastic shifts since he'd turned up with the juice and medicine. "I don't think so. I think that under that by-the-book exterior beats the heart of a genuinely nice guy."

She was almost convinced he was a man she could trust. Even after he'd caught her stealing, even after she'd fled, he had thought first of her sick child. She could see, though, that the compliment made him uncomfortable. Maybe the leniency didn't fit his own image of himself.

"What's wrong, Deputy? Afraid if word gets out, it'll ruin your reputation?" she asked, daring to tease him, hoping to catch another glimpse of that potentially devastating smile again.

"Something like that," he conceded, unsmiling.

Patsy felt an odd little shock of disappointment, then cursed herself. Was she so desperate for a friend that she was willing to trust this stranger who had the power to give her whereabouts away to her husband? He was clearly a man with a strong sense of right and wrong, a commitment to duty. He would be the worst possible choice for a friend. When it came to a choice between obligation and friendship, there would be no contest. He would choose obligation every time.

She withdrew into silence once again.

"Where are you two heading?" he asked eventually.

The question seemed innocuous enough, no more than casual conversation, except the man was a cop. Patsy hesitated.

He glanced her way and she cursed those reflective sunglasses that prevented her from getting a good look at his eyes.

"Don't you know?" he demanded. "What kind of mother leaves home with a sick baby if she doesn't have to?"

Her temper flared and she clutched Billy a little tighter. "He wasn't sick when we left home."

"When was that?"

"A few days ago," she conceded.

"And the baby's father?"

She'd known the question would come up sooner or later. She'd been praying for later, long enough to have manufactured a believable story. Forced to improvise quickly, she said only, "He's not around."

"I see," Justin said slowly, his expression thoughtful. "You know, if you don't have a place to go, Los Piños isn't a bad little town."

Startled by the suggestion, she stared. "You wouldn't object? Under the circumstances, I was sure you'd want us as far from your town as possible."

He glanced over at her. "You ever stolen anything before?"

"No."

"Why should I believe you?"

"Because it's the truth," she said fiercely. "If it hadn't been for Billy getting sick, I wouldn't have done it this time. I would have come here, found a place for us to stay, gotten a job. We're looking for a fresh start, Deputy Adams, not trouble and definitely not a handout."

Even from behind those damnable sunglasses, she could feel his penetrating gaze. It was enough to make a liar squirm. Patsy sat perfectly still and withstood it.

"What's your name?"

"Patsy Gresham," she said, resorting to her maiden name. If he checked the car tags, he'd know better, but if not, if luck was on her side, she could preserve the illusion for a little while at least.

He nodded. "Okay, then, Patsy Gresham. I suppose having you stick around won't be a problem. Just know I'll be keeping an eye on you."

She could just imagine. He'd probably spread the word from one end of town to the other that Patsy Gresham couldn't be trusted. What kind of life could she make for herself with a cloud of suspicion hanging over her head?

"I won't tell a soul about what happened today, if that's what's worrying you," he said, his expression softening as if he'd read her mind and wanted to reassure her. "You'll move into town with a clean slate."

"Why are you being so nice?"

Once more, the suggestion that he was anything other than a tough, by-the-book lawman seemed to make him uncomfortable. "Damned if I know," he said eventually. "Just don't make me regret it."

If Patsy had her way, not only wouldn't he regret it, he'd never set eyes on her again. Even in a town the size of Los Piños, it ought to be easy enough to disappear if she wanted to make it happen.

Then she took another long look at the man beside her. Of course, Justin Adams struck her as the kind of stubborn, determined man who could find whomever he set out to find. She'd just have to make darned sure he never had any reason to hunt for her.

Justin was losing it. He knew because there was no way in hell under normal circumstances he would have let a criminal off the way he was letting Patsy Gresham go free, despite what Sharon Lynn wanted.

What was it his cousin had asked? Was it the green eyes or the tears that did it? Neither, he had wanted to shout. Now he wasn't so sure.

Every time he glanced into the woman's sad, wary eyes,

he felt some subtle change deep inside him. He wanted to strangle whoever had brought such sorrow into her life. She was entirely too young to look so beaten. And yet there was a surprising strength and feistiness about her. She might be down, but she definitely wasn't out. He found such resilience admirable.

On the way back into town he'd reached a decision. Until he knew more, he wanted Patsy Gresham right where he could keep an eye on her. He could just imagine the kind of razzing he'd take for that. No one in his family would believe for an instant that his motives were altruistic. He could explain from now until every head of Adams cattle was counted that he was being cautious, trying to prevent a more serious crime from taking place, but they wouldn't buy it. Not once they got a look at Patsy, anyway. They'd blame it on his hormones and his good nature and nothing he could say would change their minds.

She was a beautiful woman, all right. Fragile and road weary as she was, there was a delicacy about her that brought a man's protective instincts surging to life. And her mouth, those luscious, sensual lips, well, it was the sort of mouth just made for kissing. Justin's gaze had been drawn to it again and again, wondering what those lips would taste like.

Right. Like he needed to get mixed up with a woman who might be an everyday, common thief. No, what he needed to do was to send Patsy Gresham packing, send her into some other jurisdiction where she'd be another lawman's problem.

The words had been on the tip of his tongue, too. He'd been ready to tell her that the second her car was brought back into town and filled with gas, courtesy of the deputy sheriff, he wanted her gone.

Instead, he'd encouraged her to stay. There were names a whole lot stronger than *fool* for the kind of man that made him. *Jerk* and *idiot* came to mind. It was also pretty clear which part of his anatomy had been doing his thinking.

"Do you have any money at all?" he asked, trying to stay focused.

"No," she admitted after a long hesitation. "At least I won't have any once I buy gas. But I'm willing to work for room and board. I just need a break, that's all. I don't want charity."

To his dismay, he realized what he was going to do the second he crossed into the town limits. A few minutes later he pulled to a stop in front of the house that belonged to his sister, Dani. She still operated her veterinary practice from one side of it, but the living quarters had been empty ever since her marriage. If he asked, Dani would agree in a heartbeat to let Patsy and the baby use the house.

But before taking Patsy Gresham and her baby inside, there were a few more questions he needed answered.

"That car of yours is pretty expensive," he said carefully, watching her intently. "Also, I'm no fashion expert, but I have enough female cousins with expensive taste to know quality when I see it."

Her chin tilted up a notch. "So?"

"The two things combined make me wonder why you appear to be in such dire straits."

"Haven't you heard? Appearances can be deceiving."

"Meaning that those things aren't expensive or meaning that you're not in dire straits? Maybe you didn't need to steal that Tylenol. Maybe you were just doing it for kicks. I've heard there are rich ladies who get their thrills that way."

Indignant color flared in her cheeks. "Of course not. You've seen for yourself. Billy is sick."

"And you don't have the money for the medicine."

"Right."

Her lower lip quivered and she looked as if she were about to cry. Justin really didn't want to deal with a flood of tears, but he had no choice.

"Hand me your purse," he said quietly.

She stared at him. "Why?"

"So I can see for myself what shape you're in financially."

She hugged the white leather bag almost as tightly as she clutched her son. "I don't think so."

"I'm ordering you to."

"And I'm telling you, you'll have to get a search warrant if you want to go poking through my things."

To his regret, she had a point. He had been hoping it wouldn't come to that, that she'd cooperate voluntarily.

"Look, if you'll just get my car back here and loan me the money for some food, I'll buy my own gas with the money I have left and be on my way. I can see that staying here isn't such a good idea. For all the pretty words, Officer, it's clear you don't really trust me."

"If you'd let me take a look in your purse, it would go a long way toward changing that," he cajoled.

"Not a chance," she said, her gaze clashing with his.

Justin debated the meaning of her resistance. She could just be a woman who knew her rights and intended to protect them. Or else she was hiding something. Maybe both. He was going to have to decide quickly whether it would be smarter to encourage her to leave town or to stay right here where he could keep an eye on her until he knew more.

He gambled on the latter. It was probably better that he not examine his motives too closely.

"Okay, come with me."

Her gaze narrowed suspiciously. "Where?"

"We're going to talk to my sister Dani about using the other half of this house. It's fully furnished and, other than crashing here occasionally after a late night with an injured animal, she doesn't use it."

There was no mistaking the quick survey she did of the white house with its neat lawn, nor the flaring of hope in her eyes. The house was small and tidy. Something told him it was nothing at all like what she was used to. He waited to see how she'd react.

"Do you really think she'd let me use it for a few days, just until I get on my feet?" she asked eagerly.

Her reaction went a long way toward reassuring him. "If I know Dani, she'll insist on it."

"Maybe you should go ask her first. It'll be easier for her to say no if I'm not standing there with Billy staring her in the face."

Justin grinned. "Which is precisely why I want you to come along. One look at you and the baby and she'll be running out to stock the refrigerator for you. Dani is a very soft touch when it comes to taking in strays. You'll see what I mean when you keep tripping over all the kittens underfoot."

"Kitty?" the boy echoed happily, coming awake again. "Where kitty?"

Justin reached down and took him from his mother's lap. The boy came to him eagerly. Justin grazed his cheek with his knuckles and noted that whatever fever he'd had seemed to have come down. "Inside, son. Want to see?"

His dark eyes regarded Justin somberly, but he nodded at once. "See kitties."

Justin started up the walk, leaving Patsy no choice but to follow.

"Hey, sis, you around here someplace?" Justin called out, striding straight through the crowded waiting room and into the back, where there was a cacophony of sound from the animals being boarded here while families went on summer vacations. A cat promptly wound between his legs, almost tripping him.

"Dani, dammit. Get these cats away from me."

His sister poked her head out of one of the tiny examining rooms, "Justin, why are you raising such a ruckus?" she demanded, then spotted Billy. "Oh, my, isn't he darling? Where'd you find him?"

Justin nodded over his shoulder. "He came with her."

His sister's gaze shifted at once to Patsy. "Ah, yes, I see," she murmured.

Justin regarded her suspiciously. "What does that mean?"

"It means Sharon Lynn mentioned you were hot on the trail of a woman and a baby."

"Sharon Lynn has a big mouth."

"I had to pry it out of her," Dani assured him. "After I'd heard about it from three other people."

Justin sighed. There were no secrets in Los Piños, not when it came to an Adams. "They need a place to stay."

"And you were thinking that they could use this place," she guessed.

He grinned sheepishly. "Well, you're never here. Maybe Patsy could look after the animals for you at night. I'm sure your husband would appreciate having you home all night long for a change."

"An interesting deal." She glanced at Patsy, who was hovering in the doorway. "How do you feel about it?"

Justin waited uneasily. There was no predicting how she would react. Patsy had been surprising him from the second they'd met. So far he'd seen no evidence of uppity, high society ways, but maybe she'd draw the line at caring for a bunch of sick animals. A part of him hoped she would.

In fact, she seemed about to argue, then she glanced his way and sighed. "I'd be grateful," she said with apparent sincerity. "And of course I'd be willing to look after the animals in return, at least until I can get a job and pay you rent."

"No need to worry about that," Dani replied. "We'll try it for a few days and see how it goes." She reached for Patsy's hand. "Come with me. I'll show you around."

Justin would have followed, but Billy patted his cheek. "Want to see kitties," he reminded Justin.

"So you shall," he promised, pausing in the kitchen where several cats were sprawled in patches of sunlight. He hunkered down so Billy could see. The boy's coal black eyes lit up.

"Kitties," he whispered with obvious satisfaction. "Nice kitty?"

Justin nodded and set the boy on his feet. "You can pet them."

Billy toddled to the closest one and bent down until he was practically nose to nose with it. "Kitty," he pronounced, and petted it gently on the head. The cat, used to the comings and goings of Dani's rambunctious stepsons, merely yawned widely and stretched before curling up again with its head resting on its paws.

Billy toddled on unsteady legs toward another and went through the same routine again. Not until he'd greeted every cat in the kitchen did he come back to Justin and hold out his arms to be picked up.

"Mama," he whispered, as if he'd just noticed she was missing. Tears began to well up in his eyes.

"It's okay, fella. Your mama's right here. We'll go find her, okay?"

A thumb went into his mouth and he nodded. "'Kay."

His mother might be all bristly caution, but Billy was so thoroughly trusting it made Justin's heart ache with unexpected longing. He'd never given much thought to marriage and kids. If he wanted to hold a baby, there were plenty to choose from in his family. If he wanted to be surrounded by laughter and love, he could invite himself to dinner at any number of homes.

There was something very different about holding a child that belonged to you, though. He'd seen it in the awed expressions of his cousins' husbands. Something told him that it might feel a whole lot like the sensation rushing over him now. And that, given how very little he knew about Patsy Gresham and her true circumstances, was a very dangerous reaction.

Chapter Three

Justin saw to it that Patsy Gresham and her baby were set-tled at Dani's. He made sure her car was filled with gas and parked out front. He even had the Italian restaurant down the block send over dinner.

And then he washed his hands of the entire situation. He'd done his good deed for the week. Maybe even for the whole year. He predicted if word got around that he'd not only let a shoplifter get away, but that he'd taken her under his wing, he'd never hear the end of it.

As it turned out, it didn't take long for word to get around. He was the butt of a fair bit of good-natured teas-ing from his uncles and cousins at the poker game that night at White Pines. Obviously Sharon Lynn had decided to spill the beans, after all. She must not have taken his threat to have a revealing talk with her fiancé all that seriously.

"Don't pay any attention to them, son," Grandpa Harlan advised, giving him a pat on the shoulder. "They've gotten so old now, they don't recall what it's like to be captivated by a pretty face."

"Except for me, of course," Harlan Patrick said. "I'm younger than Justin."

"And you've never been known to miss a pretty face," Justin retorted. "Is there a woman in this town you haven't chased after at one time or another?"

"Not since I met Laurie," Harlan Patrick said piously. "She'd poke my eyes out if she caught me looking at another woman."

"She just has you thinking she would," Grandpa Harlan corrected. "Laurie is the sweetest little gal you've ever brought around. She has a mighty nice voice, too."

"Yes, indeed," Justin agreed. "One of these days Laurie's going to run off to Nashville and leave Harlan Patrick pining away back here."

His cousin scowled at him. The remark had cut a little too close to Harlan Patrick's greatest fear and Justin knew it.

"How'd we get on my love life, anyway?" Harlan Patrick grumbled. "We were talking about you and the shoplifter."

"Don't call her that," Justin said harshly.

"Why not? Isn't that what you and Sharon Lynn caught her doing?"

"She was desperate," he countered defensively. "Besides, unless a person's tried and convicted, you shouldn't go throwing names around. She could sue you for slander."

"And probably hire my wife to do it," Grandpa Harlan warned. "Janet would just love to get her teeth into a case like that. She hates being retired from her law practice. One of these days she's going to stir up a mess of trouble, just so she can get herself into the thick of it."

"From what I've seen over the years, Daddy, you're all the trouble Janet can cope with," Justin's uncle Cody said.

Grandpa Harlan scowled. "Watch your tongue, boy. I'm not too old to throw you out of here. Maybe I'll cut you out of the will while I'm at it. White Pines can skip right past you and go straight to Harlan Patrick."

Cody took the good-humored teasing in stride. "Daddy, you've been threatening to take this ranch from me since I can remember. One of these days I'm going to call you on it. I'll hire Janet to contest the will."

"Can't do it," Grandpa Harlan said triumphantly. "It'd be a conflict of interest."

"Is anybody actually going to play poker tonight?" Justin inquired with a wistful glance at the hand he was holding. "I'm feeling lucky."

Harlan Patrick shot him a knowing look. "I'll just bet you are." He tossed some money into the pot. "Okay, let's see those cards you're so proud of."

"Oh, shut up," Justin muttered, and slapped three aces on the table to take the pot from his mouthy cousin.

From that moment on, he tolerated the jokes and proceeded to whip their tails. He walked away from the poker table a good deal richer than he had been when he sat down.

What troubled him, though, was the fact that his first instinct was to give some of his winnings to Patsy Gresham to make sure she got by until she could find a real job.

Obviously he was turning soft, which was why half a dozen people got tickets for minor traffic violations before he stopped for breakfast the next morning.

When he saw who was about to start serving up eggs behind the counter at Dolan's, he wished he'd stayed on the street and given out another dozen citations.

Patsy rose at the crack of dawn, still unable to believe her luck. The tiny house Justin had arranged for her to use was perfect for her and Billy. The furnishings were old, but cheerful with all the chintz upholstery. The rooms were bright and airy.

"I could be happy here," she thought as she stretched and pulled on her robe. It was Dani's doing, of course, and not her own, but the house felt like a home. It wasn't as lavish as the one Will had insisted on buying, but it had a warmth and charm that the house in Oklahoma had lacked no matter how hard she'd tried to turn it into a home.

She checked on Billy, then went into the kitchen where she found cereal, milk and bread, courtesy of Dani, along with a note. "Make yourselves at home. We'll talk later about what you can do to help with the animals. Dani."

A nice woman, she concluded. She'd liked her instantly the day before, just as she'd been drawn to Sharon Lynn at the drugstore. It had been a long time since she'd had girl-friends. Will hadn't encouraged her to have any life at all outside of caring for him and Billy.

Maybe these two women could become real friends in time, she thought wistfully. Maybe there would come a time when she'd be able to confide the truth about her circumstances to them, instead of living this lie. Maybe she could tell them about the fear that had been gnawing at her ever since she'd discovered her husband's violent side.

First, though, she had to make amends to one of them. As soon as she got Billy up and dressed, she postponed breakfast and headed toward the drugstore, determined to get the apology over with. They were there as soon as the doors opened. Relieved that there was no one else around, Patsy faced Sharon Lynn uncertainly.

"I came to apologize and to thank you for not pressing charges," she said. "I would never have done it, not in a million years, if I hadn't been so worried about Billy."

"I know," Sharon Lynn said, and sounded as if she meant

it. She also sounded as if that were the last word she intended to say on the subject. "How about some coffee? I could fix some cereal for Billy, if you like."

Could it possibly be that easy? Patsy thought in wonder. Still chagrined by her uncharacteristic behavior the day before, Patsy started to refuse, but Sharon Lynn was already pouring the coffee and dumping cereal into a bowl.

"Dry or with milk?" she asked, taking the decision out of Patsy's hands.

"Dry for Billy," Patsy said. "He can eat it with his fingers. Otherwise there's no telling where he's likely to fling it with a spoon."

Sharon Lynn set the bowl on the counter in front of Billy, then grinned as he grabbed a fistful and shoved it into his mouth.

"His table manners leave something to be desired," Patsy apologized ruefully.

"How old is he?"

"He just turned two."

"Then he's got a few years before people start holding that against him. Besides, once you've been to a family dinner at our place, missile strikes would probably seem tame. There are a lot of kids. We've all been brought up to have endless patience. My grandfather Harlan Adams would rather have the chaos than a clean house any day."

Patsy grinned. "Maybe he can say that because he's not the one who has to clean it up."

"Oh, I've seen him on his hands and knees chasing after cornflakes and toys a time or two. Of course, he's in his eighties now and he's not as agile as he once was, but he set a good enough example for his sons that they're pretty decent housekeepers if the need arises. They all married women who see to it the need arises every now and then, just to keep them humble."

"It must be wonderful to have so much family," Patsy said, unable to hide the wistful note in her voice.

"Your own is small?"

"Just me and my parents."

"And you couldn't go to them for help when things got tough for you and the baby?" Sharon Lynn asked.

Patsy shook her head. "No, not this time," she said, unable to meet the other woman's gaze for fear all the tears she'd been bottling up would come pouring out.

"I see." Sharon Lynn's expression softened. "I hear Justin arranged for you to stay at Dani's."

Patsy knew enough about small towns not to be surprised that news had traveled so quickly, especially when it involved family members. "For the time being, anyway."

Sharon Lynn seemed startled by her reply. "Why on earth wouldn't you go on staying there? It's a great house. It's small, but surely it's big enough for just you and Billy."

"Of course it is, and I'm truly grateful to her for letting us move in on such short notice." Patsy couldn't say that she was afraid she might have to move on, that her husband would discover her whereabouts and come after her. Instead, she said only, "But I need a job, and someone to look after Billy. I haven't even had time to check the want ads yet to see if there are any openings here. I can't stay in Los Piños indefinitely without work."

"Then you have work," Sharon Lynn said with no hesitation at all.

Patsy stared at her. "What?"

"You can work right here. I can use the help. The lunch counter's busier than ever and so's the pharmacy. The pharmacist can't keep up with prescriptions and all the gift sales we're making now that I've expanded that section."

She smiled persuasively. "So, what do you think? Want to give it a try? I can pay you a halfway decent salary and you'll get tips when you work the counter. I know Dani's not going to charge an arm and a leg for the house. No one was using it, anyway. And you'll be able to eat here, so you won't have grocery expenses."

It was more than Patsy had ever dreamed of when she'd walked through the door a few minutes earlier. Though she'd trained as a secretary, she'd known she wouldn't be able to find work in that field, not without being able to give references, and she surely couldn't list Will's firm on her résumé. This job was ideal. She didn't have to think twice about it. "I'll take it," she said at once.

"You're sure?" Sharon Lynn asked. "I have to warn you, it gets crazy in here sometimes and I'm going off on a one-week honeymoon at the end of the month. You'll be on your own. Can you cook?"

"If you'll go over the menu with me, I can do it," Patsy assured her. She'd worked in a place just like this back home one summer while she was taking her secretarial training. This job would be a breeze. "And I've run a cash register before. I'm sure I'll pick up the rest in no time."

"You don't have to sell me. I made the offer, remember?"

"I wouldn't want you to regret it."

"I won't," Sharon Lynn said with confidence. "When can you start?"

"What about now?" She glanced over at Billy, who was happily mashing cereal on the counter. "Unless you'd rather I make arrangements for him so he's not in the way."

"He's not in the way. If he gets fussy, you can leave and

take him home for a nap. Someone over at Dani's will keep an eye on him for you."

Patsy grinned at her enthusiasm and quick solutions to every possible problem Patsy suggested. "You must be really desperate for help."

"Not today, but given the daze I'm in just thinking about everything that's left to do for the wedding, desperation is not far off." Sharon Lynn grinned ruefully and admitted, "And there are any number of people in town who'll be relieved that someone else is going to help with the cooking in here. I've been a bit absentminded lately. It's given the menu some interesting and not entirely successful twists."

Patsy grinned back at her as she climbed off the stool and started to join Sharon Lynn behind the counter. "What do you want me to do first?"

"Sit back down and eat some breakfast." Before Patsy could protest, Sharon Lynn added, "That's not charity. It's just common sense. You'll be dead on your feet in no time unless you've eaten something. I think scrambled eggs, bacon, hash browns and toast ought to do it," she decided, going to work before Patsy could argue.

Everyone she'd met so far had been so kind Patsy couldn't quite believe her luck. Suddenly she regarded Sharon Lynn suspiciously. "Justin didn't put you up to this, did he?"

"Justin didn't put her up to what?" the very man in question inquired as he came through the door along with a gust of hot, dry air.

"Hiring me," Patsy explained, meeting his gaze for an instant.

For once, with his sunglasses tucked in his pocket, Justin's eyes were visible. She could read the shock registered there. Even though she knew it was justified, it hurt nonetheless.

"Really?" he asked, regarding his cousin warily. "Sharon Lynn, could we talk for a minute?" With a glance in Patsy's direction, he added pointedly, "In the back."

"No, we cannot," Sharon Lynn told him. "I'm busy." She flipped Patsy's eggs on the grill, reached for the toast and buttered it, then placed it all on a plate and slid it in front of Patsy. "Enjoy. The crowd will start coming in in about ten minutes."

Patsy nodded. "I'll be finished."

Justin slid onto the stool next to her. She wondered if he meant to intimidate her, but he merely advised, "If you gulp that down, you'll have indigestion. Sharon Lynn doesn't go light on the grease."

She glanced at him. "Worried about my health all of a sudden?"

"Obviously she's expecting to get a full day's work out of you. I don't want to see her cheated." He regarded her meaningfully.

So, there it was, Patsy thought wearily. The trust he'd promised the day before had barely lasted overnight. She leveled a look straight at him and kept it steady. "I thought you were going to give me an honest chance to start over."

He sighed. "You're right," he conceded grudgingly. "I was."

"Has something changed since last night?"

"He probably had to answer a lot of questions out at White Pines last night at the family poker game," Sharon Lynn chimed in cheerfully. "It's made him edgy."

"I am not edgy," he retorted. "I'm just trying to look out for you. Obviously I'm wasting my time. You think you know it all."

Sharon Lynn grinned at him. "When it comes to Patsy, yes, I do think my judgment's better than yours. After all, I am the one who predicted..."

Justin scowled. "Never mind."

Patsy stared at the two of them, trying to guess what the unspoken hints were all about. "Predicted what?"

"Nothing," Sharon Lynn soothed. "Justin's just the family worrywart. Why don't you get back here and fix him some scrambled eggs and a couple of pancakes? I'll pour him some nice strong black coffee. That ought to improve his mood."

To Patsy's surprise, he didn't argue. Instead he turned his attention to Billy.

"So, young man, what are you up to over there? Has any of that cereal actually made it into your mouth?"

Billy promptly abandoned the mess he was making and reached for Justin. "Up?" he pleaded.

Patsy envisioned all the goo on Billy's hands being transferred to Justin's starched uniform shirt and winced. "No, baby. I don't think so."

To her amazement, Justin ignored her and accommodated Billy. He scooped him up, apparently oblivious to the mess the baby was bound to make of his clothes. Apparently a whole lot more bonding than she'd been aware of had gone on the day before.

"He's fine where he is. You don't have to do that," she told Justin, eyeing him nervously as Billy patted his cheeks with sticky hands.

"It's not a problem."

"But—"

"I said it's not a problem."

And that, she concluded, was that.

After that, she didn't have time to worry about it. As Sharon Lynn had predicted, the counter began to fill up with regulars eager for a little breakfast and a lot of chitchat over the latest local gossip. Several speculative looks were cast her way. Ignoring them and the gentle banter that ensued, she concentrated on filling orders as quickly as Sharon Lynn passed them to her.

Even though she never once looked back, she was aware of the precise instant that Justin Adams slid off his stool and left. The prickling sensation at the back of her neck vanished and the tension in her shoulders eased.

When the crowd began to thin out, Sharon Lynn introduced her to the handful of remaining customers. At the sight of a burly man in uniform, her nerves jumped.

"This is the sheriff, Tate Owens, Justin's boss. Don't mind the scowl. He looks less fierce once he's had a couple of doughnuts."

"I wish," the man said, casting a longing gaze toward the already depleted display on the counter. "Juice and dry toast for me today. The doc put me on a diet yesterday. He's grumbling about my cholesterol again."

"How about some oatmeal?" Sharon Lynn suggested.

"Not without cream and lots of brown sugar," he lamented. "No, I'll stick with the toast today and some of that blackberry jam, if you have it."

"I keep it back here just for you," Sharon Lynn said.

Patsy noted where Sharon Lynn kept it, so she could supply it on request if she was here alone. She was about to gather up Billy and slip into the back room for a break, when the sheriff spoke directly to her.

"You're new in town."

She met his gaze evenly, fighting the sick sensation in the pit of her stomach. "Yes. My son and I got here yesterday."

"Didn't take you long to find work," he observed.

"No. Sharon Lynn's been very kind."

He nodded. "Welcome to Los Piños, then. You run into any problems, let me know."

The offer was made with such absolute sincerity that for a

fleeting instant Patsy had the absurd desire to unburden herself to this man. Who knew, maybe she'd be lucky one more time and he would see what she'd been up against. Maybe he could protect her from Will. She sighed with regret. She couldn't take a chance that it would go the other way.

Instead, she smiled noncommittally. "Thanks. I'll remember that."

"You're from Oklahoma," he noted conversationally. "What part?"

She named her old hometown, rather than Oklahoma City. "I doubt you've ever heard of it. It's tiny, not even as big as Los Piños."

"Must be," he said, his expression thoughtful. "I grew up around Oklahoma City myself and I never heard of it. Of course, my memory's not what it used to be, either. Haven't been home in years, not since my folks died about ten years back."

When he'd mentioned Oklahoma City, Patsy's heart had slammed against her ribs. It hadn't eased back into a normal rhythm until he'd said how long it had been since he'd been back.

Ten years ago Will had been just starting law school. His face—and hers—hadn't been on the front pages of the local papers until much more recently. She doubted that a mayor's race in Oklahoma City would make the local paper here in Los Piños.

"Do you still stay in touch with old friends?" she asked carefully.

"Nope. My friends and family are here now. Haven't heard from a soul back that way. Skipped my high school reunions. Couldn't think of what I'd have to say to people I hadn't seen in years."

"Too bad," she said, though the relief that washed over

her said just the opposite. "It's always sad when we lose touch with old friends."

"What about you? You still have family there?"

"Some," she said.

Thankfully, he let it go at that. Much more poking and prodding, no matter how innocently intended, and she was pretty sure she would have cracked. She just wasn't cut out for this much deception. It was a habit that had started when she and Will were first dating and trying to keep it a secret from their co-workers. She'd been lousy at it then, too. Their relationship had been discovered in no time, which was one reason they'd married in such haste. Will had wanted to quiet the gossip.

Tate Owens drew her attention again. "We'll have to compare notes sometime. It's been my experience that it's a mighty small world. Maybe we'll know some folks in common."

"I doubt that," she said. "Like I said, the town where I grew up was really small."

He nodded. "Okay. Well, I'd better get out of here. If I don't stay on my toes, Justin's going to steal my job right out from under me."

"As if he would ever try," Sharon Lynn chided. "You were his mentor, Tate. And everybody knows you're the best sheriff ever. You'll stay in the job as long as you want it. Besides, something tells me half the town is going to be mad as heck at him this morning."

Tate Owens moaned. "What's he done now?" he asked in a resigned tone.

"Last time I saw him, he was handing out parking tickets all up and down Main Street."

"Damn, I thought I'd broke him of that. The town doesn't

need the money, and I don't need the aggravation." He slapped his Stetson on his head and walked out the door.

Patsy watched him go, then turned to Sharon Lynn. "What's with the parking tickets?"

"Tate tends to ignore minor infractions like that. He thought the parking meters were a nuisance in the first place. Justin goes crazy every once in a while and starts handing out tickets. Tate spends the rest of the day soothing ruffled feathers."

Patsy shook her head. "I don't get it. If the people are breaking the law, shouldn't they get tickets?"

"Technically, yes. And Justin is a by-the-book kind of man, especially after he's done something that makes him worry whether he's listening too much to his heart," she said with a look in Patsy's direction.

"Am I supposed to understand that?"

"You're here, aren't you?"

"Yes," she said, still confused.

"And not in a jail cell."

"Oh."

Sharon Lynn grinned. "Oh, indeed. Bottom line, it's my guess that you're the one behind today's rampage with the parking tickets."

Patsy would have chuckled if she hadn't been able to imagine what everyone in town would have to say if they knew to blame her.

Sharon Lynn's expression turned thoughtful. "Something tells me you're going to be good for him," she said quietly.

"Me? I don't think so," Patsy said at once. If Justin Adams knew the truth about her, he probably wouldn't even blink before tossing her in that jail cell and throwing away the key.

Chapter Four

While Justin had been thoroughly disconcerted by the sight of Patsy Gresham working at Sharon Lynn's that morning, he told himself he'd merely found it troubling that she was becoming so intimately entwined with his family.

What really worried him more, was that quick little shiver of awareness he'd felt when he spotted her. He knew his hormones well enough to recognize a man-woman thing when he felt it, and it was the very last reaction he ought to be having to the woman, not with all those legitimate suspicions he couldn't quite dismiss.

Except for a minor fender bender in midafternoon, the rest of the day had been uneventful. It had taken all of his willpower to keep from wandering into Dolan's a few more times to make sure Patsy's hand wasn't in the till or anywhere else it didn't belong. His conscience had reminded him that he'd promised her an honest chance.

By nightfall, though, he couldn't battle his desire to see how she'd fared. The fact that he chose to get his answers from her, rather than from Sharon Lynn, meant nothing, he assured himself. After all, Patsy was right here in town, while Sharon Lynn was all the way out at the ranch. It was pure logic and convenience that sent him to her doorstep.

Yeah, right.

Dusk was falling by the time he'd showered and changed into jeans and a T-shirt. He strolled up the walkway at Dani's with his mind on the excuse he was going to have to come up with for his visit.

He was about to knock on the front door, when he heard chaos erupt in the veterinary clinic. Muttering under his breath about the fact that he'd left his gun at home, he raced around to the clinic entrance and pounded on the door. It was opened by a frazzled Patsy, backed up by a snarling dog that looked perfectly capable of tearing both of them limb from limb.

"Oh, it's you," she said, and turned back toward the dog, which was straining on its leash. "Punk, hush up. You'll get your food when it's your turn."

Her total lack of concern about the huge dog's barking brought a smile to Justin's lips. He leaned back against the doorway and admired the methodical way she was moving from pen to pen.

"If I were you, I'd take care of Punk first before he decides to turn you into dinner," he observed casually.

She shot him a defiant look that would have been wasted on Punk. "And let him win? I don't think so. He's nothing but a big bully. He'll wait his turn."

Even though she spoke with conviction, he noticed that she skirted carefully just out of the huge dog's reach as she worked. He also noticed that her hands were trembling as she scooped food into the other animals' dishes. Obviously this was some sort of test she was putting herself through. Was it possible that Punk represented another bully in Patsy's life? Perhaps one she hadn't stood up against? Justin couldn't help wondering about all the gaps in her background he hadn't been able to fill in.

"What are you doing here?" she asked as she kept on working.

"I just thought I'd stop by to see how your first day on the job at Dolan's had gone."

A smile broke across her face. "It went great. Everyone is really nice. They were very patient."

"It didn't seem to me they needed much patience. You were a whiz at the grill when I was there, better than Sharon Lynn, in fact. Have you done that sort of work before?"

"Way back," she admitted.

He grinned. "It couldn't have been that long ago. You can't be more than what? Maybe nineteen?"

"Twenty-three, actually." She turned a knowing look on him. "Probing for information again, Deputy?"

He shook his head. "Just making conversation."

"If you don't have anything better to do, maybe you could take Punk for a walk. He could use the exercise."

Justin regarded the dog warily. "You have to take him for a walk? Is Dani crazy?"

She grinned at him. "Don't tell me you're scared of a little ole dog."

"That dog is bigger than I am. He does not have a friendly demeanor."

"He still needs to be walked."

Justin sighed. He knew perfectly well he couldn't go off and leave her to handle the beast. When they found itsy-bitsy pieces of her the next morning, he'd never forgive himself.

"I'll walk him," he agreed grudgingly, "if you'll get Billy and come with me. We'll stop for ice cream."

He could read the temptation in her eyes. How long had it been since she'd had such a simple pleasure? he wondered.

How long since her son had been given any kind of treat at all? With money scarce, he doubted there had been many. Patsy struck him as a very practical sort of woman who would put the basics first.

"Where?" she asked cautiously. "Dolan's is closed and I haven't seen any other places for ice cream around town."

He grinned. "But I know the owner at Dolan's and I have a spare key for emergencies."

"Somehow I doubt this qualifies as an emergency."

"True," he agreed. "Actually, though, I wasn't thinking of Dolan's. I just bought a half gallon of rocky road and some cones. I figured we could stop by my place. It's only a few blocks from here."

That all-too-familiar wary expression clouded her eyes. "I don't know."

"Is Billy asleep?"

"No. He's surrounded by kitties and glued to a video Dani left for him. It's one of his favorites. I doubt we'll be able to pry him away from the TV."

"Sure we can. Besides he should get out and get some fresh air, too. A walk will be good for all of us."

"Obviously you haven't done much walking with a two-year-old. One of us will be carrying him before we get home."

"I can carry him."

"And control Punk?"

"That, too. Consider it a challenge."

Her eyes sparkled at that. It appeared he'd finally made the offer too tempting to resist.

"In that case, I'll get Billy. You're in charge of Punk."

He eyed the beast and wondered if it was too late to reconsider. "Okay," he said, approaching the dog cautiously. "Come on, boy. Let's go for a walk."

Apparently that was the magic word. The dog began

pulling at his restraint and barking joyously. As Justin neared, Punk jumped up and put both paws on Justin's shoulders and began trying to lick him to death. Justin managed to pull back just enough to glance at Patsy, who was grinning from ear to ear.

"You knew, didn't you?"

"Dani did mention he really, really liked to walk."

"And that he was a pussycat underneath all that snarling?" he questioned.

"That, too, but I wasn't sure I could believe her on that point."

"So I was the human guinea pig?"

"Something like that."

Justin frowned at her as the dog slobbered all down the front of him. "You'll pay for this, darlin'. I guarantee it."

Even in the face of his threat, she chuckled. "Sorry. I can't help it. You look so…"

"So what?"

"Surprised," she suggested. "Indignant."

"Wait till you see me when I'm flat-out furious," he warned.

Her grin never faltered. "You're forgetting something, Deputy. I've been there, done that."

Justin paused. So she had. And surprisingly, despite the wariness he'd read in her eyes, despite a momentary panic, she hadn't run for cover. Something told him, though, that they might both be better off if she had. There were secrets with this woman, secrets and lies. He didn't doubt it for an instant. When the truth finally came out, which of them was going to be the one most hurt by it?

Every instinct she possessed told Patsy to avoid Justin Adams and yet, when he'd proposed helping her to walk that huge dog and getting ice cream, she hadn't been able to resist. For Billy's sake, she reassured herself. It had been a long time since Billy had an innocent outing, an even longer time since he'd had one with an adult male who actually seemed to enjoy his company.

Will hadn't been the kind of father who carted a messy child off for ice cream unless there was a photo opportunity in it for him. Then the ice cream had been little more than a prop and Billy had been handed back to her the instant the cameras were out of range.

In the living quarters beside the clinic, she'd had only to mention ice cream and Billy had toddled toward her with his arms upstretched.

"Go," he pleaded, the video forgotten. "Go now."

"We'll go now, but you have to walk. I'm not going to carry you, okay?"

"'Kay," he agreed, his head bobbing. "Big boy."

She grinned at him. "Yes, you are my big boy." And the treasure of her life. Everything she was doing, the risk she was taking, starting over in a new place, all of it was for him. She wouldn't have been able to bear it if he'd been injured—even accidentally—in the cross fire between her and Will.

Justin stuck his head into the room. "All set?"

At the sight of him, Billy ran straight toward him on unsteady legs. "Hi, ya."

"Hi, yourself."

"We go for ice cream," Billy announced.

"I know."

"You, too?"

"Yep, me, too."

"Mama, Justin go, too."

"That's right, baby."

Billy raced for the clinic and passed Punk as if he weren't even there. "Le's go, Mama."

"I'm coming," she assured him. She glanced at Justin. "Are you bringing Punk?"

"Do I have a choice?" he muttered as the dog leaped on him and licked his face. "Down, you beast."

The look of stunned amazement on his face when Punk dutifully sat was priceless. "Dani also mentioned he's very obedient," she said.

"You could have told me that sooner," he grumbled as he headed for the door with the dog heeling on command.

"I wasn't sure I believed her. I figured I'd let you put it to the test."

Justin tightened his hold on the leash and both of them watched with bated breath as Billy marched up to Punk and petted him gently on the nose. "Nice dog."

Punk responded by wagging his tail so hard he shook all over, but he did nothing at all to intimidate his pint-size admirer.

As they started down the block, they passed other families out for an evening stroll. Justin spoke to everyone, but to Patsy's relief he didn't pause to introduce her. Deceiving a handful of people was hard enough. She wasn't ready to put herself to the test with everyone else in town just yet.

Being with Justin like this felt so normal, so ordinary, she couldn't believe it. This was what she'd envisioned her marriage being, the kind of life she'd anticipated with Will. That it had turned out so very differently saddened her more than she could say.

"Hey," Justin said softly. "You okay?"

"Just thinking."

"About?"

"This and that," she equivocated.

"Which made you so sad? This or that?" he inquired lightly.

"What makes you think either one made me sad?"

"There are tears in your eyes."

And now they were spilling down her cheeks, she realized with embarrassment. She brushed them away and forced a smile. "Every now and then I get lost in what might have been."

He regarded her with a troubled expression. "And what might have been makes you sad?"

"No sadder than what was," she admitted and walked quickly on ahead.

"Patsy."

His voice was soft, but something in it commanded her to stop. She hesitated, fought against a fresh batch of tears, then turned back.

"If something's bothering you, you can talk to me. In my line of work, there's not much I haven't seen or heard."

She looked into worried blue eyes and saw the sincere desire to help. As she had said to Tate Owens earlier, she repeated, "Thank you. I'll remember that."

"Something tells me you won't."

"I said I would, didn't I?" she snapped defensively.

"Do you always keep your promises?"

She remembered other promises—vows—she'd made and broken by running off. "When I can," she said quietly.

"What would it take to make you break a promise?" he asked.

"Betrayal," she said without thinking.

There was a quick flash of understanding in his eyes. "Who betrayed you, Patsy?"

"No one," she said hurriedly. "Forget I said that."

His gaze searched her face. She could see there were a hundred questions on the tip of his tongue, but he finally nodded. "For now," he agreed.

Patsy should have felt relieved, but instead the reprieve promised only a temporary solution. Sooner or later, Justin Adams was going to pursue his questioning until he had all the answers he wanted. He was too good a lawman not to. She knew he didn't totally believe a word out of her mouth.

Still she could enjoy tonight. The summer air was dry and stirred by a faint, cooling breeze. The streets of Los Piños were peaceful. The only arguments were between children squabbling over a toy or a game of hopscotch. If there were more serious fights between grown-ups, they were behind closed doors and they weren't her fights. Will Longhorn was far away and, hopefully, nowhere close to finding her. Right this minute she and Billy were safe. They had found a temporary haven, where they could get back on their feet again, where she could rebuild her self-respect.

And even though he represented a very real threat of discovery, Justin Adams also reassured her. She sensed that his quiet strength would never be used against her and, after so many months of fearing for her own safety and Billy's, that was wonderful.

Yet she couldn't help wondering what would happen if Justin knew the truth. Would he feel betrayed because he'd risked believing in her? Would he send her straight back to her husband? Would be believe the lies that Will was bound to tell to discredit her?

Or, as he had with the incident over the Tylenol, would Justin understand that she was only doing what she'd had to do? Would he protect her? Did she even have the right to expect that of him?

As a lawman, yes. It was his sworn duty to keep her safe. Thanks to Sharon Lynn and Tate Owens, she already knew how Justin felt about duty.

But as a man? In less than forty-eight hours she had come

to see him as both. Wrong as it was, she had wished, how-ever fleetingly, that she could be loved by a man like Justin Adams. She'd dismissed the thought as ridiculous and hypo-thetical, not a serious yearning for this particular man. But now, with him beside her, she wondered if the thought had been hypothetical at all, or truly wistful longing?

Forget it, she told herself. It wasn't even something she could afford to consider until she did something about her marital status. At some point, she would have to file for divorce she supposed, but that meant facing Will, dealing with him in a courtroom at the very least. Now she was too fearful of the outcome to risk it. She would live the rest of her life in limbo if she had to.

"Patsy." Justin spoke quietly as if he feared startling her.

Startled anyway, she jerked, then gazed up into those vivid blue eyes again. "Yes?"

His smile was slow and a little sad, perhaps regretful over frightening her. "We're here."

She glanced toward the neatly tended house, a low brick rambler with roses in the yard and a sheriff's car parked in the driveway. The latter was a shock, a reminder that she'd been too ready to drop her guard.

He led the way inside. Punk was eager to explore, but a soft command to stay had him flopping on the cool marble floor in the foyer.

"The kitchen's this way," Justin said, leading her through a dining room that was empty of furniture.

He spotted her quick look around, then shrugged sheep-ishly. "I can't decide if I want to use it for a dining room or a family room," he explained. "It seems a little silly to put a fancy table in here, when I never entertain."

He opened a swinging door and gestured inside. "The

kitchen's plenty big enough for a table and chairs. Everybody hangs out in here, anyway."

Patsy could see why. The antique oak table was huge and it was surrounded by oak chairs with bright cushions on the seats that matched the curtains hanging at the windows. It was a woman's touch and she wondered with a twinge of jealousy who'd been responsible. The appliances appeared to be brand-new, including a state-of-the-art refrigerator that looked big enough to stock a month's supply of food for a family of eight.

When Justin opened the humongous freezer, she had to laugh. Inside there were two half-gallons of ice cream and nothing else, except perhaps some unseen cubes of ice in the automatic ice maker.

"Kind of a waste of space, isn't it?" she teased.

He shrugged. "I eat out a lot."

"Is the other side any better?"

"See for yourself," he said, opening the door to reveal a couple of cans of soda, some sandwich meat, a loaf of bread, a bottle of ketchup, a jar of mayonnaise, and a stick of butter still in its wrapper.

"Interesting diet you have."

"I eat breakfast at Dolan's, lunch wherever it's convenient and dinner with my folks or Grandpa Harlan. This stuff is good enough for a late-night snack or an emergency lunch on my day off."

"No lady friends to cook for you?" she inquired, all too aware of yet another odd little twinge of envy that came automatically with the question.

"Once in a while," he conceded. "No one special."

She could believe it. She could also believe that he didn't entertain them here. The bare necessities weren't meant to impress anyone. And any woman with marriage on her mind would have long since added her own touches to the room and seen to it that the refrigerator was stocked with tempting dishes meant to win his heart. She wouldn't have stopped with the cushions and matching curtains.

Nope, Patsy concluded, this was the home of a dedicated, unattached bachelor, all right. She found that oddly comforting.

"Ice cream," Billy demanded.

Justin hoisted him up and settled him on the counter, then reached into a cupboard and brought out a box of sugar cones. "One scoop or two?" he inquired, the question directed at Billy, but his unsettling gaze fixed on Patsy.

"One," she insisted, overriding Billy's demand for two. "And prepare for disaster. We probably ought to eat them outside."

"We can take them onto the patio," he said, scooping the rocky road into the cones and handing two to her. When he'd put the carton of ice cream back into the freezer, he picked Billy up and opened the back door to a brick patio and a medium-sized pool that sparkled with underwater lights. Billy clapped his hands in delight.

"Swim, Mama."

"Not now, baby."

She caught Justin's surprised expression.

"He can swim?"

She nodded. "Like a little fish. He had lessons a few months ago. He loves the water." Lessons had been a necessity with the huge pool in their backyard. Even so, she had had safety locks installed on all the doors leading outside to keep Billy from wandering out unattended, lured by the water and oblivious to the potential dangers.

"You'll have to come over sometime and use the pool," Justin said.

"We'll see."

She could see that there were more questions he wanted

to ask, such as how a woman who'd been unable to pay for children's Tylenol had afforded swimming lessons or had even had access to a pool. He was probably noting that, right alongside the expensive clothes he'd already commented on and the fancy car, and coming up with a background for her that didn't add up.

"One of these days we're going to have to talk about this," he said, his gaze never leaving hers.

The comment confirmed her worst fears. Patsy sighed and nodded. "One of these days," she conceded.

He nodded slowly, accepting that for now. A plaintive *woof* from inside broke the tension and had them laughing.

"Apparently Punk is tired of being obedient," she noted.

"Should I let him join us or should we head back?"

"We'd better get back," she said reluctantly. "Billy needs to get to sleep. And I have to be up early to get to work."

He gestured behind her. "I don't think Billy's rest is an issue."

She turned and found Billy curled up on a chaise longue sound asleep, his half-eaten ice cream cone melting beside him. Panic spiraled through her at the sight of the mess.

"Oh, dear," she murmured, jumping up at once. "I'll clean it up."

"Stay where you are," he said. "I'll take care of it."

"But—"

"Patsy, it's not a problem. The fabric's washable. Even if it weren't, what would it matter?"

She thought of Will's quick, explosive anger over such minor accidents and wondered at this man who seemed to take the same thing in stride. "Are you sure?" she asked, unable to keep the uneasiness out of her voice.

"Of course, I'm sure," he said, his gaze intent and filled with unspoken curiosity. "Relax. I'll be right back."

Patsy couldn't relax, but she did manage to stay where

she was and let Justin deal with the melted ice cream. When it was cleaned up, he hefted Billy into his arms.

"Let's get this guy home and into bed." He glanced at her. "Can you handle Punk?"

"Sure," she said with sheer bravado.

The dog seemed to sense her uncertainty and tested her immediately, but one sharp command from Justin had him behaving.

Back at Dani's Justin took the baby into the bedroom and settled him, then walked back to the front door. He lifted his hand to graze her cheek with his knuckles. Longing shimmered through her, a deep yearning for more than that gentle touch. For now, though—perhaps forever—more was forbidden.

"Thank you," she said, fighting the breathless note in her voice. "I enjoyed the walk and the ice cream."

In fact, she had enjoyed the whole evening entirely too much. It had relaxed her guard around this man. It had made her want things that couldn't be. It would not do to repeat occasions like this too often, for both their sakes.

"We'll have to do it again sometime," he said.

"Sure," she said, but she knew she would have to fight the next invitation.

Tonight had proved beyond any doubt that being around Justin Adams was dangerous. One day soon he wouldn't settle for evasive answers. One day soon he wouldn't settle for the quick brush of his fingertips along her cheek, as he was doing now.

Worse, one day soon, she wouldn't, either. And that could be her downfall.

Chapter Five

Justin had a long and restless night after leaving Patsy. He'd lain awake most of it reciting all the reasons he ought to be fighting his attraction to her for all he was worth. Every instinct he possessed warned him away.

Even without the circumstances of their first meeting still fresh in his mind, he would have known that there were troubling aspects to Patsy Gresham's past. She was too leery of any questions, too skittish around him. He'd noted her easygoing manner with most of the customers in Dolan's the day before and concluded that her nervousness was directed at him. More likely, at his uniform.

There were a couple of obvious reasons for people to be afraid of a cop. Either they'd committed a crime, or they were trying to hide from someone and feared discovery. He wanted to believe it was the latter in Patsy's case.

But who? And why? He wasn't sure he was going to be thrilled with the answers to those questions, either. That probably explained why he hadn't asked them the night before. If he discovered something in Patsy's background that required reporting, he would be duty-bound to deal with it. For the moment, it seemed to him it might be better not to know.

Looking the other way was totally out of character for him. That he was even in such a position was irritating as the dickens. He left for work in a foul humor, which didn't improve when he walked through the door to be greeted by more questions about Patsy.

"Justin, how much do you know about the Gresham woman?" Tate Owens asked before he'd even had time for a decent cup of coffee.

As riled as he was by the question, Justin had anticipated it. He'd known the sheriff wouldn't let the matter rest ever since Tate had come back from Dolan's the day before. He'd found his conversation with Patsy worrisome. "The woman's in some kind of trouble," he'd said then. "I can feel it in my gut."

Justin hadn't been able to argue with him.

"Justin," Tate prodded now. "What do you know about her?"

"Enough," he said curtly.

"Did you run the tag number?"

"No."

"You're sure it's her car?"

If Justin had been the kind of man who squirmed under pressure, he'd have been doing it now. He knew he should have run the check, but he wasn't sure he wanted the answers it might yield. He hadn't even demanded to see the registration.

"Sure enough," he said curtly.

"I don't suppose you checked the registration, either, did you?"

He scowled at Tate. "No, but—"

The sheriff stared at him. "Justin, you're a better cop

than that. The woman shows up here out of the blue, tries to steal from your cousin, and you ignore the obvious way to get a clear picture of what we're dealing with? Why?" Tate studied him closely. "Damn, you've got a thing for her, haven't you?"

"Don't be ridiculous."

"Then give me one good reason for not checking her out."

"I did check. I ran through the stolen vehicle reports," he conceded finally. He'd done even that much reluctantly, praying that he wouldn't find a report on a fancy Oklahoma car in the stack.

Tate was only slightly mollified. "Anything there?"

"Nothing."

"You've spent more time with her than I have. What do you think?"

"I think she's trying her best to start over. Maybe we ought to back off and let her."

"What if whatever trouble she's in follows her here to Los Piños?" Tate inquired. "We should be prepared for it, don't you think? We can't help her, if we don't know what to be on the lookout for."

Justin sighed. He had no argument with his boss's thinking. In law enforcement, especially in a small town with limited resources, it was always better to be prepared.

"We need some answers, son. You know we do."

"I know. I'll see what I can do."

"Don't take too long. Every instinct tells me that it won't be long before all hell breaks loose. A classy woman with a baby and a fancy car, but no money…" He shook his head. "It has all the earmarks of a woman on the run from her husband."

Hearing his own suspicion put into words made Justin's

heart sink. Every time a voice in his head had started to shout the possibility, he'd tuned out, refusing to listen. He'd looked for a wedding ring, but she hadn't been wearing one. He'd wanted to believe that meant there was no husband. He was smart enough to know better. Rings would be the first thing she'd hide—or hock.

"Any sign she'd been abused?" Tate asked.

"No bruises, if that's what you mean." He had checked, surreptitiously studying every visible inch of her for fading marks on her pale skin. He'd been relieved by the absence of evidence. "That doesn't mean she wasn't, though." He thought of the way she'd reacted to Billy's accident with the ice cream the night before. She'd been too quick to leap to her feet, too panicked over such a trivial incident.

"What about the boy?" Tate inquired just as the same thought struck Justin.

"By God, I hope not," he said tightly, consumed with fury at the slightest possibility that that was the explanation for Patsy being on the run. The one good sign was that Billy had shown no fear at all of him. If he'd been harmed by his father, wouldn't he have been wary of men? He clung to that tiny shred of reassurance.

Tate cleared his throat and regarded Justin uneasily. "Son, are you sure you're the best person to be checking into this. Maybe I ought to look into it myself."

"Why?"

"Could be you're too personally involved."

"Involved? I just met the woman."

"Ever heard about lightning bolts?" the sheriff questioned. "They strike without warning. Only takes an instant to change everything."

Justin thought of the way Patsy's skin had felt under his touch the night before, of the way her soft cheek had warmed, of the flicker of desire he'd been so sure he'd seen in her eyes. And then he considered how badly his body had ached the rest of the night with wanting her, with wanting more than that gentle, fleeting brush of skin against skin.

It meant nothing, he assured himself. Just a natural, hormonal reaction to a beautiful woman's proximity.

"My objectivity's not compromised," he insisted, partly because he believed it, mostly because he didn't dare consider the possibility that it could be.

Tate's gaze met his and remained steady. Finally he nodded, accepting Justin's word. "If that changes, let me know. You don't just owe it to me. You owe it to her."

"I will," he promised. If the time ever came when he couldn't do his job, surely he would know it, surely he would do the right thing. He wouldn't let pride and pure cussedness stand in his way.

If he did, if it ever came to that, he would have to reexamine exactly who Justin Adams really was, if he really was the honorable, natural born lawman he'd always thought himself to be. Or if he was like any other man who'd bend the rules when they no longer suited him.

The vivacious woman with the sculpted cheekbones and short black hair beckoned to Patsy, then glanced around furtively.

"Where's Sharon Lynn?" she demanded in a hushed voice.

"She went out to run an errand," Patsy said, dropping her own voice to a whisper in response.

The woman's smile was relieved. "Great. Then we can talk. I'm Jenny, Sharon Lynn's stepaunt technically, but that's neither here nor there. Dani should be here any minute. We're planning a surprise bridal shower for Sharon Lynn tomorrow. Can you help?"

Patsy grinned, delighted to be asked to be in on the surprise. "Of course. What do you need me to do?"

"Get her there."

"Where? And how on earth can I get her to go anywhere?"

"Well, that's the beauty of it. We thought we'd have it at your place. I understand you've moved into Dani's old house. Sharon Lynn will never suspect that. Maybe you could invite her to dinner or something. We're going to have it right after she closes up here."

Patsy thought about it. "I suppose I could manage that. I owe her a lot for giving me this job. I'll tell her I want to repay her by having her over for dinner."

"That's perfect. Do you mind us having it there? I suppose I should have asked that first thing, but we were already planning it for Dani's and now you're there, so it didn't seem to make sense to move it. In fact, it works out even better this way, if you don't mind, that is."

"Of course not. The house is Dani's, after all. She's been wonderful about letting me and Billy stay there."

"You're invited, of course. No need to bring a present. Sharon Lynn won't expect it."

"You don't need to include me. I'll lure her over and then Billy and I can just go out to eat."

"Absolutely not. Besides, if you're the one dragging her over there, you can't turn right around and leave. And we all want to get to know you better. Seven o'clock, okay? We'll take care of everything."

"I'll have her there," Patsy promised, already looking forward to the chance to pay Sharon Lynn back for her kindness by helping with this surprise.

"Terrific. Dani said we could count on you. Got to run. I'm overdue at home and my husband tends to get restless, especially now that I'm pregnant."

She was out the door before Patsy could blink, another whirlwind Adams entering into her life and drawing her into the family circle.

Weighed down by the assignment just given to her, she was a nervous wreck until Sharon Lynn returned.

Forcing a casual note into her voice, she asked, "Sharon Lynn, do you have plans for tomorrow night?"

A frown of concentration knit her brow. "I don't think so, but let me check my calendar. I can't trust myself to remember anything these days. Why?"

"I'd like to have you over for dinner after we close. Nothing fancy, but I really want to do something special to thank you for being so nice to Billy and me. I know you won't have a spare second once all the wedding plans kick into gear."

"Oh, sweetie, that's not necessary. All I did was give you a job and work you to death."

"But after what happened the first time I came in here, a lot of people wouldn't have been so understanding."

"You've more than made up for that. You've only been here two days and already I can't imagine what I ever did without you. You're fitting right in."

Patsy warmed under the heartfelt praise. It had been a long time since anyone had complimented her. Will's constant carping had eaten away at her self-confidence, eroding it to the point that she hadn't been sure if there was a single thing she could do right at all.

"All I'm doing is scrambling eggs and frying hamburgers," she said quietly.

"It's a lot more than that," Sharon Lynn insisted. "The

customers around here can be stingy with praise, but they already love you."

To Patsy's embarrassment, she could feel tears stinging her eyes. "Stop. You're going to make me cry."

Sharon Lynn stared at her. "Just because I'm pointing out the obvious, that you're good at what you do?"

Patsy nodded. "Please," she begged. "Don't ask me to explain."

"I won't," Sharon Lynn agreed, her expression turning fierce. "But if some man has made you feel worthless, then shame on him." She drew in a deep breath, then said more quietly, "If you ever need to talk, I'm a good listener." She gave Patsy a pointed look. "So's Justin."

"I know," Patsy responded. "But there's nothing to talk about."

Sharon Lynn seemed about to argue, then she let it go. "About dinner tomorrow night, if the invitation's still open, I would love to come."

Mission accomplished, Patsy thought triumphantly, pushing aside all other thoughts to focus on tomorrow's surprise. "About seven, right after we close?"

"That will be perfect."

"What will be perfect?" Justin demanded, walking up to settle on a stool at the counter.

He had a worrisome way of sneaking up on her that constantly caught her off guard. One of these days would he overhear something that would give her away?

"Patsy's invited me to dinner tomorrow night," Sharon Lynn explained.

He glanced at her. "Is that so? What about me?"

Patsy shook her head. "Sorry. It's a girls-only night."

"Then maybe I should pick Billy up and take him out for spaghetti with the guys."

The thought of being separated even for a short time from her son panicked her. "No, really, he'll be fine with us," Patsy said at once.

"Maybe it would be fun for Billy," Sharon Lynn said. "Justin's really good with kids."

"I know that. It's just that…" It was just that she envisioned Will coming to claim him when she wasn't around to prevent it. How could she explain that?

"I'll take good care of him," Justin promised. His gaze locked with hers. "No harm will come to him while he's with me."

It was almost as if he knew, she thought, studying his expression for some clue that would tell her if he'd discovered the truth.

She thought of the real purpose for tomorrow's invitation to Sharon Lynn. The house would be crawling with other women for the shower. It really was no place for a small child. And surely the safest place in the world for Billy to be was with a deputy sheriff.

"Okay," she said at last. "Billy loves spaghetti. Just be aware that he tends to get most of it all over himself and anyone else who's in his path."

Justin grinned. "In that case, maybe I'll invite Harlan Patrick along."

Sharon Lynn laughed.

"Who's Harlan Patrick?" Patsy asked, watching their shared amusement and the conspiratorial wink they exchanged.

"My brother," she explained. "When he's not herding cattle or up to his elbows in muck, he considers himself quite a fashion plate. There's nothing Harlan Patrick likes more than a fancy new outfit that'll impress the ladies. Justin's just imagining how he'd love to have spaghetti spattered all over his best western shirt, especially since his girlfriend will be singing over at the restaurant tomorrow."

"But that's…" Words failed her.

"Dastardly," Sharon Lynn provided.

"Just plain mean," Patsy said.

"Payback," Justin corrected. "Harlan Patrick and I have a score to settle."

"And you intend to use my son to do it?"

"He and my brother always have a score to settle," Sharon Lynn said. "Goodness knows what it's about this time. Don't worry about it. Just leave them to it. When Harlan Patrick decides to get even, he won't take it out on Billy. All his ire will be directed straight back at Justin."

The idea that a family could engage in teasing and pranks without rancor was so totally alien to the way Patsy had spent the past couple of years that she was enthralled by it. She would almost rather watch Justin get even with his cousin than go through with her role in Sharon Lynn's surprise.

But it was all part of the same cloth, she realized with a sense of wonder. This was a tight-knit, supportive family, the kind she'd always dreamed of being a part of.

"Do you two have any idea how lucky you are?" she asked.

"Of course we do," Sharon Lynn said, clearly grasping her meaning at once. She gave Patsy a tight hug. "You'll see," she promised, glancing toward Justin. "Won't she?"

His gaze caught Patsy's and held. "If I have anything to say about it."

Patsy trembled under the intensity of that look. A fierce longing for what these Adams cousins took for granted rushed over her. Gazing into Justin's eyes she saw what might have been a bold commitment, a promise that was there for the taking if only she could.

If only she could.

She sighed heavily and turned away, busying herself with the last of the day's dishes, which had to be stacked and ready for the morning rush. When she turned again, she realized that Sharon Lynn had silently left, leaving her alone with Justin.

"Come to dinner with me," he suggested. "And before you start making excuses, I've already checked with Dani. She's going to be late at the clinic. She'll look after Billy for another couple of hours. She says he's having the time of his life with the animals. Her boys will be over there soon, too. Billy will be in heaven with all that attention."

"But his dinner…"

"Is taken care of. They shared a fried chicken dinner that I brought them from White Pines."

She regarded him suspiciously. "Something tells me that fried chicken was meant for you. Did you use it to bribe Dani to go along with this scheme of yours?"

He grinned. "What if I did? All it proves is that I will go to astonishing lengths to grab a few minutes alone with you."

"Don't," she commanded softly.

"Don't what?"

"Be nice to me."

"Why not?"

"I don't deserve it."

"Darlin', everyone deserves to have someone special be nice to them."

Tears spilled down her cheeks. "No, Justin. This can't be," she whispered, turning away.

She heard his quick movement, felt him behind her, but it

was a long while before she felt his hand on her shoulder. It rested there gently, reminding her of his presence, soothing her but asking for nothing. The undemanding reassurance couldn't last forever, though. Sooner or later he would want something in return—answers, at the very least.

"Patsy?"

She sniffed and reached for a napkin to wipe away the dampness on her cheeks. Slowly he turned her to face him, then tucked a finger under her chin and lifted it until their gazes met.

"Tell me," he pleaded.

"I can't."

He brushed the hair back from her face, then lingered to caress her cheek. When he grazed her lower lip with the tip of his finger, the wonder of his gentleness almost shattered her. Slowly, so slowly that she told herself she must be mistaken, he lowered his head until their mouths were a scant hairsbreadth apart.

Hurry, hurry, she wanted to shout. If he rushed, if he simply stole the kiss, she could tell herself forever after that she hadn't wanted it to happen. But this way, there was no denying the pull, no pretending that she didn't want it with every fiber of her being. There was time enough for longing and more than enough time for guilt.

At the last possible second, when she could feel the warmth of his breath fanning over her flesh, honor intruded. She jerked away, moved until the width of the counter was safely between them again. She grasped the cool Formica merely to steady herself, but held so tightly that her knuckles turned white and the edge cut into her hand....

"I'm sorry," he said.

"No," she said adamantly. "You have nothing to be sorry for."

"I do," he insisted. "I knew better. I knew it wasn't what you wanted."

"But I did," she whispered, her voice thick with fresh, unshed tears. "More than anything."

"Why, then?"

Looking into his eyes, she saw that he already knew the answer, that he'd guessed it somehow.

"Who is he, Patsy?"

"Nobody," she said at once. "There's nobody."

Something that might have been pain flared in his eyes then. His expression turned weary. "You're lying," he said softly.

She turned away because she couldn't bear to see the hurt in his eyes.

"Maybe someday you'll realize you don't have to lie to me," he told her. "Maybe someday you'll trust me with the truth."

And maybe, she thought wistfully, maybe someday there would be angels to look out for women whose hearts had been every bit as battered as their psyches or their bodies.

Chapter Six

Justin cursed himself six ways from Sunday as he walked home after leaving Patsy at her front door. She'd barely said a word to him as she'd closed up Dolan's or as they'd walked up the block to Dani's.

At least he'd been wise enough not to pressure her any more by asking to come in or by walking on into his sister's clinic to say hi to Dani and Billy. No, for once he'd done the smart thing. He'd said good-night, reminded her of his promise to take Billy out for spaghetti the next night and left.

He figured it would be days and not hours before he forgot the wounded look in her eyes when he'd accused her of lying. Even though they both knew the accusation was true, pointing it out hadn't helped anything. Now she would only be more wary of him than ever. He regretted that almost as deeply as he regretted not getting to steal that kiss.

Of course, that had been a mistake, too. Had he forgotten so quickly Tate's warning to maintain his objectivity or, if he found he couldn't, to turn the unofficial investigation into Patsy's background over to Tate himself? He'd come damned close to blowing everything. For a man who prided himself on not crossing lines, he was virtually doing a hundred-yard dash across this one.

Distracted by his dark thoughts, he was halfway up the walk at home before he realized that someone was waiting in the shadows. Regretting that he didn't have his gun, he was preparing to launch himself at the intruder, when Harlan Patrick stepped into the light cast by the streetlight on the corner.

"Hey, Justin. You're late getting home."

"Damn you, do you know how close you came to getting tackled?" Justin muttered as he brushed past his cousin and unlocked his door. "You have a key. Why didn't you go inside to wait for me?"

"Because I just got here," he explained with exaggerated patience. "I saw you coming and waited out here. What the devil's wrong with you, anyway? Why are you so jumpy? This is Los Piños, not Dallas. How many criminals wait in shadows around here? For that matter, how many bad guys have you arrested lately, not counting those sickos who dared to let their parking meters run out?"

Harlan Patrick gave Justin a knowing look. "Wait. Forget I asked that. You let the last genuine lawbreaker go free, didn't you, and it's still stuck in your craw. This does have something to do with the mysterious stranger, doesn't it?"

"It's none of your business." Justin pushed past him and went into the kitchen, where he grabbed a soda from the almost barren refrigerator. "Want one?"

"Sure."

He tossed that can to his cousin, then grabbed another and popped the top. A long, cold drink did nothing to soothe his frayed temper.

"Justin?"

"Yeah."

"Is there a problem?"

"I wish to hell I knew for sure."

"What does that mean?"

"It means every instinct tells me there is, but I can't get a handle on it."

"Or do you just not like the answers you're coming up with?"

He sighed. "That, too," he admitted.

"Want to talk about it?"

"Not especially."

"I have tremendous insight into the female mind," Harlan Patrick claimed.

Justin hooted at that. "If playing the field counts for anything, I'm sure that's true. I'm just not so sure I want to take advice from a man who doesn't know the meaning of settling down."

"I am settling down. I haven't dated anyone but Laurie for months now."

"Really? Months? That must be some kind of record."

"I'd make it permanent if she'd hear of it, but she still has this crazy idea about going to Nashville as soon as she gets some money together."

"Maybe you ought to loan her the money," Justin suggested. "Let her get it out of her system."

"No way," Harlan Patrick said. "I'm not going to help set her up for heartache."

"She'll do it on her own, then. You know she will. And in the meantime, you'll be waiting around."

Harlan Patrick shook his head. "No way. She'll wake up one of these days and realize that it's only a foolish dream. Then we'll get married and raise a family out at White Pines. She'll switch from singing country to lullabies."

Justin had only spent a few evenings with Laurie Jensen, but even he could see that his cousin had a blind spot when it came to Laurie's commitment to her music. "If you believe that, then you don't know your lady half as well as you think you do," he warned. "Where is she tonight?"

"Over in Garden City, singing at a club."

"And what's she doing tomorrow?"

Harlan Patrick scowled. "Singing here in town."

"And you don't think that means anything?"

"Sure, it does. I don't object if she wants to sing every once in a while around here."

"That's mighty big of you. When was the last time Laurie asked your permission?"

Harlan Patrick's disgruntled expression was answer enough. "Never mind," Justin said. "Wake up, cousin. The woman has the voice of an angel, a way with words and the ambition it takes to make her dream come true. Either help her or get out of her way."

"Who asked for your advice?"

"Consider it a gift from someone who's older and wiser."

"You can't be that wise, if you can't make heads or tails of what's going on with the town's newest resident. I thought cops had all sorts of ways to get answers if they wanted them badly enough."

That was the trouble, of course. Justin wasn't one bit sure he was ready to hear the answers, not from that computer down at the station, not even from Patsy's own lips.

Billy's cheeks were flushed, his straight black hair a damp fringe around his face. He smelled like talcum powder and baby.

"Which bedtime story tonight?" Patsy asked him, holding up the two books she'd taken from his shelves when they'd left home. There had been dozens more she'd left behind, but these two were Billy's favorites.

Bathing Billy had soothed her jangled nerves after that near kiss from Justin. That and the story were a familiar routine, one that had been repeated for so long, no matter where they were, that she could almost convince herself that their lives were normal.

Billy popped his thumb into his mouth and studied the covers of the books as intently as if it were the first time he'd ever seen them. "Two stories," he pleaded finally.

"No, sweet pea. Only one."

A mutinous expression crossed his face. "Two."

"Choose or there will be no story at all." She moved to put the books away.

"No, Mama. Read rabbit story."

She grinned. Forced to choose, *The Velveteen Rabbit* was always the one he picked. "You must know it by heart."

"Don't care. Read it," he commanded with the same authoritative manner as his father.

"Please," she prompted.

"Please, Mama."

As she began reading the familiar words, Billy began to drift off. She was even more surprised, then, when he murmured, "Mama, where's Daddy?"

It was the first time he'd mentioned his father since they'd left home. She'd wondered more than once if that was because Will was so often away from home that Billy was used to not seeing him or if it was because he preferred this quiet, peaceful life without his father around.

"Daddy's at home in Oklahoma."

"Wanna see him."

Patsy sat back and tried to control the shaking that began deep inside. She hadn't wanted to believe that Billy would ever miss his daddy. She'd almost convinced herself that the disruption in their lives she'd brought on by running away hadn't fazed Billy at all. After all, he and his father had spent precious little time together bonding. Obviously though, what time they had shared had had a profound impact, one that weeks of separation hadn't dimmed.

Before she could think of anything at all to say, Billy crawled into her lap. "Please, Mama."

Patsy hugged him tightly. "Oh, baby, I know you miss your daddy, but it's not possible to see him right now."

"Please."

"Daddy's far away. He can't come visit."

"Wanna see him," Billy protested, tears welling up in his eyes.

Patsy rocked him. "Shh, baby. It's going to be okay," she promised.

How? a voice inside her head demanded. How was she going to make this right? She couldn't explain to a two-year-old that his daddy was a potential threat to both of them. For almost the first time since she'd left home, doubts began to crowd in.

Maybe she should call Will. Maybe by now he would have gotten the message that she wouldn't tolerate his behavior. Maybe he'd reform.

And maybe pigs would fly, she thought sarcastically. She knew better. How many women fell into that trap? How many convinced themselves that their husbands were truly sorry, that the psychological abuse or battering would never happen again? She wasn't going to delude herself that way. She wasn't going to wait for Will to actually slam his fist into her rather than an inanimate object.

Still she could take a drive one day, call Will from a public phone and let Billy talk to him. If she made the call far from Los Piños and kept it brief, surely he wouldn't be able to trace it, wouldn't be able to find them. Didn't she owe Billy that much at least?

She glanced down and saw that her son was finally

asleep, his thumb tucked securely in his mouth. She shifted him into position on his bed, then pulled a sheet up over him. He'd kick it off in no time, but at least he could start the night covered up.

She stood for a long time, gazing down at him, then bent over and pressed a kiss to his flushed cheek. "I love you, angel. More than anything."

After she left him, she took her own bath, sinking into a sea of fragrant bubbles and trying to let her mind drift. Unfortunately, every time it did, an image of Justin Adams floated into view. Even the memory of his fingers against her cheek made her nipples hard. Recalling the exact instant when she'd known he was going to kiss her made her flesh heat. As the cooling bathwater lapped against her overheated flesh, she moaned softly.

Next time she might not be so strong. Next time she might accept the tenderness he was offering, the promise of even a few moments of gentle loving.

No. She brought herself back sharply from the provocative image. Stepping out of the tub, she toweled herself dry with rough strokes, then yanked on her robe. She didn't dare even begin to think that way about Justin. She was still married, if only in name. She was no doubt in a heap of trouble with Will, if not with the authorities. She couldn't drag Justin into the middle of all that.

Nor could she turn to a man to solve her problems. All her life, she had been relying on other people. First it had been her parents who'd set the rules and protected her from harm. She had left her hometown to prove that she could stand on her own two feet, only to fall in love with Will and let him take over the control of her life just as her parents had before him.

This time was going to be different. She was going to

solve her own problems. She would settle this mess with Will, establish a solid, respectable future for herself and her son and then...well, then, if Justin was still interested, if the attraction hadn't died, maybe there could be something between them. Not if she needed his protection, though. Only if she could come to him as an equal, a woman every bit as strong and capable as he was.

"You're getting a little ahead of yourself," she chided herself aloud. "The man tried to kiss you. He didn't propose marriage."

But something told her that a man as honorable as Justin Adams had proved himself to be took even his kisses seriously and that she would be very wise to remember that.

Patsy barely had the door at Dolan's open in the morning when Justin came in. She switched on the lights and watched warily as he crossed to the counter and settled on a stool. If he brought up that almost kiss, she wasn't sure what she was going to say to him.

"I guess the coffee's not ready yet, is it?" he asked, his manner nothing more than friendly.

Patsy let out a sigh of relief. Apparently last night was forgotten. "I'm just about to put it on. It won't take a minute. Can I get you something else?"

"Take your time. I know it's not really opening time yet. I wanted to catch you alone."

Panic, never far away, choked her. "Why?" she asked, barely managing to get the single word out.

He seemed amused by the question. "To talk."

"About?"

"It can wait. Whenever you're set, I'll take eggs, bacon, toast."

She already knew he liked his eggs over easy, his bacon

crisp and his toast the same color as his coffee—or so he claimed. She'd thought he was only being polite when she accidentally burned the first batch she ever made for him, but he swore burnt toast reminded him of home. She noticed, though, that he scraped away most of the black before eating it.

She was about to turn away to start his breakfast, when he snagged her hand.

"Patsy."

Her gaze met his, then skittered away. "Yes?"

"Maybe we should get this out of the way. I'm sorry about last night."

"There's nothing to be sorry for."

"I pushed."

"You've already apologized. It wasn't necessary then. It isn't now."

"But—"

"Justin, please," she pleaded. "Drop it."

His gaze locked with hers, questioning her even without any accompanying words. She held her breath, waiting for something, an explosion maybe. Will would have gone into a rage if she'd dared to cut him off.

Finally, to her relief, Justin simply nodded.

"For now."

It had become a refrain between them, a subtle warning that one day she would pay for all the silences. One day the questions would intensify and there would be no holding back. He would demand to know everything.

"I'll get your breakfast," she said, and hurried away.

By the time she'd fixed his eggs and bacon, Sharon Lynn had arrived and there were more customers. From then on Patsy was so busy she didn't have time to take a deep breath, much less worry about Justin and his unanswered questions.

It was well after nine before she got a real break.

"Sit for a minute," Sharon Lynn ordered. "I'll bring you a cup of coffee."

"You must be as beat as I am. Why should you wait on me?"

"Because you opened up this morning and Justin was right on your heels so I know perfectly well you haven't had a spare second since." She gave Patsy a curious look. "Everything okay between you and my cousin?"

"Of course," Patsy said a little too quickly. "Why wouldn't it be?"

"I just thought there might be some residual suspicious-ness because of that incident when you first arrived. Justin's like a dog with a bone when things don't add up to him."

Patsy's hand stilled with the coffee halfway to her mouth. She regarded Sharon Lynn warily. "And you think things don't add up with me?"

"I didn't say that."

"But you believe Justin has doubts."

"He's a cop. Doubts are second nature to him. It doesn't mean I think he's right."

Fear streaked through her. What if Justin hadn't let things rest, after all? What if he'd dug up something? What if he knew all about her past and was waiting for her to open up and admit the trouble she was in? What if...?

"Has he said something?" she asked cautiously.

"No, but I've watched him around you. One second he looks like a man who's falling hard for a woman, the next he gets this wary expression in his eyes."

Patsy couldn't deny Sharon Lynn's perception. She'd seen the same reactions all too often herself.

"I'm sorry," Sharon Lynn said. "I shouldn't have said anything. I didn't mean to upset you. I don't want you to be on your guard every time he's around."

"I'm not upset. I can't blame Justin for the way he feels.

I was shoplifting when he first saw me. I offered to move on, to leave Los Piños. He assured me he could forget what happened, but maybe he can't. Maybe I should go."

Sharon Lynn looked thunderstruck. "No, absolutely not. Where would you go?"

"I don't know," Patsy admitted.

"Then put that idea right out of your head. Nobody wants you to leave."

"Leave? Who's leaving?" Justin demanded, walking up behind them.

Patsy turned slowly. "I thought maybe it would be for the best if I did."

"Well, it wouldn't," he said succinctly.

His sharp response hung in the air. For the longest time no one said anything.

"I'll be in the back if anyone needs me," Sharon Lynn said finally, but neither Justin nor Patsy spared her a glance.

"Are you sure you don't want me to go?" she asked, searching his face.

"Yes, I'm sure. I just wish…" His voice trailed off.

"Wish what?"

"That you felt you could be honest with me."

Patsy wished that, too, more than she could say. She knew, too, that he could get most of the answers he craved just by running her license tag number. Obviously he hadn't, or he'd want to know why she'd lied about her name being Gresham, not Longhorn. Either he was waiting for her to come to him with the truth on her own or he was afraid of it.

"I can't," she said simply. "I wish I could, but I can't."

"Will you tell me one thing?"

"If I can."

"Have you broken any laws?"

"No," she said honestly. Not unless Will had manufactured a crime out of her leaving with their son.

Relief washed some of the tension out of his expression. "Then we'll leave it at that."

She grinned. "For now."

He chuckled at her repetition of his favorite warning. "Who knows? Maybe I'll just drop it for good. Maybe I'll just take it on faith that you'll tell me the whole story when you feel you can."

Patsy regarded him skeptically. "Can you do that?"

He started to answer, then sighed. "Probably not," he admitted regretfully.

"That's what makes you a good cop, Deputy."

"Maybe it doesn't make me such a terrific man. I ought to trust you. I want to."

"I've given you plenty of cause not to."

He lifted his hand, hesitated, then, looking as if he wanted to do so much more, he gently grazed her cheek with his knuckles. "You know what I wish more than anything?"

Dazed by the look of pure longing in his eyes, Patsy shook her head.

"I wish that I knew whether I had any right at all to kiss you."

She shuddered with a longing that was equal to his, then finally looked away.

Justin sighed. "That pretty much answers my question, doesn't it?"

With her eyes squeezed tightly shut to keep the tears from falling, she said softly, "Yes, I suppose it does."

It was only a tiny hint at the whole truth, but it was enough to put a bleak expression on Justin's face and send him striding out of Dolan's without a backward glance.

It was also more than enough to break Patsy's heart in two.

Chapter Seven

With Justin gone, Patsy was left all alone to battle tears and guilt and shame. How could she go on deceiving a man who had been nothing but kind to her, a man who'd already put aside his own convictions about right and wrong to give her a break? She was still wrestling with that when Sharon Lynn came out of the back.

Patsy hastily wiped her eyes and forced a smile. She didn't want this compassionate woman to be caught in the middle. It was too soon to test the strength of their friendship, especially when Justin was part of her family. She knew enough about the Adamses by now to know that they were bound tight by love and loyalty.

"Everything okay?" Sharon Lynn asked, concern etched on her face.

"Fine."

"You don't look fine. You look as if you've been crying." Her expression turned indignant. "If that cousin of mine has done anything to upset you, I'll tear him limb from limb."

The fierce promise startled Patsy, then left her chuckling. "Don't you think it would be a bit of a mismatch?" she asked.

"Hey, I grew up playing with him and my brother. I'm as tough as they are. I had to be." Sharon Lynn winked. "I'm also a better shot."

Patsy shuddered at the teasing suggestion. "Please, you don't need to prove it on my account. I don't think there will be any need to resort to guns. Justin didn't deliberately upset me. I'm the one responsible for him taking off in such a foul humor. It was all my fault."

She deliberately pushed her own concerns over Justin aside. Now seemed like a really good time to change the subject and focus on that night's surprise bridal shower before Sharon Lynn wanted to know exactly what she'd done that was so terrible.

"Don't forget we're having dinner tonight," she reminded Sharon Lynn.

For a moment Sharon Lynn seemed startled by the abrupt shift in topic. "Patsy, don't you want to talk about what just happened here?"

"No," she said honestly. "I'd rather think about the pleasant evening we're going to have. It's been a long time since I've invited company over. You haven't forgotten, have you?"

"No, of course not, but there's no reason you should cook after standing in front of the grill here all day. Why don't we go out?" she suggested. "We can let somebody else cook for both of us for a change."

Patsy thought of all the people who'd be waiting in her living room and almost panicked. "Absolutely not," she said hurriedly and began improvising. "I already have everything ready. It won't take a minute to get dinner on the table."

"But you must not get a chance to go out with friends very often because of Billy. Since he'll be with Justin, it would be the perfect time to get out and kick up your heels a little."

"Believe me, the last thing I want to do is kick up my heels," she said with heartfelt sincerity.

Patsy studied her intently, then nodded. "If you're sure..."

"I am."

The rest of the afternoon was so busy the only words they had time to exchange were about orders. By the time they closed up, both of them were dead on their feet. Even so, Patsy couldn't help feeling excited as she and Sharon Lynn headed for her place and the waiting bridal shower. She was grateful she'd been asked to play even a minor role in the surprise. It made her feel as if she belonged, as if she had a contribution to make, something she hadn't felt in a very long time.

When they reached the house, she was taken aback by its deserted look. Not even Dani's car was in the driveway, and there were no extra cars parked along the block. Where was everyone? Had she gotten it wrong, after all? If she had, the big surprise for Sharon Lynn was going to be the fact that there was no dinner waiting in the fridge.

Taking it on faith that there was a surprise party waiting inside, she unlocked the door, then led the way into the living room. It wasn't dark yet, but the room was filled with shadows. Just as she was about to reach for a light switch, someone else turned on the overhead light and the room erupted with noise. People burst in from the clinic, where they'd obviously been hiding. All the shouts of "Surprise!" set off the animals. The dogs began howling and the cats scurried for cover.

In the midst of the chaos, Sharon Lynn stared around at all of her friends and family, then burst into tears.

"Oh, dear," Patsy murmured, stunned by the reaction. She put an arm around her. "What's wrong? Please, don't cry."

Sharon Lynn waved off the sympathy. "I'm okay. It's just..."

"It's just that she's never gotten this far before," Jenny said, coming over to envelop her in a hug. "It's only a little over a week and counting to the big day."

Sharon Lynn mopped at her eyes. "I'm actually beginning to believe it's going to happen this time." She turned to Patsy and said with mock severity, "As for you, you are a very sneaky lady. I had no idea what you were up to. No wonder you turned down my offer to go out for dinner."

"Thank goodness you didn't insist on it. I'm not sure what I would have come up with to get you over here. As for the rest, I didn't really do anything," Patsy said. "Jenny and Dani did all the planning and the work. I was just brought in at the last second to deliver you. I still think I ought to get Billy and go out to eat, while you all celebrate."

"Absolutely not," Dani said, joining them. "Besides, Justin already has Billy. The boy has my brother wound around his little finger. I believe they were going to stop at the toy store on the way to dinner. Justin saw a remote control police car in there he wanted to check out."

"Oh, dear," Patsy murmured. "Maybe I should—"

"You should relax and enjoy yourself," Jenny told her. "Let Justin spend a little of his money for a change. It'll do him good to hang out in a toy store. Maybe he'll rediscover the kid inside. He's not even thirty and already he's turned into a straitlaced old man."

"You've got that right," Sharon Lynn said. "When I think of how much mischief he and Harlan Patrick used to get into, it's hard to believe it's the same person."

"Come on, ladies," an older woman with the same dark hair as Jenny said. "I'm starving and you know your grandfather will start worrying if I'm out too late. Next thing you know he'll use it as an excuse to come looking for me. As it is, he's very put out that he wasn't invited to the shower. Just give him the slightest excuse and he'll race into town."

"Maybe it would be worth it," Dani said with a wicked twinkle in her eyes. "I can just see Grandpa Harlan's expression when Sharon Lynn starts opening packages filled with slinky lingerie."

"If Mom's half the woman I know she is, it won't be anything he hasn't seen before," Jenny teased, bringing a blush to the older woman's cheeks.

"Patsy, have you met Janet yet?" Dani asked. "She's married to Grandpa Harlan and she claims to give him a run for his money, but as you just heard, the man has the original feminist in the family on a short leash."

Janet winked. "I just let him think that. Now that I've closed my law practice, I do my level best to drive him crazy. It's the only thing I have to look forward to."

Patsy regarded her intently. "You're a lawyer?"

"One of the best in the business," Jenny said proudly. "She was also a real activist for Native American rights. If you ever have a legal problem, you couldn't find anyone in town to give you better advice."

Patsy tucked that piece of information away for another time. Could this woman with the wise face and kind eyes be the answer to her prayers? If she knew a lot about Native American affairs, wouldn't she also know if Patsy's position would be weakened in a custody battle because she wasn't Native American? The fear that tribal law would come into play had been nagging at her from the moment she decided to run. She had been terrified that that was the unspoken threat Will would use to take her baby away.

"Hey, why so solemn?" Jenny asked, studying her worriedly.

Patsy forced a smile. "Sorry. Don't let my mood spoil the party."

"She and Justin had a little set-to earlier," Sharon Lynn explained.

"Oh, really?" Janet said, her expression thoughtful. "I haven't seen Justin riled up much. He's always been a pretty even-tempered guy."

"Put him in a room with Patsy for ten minutes and watch the fireworks," Sharon Lynn suggested.

"Interesting," Janet said.

"Okay, enough of this. Forget Justin. He's just a man. Nothing is going to ruin this shower," Jenny said adamantly. "It's been too long coming, right, Sharon Lynn?"

"Way too long," Sharon Lynn replied fervently. She beckoned to Patsy. "Come with me. I hear there's a huge Tex-Mex buffet in the dining room and the word is that the housekeeper at White Pines made the food. Maritza's enchiladas are to die for."

From that moment on, everyone made a deliberate effort to include Patsy in the celebration. By the time it was over, she had pushed aside the words she had exchanged with Justin and her worries over a custody battle for Billy. For a couple of hours, she actually managed to live in the moment. More than being accepted as a stranger in their midst, she felt as if she were part of this large extended family.

If only it were true, she thought wistfully as the last of them left. Surrounded by their strength, she was pretty sure she could face just about anything.

As she helped Sharon Lynn pile the last of the packages into the back of her car, Justin came up the walk, carrying a sleeping Billy in his arms. He grinned at Sharon Lynn.

"Looks like you picked up a lot of loot. Any sexy lingerie in there?"

"None that you'll ever see," Sharon Lynn told him. "You find your own woman and your own sexy lingerie."

Justin's gaze shifted instantly to Patsy. She could feel her cheeks burning as he studied her thoughtfully. To cover her rush of embarrassment, she reached for her son.

"I'll take Billy."

"No need," Justin countered, his expression turning stubborn. "I'll carry him in to bed." He held out a huge sack. "You can take this, though."

She reached for the bag and almost dropped it. "What on earth?"

"Billy and I did a little shopping."

Remembering what Jenny had said earlier, she asked, "For yourself or for him?"

He grinned. "He's promised to let me come over and play with his new toys every now and then."

"Justin, you really shouldn't have."

"Of course I should. I haven't had so much fun in years. Wait till you see this really nifty police car. It even has a siren."

Sharon Lynn regarded him with amusement. "I thought you had your own police car with a siren."

The comment didn't seem to faze him. "Yeah, but Billy didn't," he said matter-of-factly.

As far as Patsy knew, Billy had never expressed any interest in having a remote control car. As Jenny had suggested earlier, she suspected the toy really was for Justin, bought under the guise of a gift. She hefted the bag, which weighed a ton.

"There's more than a car in here, isn't there?"

"We saw a basketball set that was pretty snazzy, too."

Patsy stared. "Basketball? Billy's two. It'll be a long

time before he can even hold a basketball, much less play hoops with someone your size."

"This is a toddler basketball set. The net's only as high as my waist and the ball weighs about five ounces. It's not exactly regulation."

"I see. Anything else?"

"A surprise for you. Billy picked it out."

"At the toy store?"

"Yep."

Sharon Lynn regarded them both with tolerant amusement. "Looks like it's your turn for surprises, Patsy. I'll just run along now and leave you to it."

"Don't go," she said in a rush. She didn't want to be left alone with this man whose every action charmed her and reminded her of how long it had been since anyone at all had given a thought to what might make her happy.

"I have a long drive," Sharon Lynn said, ignoring the plea and getting into her car. "See you two in the morning." She blew a kiss in Patsy's direction. "Thanks again for everything."

After she'd gone, Patsy seemed to be rooted to the spot. It was Justin who finally said, "I think maybe I ought to get Billy into bed before he wakes up."

Flustered, she murmured, "Yes, of course."

Inside, she followed him into Billy's room. She took off Billy's shoes and socks, then stripped off his shorts. She left his spaghetti-stained T-shirt on, fearful that removing it would awaken him. He settled onto his tummy, his thumb going instinctively into his mouth.

She glanced up and caught an odd expression on Justin's face, something that might have been longing.

"He's a terrific kid," he said softly.

"He's the light of my life," she said. "I don't know what I'd ever do if something happened to him."

Justin's gaze shifted to her. "What could happen?"

Realizing that she'd almost given her very real fears away, she said, "You know, any of the million and one things that can happen to a kid."

Justin shook his head. "You sounded as if you had something very specific in mind," he said, seizing on her slip of the tongue.

"No," she protested. "Just the usual worries any parent has."

His piercing gaze was unrelenting. "Why don't I believe you?"

"Because not believing me has become second nature to you."

He continued to study her intently, then finally sighed and relaxed. "Okay, maybe my cop's instincts have been on overdrive since we met. I'll try to let up."

Patsy recognized it for the futile promise it was. Rather than debating it with him again, she poked at the bag she'd dropped on the floor. "Okay, where's my surprise?"

Justin picked up the sack and carried it into the living room. "Close your eyes."

She did as she was told and waited with as much anticipation as she might have the promise of a kiss. Her heart skipped a beat. Her pulse pounded.

"Hold out your hands."

She held them out in front of her. A second later she felt something soft and fluffy being placed in her hands. She opened her eyes and saw a toy dog that looked so real she was certain it would begin to bark at any second. The terrier look-alike was caramel colored and had a pink tongue so real looking she expected him to lick her fingers.

"He's wonderful," she said, hugging him to her.

"Billy said you liked dogs. I figured I shouldn't try getting you a real one without discussing it with you, but this looked like the next best thing."

"He feels real," she said, running her fingers through the curling plush hair. "And look at these eyes. He's staring right at me."

"Have you ever had a dog?"

She shook her head. "My parents both worked. They didn't think it was right to leave a dog home alone all day." And Will hadn't wanted anything that might mess up the house and spoil his image if a reporter happened to drop by unexpectedly.

"You could have one now," Justin suggested.

She gestured toward the cats that were curled hither and yon in the living room. "What about them?"

"They're used to every kind of animal under the sun. Dani's a vet, remember? She's spent her whole life taking in every stray that wandered by. She might have one next door even as we speak."

"Several," she conceded, thinking of the cacophony of sound they'd set off earlier. She grinned. "There's always Punk."

"That's not a dog. That's a beast."

"He has his own home, anyway. His owners are due back any day now."

"You sound sad about it."

"I've gotten used to him. Punk and I have an understanding. I sneak him treats and he doesn't lick me to death."

Justin grinned. "See what I mean? You're a natural pet owner. Think about it," he encouraged.

Getting a dog of her own would make a statement of sorts, she realized, if only to herself. It would mean that she intended to stay right here, that she was beginning to put down roots. It would also finalize her decision never to return to Will.

"I'll think about it," she said, then stroked the toy dog in her lap. "In the meantime, Chester here will do just fine."

"Chester?"

She shrugged. "I have no idea why. The name just came to me."

He grinned. "Don't expect me to argue with divine inspiration." He stood and headed for the door, then paused. "I'm glad you like the surprise."

"I *love* the surprise," she said emphatically. It was the very best one she could remember.

With Sharon Lynn's wedding only a few days away, the burden for running Dolan's fell on Patsy's shoulders. She was grateful for the responsibility. It kept her so busy she didn't have time to think about how much longer she could continue with this charade before Justin found out the rest of the truth.

"You're sure you can handle things if I'm gone today?" Sharon Lynn asked for the umpteenth time.

"I can handle it," Patsy repeated, also for the umpteenth time.

"You remember how Mrs. Jenkins likes her eggs?"

"Scrambled moist," Patsy dutifully recited.

"And Tate prefers—"

"Rye toast, not plain."

"What about Doc Dolan?"

"He likes egg salad on white for lunch with a scoop of potato salad on the plate."

Sharon Lynn nodded. "Yes, perfect." She started for the door, then turned back. "I won't be back from Dallas before seven. I've got the fitting for the wedding dress, then a meeting with the florist and a late lunch with two of my bridesmaids, women I went to high school with who're living in Dallas now."

"I can close up," Patsy reassured her. "I'll leave the day's deposit in the night drop at the bank. You've shown me what to do."

"I know. I just hate dumping all this on you."

"You're not dumping anything on me. You told me, when you hired me, you were getting married and that I'd have extra work. Stop worrying and get going before you miss your final fitting."

"Given the number of times Kyle and I almost made it to the altar in the past, you'd think I'd have this down to a science by now."

"Well, this time's the charm. It's less than a week till the wedding and everything's going smoothly, right?"

"I suppose."

Patsy studied her intently. "Sharon Lynn, is there something else worrying you?"

"Not really. I suppose it's just panic. There's been one crisis or another every time the wedding date got close. I'm afraid we're jinxed."

"I don't believe in jinxes. Now go, before your uncle Jordan pitches a fit. He is flying you over, isn't he?"

"Yes, and you're right. He's always in a rush. I'll call you later just to see if anything's come up."

"If you call, I'll be insulted."

Sharon Lynn grinned. "Okay, okay." She paused to hug Patsy. "Thank you. You've been a godsend."

"So have you," Patsy replied quietly. "More than you know."

Sharon Lynn gave her an odd little look, but she let whatever questions she had die on her lips. Finally she smiled and said again, "Thanks."

"Go."

"Let me check—"

"Sharon Lynn!"

"Okay, I'm out of here."

Justin met her in the doorway. "It's a good thing," he said. "I just got a call from Dad. He's at the airport and he's getting really irritated. You were supposed to be there a half hour ago. He has a business meeting he's going to miss if you don't hit the road right this second."

"Why didn't he call me?"

"Because apparently your phone is dead or off the hook."

"Oh, my God," she murmured as the color drained from her face. She raced into the back room.

Patsy and Justin exchanged an amused look, then followed. They caught Sharon Lynn putting the receiver back into place.

"I laid it down to look for my wedding checklist while I was talking to Mom," she explained sheepishly. "I guess I got distracted."

Justin shook his head. "Which explains why I had a call from your mother, as well," he said with tolerant amusement. "Maybe I'd better drive you to the airport."

Sharon Lynn looked oddly relieved. "Would you? You're a doll."

Justin turned and winked at Patsy. "Remember that, would you?"

"No need," she said. "I already knew it."

He seemed startled by her reply. He hesitated as if there were something more on his mind, but Sharon Lynn clutched his arm and dragged him away.

"I'll be back," he promised. "And I won't forget what you said."

Patsy's heart skipped a beat. He was making far too big a thing out of a casual admission, she thought. Had she known he would? Was that why she'd said it?

Of course not, she consoled herself. It had just been a teasing response to his own deliberate taunt. It had been so long since she'd engaged in even the most innocent flirting, she'd forgotten that it could be taken seriously. She hadn't meant to light that fire in his eyes. Surely she hadn't meant to undo all she'd done to keep him at a distance. Justin had simply read too much into it.

The fact remained that he was going to be back here in no time and he was going to have expectations of one sort or another. And she was going to have to think of yet another lie to push him away, when all she really wanted was for him to sweep her into his arms and never let go.

Was that why she'd tempted fate just now? Had she wanted him to take the decision out of her hands at last? Had she deliberately prompted him into making a move so that she wouldn't have to hold herself accountable? Was that the kind of woman she'd become?

She was still debating with herself and not liking any of the answers she came up with, when a man with white hair and the impish grin of every Adams she'd ever run across walked in and sauntered up to the counter. He settled on a stool, then looked her over with blatant fascination.

"Can I help you?" she said, trying not to flinch under that penetrating scrutiny.

"That depends. Are you Patsy Gresham?"

She nodded.

"I'm Harlan Adams. Since no one's seen fit to bring you

by the ranch to meet me, I figured it was up to me to perform the introductions. I'm Justin's granddaddy."

"Yes, sir."

His gaze never wavered. "And you're the woman who's managed to tie that boy into knots." Another grin broke across his face. "Congratulations!"

Patsy swallowed hard. "Sir, I don't know what you've heard, but I think you've got it all wrong. Justin and I are just friends. Acquaintances, really."

"Girl, I don't care what you call it, as long as you bring some joy into his life."

She was stunned by his analysis. "Actually, all I've brought into his life so far is aggravation," she said, to set the record straight.

He chuckled at that. "So much the better. Now I want you to come to White Pines for dinner tomorrow night. Bring that little one of yours, too. The place will be crawling with my grandbabies. One more won't make a bit of difference. In fact, the whole family will be there."

"Then won't I be out of place?"

"I invited you, didn't I? Besides, it's a little get-together in Sharon Lynn's honor. You belong there."

"Yes, but—"

He got off the stool and headed for the door. "Seven o'clock sharp. Maritza gets downright testy if her food gets cold."

He was gone before Patsy could argue. One thing his visit had proved, though. The Adams men were bossy as the very dickens and she was pretty sure most of them always got their own way. It was one more thing she needed to keep in mind when she was dealing with Justin.

Chapter Eight

Justin's day went from bad to worse. After he dropped Sharon Lynn off at the small local airport, he got a call about a prowler at the home of an elderly woman. More than likely it was her overly vivid imagination, but he couldn't ignore the call. Once Letty Jane got to talking, though, it took an act of God to get him away from the place. Literally.

A late-morning thunderstorm rolled in with unexpected force, toppling a line of trees. Everyone vowed it hadn't been a twister, but Justin couldn't prove that by the damage the wind had done. It had upended a trailer on an acre of isolated property on the opposite side of town from Letty Jane's. He spent all day running to and fro, from one crisis to the next, never settling in one place long enough even to call Patsy and explain why he hadn't gotten back.

Not that she was likely to mind, he conceded. He'd seen the quick flaring of panic in her eyes when he'd promised to return. He'd known he was pushing again, but he hadn't been able to help it. There was something between them and he intended to do whatever it took to force her to admit she felt it, too.

After that, they could worry together about the consequences, assuming there was anything that needed worrying about.

Which he still didn't know, he reminded himself with a weary sigh.

As he drove back into town he told himself it was only natural to be going down Main Street just to see that all was right with his little world, even though a shortcut would have gotten him home more quickly. It didn't have anything at all to do with hoping to catch a glimpse of Patsy, either at Dolan's or at her own place.

Unfortunately, the drugstore was locked up tight, the only light the red glow of the exit sign inside the door. Patsy's was just as dark. He tried to tell himself it was just as well. He was exhausted and filthy. Even if she'd opened her arms and invited him in, he was too damned tired to do much about it. He satisfied himself with just knowing that she was all tucked in for the night.

He drove on to the sheriff's office. He could get a cup of coffee there, do his paperwork and head on home for a shower and a good night's sleep. Tomorrow would be soon enough to pursue things with Patsy. Tomorrow or the next day.

Or the day after that, if she had her way.

"My, my, you're a pretty sight," Tate Owens observed when Justin dragged into the station.

"Fortunately, you're not paying me according to my appearance," he retorted. "This is what happens when you slog around in a foot of mud for a few hours chasing down a woman's belongings."

"It surely was a mess out there," Tate agreed.

"I noticed you didn't linger long enough to muss the crease in your trousers," Justin commented good-naturedly. They both knew that Tate wasn't above getting filthy if there was a need for it. Today Justin had had things under control without his help.

Despite the jest, Tate's expression turned serious. "Becky called. Something came in over the wire she thought I ought to see."

A solemn note in Tate's voice alerted Justin that it was something he needed to see, as well. "About Patsy Gresham?"

The sheriff nodded and handed over a flyer. "Her name's Longhorn," he said. "And she's got a husband over in Oklahoma who's been looking for her for a while now. Seems like she's been gone since just a little before she showed up here."

Justin stared blankly at the missing persons flyer. The picture was a family portrait—Patsy, Billy and a man who had to be her husband, Will Longhorn, according to the information at the bottom. For some reason that picture reminded him of a damned campaign poster. Even though the three of them were at some sort of outdoor picnic, there was a posed quality to it, a perfection to the lighting that suggested it had been taken by a professional, rather than some family member or a cooperative stranger.

"They look happy enough, don't they?" Tate said, his tone gentle.

Justin told himself it was his boss's tone, the hint of pity, that made him want to start throwing things. It had nothing to do with the gut-sick feeling in the pit of his stomach at the sight of Patsy with another man.

"You going to talk to her about this or am I?" Tate asked.

Justin stared at him in surprise. "You haven't reported her to the Oklahoma authorities yet?"

"Hell, no," Tate declared. "I figure she's a grown-up woman. If she's here, instead of there, there must be a reason for it. I'm not turning her over to them until I know a hell of a lot more than I do right now. You see anything on there about a crime? No. She's just a missing person. And while I think her family probably has a right to know she's safe, I don't think it's my place to go about giving her away until I hear her side of it." His gaze was steady. "Or until you do."

"I'll talk to her," Justin said, his heart aching. The poster in his hands was proof that Patsy Gresham—Patsy Longhorn—was more out of his reach than ever. "How much time do I have?"

"I can bury that poster on my desk. Given the amount of paperwork piled up, it could take me a mighty long time to find it again. On the other hand, my conscience says a week at the outside."

Justin nodded. It was more than he'd hoped for. "I'll get the answers we need," he said grimly. "You can count on it."

Patsy had never met anyone like the Adams clan. They stuck together. And while there seemed to be a whole crowd of them, there was always room for a stranger in their midst.

The dinner she'd been invited to at White Pines had been a revelation. Harlan Adams's ranch was bigger by far than the ostentatious house Will had insisted they buy, yet White Pines was a home. There was no mistaking the warmth and love in every single room.

To her amazement, though, there had been no sign of Justin by dinnertime. No one had made excuses for him, either. When he'd appeared just in time for dessert, everyone had accepted his arrival without question.

If he'd been surprised to see her, he hadn't shown it. But he'd also seemed to be avoiding her the past few days, making her wonder if he was angry about her inclusion in the family event. Maybe she'd misread his intentions toward her, or maybe they'd just changed.

It was obvious he'd been startled again today when she'd walked into the wedding reception for Sharon Lynn. She hadn't made it to the church, because she'd filled in at Dolan's in the morning so everyone else could go to the service. But Sharon Lynn and Doc Dolan had insisted she close up and come to the reception. Neither of them had taken no for an answer.

"I intend to toss my bouquet straight at you, so you'd better be prepared," Sharon Lynn had told her.

The teasing remark had brought tears and a fresh bout of guilt she hadn't been able to explain.

The dance music was just starting when she walked into the huge tent that had been set up on the lawn at the ranch. Justin had been laughing with his cousins, but the laughter had died when he'd spotted her. This time, though, it seemed he didn't intend to avoid her. He made his way across the room and ended up at her side.

"What a wonderful party," she said, forcing a smile to go along with the lighthearted small talk. "Sharon Lynn looks radiant. And Kyle looks dazed."

"I don't think he can believe it's finally happened. It took them a long time to make this trip down the aisle. They deserve to be happy." His gaze locked with hers. "Everyone does."

She sensed at once that there was a deeper meaning behind his words, but for the life of her she couldn't imagine what it was. There was a vague hint of the old suspicion, the old caution, back in his expression, too.

Rather than ignoring the undercurrents as she once would have done, she addressed them directly. "Justin, are you upset that I came?"

He looked vaguely guilty at the pointed question. "No, of course not."

"Are you sure? I know there's nothing between us."

"Not for lack of trying on my part," he said.

She persisted, determined to apologize for intruding where she didn't belong. "I'm sorry if finding me at all these family functions the past few days is making you uncomfortable. Your grandfather and Sharon Lynn, they insisted I come."

"I'm sure," he said ruefully. He shook his head. "No, I'm the one who should be apologizing. We're a family of meddlers. With Sharon Lynn married off tonight, I'm the next logical target. Next week or next month it'll be Harlan Patrick's turn. I'm sorry you got caught in the cross fire."

"I don't mind," she confessed with a catch in her voice, uncertain what sort of reaction the admission might draw.

He regarded her with surprise. "Really? Now that is a change."

"It's true."

In fact, if the truth were known, she liked being linked to this strong, decent man whose temper never seemed to get the better of him. She'd seen his patience tested to the limits—by her, in fact—but he'd never once raised his voice. It was a welcome relief after Will.

If things were different, if she were free, a man like Justin Adams would be the kind of man she'd like in her life.

If she were free...

But she wasn't, and because she wasn't, she turned and hurried away, ignoring Justin's commands for her to stop. She didn't slow until she was locked in a bathroom upstairs, far from the crowd of well-wishers.

She should leave, not just White Pines, but Los Piños. There was something different about Justin tonight, something that warned her away, told her that she'd stayed too long, tempting fate.

But if she took even a second to look into her heart, she knew that no matter the consequences, she couldn't go. The time for running was over.

"Getting any ideas, son?" Grandpa Harlan asked Justin as Sharon Lynn and Kyle moved into each other's arms for the first dance at the reception.

The question's timing couldn't have been worse, because he was getting ideas, had had them for a long time now, but he now knew for a fact they would never be. That poster on Tate's desk was evidence of that. Patsy belonged to another man. He'd guessed it weeks ago, but the proof had torn him apart.

"Don't you start, old man," he said, trying to take the sting out of his words.

His grandfather was made of hearty stuff. The order didn't faze him.

"I've seen the way you look at that pretty little gal from Oklahoma," he said, casting a sly look across the room to where Patsy was standing all alone. "You've got a thing for her. Why not admit it?"

Justin sighed. "Because there are things you don't know, Grandpa Harlan, things I'm not even sure about. Seems like we just weren't meant to be."

"Such as?"

Justin hesitated, then decided that his grandfather might be the one person on earth who could give him the kind of levelheaded advice he desperately needed right now. "I think she's on the run."

His grandfather took that news in stride. "From the

law?" he demanded indignantly. "I don't believe it. If that girl's some sort of criminal, then I'm no judge of character."

"Maybe not from the law," Justin conceded. "More likely from a man, possibly her husband."

That did raise his grandfather's eyebrows ever so slightly. "She's married? You know that for a fact?"

There was the missing persons report, but that was only one side of the story, just as Tate had suggested. "Not exactly," he said eventually.

"Well, if you suspect it's the case, why the dickens haven't you asked her? From what I've seen, both of you have a lot riding on the truth."

"I'm not sure she'd tell me the truth," Justin admitted. "I see how skittish she is around me whenever I'm wearing my uniform. Tate flat out terrifies her. If she's going to open up, it might not be to one of us."

What if she knew about the poster, guessed they'd seen it? he wondered. Would she run again? Was she that desperate to get away from her husband? He sighed. He couldn't get into that with his grandfather. He'd probably told him more than he should as it was.

"I keep hoping she'll explain on her own and let me help."

His grandfather regarded him with sympathy. "I think I see the position you're in. There's your duty as a sworn lawman. And, then, there's your duty to a woman you care about."

"Which one's more important?" Justin asked, aware that the question sounded a little plaintive. "I always thought for sure I knew. The law's the law."

"It's a delicate balancing act, all right," his grandfather said. "Maybe there's a way for both to be the same."

"How?"

"You won't know until you know all the truth. Talk to her, son. Do it now, tonight, before your courage fails you and before the answers can cut too deep."

"Too late for that," Justin said. "I'm already in way over my head."

"Then you'll find a way to make things right," his grandfather said with absolute confidence. "For both of you."

"I hope you're right."

"Well, of course I am," his grandfather said with exaggerated indignation. "You don't get to be my age without learning a thing or two. Now, go along. Talk to her. Unless I miss my guess, she's as torn up inside as you are."

Justin knew his grandfather was right. There was no way around it. This was one time he couldn't afford to be endlessly patient. Lives and futures were at stake. Patsy's and Billy's, maybe. His own for sure.

He weaved through the crowd, his gaze locked on the woman who stood all alone on the fringes. She looked more fragile than ever in a pale blue slip dress that skimmed over her body in a silken caress. The dress was the epitome of costly simplicity. It practically had designer stamped all over it. The cop in him had wanted to check for a label and demand explanations once again for the inconsistencies in her life-style. The man simply wanted to slide it over her head and run callused hands over the woman beneath.

If he listened to the throbbing in his veins, that dress would be merely an inconvenience. If he listened to his head, he would escort her somewhere very public for the conversation that had been too long coming. By the time he reached her side, he still wasn't sure which side had won the mental debate.

"Everything okay?" he asked, his tone cautious.

"Of course," she said, a little too brightly.

"Where'd you run off to?"

"The ladies' room."

"I thought maybe you were running away?"

Alarm flared in her eyes, but she quickly hid it. "From what?"

"Me."

"You don't scare me."

"I should."

"Why?"

"Because I want you."

She swallowed hard at the bold assertion. "I know."

"Any objections?"

Her hesitation—combined with the pure desire written all over her face—was enough to tell him as much as he needed to know. She wanted him all right, but she was going to do the honorable thing—the *wifely* thing—and say yes. She was going to tell him to take a hike.

Before she could say anything, he said quietly, "Let's go somewhere for coffee."

She blinked in surprise. "Coffee?"

"Don't argue. You don't want the alternative."

Her gaze locked with his. "I didn't say that."

His smile was forced. "You didn't have to. Come on, darlin', before I change my mind. Sharon Lynn and Kyle will be leaving any minute now, anyway."

Before she could object, he clasped her hand and dragged her along behind him, nodding politely to everyone they passed. It was a neat trick to get away from White Pines without being subjected to a million and one questions, but he managed it.

As he headed for his car, Patsy began to voice her first objection. "My car—"

He refused to relinquish his grip on her. "I'll have someone drive it into town in the morning."

Only after they were in his car with the radio playing at top volume to drown out any need for conversation did she speak again. Raising her voice to be heard, she asked, "Justin, what's going on?"

"We'll talk when we get into town."

"What's wrong with here?"

"I can't concentrate on you and the road at the same time."

He thought he caught the beginnings of a smile at that.

"Ever heard of small talk?"

"That's the last thing I want to engage in with you." To make his point, he reached for the volume and turned it up another notch. Now there was nothing in the car but the sound of George Strait and a sizzling tension for which there would be no relief.

In town, he parked in front of the Italian restaurant, knowing that it would be virtually empty at this hour, especially with half the folks in town out at White Pines at the wedding reception. The coffee was strong enough to keep them both wide-awake until they'd hashed this mess through from beginning to end.

He led the way to a booth with Patsy trailing along behind, silently fuming. He could practically feel the anger radiating from her. He couldn't say he blamed her, but he wasn't exactly dancing with joy tonight himself.

"Two coffees," he told the waitress in a tone that warned her not to linger.

"Sure, Justin." She left without asking about the wedding, returned with two cups and a whole pot of coffee, then retreated all the way into the kitchen.

"Look," Patsy began, scowling at him, "I don't know

what has you in such a snit tonight, but you don't have any business taking it out on her, or on me, for that matter."

Justin sighed. "You're right."

"Then what's this all about?"

He looked into her eyes and saw the beginnings of wariness again. "Same old thing," he said, trying to make light of it.

"You think I'm hiding something."

"I *know* you're hiding something," he corrected.

She began twisting the napkin she was holding into a tight knot. She looked everywhere in the restaurant except at him. When the napkin shredded, she stared at it in dismay.

"Patsy, please, can't you tell me the truth after all this time? Maybe I can help."

The tears welling up in her eyes were almost his undoing. He wanted to take back all the questions. He wanted to promise that he would never pry into her past again, but it was too late for that. If he didn't, Tate would. It was better if he did it, if the truth was something shared between them, instead of a barrier they could never overcome.

"You can't," she whispered finally. "You can't help."

"I can try."

She shook her head. "This isn't the kind of problem you can fix with a screwdriver or even a hankie," she said, accepting the one he offered with a rueful smile.

"Neither of us will really know that until you tell me." He looked directly into her eyes then, willing her to begin at the beginning and tell him everything.

She opened her mouth, about to speak, when his beeper went off. He ignored it, but it went off again and then again.

"Damn," he muttered. "I've got to call the station. I'll be back in a second."

Relief washed over her face at the reprieve.

"I will be back, though, and we will finish this conversation," he vowed as he went toward the pay phone to call the station.

Justin quickly placed a call to the station. "Justin, I'm sorry to call you, but I thought you'd want to know," the late-night dispatcher said.

"What? Couldn't it wait until morning?" he asked impatiently.

"There's been an accident on the highway coming into town from White Pines. It's Sharon Lynn and Kyle."

Cold dread settled in the pit of his stomach. "Are they okay?"

"It's bad, Justin. Real bad. I think you'd better get out there."

He slammed the phone down and walked slowly back to the table. "I have to go," he said, his voice cracking on a sob he hadn't even known was bottled up inside.

Patsy jumped up and followed him. "Justin? What is it? You're white as a ghost."

"An accident," he said. "Sharon Lynn and Kyle."

All of the color drained out of her face, too. "I'm coming with you."

"No. There's no need. I can drop you at your place."

Her chin shot up. "I'm coming with you," she repeated. "Are you going to waste time standing here arguing?"

He realized then how desperately he wanted her with him, how very badly he would need her to hang on to if the news was as grim as the dispatcher had made it sound.

"Buckle up, then," he said grimly as she climbed into the car and shot him a look that dared him to argue.

"You won't help anyone by getting killed en route," she said softly as he took the corner on two wheels and shot down Main Street.

He slowed, but only to the point of reason and well in excess of the speed limit. He'd done enough training and high-speed chases to know precisely what his own limits were on the road. He drove with total concentration, allowing his mind to wander only long enough to utter a few fervent prayers that Sharon Lynn and her new husband would be all right.

What in God's name had happened? Kyle was a good driver, the roads were practically deserted this time of night and he'd bet the ranch that neither of them had had more than a glass of champagne during the reception.

"I see the flashing lights up ahead," Patsy murmured, fear in her voice. "It looks as if there's a lot of them."

"That just means they're getting all the help they need. Nothing to panic over." He said it as much for his own benefit as hers.

They arrived just as an ambulance sped off toward Garden City in the opposite direction, siren blaring. There were two more on the scene and paramedics seemed to be everywhere, most of them volunteers who'd come scrambling in pickups, lights flashing on their dashboards and casting an eerie glow in the dark.

A huge spotlight was shining on the twisted wreckage of Kyle's car, guiding him through the maze of rescue vehicles, police cars and ambulances. One glimpse was enough to make Justin want to retch. He heard Patsy's gasp beside him at the sight of the crushed passenger compartment.

"Get back into the car," he said. "There's nothing you can do to help. I'll find out what's happening."

"Sharon Lynn," she began in a whisper every bit as tormented as his own thoughts.

"Shh, don't think the worst. Let me get some answers."

He herded her back toward his car, then moved again through the tangle of debris and people. He saw the expressions of sympathy and knew then that the news wasn't going to be good.

Swallowing hard, he forced himself to face the deputy in charge. "My cousin," he began. It was all he could say without falling apart.

"Sharon Lynn's badly injured, but she's going to make it," Dusty assured him. "She's unconscious, but her vital signs were good. She's already on her way to the hospital."

Justin's gaze was drawn back to the collapsed mass of metal on the passenger side. "But how?"

"She was driving," Dusty said succinctly. "The air bag saved her. Kyle took the brunt of the impact." He looked as if he wanted to cry, too. "He…he wasn't so lucky, Justin. There was a faint pulse when we got here, but we couldn't get him out in time to save him. The guys did everything they could."

Justin felt the world begin to spin. Sheer will kept him upright. "Do you know what happened?"

"A drunk crossed the center line. It looked as if Sharon Lynn tried to get out of his way, but with no shoulders and those deep ditches, there was no place to go."

"Is he dead?"

Dusty looked startled that he cared. "The drunk driver?"

Justin nodded.

"No, he's over there. Some minor cuts and bruises. He'll walk away."

Pure rage made Justin see red. He turned in the direction the deputy had indicated, ignoring Dusty's commands to stop, to let it go. He had to see for himself, had to look into the face of the man who'd murdered his cousin's husband, who'd almost killed her, as well.

And then he might very well beat that face into a bloody pulp.

Chapter Nine

Patsy saw Justin walking toward the side of the highway. There was something about his jerky, dazed progress that brought her scrambling from the car and heading straight for him. She reached him just as a deputy she recognized as Dusty Patterson got to his side and clamped a hand on his shoulder.

"Get away from me," Justin demanded, his voice like ice.

"Don't do this," Dusty pleaded. "You're not thinking straight."

Anger radiated from Justin in palpable waves. Even without knowing what was going on, Patsy sensed that he was about to do something he would come to regret. Instinctively she stepped in front of the two men.

"Justin?"

When he didn't even glance at her, she spoke his name again, more sharply this time. As if he'd been drawn out of some distant hell, his gaze finally shifted to clash with hers. The sight of the tears streaking down his cheeks was almost her undoing. There was no doubt in her mind now that something truly terrible had happened to Sharon Lynn and Kyle. What else could create such despair in such a strong man?

She reached up and touched his face. "Come with me, please," she begged.

For the longest time, she wasn't sure he would agree. He seemed torn between anger and a distress so deep and heart wrenching, she could only fear its cause. At last, he turned away and went with her.

He got into the car and leaned forward, his head resting on the steering wheel. Quiet sobs shook his shoulders. Patsy scrambled across the seat and put her arms around him. As desperately as she wanted to know what had happened, how badly Kyle and Sharon Lynn were injured, she kept silent, letting Justin do his grieving in silence while she fought her own fears.

It seemed they remained like that forever, but in truth it was no more than a minute or two, she realized, before he drew in a shuddering breath and faced her.

"We have to go to the hospital."

"Sharon Lynn and Kyle are there?"

He shook his head. "Only Sharon Lynn."

The implication of that tore through her. "Oh, my God. Kyle?"

"Didn't make it." He looked so shattered that all she wanted to do was reach over and hold him again, but he was already starting the engine. The grim set of his mouth told her he wouldn't appreciate a show of sympathy right now, that he'd only tolerated the first display because he'd been nearly oblivious to it. All she could do was stay with him, be there when he needed someone and be there for Sharon Lynn, whose world had just come crashing down around her head. She thought of Sharon Lynn's terrible premonition that her future with Kyle was jinxed and realized the enormity of what lay ahead for her.

At the hospital, they found the rest of the family already gathered, most of them still in the clothes they'd worn to the wedding. Patsy faded into the background once she was certain that Justin was being taken care of by his family.

She wandered from the emergency room waiting area and went in search of a chapel. When she found it off the main lobby, she went inside and found Janet Adams already there, her face damp with tears.

Patsy started to tiptoe out again, but the older woman spotted her and held out her hand. "Come, sit with me. I just came to tell God how grateful we are for sparing Sharon Lynn."

"What about how angry we are that Kyle was taken from her?" Patsy asked, unable to hide her own bitterness on her friend's behalf. "How could this happen to someone as decent and kind as Sharon Lynn?"

"God never gives us any pain he doesn't think will make us stronger."

Patsy wondered about that. Then she thought of her own life up until now. When she'd been caught up in Will's web of snide remarks and psychological abuse, she'd thought only about the terrible sense of failure he was instilling in her. When she'd run, she'd felt more like a victim than ever and she'd cursed him for that, hating him every bit as much as if he'd hit her.

But she was stronger now and her strength had come out of that pain. Would the same be true for Sharon Lynn? She could only pray that Janet was right.

They sat quietly side by side, lost in their own thoughts, taking comfort from each other's presence. It was a long time before she looked up and saw Justin standing hesitantly in the doorway. "I heard this was where you'd gone," he said, still not coming into the quiet, dimly lit chapel.

Janet regarded him with sympathy. "I'm sorry you had to be there tonight. It must have been terrible for you."

Anger flashed in his eyes. "I'm not the one who needs your pity. Save it for Sharon Lynn. I only wish I could have killed the man responsible when I had the chance."

"You don't mean that," Janet said gently. "The courts will hand down justice. It wasn't up to you. You know that's the way it has to be."

"Do I?" he asked bitterly. His gaze shifted to Patsy. "There's nothing more we can do here tonight. I'll take you home."

She nodded and squeezed Janet's hand. "Thank you for what you said. It meant a lot to me. If there's anything I can do for any of you, let me know."

Janet glanced toward the doorway. "Stay with Justin," she said, her expression worried. "He's going to need you. You heard him just now. This doesn't fit with his sense of justice at all. It won't be easy for him to reconcile it." She sighed. "If I'm being totally honest, no matter what I said before, even I know it won't be easy for any of us."

The next few days went by in a terrible haze. Patsy did the only thing she could think of to do that might help. She kept the lunch counter at Dolan's running smoothly from dawn to dusk. The news on Sharon Lynn was more positive each day and by the beginning of the following week she had been released from the hospital. Patsy went to visit her at the ranch, where the whole family was hovering over her. When she went into Sharon Lynn's room, she was horrified by what she found.

Though Sharon Lynn's injuries were healing nicely and the bruises had begun to fade, she was lying in bed staring dully at the ceiling. When Patsy had walked into the room, her friend had not even glanced in her direction.

"Hey," Patsy said softly. "I'm so relieved to see you safe at home again."

Sharon Lynn nodded, her expression blank. "Thanks," she murmured with no emotion in her voice at all.

"Everyone at Dolan's misses you like crazy. They're asking when you'll be back."

No response. Patsy tried again.

"What is the doctor saying about getting back on your feet again?"

"Not much."

Patsy didn't know too much about clinical depression, but it seemed to her that Sharon Lynn was sinking into the kind of dark despair that needed quick attention. She wondered if anyone had broached the subject with her, then wondered if she dared do it herself. She was still debating whether she had any right or even an obligation to say something, when Sharon Lynn spoke.

"I killed him, you know." She whispered it matter-of-factly.

Patsy reacted angrily. "Don't be absurd. Kyle was killed by a drunk driver. Don't you ever think otherwise."

"But I was driving our car. I should have done…" Her voice trailed off before she finally added forlornly, "Something. I should have done something."

Patsy reached for her hand. It was ice-cold and limp. "There was nothing you could have done, no place you could turn," she insisted. "The road's narrow, and there are deep ditches on either side. The only person responsible for this tragedy was the other driver."

The door to the room opened just as she spoke.

"Damn right!" Justin said fiercely. He came over to the bed and reached down for Sharon Lynn's hand. "Don't you dare blame yourself. The slime who did this should be locked up for a long, long time. The sheriff will see that he is."

Sharon Lynn retreated visibly, staring back up at the ceiling again, her expression blank. Patsy beckoned to Justin and led him from the room. It was the first time she'd seen him in days, as well. He looked only marginally better than his cousin. She wanted to throw her arms around him and hold him. It was a strange feeling to think of herself as the strong one after so many years of believing herself to be weak.

"Are you okay?" she asked quietly.

A ghost of a smile came and went. "Better now that I've seen you."

"You don't look as if you've slept a wink in days."

"You mean I'm not as handsome as ever?" he asked, a twinkle bringing a momentary light to his eyes.

"Oh, you'll always be handsome enough, Justin Adams, but right now you're pale and drawn. Haven't you been eating? You haven't been by Dolan's since this happened."

He did smile at that. "Did you miss me?"

"Of course not. I just worried that the thieves were going to start getting ideas now that there hasn't been a lawman parked at the counter for days."

"So it's my badge you've been missing," he teased. "I'm surprised. I always had the feeling it made you nervous."

Patsy's pulse thudded dully at the taunt. It was too close to being squarely on the mark.

"I don't hear you denying it," he said.

"Because it's so ridiculous it doesn't deserve a reply," she said, trying to brazen it out. She met his gaze unblinkingly.

Eventually he grinned. "If you say so, darlin'."

"Can we talk about Sharon Lynn for a minute?" she asked.

She knew it was a topic that would fully capture his attention and get the glare of the spotlight off her for a bit. As she'd anticipated, a worried frown creased his brow. "What about her?"

"I think maybe she's going to need some help getting through this."

"She's getting help. We're all here. All she has to do is say the word and any one of us will get her whatever she needs."

"I'm not talking about soup or some custard when she says she's hungry. I'm talking about professional help."

"A shrink?"

She nodded.

"That's crazy," he said indignantly. "Anyone would be upset after a tragedy like this. Sharon Lynn's strong. She's an Adams. She'll pull herself together in time."

Patsy was doubtful. "Will she? She's eaten up with guilt. She told me she killed Kyle. You heard her yourself."

"That's the grief talking. She'll put this into perspective. Once the other driver is convicted and locked away, she'll see it wasn't her fault."

Patsy remained silent in response. Finally Justin said, "You don't believe that, do you?"

"No, I don't. There's something about the way she's staring off into space, as if she's slowly disconnecting from the world. It worries me. Maybe it's just grief, but it seems to me it goes deeper than that. It's not just that she's lost

Kyle." She struggled to put it into words. "It's as if she's lost her reason for living."

"And you got all that from a five-minute visit?" Justin asked, his expression incredulous.

Patsy refused to back down, even in the face of his blatant skepticism. "Okay, it's just my opinion and I'm not an expert. I'm just saying an expert would be able to say once and for all if she needs some counseling. Don't trust my judgment, just ask yourself if you want to take the chance that I'm right."

Justin sighed and ran his fingers through his close-cropped hair. "Hell, I suppose you could be right. It's just that Adamses solve their own problems."

"Sometimes the solution is asking for help," Patsy said.

"I'll mention it to the family and see what they think," Justin promised. He reached over and tucked a stray curl behind her ear. "By the way, has anyone thanked you for pitching in and taking over at Dolan's?"

"I don't need to be thanked. It's my job. Dani's staff has been great about helping with Billy so I could be there longer hours."

"Don't work yourself to a frazzle," he warned. "You need to look after yourself, too."

She gazed into his eyes and saw genuine concern there. It was the first time in as long as she could remember that anyone had been truly worried about her well-being. It had mattered to Will only as far as her ability to campaign on his behalf.

"I'm fine," she reassured Justin. "But I'd better be getting back into town. With the hours I'm putting in at Dolan's, I don't like to leave Billy with a sitter in the evenings, too."

"Mind if I come along?" Justin asked. "I promised him I'd be by to play with those toys we bought. I haven't had a chance up until now. Frankly, I could use a break from all this."

"He'd like that."

"And you? Would you like that, too?"

She knew what he was really asking, but she wasn't sure she entirely trusted his motives. Did it really matter to him whether she was beginning to care for him or was he simply trying to test her again? Even though it had been days since their last talk and despite all that had happened, she doubted Justin had forgotten all the questions he had about her past.

"Of course," she said cheerily. "If you haven't eaten yet, you can share a pizza with us."

"Why don't I pick it up on my way and meet you at the house?"

"I can do it."

"Why should you when I can and you can get home to Billy that much sooner?"

She grinned. "Okay, when you put it like that, how can I argue? But I insist on paying for it."

"We'll discuss that later."

"Justin!" She took a twenty from her purse and tried to press it into his hands. He jammed his hands into his pockets and defied her to follow with the money. She was tempted to do just that, but the prospect of finding her own hand trapped between his and his body with only a layer of denim in between rattled her too badly. That jittery temptation was proof enough that she had no business getting in any kind of intimate contact with him.

She sighed. "Okay, you win. We'll discuss it later."

He grinned. "It's nice to see that you can compromise."

"Is that what you call it?"

"Sure, darlin'. I have it on the best authority that compromise is very important in any relationship."

Patsy didn't know whether to cheer or turn tail and run at the mention of the word *relationship*. She and Justin weren't having a relationship. It was impossible.

But, oh, how she wished it weren't.

"Patsy?"

Startled, she glanced up and met Justin's worried frown. "Everything okay?"

"Sure," she lied. "Just trying to remember how big a mess the house is in. I'd hate for you to walk in and wonder if a tornado blew through. After all, it is your sister's place. I'd hate to have her evict me."

"There's no chance of that," he assured her. "And don't worry about the state of your housekeeping. With all the nieces and nephews running around in this family, no one knows the meaning of tidy anymore."

"Not even you? You live alone and, as I recall, your place was spotless the one time I came over."

"That's because I'm never there. And it's not tidy. It's sterile. Give me chaos any day. It's what makes the difference between a house and a home."

"Maybe I should let Billy come and visit for an afternoon. The resulting mess ought to send you into raptures."

"I'd love it," he said, much to her amazement. "In the meantime, let's get into town. Suddenly I'm starved for the first time in days."

The gleam in his eyes was a reminder that food was not the only thing a man could be starved for. Patsy was drawn to that look, wanted desperately to respond to it, but decency prevented it.

She had the whole long drive into town to wonder how long she could allow this marital limbo to drag on. It was unfair to Billy and to her. Maybe even to Will. Most of all, though, it was unfair to Justin, because he didn't even know what he was up against.

How was she going to resolve it? Could she simply file for divorce long-distance and pray that Will went along with it? Thinking he would was a foolish idea. He was a very possessive man. Even though she knew he no longer loved her—if he ever had—he would fight the divorce if only because he would fear the damage to his image if he let her go. He would demand custody of Billy for the same reason.

Her feet were dragging as she walked into the house, not just from exhaustion, but from despair. How could she ever truly move on with her life, build a real future for herself and her son, unless she resolved things with Will? She'd been crazy to think that simply running away would solve all of her problems. It had removed her and Billy from harm's way, but it had created a whole new set of problems.

Still the thought of seeing Will again under any circumstances terrified her. She had weathered a lot in the past couple of months. She was far stronger than she'd been when she'd run from Oklahoma, but was she strong enough for the battle that was likely to ensue?

Before she could reach any conclusion at all about that, Billy came running toward her, arms held high, a piece of paper clutched in one tiny hand.

"Mama, Mama, Mama," he chanted. "Me drew picture for you. See?"

She took the paper and looked at the colorful scribbles. They were meaningless to her, but clearly not to her son. She hunkered down beside him. "This is beautiful," she said admiringly. "Tell me about it."

"I drewed us. We're a family. See?" He pointed to the littlest batch of swirls and lines. "That's me. And that's you."

"Ah," she said, seeing the relative difference in sizes, if not the identifying details. "And this?"

"That's Daddy." There was a mulish lift to his chin when he said it, then added, "Want to see Daddy."

"Daddy's far away," she reminded him.

"Want to see him."

"Maybe we can call him later."

"Now," Billy demanded. "Call now."

Patsy sighed. She had promised him days ago that they would call his daddy, but there had never been time to take a trip to some out-of-the-way pay phone that couldn't be traced. Obviously she would have to make the time.

"Tomorrow," she promised. She would get one of the women who'd volunteered to help out at Dolan's in Sharon Lynn's absence to fill in long enough for her to take Billy to make the phone call. "Now why don't we get you cleaned up? Justin's coming over and he's bringing pizza."

The mention of his favorite food—to say nothing of his favorite grown-up playmate—was enough to distract him. She went into the living room where Flo Bartle was waiting. Flo lived next door and, since the accident, had taken over baby-sitting duty when Dani's staff left for the day.

"Flo, I can't thank you enough for looking out for Billy for me."

"No problem. He's an angel. You do whatever you need to do to help out Sharon Lynn. There are plenty of us who can pitch in and help with Billy. All I'd be doing at home is watching my husband snooze through the national news. Believe me, I'd rather be here."

"Justin's bringing a pizza by. Would you like to stay?"

"No, indeed. I'd have heartburn the rest of the night." She winked. "Besides, I doubt Justin's coming by so he can look at an old lady across the table."

"It would be fine," Patsy insisted. "Justin and I are just friends."

"If you say so, dear. Just remember there are friends and then there are *friends*."

"Hey, Mrs. B.," Justin called out as he came up the walk carrying a huge pizza box. "You get more beautiful every time I see you."

"Then your eyesight's going, boy, or else you're as full of blarney as every other male in your family."

He dropped a kiss on her cheek. "I'm a deputy sheriff, Mrs. B. I'm sworn to uphold the law and to tell the truth, so help me God."

The teasing comment put a sparkle in her neighbor's eyes, but it sent a shiver down Patsy's spine. Once again she'd been reminded of the position she'd been putting Justin in since the day they'd met. It had to stop.

Tomorrow, she vowed to herself as she had to Billy earlier. Tomorrow, when she called Will, she would test the waters and see if there was any way to put an end to all the lies and deception or whether she was doomed to a life in limbo.

Chapter Ten

It was the first time since the night of the accident that Justin had let himself relax. He was stretched out on the floor in Patsy's living room, his back braced against the sofa, the empty pizza box off to one side, as he watched Billy struggle to build a tower with a new set of blocks.

One block, two, then eventually six, stacked in a way that virtually assured disaster. With awkward fingers Billy tried to put the seventh block on top, only to set the whole stack to teetering dangerously. Justin reached over and steadied it, but balance was elusive. It toppled over, sending Billy into fits of giggles.

"Again," he insisted, putting the first block into place.

"Maybe it needs a bigger base," Justin suggested idly.

"What's a base?" Billy demanded.

"More blocks on the bottom." He reached over and set four of the colorful plastic blocks into a square, then stacked two on top of that. "See, like this."

"Won't fall down?" Billy asked skeptically.

"Nope."

"'Kay," Billy agreed, and added another block to the pile, then another.

When it all teetered and fell again, he stared at it with a look of such betrayal in his eyes that Justin felt like a heel. This time tears, rather than giggles, accompanied the architectural disaster.

"Maybe I'm not as good an engineer as I thought," he apologized.

"Or maybe your work crew isn't past the apprentice stage yet," Patsy suggested, grinning at them. "It's Billy's bedtime, anyway."

"No," Billy said at once, even though his eyelids had been drooping for the past half hour.

"I'll put you to bed and tell you a story," Justin offered.

Billy's eyes widened. "You will?"

"Indeed, I will. I'll tell you the story about a girl named Little Red Riding Hood and this big, bad wolf."

"No. Want rabbit story."

Justin shrugged. "Then the rabbit story it will be, but I gotta tell you, kid, the big, bad wolf is much more of a guy thing."

"He might be a little young for guy things," Patsy said, her expression amused. "And you won't be the one left to deal with the nightmares."

"Okay, Mom. I bow to your superior knowledge on the subject," he said, scooping Billy up and tickling him until he giggled. The sound was pure delight, so he kept it up. It reminded him of things like innocence and simple pleasures. It reminded him of all the things he wanted and that were out of reach.

"You realize, of course, that if you do that much more he'll never get to sleep," Patsy observed.

Justin shook his head and gave Billy a sympathetic look. "Moms just don't get it, do they?"

Billy shook his head. "Don't get it."

He carried Billy into his room and helped him into his pj's, then settled him in bed. He'd done the same thing a hundred times with his nieces and nephews, but there was something different about putting Billy to bed. The kids in his family all had adoring dads of their own. He was just a welcome variance in their routine. With Billy he sensed that having a man put him to bed was a whole new experience. He seemed wide-eyed that Justin would want to, and pitifully eager to prolong the storytelling as long as possible.

"Read it again," he begged, even though he could barely hold his eyes open after the second time.

"Close your eyes and go to sleep," Justin countered. "I'll read for five more minutes, but you'd better be snoozing when I'm done."

Billy smiled contentedly and snuggled down beneath the covers. He dutifully closed his eyes. As Justin had expected, he was sound asleep before Justin had finished reading the first page. Justin sat for a moment longer and stared at the boy, amazed by the sense of yearning that came over him.

Why had he waited so long before claiming nights like this for himself? He'd been dating forever—maybe not as extensively as Harlan Patrick, but enthusiastically. The idea of settling down had never once crossed his mind until now.

He sighed heavily. It would have to be a woman with secrets and a boy with coal black eyes who drew him. Something told him that down that path lay heartache. The new report that had landed on Tate's desk today confirmed it. Will Longhorn was now claiming that Patsy had kidnapped their son. The stakes had escalated way past his own needs and longings.

He was still sitting there when he sensed Patsy behind him. He jolted when her hand came to rest on his shoulder. The touch was as light and tentative as the flutter of a bird's wings, but he felt as if it were the most intimate caress he'd ever shared.

"You guys finish your story?" she whispered.

"Twice," he admitted.

"Dani was right. He does have you wound around his little finger. I thought you were made of tougher stuff than that."

"He gets to me."

"Why?"

He shrugged. "I'm not sure. Is it possible for a man to feel an instinctive bond with a child who's not his own?"

"Adoptive dads do that all the time."

"True." He glanced over his shoulder into her eyes. "Maybe I'm just getting to a time in my life when I'm thinking about a family and wondering when I'll have one of my own."

"You will when you want to," she said. "You come from a long line of men who go after whatever they want. They're all family men, with deep roots. You're no different."

"What happens if I pick the wrong woman?" he inquired softly, meeting her gaze evenly. "What if I pick someone who's not free to love me back?"

He saw the flare of alarm in her eyes, the sudden rush of dismay that stripped the color from her cheeks.

"What are you saying?" she asked, her voice shaky.

He refused to look away or to yield to her obvious panic. "I'm just wondering, hypothetically, what would happen to my dreams if I fell in love with a woman who's not available? Where would that leave me?"

Rather than answer, she whirled and left the room. Justin followed slowly. He found her on the front porch, staring out at the night sky. He walked up behind her and rested his hands on her shoulders, much as she had done to him earlier. He could feel her trembling, felt the buck of her pulse where his thumb rested against her neck.

And then he felt the hot splash of a tear on his hand. It almost brought him to his knees. He hadn't meant for her to cry, hadn't meant to shake her so badly that she would run from him. He'd just wanted to prod her into opening up at last. Maybe a direct, straightforward question would have been better, after all.

He turned her gently, then pulled her into his arms. She resisted for no more than a heartbeat, then rested her head against his shoulder.

"I'm sorry," he apologized.

"For what?"

"Pushing again."

"It's not that."

"What then?"

She drew in a deep, shuddering breath, then whispered, "You know, don't you? I've sensed it for days now."

His own breath caught in his throat. At last, he thought. At last there would be truth between them.

And then what? he wondered to himself. What the hell would he do when the truth was out? There would be no turning back, then. What if it started them both down a path that destroyed any hope of the future he'd been envisioning just a short time before?

"Know what?" he asked, because he had to, because it was the only thing to do. The kidnapping charge was too serious to be ignored, no matter how ridiculous he might believe it to be.

"About me." She drew in a deep breath, then blurted, "That I'm married."

He sighed. He'd hoped, prayed, that he'd been wrong about that, that she was divorced at least, but the report on

Tate's desk hadn't lied. Will Longhorn was still her husband. What was the rest of the truth, though? Were they in the process of getting a divorce? Was there a battle for custody? Had she kidnapped their son to avoid losing him to her husband? Justin didn't believe that, even though it would explain the skittishness, the use of her maiden name, rather than her husband's. He would lay odds that she had every right to have that boy with her.

"Maybe I'm the wrong person for you to talk to about this," he said finally.

She regarded him incredulously. "You forced this into the open and now you don't want to talk about it?"

He touched a silencing finger to her lips. "It's not that I don't want to hear everything. I just think maybe it would be best if you talked to Janet."

"Why?"

"Because she's an attorney and a damned fine one. If you're in trouble, she can help. She'll want to, you know that. You won't go wrong listening to her."

"Who says I need an attorney?"

"I do," he said, a gentle hand on her cheek. "Listen to me. Talk to Janet."

"Justin, how much do you know?"

"Not everything," he admitted. "I know that your husband is looking for you."

She sighed. "I thought he might be. What else?"

"He's accusing you of kidnapping your baby."

She stared at him in shock. "Kidnapping? That's absurd. Billy is mine as much as he is Will's. There's been no divorce, no custody battle. There's no way he could accuse me of kidnapping my own son." She regarded him with a panicky expression. "Could he?"

He rushed to reassure her. "He can make all the accusations he wants, but it remains to be seen if any of them will stand up in court. That's why I think you should talk to Janet."

"I can't," she whispered. "What if she says I have to go back? What if she tells me he can take Billy away from me, that I have to give up my son?"

He studied her intently, recognizing the genuine fear in her eyes. "Has Will Longhorn ever hurt you?"

His heart was in his throat as he waited what seemed to be a lifetime for her to slowly shake her head.

"Not physically, no. He's come close. His temper gets out of control. He's threatened me, my parents. It was terrifyingly real."

And then she burst into tears and buried her face in her hands. All Justin could do was wait out the storm, his arms around her, his shirt growing damp with her tears. Eventually, when the sobs subsided, he handed her a handkerchief. She blotted her eyes and scrubbed away the dampness on her cheeks.

"I'm sorry."

"There's nothing to apologize for," he insisted.

Patsy sighed heavily. "I knew I should have dealt with this straight on, but I was so afraid, Justin. I was afraid he'd take my baby. That's what he threatened to do."

Once the words were out, it was as if a dam had burst. She told him everything, about meeting the attractive, ambitious young attorney, about working for him and falling in love, about marrying him and joining him in his political rise, only to have their home life disintegrate.

"I was his trophy wife, the all-American girl. I know it wasn't true, but sometimes I wondered if he hadn't married me because his political advisers told him to. He resented me that much."

Justin heard pain and confusion in her voice, but not the bitterness he'd expected. That was a surprise. He touched a hand to her cheek. "Are you still in love with him?"

She stared at him in shock. "In love with Will? No. He killed whatever love there was between us a long time ago."

Relief washed over him. He'd had to be sure. If there was even a lingering trace of love for the man back in Oklahoma, then his advice might have been different. Instead, he advised one more time. "Talk to Janet. She will tell you what your legal options are."

"I'll think about it," she promised.

"Do it," he said more sharply than he'd intended. He sighed. "Sorry. It's just that I can't bury these notices forever and neither can Tate."

She stared at him, her expression horrified. "Tate knows?"

Justin nodded. "He found the first report. He's left it up to me to take care of this for the moment, but it can't wait forever. Earlier today it escalated from a simple missing persons report to a kidnapping charge. It sounds as if your husband's getting desperate."

"I've put you in a terrible position, haven't I?"

He noticed that she put concern for him ahead of concern for her husband. That was something to hold on to in the days ahead. There was no question it was going to get messy. Any man who would threaten his wife with violence as Will Longhorn had was dangerous. He was also a lawyer with political connections. It was impossible to tell what lengths he might go to before everything was sorted out in a courtroom.

"I want you to think about moving out to White Pines," he said carefully. "Billy will have a wonderful time on the ranch and there will be people around."

"You think this is going to get ugly, don't you?"

"Hasn't it already?" he asked dryly.

"But I can't involve your family. It's bad enough that you're in the middle of this."

"I made the choice," he said. "I could have called the Oklahoma authorities the second I knew who you were. So could Tate."

"Why didn't you?"

His mouth curved slowly. "Darlin', if you don't know that, then you're not half as quick as I've been giving you credit for being."

A faint smile touched her lips, then faded just as quickly. "And Tate?"

"Tate's a lot like Grandpa Harlan. He's the kind of a man who trusts his gut instincts. And when it comes to a choice between that and a piece of paper coming in over a fax machine, he'll go with his gut every time. He likes you. He believes there's more to the story than what's on those papers and until his back's to the wall, he'll do everything he can to protect you. In the meantime, I'd feel a whole lot better if you were out at White Pines."

"I can't impose like that, especially not if things start getting ugly."

"That's exactly why you need to be there. Grandpa Harlan will stand up to the devil himself to protect those he loves. Cody's there and Harlan Patrick, not that I want you seeing too much of him."

"No," she said, that familiar stubborn tilt to her chin. "This is my fight, not your family's."

He regarded her soberly. "I'm making it mine."

"No," she said again, though a little less forcefully.

Justin grinned. "Yes. Don't fight me on this, darlin'.

My mind's made up and nobody on earth's more stubborn than an Adams."

"We could debate that," she teased, her expression brightening for the first time since the conversation began. "I'm not exactly a pushover."

"No, you are anything but a pushover," he agreed, amused. "Let's just say you've met your match."

He'd made the remark lightly, but the words hung in the air and set off a sizzling tension. Patsy's gaze locked with his.

"Yes," she said very quietly. "I think maybe I have."

After that soft-spoken admission, it took every last bit of willpower Justin possessed to walk away from her and go back to his own place. It was late. He was exhausted. Stress piled on top of stress for days now had left him thoroughly drained. And yet he knew he wouldn't sleep.

He was a man who liked to control his own destiny and too much of his future hinged now on other people. For the first time since he'd put on a badge he regretted it. It kept him from being able to track down Will Longhorn and bloody his nose for the hell he'd put Patsy through and the likely anguish that was yet to come.

Even with right on her side, there was no way to be sure that things wouldn't get twisted around in a courtroom with Patsy coming out the loser. That was why she needed Janet at the moment, even more than she needed him. He could love her—and God knows he'd finally recognized that he did—but he couldn't protect her from the fallout of her own impetuous decision to run. Not that he blamed her for not wanting to square off against her husband when all the odds were stacked in his favor.

That, at least, was no longer true. With the considerable

force of the Adams name behind her now, Patsy stood a better than even chance in a legal battle.

But what if she lost? He had to consider that possibility. Nothing was certain when it came to the whims of judges. He'd seen too many black-and-white cases dismissed on a technicality. He had to believe, though, that she would win. If she didn't, then nothing he worked for as a law enforcement officer was worth anything.

If the legal system went awry, what then? What if he was forced to choose between a misguided legal decision and what he saw as Patsy's God-given right to have her son? God help him, what would he do? Encourage her to take Billy and run again? Go with them, leaving behind his family, his principles?

It won't come to that, he reassured himself time and again. It would be too cruel.

But fate could take cruel twists. Just ask Sharon Lynn. She'd waited for years to finally marry the man she loved, only to lose him on her wedding night. Where was the justice in that?

He thought back to those few brief hours earlier in the evening when he'd actually felt at ease for the first time in days. Why the devil had he insisted on opening up this whole blasted can of worms? Maybe ignorance really was bliss. A few hours ago he'd only suspected the tangle of problems facing Patsy. Now he knew for sure what was ahead of her, ahead of both of them.

How could he possibly seize control of this before things got out of hand? Other than pounding some sense into Will Longhorn, that is? Longhorn held the answers, though. And Justin was a cop with all sorts of investigative skills at his command.

His spirits brightened. Maybe he couldn't do anything

officially, but unofficially? Yes, indeed, he could find out if there was so much as a parking violation outstanding in the man's past. If there was anything, anything at all, he would hand it to Patsy and Janet as ammunition for the battle ahead.

With something concrete he could do to help Patsy, his mind eased and he finally fell into a deep sleep. Unfortunately, it lasted little more than half an hour before the alarm was going off and the phone was ringing.

"Justin, I'm sorry to wake you," Becky apologized. "But you'd better get over to Dolan's right away."

He struggled to shake the cobwebs from his mind. "Dolan's? Why? What's happened?"

"Patsy just called. She was too upset for me to make much sense of it, but I think she said someone's trying to break down the front door."

He glanced at the clock. Patsy wasn't due at work for another half hour. "She's there?"

"Locked in the back room is what she said. I could hear the glass breaking."

"I'm on my way. Have you called Tate?"

"Not yet. I got Dusty rolling first. He was just coming back into town from a patrol on the highway. He's on his way. Should be there any second now."

"I'm on my way," he said, and hung up. He was still pulling on his clothes as he ran out of the house. He had his service revolver tucked into his waistband.

It took him less than five minutes to reach Main Street. He could hear the commotion as he made the turn. Glass was shattering and someone was laying into whatever remained of the front of the store with something heavy, more than likely a crowbar or tire iron. Dusty was shouting commands that were being ignored. Instead, more debris flew, amid a flurry of curses and threats.

Justin made the turn on two wheels, then slammed to a stop behind Dusty's patrol car. He stared at the mess in disbelief.

"What the hell's going on?"

Dusty turned, his expression shaken. "Beats the hell out of me. Looks like the guy just lost it. Either he's got a grudge against Doc or he's a junkie out of his mind and desperate for drugs. Do you recognize him?"

Justin surveyed the man, from his pitch-dark black hair to his sculpted cheekbones, angled jaw and well-tailored suit. This was no thug or drifter. In fact, he concluded with a sinking heart, he would bet the ranch that this was Will Longhorn. He glanced up and down the block until he spotted a very fancy car that was almost exactly like Patsy's, just shiny black to her white one.

"Can you see the tags on that car?" he asked Dusty, who had a better angle on them.

"Oklahoma."

"Damn."

"What the hell is going on here?" Tate demanded, joining them.

"Unless I miss my guess, we're about to meet Will Longhorn," Justin said.

Tate's eyebrows rose. "Patsy's husband?"

"The one and only. It appears he's come calling, though I have to say his courting leaves a little something to be desired."

The sheriff's expression cheered considerably. "Well, well, well. It will surely be my pleasure to lock him up." He glanced at Justin and Dusty. "Shall we?"

"Oh, yeah," Justin said grimly.

Tate gave him a sharp look. "You don't lay a hand on him. Understood?"

Justin grimaced, then sighed. "Yes, sir."

"Then let's do it," Tate said.

It was an uneven fight, three against one with the three armed, as well. Tate had slapped handcuffs on the man before he even realized he was being taken into custody. When he heard the click and felt the cold metal around his wrists, he whirled on Tate.

"What the hell do you think you're doing?"

"Arresting you," Tate said evenly. "We can start with destruction of property and go from there." He began reading him his rights.

"Do you know who I am?"

"I don't give a damn if you're the governor or the president of the U.S. of A., nobody pulls a stunt like this in my town," Tate retorted.

Justin didn't waste time listening to the rest of the exchange. He stepped over glass shards and broken toys from the window displays, then used his own key to the drugstore. As he went inside, he called out to Patsy. The door to the back room cracked open.

"Justin?"

"It's me," he said, and opened his arms.

Patsy ran straight into them and clung. "Oh, my God, did you see him? He's lost his mind. He must have."

"I take it that's Will."

Her head bobbed against his chest.

"It's okay, darlin'. Tate has him in custody. He won't hurt you."

"But this place," she murmured, gazing around in horror. "Look what he's done."

"As long as you're all right, it doesn't matter. We'll have it cleaned up in no time."

"I can't believe this. It's all my fault."

"It is not your fault," Justin said. "He's an adult. He's responsible for his own actions, and believe me, this is not going to look good when you go into court and ask for your divorce. You have three cops as witnesses to the violence he's capable of. You can't get any better than that."

Patsy regarded him sadly. "It won't be that easy. He won't let it be."

"I know. But I'll be right here with you." He tilted her chin up and gazed into her eyes. "Believe it or not, this is a good thing."

She stared at the broken glass and demolished displays. "You'll pardon me if I can't quite see it that way."

"Darlin', I think I could forgive you just about anything. Now get a couple of brooms and let's get busy."

"Don't you have to go down to the station?"

"Not yet. Tate can handle your husband. When things settle down a bit, you and I can go down there and you can press formal charges against him. Doc Dolan can press whatever charges he wants to for the damage to the store. Then you can see Janet and we'll find out just what kind of a case she can put together for you." He brushed a wayward curl from her cheek. "It's almost over, Patsy. I guarantee it."

But, of course, it was just beginning.

Chapter Eleven

The last place on earth Patsy wanted to be was the sheriff's office. Even with Justin by her side, she dreaded confronting Will after the scene and destruction he'd caused. She was thoroughly embarrassed, not only for herself, but for him. He'd always been such a proud person. She didn't like thinking that she was to blame for him being reduced to this out-of-control mockery of a man.

"Want me to come in with you?" Justin asked as she hesitated at the doorway to the cell block.

Overcome with a sense of foreboding and trepidation, she almost agreed. It would be so easy to rely on his strength, to accept his protection. Then she thought better of it. She squared her shoulders and shook her head.

"No," she said. "It would only outrage him."

"So what?" Justin retorted with a touch of defiance. "Let him be outraged. Let him take a swing at me and give us one more thing to charge him with."

"No," she repeated, certain now that this was a confrontation she had to face alone. "I'll be safe enough."

Despite her claim, though, she was grateful that the cell

door between them would be locked. Today's scene had proved her worst fears about Will's temper.

After taking one last look at Justin, she drew in a deep breath and went to see her husband, all the while trying to remember that this was a man she had once loved with all her heart.

Since she'd seen him being led away from Dolan's, all of the fight had drained out of him. He was sitting on the cot in his cell looking dazed, as if he weren't quite sure how he'd gotten there. He looked surprisingly chastened.

In the months since she'd last seen him, he'd aged. There were even premature hints of gray in his straight, coal black hair. There were shadows under his eyes and lines of weariness etched on his face. And yet, despite the obvious exhaustion, he was as handsome as ever, his clothes perfectly tailored, if badly mussed from his rampage at Dolan's. He would hate it when he realized how filthy and wrinkled he was.

"Will," she said softly.

His head jerked up and for a brief instant she saw the hint of vulnerability, the flash of a boyish smile that had made her fall in love with him when they'd first met. Then, as if he suddenly remembered the circumstances, his expression hardened and the light in his eyes died.

"You'll pay for this, Patsy," he said coldly.

"No," she said, refusing to cower under the threat. "You brought this on yourself. I wasn't the one smashing things up at Dolan's."

"If you'd opened the damn door..."

"You were out of control," she reminded him patiently.

"Because of you. You took my son. You ran away from our marriage and you did it when it would hurt me the most, right in the middle of a campaign. You deliberately humiliated me."

"You're wrong," she said, and met his gaze evenly. "I wasn't even thinking of you."

"There, you see. It didn't matter a damn to you that your leaving could cost me the election."

"No, it didn't. I was only thinking about saving myself and Billy."

He gazed at her incredulously. "From me?"

"Yes, from you. You'd turned our house into a war zone. I left you once because of it, but rather than change, you just threatened me and my parents. You virtually blackmailed me into coming back. This time I just made sure there was nobody else involved and I came to a place I prayed you'd never find me. Obviously it wasn't far enough."

His expression turned triumphant. "You should have known better than that. I have the resources to find you no matter where you try to hide. It would be wise of you to remember that if you ever get a crazy idea about leaving again."

Patsy wrapped her arms around her middle and forced herself not to show how terrified she was that he might try to make her go home with him again.

"I'm not coming back to Oklahoma, Will, and neither is Billy." She said it firmly, her gaze fixed on his face as she waited for the explosion of temper likely to follow. To her amazement—and fear—there was no explosion, just a cold, cruel look.

"I guess we'll see about that," he said in a soft, lethal tone. "Have you noticed that this cell has a window? It has a perfectly fascinating view of Main Street. I saw you and your boyfriend."

Patsy barely contained a gasp of dismay. Surely he

wouldn't drag Justin into the middle of their fight. She stared into his unrelenting eyes and sighed. Of course, he would.

"He is not my boyfriend," she said, hoping to persuade him.

"Oh, I'm sure I can find folks who'd say otherwise."

"Pay them to, you mean."

"If necessary."

"It won't hold up, Will."

"Are you willing to risk that? Is he worth losing Billy?"

Fury outdistanced fear. "You will never take my son. *Never!*"

"Try me."

"You won't win."

"Oh, but I will. I have money and power and influential friends. I can give Billy everything. He's half Native American. That'll work in my favor, too. Living with you would rob him of his heritage, keep him from understanding his father's culture. Tribal law—"

She cut him off. "Since when are you so concerned with your culture?" she snapped. "The only time it's mattered to you is when it can be exploited for your own political gain. Beyond that, you've turned your back on your people. When was the last time you spent even five minutes with your parents on the reservation? When did you ever give a damn about the customs of your people?"

As soon as the words were out of her mouth, she knew she'd made a mistake. She had touched a raw nerve. In fact, she suspected that most of her own problems with her husband arose from the fact that he knew in his heart that marrying her had been a betrayal of his roots, the final slap in the face of his family. He'd been proud of winning her love, only to resent the fact that he'd needed her by his side to become a more acceptable candidate for office.

"Then the best way to make amends will be to insure that my son is raised by his Native American family," he retorted. "It will happen, Patsy. Count on it."

"Will," she began, ready to beg. Then she caught herself. That was what he wanted. He wanted to see the fear in her eyes, wanted to hear it in her voice. She wouldn't give him the satisfaction, even though she was quaking inside. Instead, she said quietly, "I'm sorry it's come to this. I really am. There was a time when I truly loved and respected you."

For a moment he seemed taken aback, but Patsy didn't wait to see what he might say next. She had to get away from him before she made things worse than she already had. Head held high, she walked out of the cell block. Only when she was back in the lobby with the door firmly closed behind her did she sag against it. Justin was there at once, concern written on his face as he led her to a seat beside his desk.

"What can I get you? Want some coffee? It's foul, but the caffeine might jolt some color back into your cheeks."

"No, thanks."

"What happened in there? What did he say to you?"

"The same old thing," she said wearily. "He's going to take Billy from me."

"Over my dead body," Justin said fiercely. "That is the one thing that will never happen."

"You can't guarantee that."

"Okay, maybe I can't," he conceded, "but Janet can." He tucked a hand under her elbow and hauled her to her feet. "Come on."

All Patsy wanted to do was go home and hold her baby,

then crawl under the covers and hide for a month. But that was what the old Patsy would have done. She was stronger now. She had to keep reminding herself of that.

"Where are we going?" she asked as Justin half dragged her from the station.

"To see Janet. I've already called. She'll meet us at her office."

"I thought she'd retired."

"There's retired and then there's Janet's version of retired. She's giving it lip service for Grandpa Harlan's sake, but, believe me, she can't wait to find a case she can get her teeth into."

He grinned. "That's why she never quite got around to putting her office on the market, much less moving out her desk and files and law books. Personally, I think she sneaks into town and hides out there after telling Grandpa Harlan she's gone shopping, but I can't prove it. I've never caught her there. Then, again, I've never seen her carrying a lot of packages to her car, either."

"I don't want to be responsible for the two of them fussing with each other," Patsy said, still reluctant.

"Oh, Grandpa may bluster some, but he knows deep down that Janet loves being a lawyer too much ever to walk away from it entirely. At least he's gotten her to slow down, and he thoroughly enjoys letting her think she's putting something over on him."

Patsy sighed enviously. "They have a wonderful marriage, don't they?"

"The best. It's set a great example for the rest of us. As I understand it, my grandmother Mary adored my grandfather. She was the epitome of the traditional wife. She devoted herself to him, almost to the exclusion of their sons. When she died in a riding accident, Grandpa was devastated."

He chuckled. "Then, thanks to Jenny stealing his car, he met Janet."

Patsy stared at him, flabbergasted. "Jenny stole his car?"

"Oh, yeah. She was fourteen at the time. She crashed it into a tree."

"I'll bet that got his relationship with her mother off to a rocky start."

"You could say that. Janet was definitely not the kind of woman Grandpa was used to. For one thing she didn't bow to his every whim. I was pretty little when they met, but the stories are legendary about their courtship. Best of all, the sparks are still there. You can feel it whenever they're in the same room." He met her gaze. "Just like us," he added softly.

Patsy had always wanted to believe that a relationship like that was possible. Her own parents had been married for years, but it was as much habit as love that kept them together. There was none of the warmth and tenderness she had witnessed between Janet and Harlan Adams. Theirs was the kind of relationship she'd always dreamed of, the kind she could almost imagine having with Justin if things were different. Maybe someday, though, as soon as this mess was straightened out once and for all.

They reached Janet's office and paused on the sidewalk out front.

"You ready?" Justin asked, tucking a finger under her chin to tilt her face up so he could study it.

Thinking of Will's view of the street, she backed away, ignoring the flash of hurt in Justin's eyes. "I don't have any choice, do I?"

"Not unless you're willing to go back to Oklahoma with him and go through the same thing all over again."

"Never," she said adamantly.

"Then let's do it." He held open the door.

Inside, Janet rose to greet them. She gave Justin a kiss on the cheek, then enfolded Patsy in a hug.

"Justin's filled me in on the basics. It's going to be okay," she promised, her expression radiating a quiet serenity.

And for the first time in months, Patsy actually felt as if it might be.

Before Patsy realized what was happening, Janet was ushering a protesting Justin out the door.

"He can stay," she said, responding to the indignation on his face.

"No," Janet countered. "It will be best if we have this conversation in private."

"But—" Justin began, only to be cut off again.

"Go," Janet said. "You've done your part by bringing her here. Now, go away and have a cup of coffee or something."

Justin's gaze sought Patsy's. "You're okay with this?"

Patsy nodded. "Thanks to you, I'm in good hands."

"Well, of course. That's not the issue."

Janet smiled tolerantly. "Justin, go," she commanded softly.

He bent and brushed a kiss across Patsy's forehead. "I'll be at the office if you need me."

After he'd gone, Janet turned a thoughtful look on Patsy. "He's very protective of you, isn't he?"

"That's just his nature. It's probably why he became a cop."

"Sweetie, I don't think this has anything to do with his job. Whether he knows it or not, he's falling in love with you."

Patsy stared at her in shocked disbelief. "You're wrong. I mean, I know he cares about me and Billy, but love? No, it can't be."

"Why not? Because you don't love him?"

"I never said that."

Janet grinned. "Good, then we won't be starting out with any lies and half-truths between us."

Patsy studied her intently. "You tricked me, didn't you?"

"I suppose. I just wanted to be sure where things stood. I don't want Justin to be hurt. He has a tender heart." She shuffled some papers on her desk and got out a pen. "Now, tell me about you and Will Longhorn. From the beginning."

An hour later Patsy was still talking. She told Janet every single thing she could recall about their relationship, from the moment she'd gone to work in Will's office until she had run away and sought refuge for herself and her son in Los Piños.

Janet rarely interrupted and then only to ask very pointed questions about something Patsy had said. When Patsy was finished, she regarded Janet evenly. "It's not a very pretty story, is it?"

"I've heard worse. How much of this does Justin know?"

"All of it." She hesitated, then said, "There is one more thing you should probably know. Will saw me with Justin earlier. He's threatened to drag him into it."

To her surprise, Janet chuckled.

"That will certainly make his day," she said. "He's already spoiling for a fight with this man. Heaven help Will Longhorn if he gives Justin an excuse."

"Justin can't be involved," Patsy said fiercely. "He's already paid a price for keeping silent rather than reporting me to the Oklahoma authorities. I know he struggled with his conscience every day over that."

"Justin knew you were wanted for kidnapping your son?" Janet asked, clearly surprised.

Patsy nodded. "It put him in a terrible position."

"Did you ask him to keep silent?"

"No, of course not. I didn't even realize how much he knew until yesterday. That's when he admitted that both he and Tate knew all about Will's claim. I guess Tate had buried the paperwork."

"Well, well, well," Janet murmured. "I've always known that Tate Owens was a good man, but to tell you the truth I've wondered when Justin would get the perspective he needs to do that job right."

Patsy was startled by the implied criticism. She rushed to Justin's defense. "Justin is an excellent lawman. You have to know that. He believes so fiercely in right and wrong."

"Exactly," Janet said. "Up until now it's been black-and-white with him. You're either obeying the law or you're breaking it, in spirit or in deed. Apparently he's finally discovered that there are some actual gray areas in life. It will make him a better policeman. Maybe he'll even find a way to forgive the man who hurt Sharon Lynn and killed Kyle."

"Has Sharon Lynn been able to do that?"

Janet looked deeply troubled by the question. "I'm not sure she ever thinks of him at all. She's still blaming herself."

"I was afraid of that. Do you think she needs to see a psychologist?"

"It doesn't matter what I think," Janet responded. "Sharon Lynn has to want to move on and right now she's too consumed with guilt to think about the future."

"Is she better physically?"

"She's getting stronger every day. She needs to start getting up and getting out."

Patsy gave that some thought. "I have an idea."

Janet's expression brightened. "Tell me."

"I know she'd been thinking about buying Dolan's. What if she were to think that Doc was about to leave and the rest of us were going to be out of jobs. She loves that place. Would she be able to bear the thought of it closing down?"

Janet pondered the idea, then nodded slowly. "It just might work. Particularly if you were the one to tell her, maybe lay it on really thick about how important the job is to you, especially now with the custody fight and your very expensive lawyer." She added the last with a grin.

"How expensive?" Patsy asked. "Are you really going to help me? Do we have a case?"

"Don't worry about my fee. We'll work something out. I'm grateful to have a case that my husband can't possibly disapprove of my taking. As for winning it, there's something you need to understand about me. I have never accepted losing as a possibility. That doesn't mean I haven't lost a time or two, but I always fight to win."

"But the system—"

"The system requires a fair fight. With all due modesty, with me on your side, the fight will be more than fair. I know how to handle the Will Longhorns of the world." She met Patsy's gaze evenly. "Tell me this, what are you most afraid of?"

"That Will will try to take the baby, insist on him being raised by the tribe. Isn't that what's happening with babies who are part Native American?"

"They won't take the baby from its natural mother. I promise. And given what you've told me about your husband, I doubt he'll fight the divorce or even whatever custody arrangements we want, not if he wants to run for political office," she said grimly. "He won't want all the details of his abuse made public."

"But—"

"No buts. Even if he tries to claim that the charges are false, he'll never be able to wash away all the mud on his reputation," Janet said with confidence. "If he's smart and his advisers truly believe in him, they'll convince him to settle this quietly and with as little publicity as possible. From everything you've said about him, I doubt Will Longhorn will be vindictive enough to throw away everything he's ever wanted just to get even with you."

For the first time since she'd fled, Patsy began to hope that she could finally stop running. Relief coursed through her. "Will I have to go back to Oklahoma?"

"No. We'll file the divorce papers right here. I'll have him served before he even gets out of jail." She came around the side of her desk and clasped Patsy's icy hands. "You and Billy will be fine, and you *will* be together. Trust me."

"He'll be furious when he gets the papers." She thought of his temper. "What if he comes to the house?"

"I'll ask for a restraining order."

Relieved, Patsy was ready to grasp at the option and then she thought of Billy. He wanted so badly to see his daddy. Could she keep them apart? Or did she owe it to Billy to let him maintain some sort of relationship with his father, however carefully guarded?

Finally she voiced her concerns out loud. "Billy's been asking to see his father. With Will right here, what should I do?"

Janet considered the question for some time. "We can work it out, if it's what you want. It might be for the best, prove how reasonable we intend to be."

"Not alone, though," Patsy said hurriedly. "I don't want Will alone with him. He might take him and run."

"A supervised visit, then. I think I know of a sheriff's deputy who'd be happy to hang out with the two of them or all three of you, if that's what you'd prefer."

"Yes," Patsy said at once, thinking of the likely need for a buffer between the two men. Will was going to resent Justin's right to be there, and Justin was clearly itching for an excuse to slug him. "I'd better be there."

"Then when Will's released, we'll arrange for him to come to the house to see his son."

"Thank you," Patsy said. "For everything."

"No need. I'm doing this as much for Justin as I am for you. You're good for him."

"I've brought him nothing but trouble."

"No," Janet corrected. "You've opened up his heart."

Chapter Twelve

When Patsy emerged from Janet's office into the bright sunlight, she couldn't help comparing it to emerging from the darkness of the nightmare Will had put her through these past few years. At last, though, the future was bright again. The debt she owed to the Adamses was enormous, beginning way back with Sharon Lynn.

Instead of heading directly to Justin's office, she went to Dolan's and found the elderly pharmacist filling prescriptions as methodically as ever, evidently unconcerned about the mess in the front of the store.

"Doc, I'm truly sorry about all of this. I'll pay for fixing it."

He peered at her over his reading glasses. "You didn't do it, did you?"

"Well, no, but—"

"Then I'm not laying the blame on you. It'll get fixed up. The glass cutter's already been here. Justin saw to it."

"But I should be the one—"

He grinned. "You're wasting your time arguing with me, young lady. If you disagree with the plan, you'll have to talk to Justin."

Patsy sighed. He was doing it again. He was fixing things for her. On the one hand, she was grateful. On the other, it was a reminder of too many years of weakness and dependence on other people.

"I'll speak to him," she said grimly.

The older man grinned. "Let me know how it turns out. It's been my experience that once an Adams makes up his mind, there's not much use in fighting him."

"We'll just see about that," Patsy retorted. "Before I go to see Justin, there's something else I want to discuss with you." She explained her idea for lighting a fire under Sharon Lynn and hopefully jolting her out of her depression. She didn't mention that the plot was helping her to keep her own mind off whatever was going on with Will down at the sheriff's office.

"Are you sure you're not an Adams?" he asked when she'd finished. "You're sneaky just like they are."

"You disapprove?"

"No, indeed. Not if it'll get the job done. I'll go along with anything that'll get that pretty little gal out of her bed and back among the living. I've just been putting off my retirement until she made up her mind whether she wanted to take this place off my hands."

Impulsively Patsy hugged him. "Thank you. Since the lunch counter's already covered, I'm going out to White Pines now, if you don't mind."

"Go. Be sure to let me know how it turns out."

"If I go about this right, you won't need me to tell you. Sharon Lynn will be busting down the door before the afternoon's over with."

"Lordy, I hope not," he said with mock horror. "One busted door in a day is about all an old man can cope with."

"You know perfectly well what I mean."

"Yes, I do. Now, get along with you."

When she arrived at the ranch, she went straight up to Sharon Lynn's room in the main house. She found her friend still in bed, still gazing blankly at the ceiling.

"Hey, sweetie, how're you feeling?" she asked, pulling a chair up beside the bed.

Sharon Lynn cast a distracted look her way, then gazed off in the distance again.

"I have some news," she said, deliberately injecting a somber note into her voice.

The statement drew no response.

"It's about Dolan's."

There was a flicker of interest in Sharon Lynn's eyes, but nothing more.

"The Doc told me today that he intends to close it down."

Sharon Lynn blinked rapidly at that, then turned slowly to face Patsy. "He's closing it?"

"Well, you know he's been thinking of retiring for some time. You told me that yourself. I guess he's decided it's time."

Sharon Lynn frowned. "But he knew I was thinking about buying it."

"I guess he figured since the accident and all, you wouldn't be interested, and he didn't want to wait around until another buyer showed up. I guess he's anxious to move on down to the Gulf Coast and go fishing."

The news clearly agitated her friend. Sharon Lynn began to fiddle with the pretty flowered comforter that was drawn up to her chin.

"This couldn't have come at a worse time," Patsy said sorrowfully.

"What do you mean?"

"I guess you haven't heard. My husband, Will, he showed

up in town today and bashed down the door at Dolan's."
Her shudder at the memory was only slightly exaggerated
for Sharon Lynn's benefit. "Maybe that was the final straw
for Doc. I don't know. Anyway, Will's in jail, and Janet's
about to file divorce and custody papers. It's going to be
expensive, and I'm out of a job again."

"You don't need to worry about that. Janet won't take
your money, anyway."

"Of course she will. I'm not accepting charity. It's important to me to prove I can stand on my own two feet.
I'm sure you can understand that. Dolan's has always represented a certain amount of independence to you, too,
hasn't it?"

"Yes, I suppose it has. I've never thought about it that
way before. I just knew I liked working there. It gave me
my own identity away from the family's ranching. Plus I
was following in my mother's footsteps. She and Daddy
did most of their courting in that place while she ran the
lunch counter."

"There, you see?" Patsy said brightly. "I knew you'd
understand." Then she sighed heavily. "Of course, I can
probably find another job in another town."

Sharon Lynn appeared genuinely shocked by the suggestion. "And leave Justin? You would do that to him?"

"Well, I wouldn't want to, but—"

The next thing she knew, Sharon Lynn had tossed off
the comforter and was climbing out of bed. She brushed
past Patsy.

"Oh, for heaven's sake, get out of my way."

Patsy barely contained a hoot of triumph. "Why? Where
are you going? Should you be out of bed?"

"I should have been out of bed days ago. As for where
I'm going, you know perfectly well, I'm going to have a talk

with Doc Dolan. I will not let Dolan's be closed down, and if anybody's going to buy that place, it's going to be me."

Patsy regarded her innocently. "If you're sure…"

"I'm sure."

Patsy kept up a steady barrage of doubts all the way to the front door, right past a gaping Harlan Adams. After they'd waltzed past him, Patsy turned around and caught his wink. Obviously Janet had filled him in on the plan, though he was clearly stunned to see it had worked.

"I really don't know if you should be going all the way into town your first day out of bed," Patsy said, along with half a dozen other protests designed to keep Sharon Lynn just irritated enough not to back down.

"Oh, will you just shut up," Sharon Lynn finally snapped. "I'm going and that's final."

"If you say so."

"Well, I do."

Outside, though, Sharon Lynn came to an abrupt halt. Patsy regarded her worriedly. "What is it? Is something wrong? Are you feeling faint?"

"I don't have a car," she whispered, her voice cracking. "And even if I did, I couldn't… I don't think I can ever drive again."

Patsy reached for her hand and squeezed. "Then isn't it a good thing that my car is here? I'll drive you into town, if that's what you want."

For a moment, Sharon Lynn looked as if she might back down, but then she squared her shoulders. "Perfect. I'm sure Justin or someone in the family will be coming out this way later. I can hitch a ride home with them."

"Or I'll bring you back. It's not a problem."

"Whatever." She walked over to Patsy's car and reached

for the handle of the passenger door, then faltered. She swallowed hard. "I'm not sure…"

Patsy sensed that Sharon Lynn had to do this today or she might never try again. "You'll be fine. I'll drive very carefully."

"Of course you will. It's not that."

"Let me ask you something. Have you ever fallen off a horse?"

Sharon Lynn regarded her impatiently. "I grew up on a ranch. What do you think?"

"And what did your dad or grandfather tell you?"

"To get up and get back on."

"Same thing after an accident," Patsy said lightly, praying that she was giving the right advice.

"I'll never get behind the wheel of a car again," Sharon Lynn said fiercely, her expression anguished.

"You don't have to drive, if you don't want to, but you're bound to want to go places. How will you get into town every day, if someone doesn't bring you?"

"I'll move to town."

"Then how will you get back out here for family dinners and holidays?" Patsy asked reasonably.

"Oh, for heaven's sake," Sharon Lynn finally grumbled, and opened the door. "Let's just go and get it over with."

She maintained a white-knuckled grip on the edge of the seat all the way into town, but she didn't utter another protest. Still there was no question she was relieved when Patsy parked in front of the drugstore. She rushed out of the car as if she'd just been advised there was a bomb under the hood.

Thankfully, the glass cutter had been busy while Patsy had been at the ranch. Though the window displays hadn't been redone, at least there were shiny new windows in place. Sharon Lynn viewed the residue of the disaster with lifted brows, then walked inside. Heads turned as she sailed past the lunch counter and straight to Doc Dolan's place behind the prescription counter.

"We need to talk," she said in a no-nonsense tone.

"As soon as I finish getting Mrs. Phelps's pills ready for her," the pharmacist said without looking up.

"Now!" Sharon Lynn said fiercely.

"Sounds like she's back to her old self," Justin observed, coming up behind Patsy.

"Not yet, but I think she's getting there."

He rested his hands on her shoulders and turned her to face him. "You're a good friend, maybe even a bit of a miracle worker."

"There were no miracles involved. I just thought of a reason for her to get out of that bed. Thank God, it was the right one." Satisfied that everything had been set into motion at the back of the store, she met Justin's gaze. "Anything happen at the jail I should know about?"

"Your husband got the divorce papers."

Stunned by the speed with which Janet had worked, she asked, "Is the building still standing?"

"It was when I left. He's demanding a conference with Janet."

"Oh, dear."

"Not to worry. Janet was sitting in Tate's office waiting. She'd anticipated the request. She looked downright eager to have a little face-to-face with him."

"Did she tell you about the visitation with Billy?"

"I'll be there," he said softly. "Don't worry about it."

She regarded him worriedly. "You won't be looking for an excuse to shoot him, will you?" she asked, only partially in jest.

He grinned. "Not as long as he keeps his temper in check and Billy's glad to see him."

"Any idea when he'll be free to come over?"

He nodded. "That's why I came looking for you. He's going to be released right after his meeting with Janet. I thought you might want to go home to prepare Billy."

Patsy's knees turned weak at the prospect. She hadn't expected it to happen so soon, not on a day that had already been a roller coaster of emotional ups and downs. "Tonight?"

"Yes. Then with any luck he'll leave town. That's the deal for his release. Doc Dolan won't press charges if Will heads back to Oklahoma and never sets foot in Los Piños again except for liberal court-approved visits with his son." He stroked a finger down her cheek. "It's going to be over, Patsy. By this time tomorrow, it's finally going to be over."

She wanted to believe that, but she couldn't. Not yet. Not until she saw Will actually get in his car and drive away. Maybe not even then. Maybe not until he'd been gone for weeks or months and there'd been no attempts at payback.

The first step to insuring that Will would stick to their bargain and leave was to let him see Billy tonight. Needing Justin's strength, she reached for his hand and said in an unsteady voice, "Let's go home."

"I'll walk you over, then head back to the station," Justin said. "I'm going to escort him officially to your place after his release. After that, he'll stay overnight at a motel, then if all the details are ironed out in the morning and all the papers are signed to Janet's satisfaction, you can say goodbye once and for all."

If only it would go that smoothly, Patsy thought wistfully, but this was Will they were talking about. He didn't give up anything he considered to be his that easily.

* * *

Justin stood idly by as Will Longhorn signed himself out of jail. Tate made it a point to remind the lawyer of his agreement to be gone by the next day. For a brief instant, the man's arrogance threatened to erupt, but he finally set his jaw and nodded.

"If you're ready, I'll take you by Patsy's," Justin said when the last paper was signed.

"I can get there on my own," Will said, dismissing him.

Justin stood his ground. "Afraid not."

"More rules?" Will demanded sarcastically, but he followed Justin to the waiting patrol car. "What kind of town is this? Do you all just make up these regulations as you go along? Or are you taking particular pleasure in tormenting me?"

"We believe in the kind of justice it takes to get the job done," Justin said evenly as he drove the few blocks to Patsy's and pulled up to the curb in front. "If it requires a little creativity, so much the better."

Will glared at him. "Believe me, I know exactly what your agenda is. You think you're so smart, don't you? You think you've won."

"Where you're concerned, I don't have to win. This is all about your wife and son and what's right for them. If you've got a shred of decency in you, you'll set them free."

"It's not up to you."

Justin feared prolonging the debate would only make the other man's hackles rise. He was clearly spoiling for a fight and Justin was a handy target. If Justin thought about accommodating him, it might be enough to cause him to back out on whatever deal he'd agreed to with Janet. To prevent that from happening Justin remained tight-lipped.

"Nothing to say to that?" Will taunted.

"Maybe you should stop worrying about me and concentrate on your boy," Justin said mildly, gesturing toward the window where Billy was watching for them.

Even as they looked, Billy scrambled down and raced out the front door.

"Daddy, Daddy," he shouted as he toddled unsteadily down the walk.

To Justin's surprise, Will Longhorn bolted from the car, knelt down on the sidewalk and scooped his son into his arms. There were tears in his eyes as Billy's arms locked around his neck.

"I missed you, Daddy. I missed you lots."

"I missed you more," Will murmured, his voice thick with tears.

Justin felt his throat squeeze tight as he watched the two of them. The sight had shaken him more than he cared to admit. It was yet another reminder that not everything was as black-and-white as he'd always believed. His view of Will Longhorn had been colored by what he knew of the man's shabby treatment of Patsy. Now, seeing him with his son, he realized that whatever his faults, Will Longhorn loved his son and Billy returned that love. It wasn't a bond that could be broken lightly.

He glanced up and saw that Patsy was watching the scene with tears in her eyes. He went past the man and boy to stand beside her.

"How can I do it?" she wondered aloud. "How can I keep them apart? Billy still brings out the good in him."

"That's a heavy burden for a two-year-old. Will needs to find the good in himself some other way."

She sighed. "I know you're right, but—"

"No, darlin'. You're doing the right thing. I suspect if he's honest with himself, even Will sees that."

"I hope you're right," she said as Will stood up with Billy in his arms and started toward the house. Despite whatever trepidations she might be having, she managed a smile for them. Justin had never been prouder of her.

"Daddy's going to stay for dinner," Billy announced. "S'ghetti."

"That's right, munchkin. Your favorite."

Justin hid a smile. He'd seen the damage Billy could do to the surrounding area with a plate of spaghetti. He wondered how Will would feel when it wound up splashed all over his fancy clothes, even if they were a little the worse for wear.

He was in for a surprise on that score, too. Will never batted an eye when sauce splattered off Billy's exuberantly wielded fork. Patsy started out of her chair at the sight of the red stain, but Will waved her off.

"It's a suit," he said mildly. "It'll clean, or I'll get another one."

She stared at him in blatant amazement. Even Will grinned at her reaction.

"Okay, so I'm mellowing. Maybe I've finally started getting my priorities in order." He regarded her wearily. "Too bad it's too late, isn't it?"

"Yes," she said softly. "Yes, it is." And then she turned and gazed at Justin.

There was no mistaking the message in her eyes, and Will didn't pretend not to get it. He rose from the table and picked up his son. "I'll give Billy his bath and put him to bed, if you two don't mind. Then I'll be on my way."

"Fine," Patsy agreed, watching as he left the room and headed toward the bathroom with Billy pointing the way.

After he'd gone, she gazed at Justin. "He's changed."

With an odd, cold sensation in his chest, Justin stared at her evenly. "Enough?"

"No," she said, reaching out to lay a hand against his cheek. "It can never be enough."

Relief swept over him then. They weren't at the end of her troubles yet, but they were getting there. And when they did, Justin vowed that he would be waiting.

When it was time to escort Will to his motel, Patsy beckoned Justin back inside for a moment. He studied her expression, trying to guess what was on her mind.

"Second thoughts?"

"About Will and the divorce? No. I just wanted to ask you if you could come to dinner tomorrow night, alone, just the two of us?"

Justin's heart lurched and his blood began to pump a little faster. He had a thousand questions begging to be asked, but with Will waiting, there was no time. "Seven o'clock?" he asked.

She nodded. "That will be perfect."

"I'll be here."

Back outside he glanced at his watch and noted that it was already after nine. Less than twenty-two hours until he could return and by then Patsy Longhorn would be well on her way to becoming a free woman. He wondered if she could possibly be looking forward to that any more than he was.

Chapter Thirteen

Justin couldn't seem to make himself wait until dinner-time before catching a glimpse of Patsy. He strolled into Dolan's first thing in the morning and was stunned to find Sharon Lynn at work behind the counter. Even though he'd seen her talking to Doc Dolan the day before, he hadn't expected her to return full-time anytime soon.

"Hey, sweetheart, what are you doing here?"

She gave him a wry look. "I work here, or had you forgotten?"

Her tone suggested she didn't want to get into anything connected to her absence. Justin followed her lead. "Seems to me I do recall seeing you here a time or two. You cook a mean hamburger."

"I'm glad you approve, because I just bought the place."

Justin stared. This was a wrinkle he hadn't really anticipated. He knew she'd been toying with the idea, but to actually do it, especially considering her recent state of mind. He prayed she hadn't been pushed into making a hasty decision she would come to regret.

"You bought it?" he repeated slowly.

"Yesterday. Doc will stick around for a few more months

until he's sure I understand how his part runs and until I find a replacement pharmacist, but it's all mine as soon as the bank works out the financing."

"Are you sure you're ready to take this on?"

She met his gaze evenly and her chin jutted stubbornly in typical Adams style. "I need it, Justin. Now more than ever. I couldn't lose it, too. Not after…" Her voice trailed off.

"Not after Kyle?" he asked gently.

She shook her head, blinking back tears. "He was my…"

"I know, sweetheart. Kyle was your world." He went around behind the counter and hugged her fiercely. "Do you know how proud I am of you?"

"Me? I haven't done anything."

"Sure you have. You've taken the first step toward getting on with your life. That's the hardest one. I guess for a minute there I was just surprised you'd taken such a big one."

"You can thank Patsy for that. She's a very clever woman."

He grinned. "I've noticed."

Sharon Lynn snagged a handkerchief from his pocket, brushed away tears and gave him a penetrating look. "Speaking of Patsy, I hear I'm not the only one who's getting on with her life."

"I have no idea what you're talking about," he claimed innocently.

"Yeah, right."

"By the way, where is she this morning?"

Sharon Lynn shot him a look of triumph that could have rivaled one of Grandpa Harlan's. "So much for the innocent act. And here I thought you'd stopped by just to visit with me."

"Just tell me where she is."

"Meeting with Janet and Will." She surveyed him knowingly. "Then she's taking the rest of the day off to get ready for her big date."

"Oh, you've heard about that, too, have you? The grapevine must be in really top form these days."

"No need to worry about that. She just discussed it with me to arrange for the time off."

"And you haven't been burning up the phone lines out to White Pines?"

"Not a peep," she swore.

"I would be eternally grateful if that remained true," he said.

She feigned disappointment. "For how long?"

"How about the next year?" He grinned at her shock. "Okay, at least until tomorrow."

Sharon Lynn nodded. "I can do that."

Justin slid onto a stool. "Now what does a guy have to do to get a cup of coffee around here?"

"Begging would be a good start."

"How about if I ask nicely and leave a big tip?"

"That would work, too."

Patsy was a nervous wreck. In a few minutes she was going to walk into Janet's office and the details of her divorce agreement with Will were going to be finalized. It would be over. Oh, there would be a wait for the final decree, but with Will not contesting, she would be free to move on with her life. Once the wheels had been set into motion, it had all happened so quickly her head was spinning. She could thank Justin and Janet Adams for that.

Janet claimed that dueling wits with Will Longhorn had been sheer pleasure and that no thanks were necessary, but Patsy intended to offer a more personal sort of thanks to Justin that night. She was going to show him how very grateful she was for everything he had done for her, from giving her a break on her first day in town, to arranging for Janet to intercede with Will.

In the meantime, though, there was one more thing she had to do. She had to talk to Will and try one last time to understand where everything in their marriage had gone so wrong. How much of it had been her fault? For too long she'd been willing to shoulder most of the blame, but she knew better now. Will was the one who'd changed and made their lives into a hell.

On the sidewalk outside of Janet's office, she drew in a deep breath, then turned the doorknob and walked in. She crossed the empty reception area and rapped on the office door even though it was wide-open. Janet and Will looked up at her knock.

"Good, there you are," Janet said, giving her a reassuring smile and beckoning her inside. "We were just going over the last little details."

"Everything's okay, isn't it?" she asked, the question directed at Janet but her gaze on Will.

He gave her a rueful smile. "I suppose that depends on your point of view, but in general everything is just fine. I'm not fighting you on anything. You've been generous with the visitation schedule, probably more generous than I deserve."

"Thank you for not fighting me."

"Don't thank me. I figure I owe you, and your lawyer has seen to it that I remember that."

"I don't want your money, Will." She turned to Janet. "I thought I made that clear."

"We've only asked for child support," Janet reassured her. "Billy deserves that."

"And I insist on it," Will said, his expression defiant.

"Yes, you're right," she said, backing down. "Of course there should be money for Billy. I can put it into a college fund."

Janet slid the papers across her desk. "Then let's get the last of these signed and everything will be official. I can file it with the court this afternoon."

Will cast one last look at Patsy, then turned back and signed the papers. Patsy followed with her own signature wherever Janet indicated.

"That's that, then," Janet said. She glanced at Patsy. "Would you two like a little time alone?"

Patsy nodded. "Please."

"I'll be in the next room, if you need me for anything."

After she'd gone, Will said, "An amazing woman, isn't she?"

"Yes, she is."

"I'd heard about her, of course, but the stories didn't do her justice. Seeing her in action reminded me of what being a good lawyer is all about." He met Patsy's gaze. "She's very protective of you, too. Is that because of Justin?"

"It's because she's a good lawyer, just as you said."

He shrugged. "I suppose."

"Can I ask you something, Will?"

"Why not?"

"What went wrong?"

He sighed heavily. "I wish I could begin to understand that. I certainly never meant to hurt you or Billy. I guess I didn't even realize how deeply words could cut or the kind of scars they could leave. I'm sorry,"

There was a raw anguish in his expression that Patsy had never seen before. "Can you just explain why you seemed to hate me so? Was it because I'm not Native American?"

"Amazing," he said, clearly startled by the question. "I wonder if you hadn't figured that out long before I did. I began dating you, married you, for all the wrong reasons. You fit the image I thought I needed to go someplace. All those advisers I had around me concurred. They were ecstatic about our relationship. One day I just woke up and saw it as a betrayal of who I was. I blamed you for it, when the fault was my own." For the first time he looked directly into her eyes. "Can you forgive me?"

Patsy thought of Justin, a man whose self-esteem was so strong, whose sense of family had never been tested. He would never struggle with who he was as Will had. And he was able to share his family and his strength with her. She'd never thought it possible, but she actually pitied Will for struggling to find a place in two sometimes incompatible worlds.

"Of course, I can forgive you," she said eventually. "More important, though, can you forgive yourself?"

His smile was a mere ghost of the trademark Longhorn smile, the one that lit up his campaign posters and would no doubt seduce thousands of voters. "I'm working on it." He moved closer and gently touched her cheek, his expression turning unbearably sad. "See you around, Patsy."

"Yeah. See you around."

And then he was gone and in the blink of an eye she was on her own again. This time, she vowed, she was going to make sure she got it right.

Justin got through the rest of the day cruising on automatic. His mind certainly wasn't on work. It was fortunate for everyone that it was a quiet day. Everybody parked where they were supposed to and no one violated so much as the speed limit, much less any more serious laws. He spent most of the day catching up on paperwork.

"You still here?" Tate asked at six o'clock when he found Justin at his desk.

"Just killing a little time."

"Until your date with Patsy?"

"How the hell did you know about that?"

"My wife saw her picking up a couple of steaks at the supermarket. Plus she wasn't at work today and I saw Dani leaving the house a few minutes ago with Billy." He grinned. "Doesn't take a genius to add all that up, and I am a highly qualified sheriff. I make deductions a whole lot trickier than that all the time."

"You're also entirely too smug for your own good."

"So why aren't you at home getting ready?"

"How long can it take to shower and change?"

"What about stopping off to buy some flowers, maybe a box of candy? Women like those little touches. Trust me."

"When I want advice on my love life, I'll go to Grandpa Harlan. You may be a good cop, but he's a grand master at mapping out a courtship strategy. Of course, he rarely bothers with notifying the principals of his intentions where they're concerned. I'm just grateful he's left Patsy and me pretty much on our own."

"Once his wife mentions that those divorce papers got filed in court today, he might not be so reticent. I'd suggest you take advantage of the time left to you before he starts meddling."

Justin nodded. "Good point. I'm out of here." He glanced at the clock and muttered a curse. It was after six.

Tate grinned and said innocently, "By the way, I told Millie at the florist's you might be by for a bouquet of flowers. She's staying open till you get there."

"Remind me to thank you one of these days."

"Just make sure I get an invitation to the wedding."

Justin was halfway down the block before Tate's words sank in. Who'd said anything about a wedding? Certainly not him. To be perfectly technical, this would be his very first date with Patsy. No one proposed on a first date, not when the ink wasn't even dry on the woman's divorce petition. Even with all the tricks at Janet's command it could be weeks or even months before the decree was final.

Still he couldn't seem to shake the idea once it had been planted. Wasn't that what the past few months had been leading up to? There wasn't a doubt in his head about how he felt about Patsy. Like all the Adams men, he might be a little slow at recognizing love when it was staring him in the face, but once he did, he couldn't see a whole lot of reasons for delaying the inevitable. Patsy, however, might not be quite so anxious to plunge into another marriage.

He was still reminding himself of that when he rang her doorbell promptly at seven, a huge bouquet of daffodils and bluebonnets in his hand. When she opened the door, she took his breath away.

She was wearing a pale yellow sundress that bared just enough of her shoulders and cleavage to make his mouth go dry. Her hair fell in waves to her shoulders, and moist color on her lips had turned her shy smile sexy. He swallowed hard.

"You look beautiful," he finally managed to say.

"So do you," she said, then blushed furiously. "I meant the flowers. They're lovely."

He shoved them into her hands, then cursed the fact that he suddenly felt like an awkward adolescent on his very first blind date ever, instead of an experienced man having dinner with an attractive woman he'd known for months.

"Dinner will be ready in a few minutes," she said, turning and leading the way through the dining room.

"Steaks," he said even before they reached the kitchen.

She glanced over her shoulder. "How did you know?"

He winced at the slip of the tongue. He absolutely refused to tell her that half the town probably knew. "I can smell the charcoal," he improvised. "Want me to throw them on the grill?"

"Would you mind? I'll finish up the salad."

Justin almost chuckled at her eagerness to get him out onto the patio and out of her way. It was clear she was every bit as nervous as he was. He found that as endearing as everything else about her.

He had the steaks on a plate and was about to come back inside just as she came through the screen door. They were standing toe to toe, gazes locked.

"I was just coming to check…"

"The steaks are done. I was just coming back in to…"

She covered her face and turned away. "Oh, God, I can't do this."

Justin stared at her, appalled. "Can't do what?"

"Nothing."

He brushed past her and set the platter of meat on the kitchen table, then turned to draw her into his arms.

"What's going on here?" he asked.

"I wanted everything to be perfect."

He was still confused. "It is perfect."

"No, it's not," she mumbled with a sniff. "I've ruined it."

"How? We haven't even sat down at the table yet."

"I don't mean the dinner."

Now he was more confused than ever. "What then?"

She gazed up at him with tear-filled eyes. "Justin, would you do something for me?"

"Anything."

"Kiss me, please."

He stared at her for no more than a heartbeat, before murmuring, "Now, darlin', that would be my pleasure."

He lowered his head and brushed his lips across hers, tasting the salty dampness of tears on her skin. It was the first tentative hint of a kiss, no more, but it might as well have been the most passionate one he had ever shared. Heat and yearning and desire slammed through him. He wound his fingers through her silky hair and stilled her head beneath his as he continued to explore the exquisite texture and taste of her mouth.

She moaned softly and opened her mouth to his tongue. Her body molded itself to his, every curve fitting snugly against the hard planes of his body. The intimate contact sent images streaking through his mind of the two of them tangled together in his bed.

"We have to stop," he said on a ragged breath, pulling away.

"Why?"

"Because this is happening too fast. It's all wrong."

"It's not wrong," she insisted. "Not if we both want it."

Holding her at arm's length, gazing into her eyes, he admitted to himself for the first time without reservations that he had fallen deeply in love with this fragile yet brave woman. Whether she loved him, though, was another matter. What he saw in her eyes was nothing more than gratitude, mixed in perhaps with a whole lot of lust.

"Is this what tonight was about?" he asked gently. "Did you ask me over so you could seduce me?"

"You want me," she said. "I know you do."

"That's not the issue."

"What else is there?"

He smiled ruefully. "If you have to ask that, then we really are on the wrong wavelength."

"I want you to make love to me, Justin."

He heard the urgency in her voice, but it wasn't the urgency of desire. It was, he was sure, the need to settle a debt and it broke his heart.

"Not like this," he admonished her softly.

"Like what?"

"This isn't the way to say thanks, Patsy. Dinner will do for that just fine."

She started as if he'd slapped her. "You think I was offering myself to you out of gratitude?" she demanded.

"Weren't you?"

The question hung in the air, adding to the already high tension. Her expression faltered under his steady gaze.

"Okay, yes," she said finally. Eyes blazing she met his gaze. "But it was more than that. It is more than that."

"Tell me, then."

Her temper died slowly and only then did she murmur in a voice so low he could barely hear it, "I think I'm falling in love with you. It scares me to death, but there it is," she said with a defiant tilt to her chin.

Justin's heart flipped over. With some other woman maybes might have been enough. Not with this woman. With Patsy he wanted it all. He wanted love, commitment, permanence. He wanted a family and forever, with no doubts at all.

He bent his head and touched his lips to hers, then headed for the door because he knew he didn't dare stay. He glanced back, saw her shattered expression and almost changed his mind, but something warned him that it would be the worst mistake of his life.

After taking one last look at this woman who'd stolen

his heart, he sighed, then said, "Let me know when you're sure."

He almost made it out the door, but her softly whispered cry of his name stopped him. He turned slowly back.

"I know now," she said, her eyes bright.

He smiled. "So fast?"

She nodded. "Because you were willing to walk out of here when I know you didn't want to. I knew in that instant."

He wanted desperately to believe her.

She held out her hand. "Please stay. Just for dinner, if that's all you're interested in."

"You know better than that."

"Please stay," she repeated.

Still wondering if he could trust himself, he grinned. "No hanky-panky?"

"Absolutely not." She sketched an X across her heart, then regarded him innocently. "Unless you change your mind."

"The steaks are probably ruined," he noted.

"We probably shouldn't be eating meat, anyway."

"Don't ever say that out at White Pines," he warned. "Grandpa Harlan will surely take offense. He does run a cattle empire, you know."

"I'll remember that." She tilted her head. "So was that a yes? Are you going to stay?"

He considered the question for some time, debating the wisdom of his decision, weighing desire against reason. Finally he nodded.

"Against my better judgment."

She laughed at his somber tone. "What's the matter, Deputy? Don't you trust yourself around me?"

"You've got that right."

"I'll do my best to see that you don't go against any of those important principles of yours."

"There's only one principle that applies to this particular situation," he told her.

"What's that?"

"I don't want to do anything that either one of us is going to regret in the morning."

She stepped up close then, deliberately crowding him, and rested her hand against his cheek. His skin heated under her touch. "There is nothing we could do, Justin, *nothing*, that I would ever regret."

She said it so fiercely, with so much passion that Justin's only choice was to kiss her. He moved quickly, before he could think, before second thoughts could come roaring back. And when he claimed her lips this time, he knew there would be no turning back.

Until the very instant when Justin's mouth had come crushing down on hers again, Patsy had been terrified that he would walk out the door. She had also been very much afraid that she would never again have the courage to go after him. It had been a long time since she'd taken an emotional risk. Her confidence was shaky.

She had been astonished earlier when he'd read her so easily, when he'd guessed that she'd wanted to give herself to him out of gratitude. Men weren't supposed to be so perceptive. Then, again, this wasn't most men they were talking about. This was Justin. He'd always struck her as a cut above the rest and tonight he had proved it.

She wanted him so desperately. She wanted the physical connection, knowing that it would come with the emotional commitment. She had been so sure that she was doomed to a life of solitude, a life on the run, an unending marital limbo. Because of Justin, all that had changed. He had given her back her life, given her back her heart. So, yes, she was grateful.

She was also wildly, passionately in love with him. There wasn't a doubt in her mind about that now. She had told him the honest-to-God truth about that. She had known, though, that he was really asking more than that. He was asking not just about her feelings, but about her readiness to face the future, a future with him very much in the middle of it. Could she answer that question as easily? Truthfully, no. She'd made so many resolutions about standing on her own two feet. It was important to keep them.

But with Justin's mouth covering hers, with his hands dancing over her skin and setting off wildfires in the wake of his touches, the only answer she could give was with her body and she gave it eagerly.

Clothes were shed in a frenzy, his, hers, flying through the air and landing who knew where. His heated gaze was as seductive as his caresses, lingering on every inch of bared flesh, stirring her.

He slowly slid his hand along her belly toward the hook of her bra. He flicked it open, then slowly brushed away the scraps of lace. She watched the muscle in his jaw work as he stared at her breasts.

"You are so beautiful," he whispered for the second time that night, his breathing ragged. "I want to make love to you right here, right now."

"In the kitchen?" she said on a gasp that was as much pure pleasure as shock as he skimmed his finger across an already hardened nipple.

"You'll never prepare a meal in here again without remembering," he teased.

"I'm not sure my heart will be able to take it."

"Now, see, there's something I didn't know about you. You're very traditional."

Patsy glanced at the counter, then considered that they were both already mostly undressed. "I can change," she said thoughtfully. "It could be fascinating."

He chuckled. "You've turned daring now? In the blink of an eye?"

She felt laughter bubbling up. "It's been that kind of day."

"Come here then," he suggested, stealing away the last scraps of clothes she was wearing and hoisting her onto the counter. The tiles were cold, a startling contrast to the fire burning inside her.

When he lowered his head to take her breast in his mouth, she rocked back, stunned by the sheer magic of it. He shucked off his jeans and briefs, guided her legs around his waist and then he paused. Anticipation had her ready to plead with him, but then she saw that he was only reaching for a foil packet in his pocket.

And then, before the heat had cooled even so much as a degree, he was inside her and it was building again. So much heat, so much urgency. Patsy was trembling from the inside out, straining toward an elusive goal that promised release. She kept thinking about the magic of it, the wonder of being touched by a man who was totally, thoroughly dedicated to her pleasure.

And then she wasn't thinking at all, just feeling as Justin's thrusts went deeper, as tension coiled in her belly, then sent shock waves ricocheting wildly through her. The intensity of it shattered her, leaving her panting and sated and awed by the wonder that was Justin.

Chapter Fourteen

It was morning before Justin was finally able to force himself to leave Patsy's bed. They had finally made their way into it long after midnight. In the meantime, they had used Patsy's newfound daring to make love in several spots along the way.

Gazing at her with the morning sun splashed across her body, he was struck anew by what a remarkable woman she was. Definitely full of surprises, that was for sure.

He dressed quickly and paused beside the bed for one last, lingering look. She stirred as if she'd felt his gaze. She came awake slowly, stretching like a sinuous cat and setting his blood to roaring through his veins all over again. When her eyes finally focused on him, she blinked.

"You're already dressed."

"I need to get to work and I have to stop by the house first to change into my uniform."

She glanced at the clock. "Oh my gosh, I'm going to be late, too."

"Take your time. I've got an in with your boss."

She scowled. "Which you are not to use. Getting there on time is my responsibility. I'm supposed to open up.

Sharon Lynn's not ready to be back full-time yet." She yawned.

"The impression I got is that she's anxious to be busy."

"I'm going in," she repeated emphatically.

Justin decided he'd better not argue with her. He'd seen evidence of this stubborn streak before, and after growing up with a whole clan of control freaks, he knew better than to take her on over the inconsequential stuff.

"Just don't burn the coffee."

"You can't burn coffee."

"You can if you forget to put any water in the pot. Ask Sharon Lynn. She has firsthand experience."

"When she was distracted by the wedding preparations?"

"Oh, yeah. And that was just the tip of the iceberg. Suffice it to say, you will always be regarded as something of a savior of the public health in this town."

She tilted her head. "Is that how you think of me?"

"No way, darlin'." He leaned down and whispered in her ear, chuckling when her cheeks turned bright red. "That's how I will think of you from now on."

"Well, I certainly hope you're the only one who feels *that* way."

"I'd better be," he concurred. He leaned down and delivered a hard, quick kiss that made up in intent what it lacked in passion. It was meant as a final reminder that she was his now. The dazed look in her eyes suggested he'd gotten his message across.

"See you in a while," he said.

"Justin, we are going to keep quiet about this, aren't we? For now, at least?"

He grinned, knowing the futility of it. "We can try."

She sighed. "I was afraid you were going to say that."

* * *

The whole blasted town was jumping to conclusions. Patsy realized it when half a dozen people asked very pointed questions that morning about her dinner with Justin and none of them had even witnessed the warm, personal greeting he gave her when he stopped by for a quick cup of coffee just before nine. Nor had most of them seen the way she'd brightened at his entrance. No, indeed, their probing had been sparked by something else entirely.

Thoroughly embarrassed at having her private life made public, she mumbled evasive answers to the prying questions and retreated to the back room at Dolan's every chance she got. Obviously Justin had known what he was talking about. There hadn't been a chance in hell of keeping anything secret in this town. It was all too reminiscent of being the wife of a promising political candidate.

"Hiding out again?" Sharon Lynn inquired, peeking through the partially opened door.

"I am not hiding out."

"Sure you are. Can't say I blame you. The folks in Los Piños do like their breakfast served up with gossip."

Patsy sighed. "What I can't figure out is how they even knew Justin and I were having dinner last night."

"That's a no-brainer."

"Explain."

"Did you shop at the grocery store?"

"Of course."

"Enough food for two, maybe something a little special, like thick steaks?"

She began to see where this was heading. "Yes."

"Did he bring you flowers?"

"Yes, but—"

"Did I cover for you in here yesterday afternoon?"

She got the picture. "Oh, good grief," she muttered impatiently. "Am I going to have to buy food in the next town before I invite him over again?"

Sharon Lynn grinned. "It won't help. We have sources there, too." She sat down on a stack of boxes. "So, tell me, how did it go?"

"We had a great time."

"Did you sleep with him?"

"Sharon Lynn!"

Her friend—and his cousin, she must never forget that—grinned impudently. "Never mind. I think you've just answered that question."

"I did not."

"That bright pink color in your cheeks did."

"Maybe I was just embarrassed that you would even think such a thing."

"If you're trying to persuade me I'm wrong, it's not working. Justin couldn't look me in the eye and give me a straight answer, either."

"You asked him, too?"

"Well, of course I did. I love both of you. I want this to work out."

"Then maybe you should just leave us alone. Knowing there's a fascinated audience panting for a play-by-play won't help."

"If you think I'm nosy, wait until you run into Grandpa Harlan."

"Did I hear somebody mention my name?" the very man in question called out. "Where the dickens are you, girl? You hiding in the broom closet like your mama and Cody used to do?"

Patsy sent a panicked glance toward the door. "I am absolutely not going out there."

"Of course you are," Sharon Lynn said, clearly eager to throw her to the wolves—or one wolf in particular, at least. "Your break's over. Mine's just beginning."

Before Patsy could argue that point, the door pushed open and Harlan Adams poked his head in. He was evidently tired of waiting for either of them to appear.

"I knew it," he gloated. "What is it about this room that lures everybody back here?"

"Maybe they're hoping for a little privacy," Sharon Lynn teased, going over to give him a kiss on the cheek.

He seemed fascinated by the explanation. "You two indulging in a little girl talk? Mind if an old man sits in?" He glanced at Patsy. "I have a few questions about you and my grandson."

"Sorry, sir. You'll have to get those answers from Justin," Patsy said, slipping past him with the finesse and speed of a very crafty running back.

"Dadgumit, he wouldn't tell me a blasted thing, either," he grumbled irritably.

"Bless his heart," Patsy murmured.

"What was that?" Harlan Adams asked.

"She said he's a wise man, Grandpa. What she had the good grace not to say was that you're being a nosy old man."

He scowled at her. "Like you haven't been poking at her all morning long."

Sharon Lynn shrugged. "I'm her friend. I'm entitled."

His gaze narrowed. "Did she tell you anything?"

"No, I did not," Patsy said, giving Sharon Lynn a warning look. "Some people just enjoy making assumptions."

"How the devil is a man supposed to plan a wedding, if nobody will tell him anything."

Patsy halted in her tracks. A wedding? Who the hell

had said anything about a wedding? Sharon Lynn shot her a sympathetic albeit an I-told-you-so look.

"Maybe you should let the people involved make their own wedding plans, Grandpa, if there are any to be made."

He stared hard at Patsy. "That what you want?"

"I think it would be best," she agreed, then relented just a little at his look of disappointment. "I will tell you one thing, though. If and when Justin and I talk about getting married, you will be the first to know."

He gave a little nod of satisfaction. "Good enough." He bent down and kissed Sharon Lynn's cheek, then Patsy's. "I'd best be getting back to White Pines. Janet's been moping around out there this morning because she doesn't have a case to work on. I've got to come up with something to keep her occupied or she'll be back here in town practicing law full-time before I can blink. That case of yours sparked her hunger to work again."

Sharon Lynn winked at Patsy. "Maybe you should compromise, Grandpa. Let her take on a case now and then."

"She is a very good lawyer," Patsy offered. "It's a shame not to take advantage of all that legal knowledge."

"You two are just too danged liberated for your own good. Her place is home with me. It's taken me too darn long to get her there as it is."

"She'll be happier if she's feeling fulfilled professionally," Sharon Lynn said.

"Which means she will be very, very grateful to you for suggesting that she go back to work part-time," Patsy said slyly. She did not mention just what form that gratitude might take, even though she had some very recent experience with it.

He regarded Patsy with a twinkle in his eyes. "I do like

the way you think, girl. I hope you and my grandson hurry up and get this show on the road."

"Why don't you forget about Justin and Patsy and pester Harlan Patrick," Sharon Lynn suggested. "Now there is a man just ripe for matrimony."

"Never you mind your brother. He's right on track with Laurie Jensen, as far as I can tell."

"And you would know, I'm sure," Sharon Lynn teased.

He scowled at her. "I have to see to it that all my babies are settled, don't I?"

"You think you do, anyway," she agreed.

Harlan Adams's expression sobered. "What about you, darlin' girl? You doing okay?"

The smile on Sharon Lynn's face faded faster than the sun dipping below the horizon. Patsy gave her hand a squeeze.

"She's doing fine," Patsy said, trying to bring a quick end to the subject. She was all too aware that Sharon Lynn's tears were too close to the surface and that the slightest reminder of Kyle could bring them coursing down her cheeks again. She'd dashed into this back room a few times herself today, when a customer's sincere expression of sympathy had gotten to be too much for her.

Thankfully, Harlan Adams glanced at Sharon Lynn and took Patsy's hint. He rose to his feet, again kissed his granddaughter on the cheek, then pressed another kiss on Patsy's cheek.

"I'll be getting on home now. As for you two, you might want to come out of this broom closet every now and again. It looks to me like there are some impatient folks sitting out here wondering what happened to the help."

"I'll go," Patsy said at once, brushing past him to discover that the only impatient person in the store was Justin. Her heartbeat accelerated. She forced herself to walk slowly back to the counter, pausing to grab a cup and the coffeepot on her way to where he sat.

"Back so soon?" she asked.

"Had to get my hourly fix of the prettiest woman in Los Piños," he teased.

"Sharon Lynn, get out here," Patsy called. "Justin's looking for you."

He grinned. "Very funny."

He looked past her just then and spotted his grandfather. To Patsy's amusement, he regarded him suspiciously.

"What are you doing here?" he asked.

"Do you think you're the only one in the world who appreciates a beautiful woman?" his grandfather asked.

"Go find your own. This one's mine," Justin said.

"Says who?" Patsy inquired.

"Whooee," his grandfather said, grinning. "I like this girl."

Justin turned his gaze from his grandfather to Patsy. His expression sobered. "So do I, Grandpa. So do I."

"Then I'll just run along and leave you to see what you can do about getting her to change her mind about you."

After he'd gone, Justin focused on Patsy. "So, what about it? Can I change your mind?"

"About?"

"Being mine."

Something in his tone told her the question wasn't being asked in jest. And as desperately as one part of her wanted to say yes, another part reminded her that once before she'd been too eager to jump into a relationship. She hadn't even fully extricated herself from that mistake yet.

"Maybe one of these days," she said. She glanced around to make sure they were unobserved, then leaned across the counter to brush a kiss across his lips. "You are aw-fully cute."

When she would have drawn away, Justin tucked his hand around the back of her neck and held her still long enough to deepen the kiss into something wild and sweet.

"Have dinner with me tonight," he suggested when he released her.

"Two nights running. People will talk," she teased.

"Darlin', I'm beginning to think it's our civic duty to give them something fascinating to talk about."

"That sounds a little too self-serving to me."

He grinned. "I was going for noble. What about it, though? Will you have dinner with me? We'll go some-place quiet and romantic."

Patsy had been to most of the restaurants in town. None she knew qualified. "Where?"

"You'll see."

"Justin, I really think you ought to tell me. I have a son to consider."

"Taken care of. He's going out to the ranch to spend the night. Janet says she can't wait."

Once again, he was taking over, smoothing things out to get his own way. Maybe under other circumstances she would have found the gesture touching. Instead, it rankled.

"Don't you think you should have consulted me before making arrangements for my son?" she asked testily.

"The plans aren't cast in stone," he replied, his tone rea-sonable. "If you have a problem with them, we'll change them."

"That's not the point."

"Then what is the point?" he asked patiently.

"I don't need somebody to run my life for me, Justin. I've been there, done that, and I didn't like it."

He nodded slowly. "I see."

"Do you really?"

"I think so. Will pretty much set the agenda for your lives and expected you to fall in line. How am I doing so far?"

There was that perception of his kicking in again to surprise her. "On the money," she admitted.

"I'll try to be more sensitive to that in the future," he promised.

She shrugged, not entirely trusting an easily made and easily broken promise. The proof would have to come over time.

He gave her one of his crooked, endearing smiles. "Can we start this conversation over again?"

She hesitated, then grinned back, unable to resist him in the end. "What the heck, give it a try."

"Patsy, would you care to have dinner with me tonight?"

"I'd be delighted," she said, because she could recognize the stupidity of turning down a date with a man she loved just to make a point.

"What about a baby-sitter for Billy? Need any help in making arrangements?"

"I'll volunteer," Sharon Lynn offered, joining them.

It was impossible to tell how much of the earlier conversation she'd overheard, but Patsy was grateful for the offer. "Are you sure you won't mind?"

"Heavens, no. It'll be fun. I can even stay over at your place. That way I won't have to have someone from the ranch come into town to pick me up tonight and you won't have to rush back home." She grinned. "In fact, you could stay out all night if you wanted to."

Patsy almost laughed at the hopeful expression on Justin's face. "Okay, it's a deal," she said. "Thank you."

"No," Sharon Lynn said softly. "You're the one doing me a favor."

Her expression was so sad that Patsy was taken aback. She had seen firsthand how getting into a car had panicked Sharon Lynn. Now she realized just what a toll the trips into town and home again were taking. Suddenly she knew that if she weren't staying in Dani's old place, Sharon Lynn would have snatched it up for herself to rid herself of the frightening commute.

Before she could second-guess herself, she said casually, "You know, Sharon Lynn, if you wanted to, you could stay with Billy and me for a while."

The suggestion startled both Justin and Sharon Lynn, but Sharon Lynn seized on it with such a look of relief that Patsy knew she'd done the right thing.

"Are you sure you wouldn't mind? It would save me..." She hesitated, then sighed, not quite meeting Patsy's gaze. "It would save a lot of time."

Patsy met her gaze evenly. "I understand, and it would be fine with me. And I have no intention of thinking of you as a built-in baby-sitter. I'll enjoy the company."

"What about my company?" Justin demanded irritably.

"You, cousin dear, are an entirely different kind of company," Sharon Lynn teased. "And I'm sure she enjoys that, too."

"I do," Patsy assured him.

"Then we're on for dinner?"

"We are definitely on for dinner."

He grinned. "And after?"

"Don't push your luck, lawman. We'll negotiate the details over dinner."

He touched a finger to his Stetson in a mock salute as he

put it back on. "I'll be looking forward to it, ma'am. What time shall I pick you up?"

"Why don't I pick you up?" she suggested, as a perfectly fascinating idea occurred to her.

"Why not? I'm a flexible kind of guy."

"That'll be the day," Sharon Lynn taunted.

He scowled at his cousin, then said to Patsy, "Don't listen to a thing she says about me. She's never forgiven me for laughing when she fell off a horse in front of…" The teasing light in his eyes died. "Oh, God, I'm sorry, sweetie."

Tears welled up in Sharon Lynn's eyes, but she reached over and touched Justin's lips. "Don't be sorry. Don't ever be sorry for reminding me of the good times. It's just that…"

"It's just that the wound is still raw," Justin said. "But you're going to be okay, you know that, don't you?"

"Sure," she said, forcing a wobbly smile. "We Adamses are made of tough stuff."

"The toughest," Justin concurred.

But looking at the tenderness in Justin's expression as he watched Sharon Lynn, Patsy knew he was wrong. Justin Adams, at least, had the softest heart she'd ever seen.

Justin had no idea why it had been so important to Patsy to pick him up that night, but he was going nuts waiting for her. Was this how women felt all the time waiting for their dates to arrive? No wonder some of them were itching to turn into control freaks.

Oh, he'd recognized what that whole discussion at Dolan's had been about that afternoon. Will Longhorn had dictated every aspect of his wife's life and she didn't intend to let it happen again. He had to wonder, though, how long these bids for independence were likely to go on. Would she refuse to marry him just to prove she could get along on her own? Or could he persuade her that it was possible to be half of a whole without losing her own identity? Tonight would be a fascinating test of his theory that she needed to know that at least some of the decisions in their relationship were hers to make.

When the doorbell rang at last, he bolted to answer it. To his astonishment, in spite of the humid evening air and clear skies, Patsy was wearing a raincoat.

"Expecting a storm?" he inquired lightly.

She gave him an enigmatic look. "In a manner of speaking. May I come in?"

He stepped aside. "Be my guest."

She sailed past him in a cloud of very seductive perfume. By the time he could recover from that and had closed the door, she had disappeared.

"Patsy?"

"Back here," she said in a tone that could have lured ships to crash into rocky cliffs.

There was no question that her voice was coming from the bedroom, his bedroom, unless he missed his guess. He swallowed hard. Something told him that dinner was going to be very late and was going to consist of whatever was in his freezer.

When he got to the door to his room and glanced inside, his mouth gaped. Patsy was standing in the middle of the room in a black negligee so scanty he thought for sure his heart would slam to a stop if he stared at her too long.

"Won't you get cold at the restaurant?" he asked when he could find his voice.

Her confident expression faltered just a little. "You still want to go out?"

He barely held back a grin at her wistful tone. "Not if you don't."

"I thought I was making myself pretty clear."

"It wouldn't be the first time we've gotten our signals crossed."

"Justin, you will never make sheriff if you can't read a clue this obvious."

He grinned. "Okay, let me try." He paused thoughtfully. "You are less interested in dinner than you are in seduction."

She stepped toward him and nodded. "Very good," she praised.

She slid her arms around his neck. "And this?"

"No waiting?"

"Oh, yes," she murmured just before she stood on tiptoe and kissed him with an enthusiasm that left not a single doubt in either of their minds about how they were going to spend the rest of the evening.

Chapter Fifteen

Patsy was very proud of the way she'd managed to render Justin Adams totally speechless. Lying next to him in his bed, she felt as if she'd finally come home, finally met a man who thought of her as an equal, a partner. Maybe she was being a fool for setting some artificial time constraint on the relationship.

"Satisfied?" he asked, regarding her with an amused look.

"Oh, my, yes," she said.

"What happens now?" he asked.

Her expression faltered. "I guess that depends on you."

"Oh, no, you don't, Patsy Gresham Longhorn. For the past twenty-four hours you've been telling me every way you knew how that you are capable of making your own decisions, capable of taking the initiative, capable of standing on your own two feet, that you *insist* on standing on your own two feet, come what may."

"There are still some things that are a man's prerogative," she admitted unwillingly.

"Such as?"

She was not going to put these words into his mouth.

Nor was she quite brave enough to demand that he marry her and make an honest woman of her. Maybe if neither of them could put the question into words, there was a reason for it. Maybe it really was too soon after Will.

Even if she did absolutely adore being in his bed, with his arms around her and her head resting against his chest.

She sighed, rolled over and stood up. Justin regarded her with surprise.

"Where are you going?"

"You promised me dinner."

"Sorry, darlin'. The cupboard's practically bare." He grinned. "We could order in. That would certainly make Angie's day over at the Italian restaurant. Or we could call Rosa and ask her to deliver some Mexican. Of course, she is related to the housekeeper at White Pines, which means there would be more talk."

"Are you saying there is not one tiny little scrap of food in this house?"

"Not even a cracker." He surveyed her thoroughly. "And you're not exactly dressed to go to the restaurant I had in mind." He beckoned to her. "Maybe if you climb back into bed I can make you forget all about your growling tummy."

"I'm sure you could," she agreed. "But without food neither of us will survive another round of really energetic sex."

"Then we'll take it nice and slow," he said in a provocative way that set her blood to pumping furiously.

She was still standing there debating the wisdom of that when Justin's beeper went off. In an instant, he was all cop. He grabbed the beeper from his nightstand, reaching for the phone at the same time.

"What is it?" he demanded, even as he scrambled to

find clothes. His expression sobered. "I see. Okay, I'm on my way."

He slammed the phone down, pulled on his shirt and unlocked the drawer to get his gun. Patsy watched him and shivered. It was a full minute before he glanced her way and noticed her expression.

"I'm sorry," he said.

"No, it's okay. Of course, you have to go. What's happened?"

"We've got a high speed chase on the interstate heading this way. Tate wants me to set up a roadblock."

Patsy's blood ran cold as images of Sharon Lynn's wrecked car came whirling back.

He touched a finger to her cheek. "Don't worry. I know what I'm doing."

"I know. It's just that..."

"The accident," he said succinctly. "I'll be fine, Patsy. We have important things left to finish here tonight. I'll make sure I get back before you even miss me."

"Not possible," she told him softly. He wasn't out the door and she missed him already.

The instant he was gone, panic began to set in. What if he never came back? What if something happened and she'd never told him just how desperately she loved him? What if she'd wasted precious time while trying to declare her independence? Would it be worth it?

Maybe, she told herself as she sat huddled in a blanket on the sofa waiting for him, maybe when something was so clearly right, only a fool would take a chance on throwing it away.

When the clock ticked on slowly and still Justin hadn't returned, Patsy could no longer sit still. Despite his earlier claims that there was no food in the place, she went into the kitchen in search of something to eat.

When that proved fruitless, she went back to the bedroom and began straightening up. It didn't take long. Justin was invariably neat. Only the clothes they'd worn earlier were scattered about. Her negligee and raincoat seemed ludicrous now, when she'd been reduced to wearing one of his shirts. Why hadn't she at least tucked an overnight bag with a change of clothes into the back of the car? Had she planned on leaving here in broad daylight wearing virtually nothing? The truth was, she hadn't thought about leaving at all, only about getting here and stunning him speechless.

She picked up his slacks and when she did, something dropped out of the pocket, then rolled under the bed. She scrambled after it. When her hand closed around it, she realized it was a small velvet box. Her heart stood still.

She rocked back on her heels and stared at the red velvet in wonder. This was what he'd had in mind for tonight, she realized. A romantic dinner and then this. With fingers that trembled, she flipped open the lid and gazed at a stunning solitaire diamond on a wide gold band. Even though the stone was large, there was nothing ostentatious about it. It was elegant and simple, a declaration not just of love, but of understanding.

"He knew," she murmured as tears began to build. He had understood that all of Will's gestures had been for show—the gaudiest diamond, fanciest car, biggest house. This ring just said that Justin Adams loved her and nothing more.

"Oh, Justin," she whispered, her throat tight.

What if she never got to say yes? What if the divorce dragged on, for some reason? What if…? She couldn't bear to say it, not even to think it. Instead, she slid the ring onto her finger. Somehow, she thought, somehow he would know her answer, no matter what. When the decree was final—when Justin was safe—they would start to plan their future.

It was nearly daybreak when she heard the front door open, then close quietly. In a heartbeat, she was on her feet and racing toward the living room. She skidded to a stop at the sight of him. He looked as if he'd been mauled by a particularly cantankerous bull. There were cuts and gashes and dirt. His uniform was in tatters, but he was alive, she told herself. He was blessedly alive.

He glanced up and saw her then and the exhaustion vanished. His eyes lit up.

Patsy moved toward him, then hesitated, all too aware of the state he was in. "How badly are you hurt?"

"Just a few bumps and bruises. The guy took exception to being arrested. I had to chase him down and wrestle around with him near a barbed wire fence. The fence won."

"And you? Did you get your man?"

"Of course," he said, his expression smug. "The good guys always win." He reached for her gingerly, then searched her face. "Don't they?"

"Depends on what they're after, I suppose."

"You know what I'm after," he said. "Are you ready for me to spell it out?"

She held out her hand. "Does it have anything to do with this?"

He stared at the ring in surprise. "You found it?"

"I was straightening up. It fell out of your pocket."

He grinned. "And you assumed it was meant for you?"

She scowled. "And who else would it have been meant for?"

"Maybe some woman who knows her own mind."

"I know my own mind."

"Do you?"

"Always have." She circled his waist with her arms and held on, relishing the sense of security that swept over her. "It just took me a while to figure out I could trust my own judgment. I have had reason to question it, you know."

"You can trust yourself this time, darlin'. I will love you till my dying breath, Patsy Longhorn. I will never hurt you. I will treat Billy as if he were my own and I will make absolutely sure that we have a house crawling with brothers and sisters for him, if that's what you want."

"Oh, it is definitely what I want," she assured him. She gazed into his eyes. "No doubt about it."

He lifted her hand and admired the ring that fit perfectly. "You stole my thunder. I was going to ask you last night," he said. "But you had other plans for the evening."

"I didn't hear any complaints at the time."

"No way. Now, though, I want your full attention. No funny business, okay?"

"Okay."

He surveyed her from the open collar of his shirt to her bare thighs. She could feel the heat of his gaze everywhere it touched.

"Maybe you ought to get dressed."

She grinned. "My choices are pretty limited. It's this shirt, the negligee or the raincoat."

He groaned. "Never mind. I'll just have to concentrate a little harder."

"Can't remember what you had in mind?" She waved the ring under his nose, then dropped it into his palm. "Does it have anything to do with this?"

Justin looked as if he'd never seen the diamond engagement ring before in his life. "This? Yeah."

His reaction, his inability to focus on anything but her

couldn't have pleased her more. Will had always acted as if half his attention was on a speech he had to make later in the day.

"How about the future?" she coached. "Does it have anything to do with that?"

"You're beautiful, you know that."

"The future, together, you and me," she persisted, refusing to allow him to distract her, too.

"Mmm-hmm," he said, and reached for her.

Sometime later, Justin finally managed to get out the words and get the ring on her finger, but the moment was almost anticlimactic. She'd given him her answer long before, in his arms, when she'd murmured yes over and over in his ear. And one day soon, when her divorce was final, the whole world would know, too.

The wedding plans had been taken completely out of her hands the very instant the divorce decree was final, but for once Patsy wasn't feeling the least bit defensive about losing control over her life. It gave her more time to spend with Justin and Billy, more time to indulge in the incredible romantic fantasy her life had become.

Watching her son with his prospective stepdaddy always brought a lump to her throat. And listening to Will explain to Billy that he would always be his daddy, but that it was okay with him if Billy loved Justin did bring tears to her eyes.

"Thank you," she told Will as he walked to his car after his visit.

"You deserve to be happy. Your being happy will insure that Billy's happy, too. How could I want anything less for my son?" He gazed into her eyes. "There's something I need to thank you for, too."

"What's that?"

"For snapping me back to reality and for agreeing to let Billy spend time with me and my family while you're on your honeymoon. I think it's time both of us learned something about our roots."

"You've always known who you were, Will. You just got lost for a little while."

He grinned sheepishly. "Well, that's one way of looking at it, I suppose." He gave her a peck on the cheek. "Good luck, sweetheart. I think you're getting a better deal this time around."

Patsy didn't say it, but she knew she was. Her gaze lifted just in time to see Justin coming toward them. Will turned slowly and met Justin's gaze steadily.

"Make her happy," he said.

"I intend to."

"Okay, then, I'll see you two tomorrow night, right after the wedding reception."

"Are you sure you don't want to come?" Patsy said.

"You'd be welcome," Justin added.

Will seemed startled by the sincerity of the gesture. "No, but thanks. Patsy ought to start her new life without a reminder from her old one staring her in the face."

He got into his car then and drove away, leaving Patsy staring after him, her expression thoughtful. "Maybe he's not such a bad person, after all. Maybe it was just the circumstances and the timing."

"I don't know about that," Justin said. "The only timing I'm concerned about now is seeing to it you make it to the church on time tomorrow."

"Sharon Lynn is staying with me. Janet has a timetable posted on the refrigerator door. There's no way I'll be late," she promised.

Of course, she hadn't counted on getting stopped for speeding halfway to the chapel. Even as she hit the brakes, she glanced at the speedometer and noted that she was barely exceeding the posted speed limit.

Ready for an argument, she glanced up into Tate's amused eyes.

"Going somewhere in a hurry, aren't you?"

"You do realize if you keep me out here on the side of the road, I will be late and Justin will worry and the whole family will get in on the act?"

He grinned. "Which is why I decided to be your escort. I don't want any other law enforcement officer coming along and delaying this wedding."

She regarded him curiously. "Why is my marrying Justin so important to you?"

"Because the second you get back from your honeymoon, I'm going to follow Doc Dolan down to the Gulf Coast and spend the rest of my days fishing. Already have my place picked out and my wife's chomping at the bit to get going."

"Which means what for Justin?"

"That he'll be sheriff, if he wants the job."

"Have you told him that?"

"Nope. It's my wedding present. I'll tell him at the reception."

Patsy grinned. "It's better than another blender, I'll give you that."

"Come on, then, girl. We're wasting time. If you're late, Harlan Adams will have the state troopers, the Texas Rangers and Lord knows who else out here looking for you."

When they reached the church, Justin was indeed pacing around outside, with his grandfather right on his heels. The pair of them glared at Tate, who wisely scooted inside without getting dragged into a discussion over his role in her delayed arrival.

"You can go on in now, Grandpa. The wedding's about to start," Justin said, his relief evident.

When they were alone, he scowled at her. "I ought to have you arrested, you know."

"For what? I haven't done anything."

"Sure you have. You stole my heart."

Patsy reached up and cupped his face in her hands. "For a lawman, you sure do have a way with words."

And then she kissed him, which was why, forever after, everyone in Los Piños would talk about the fact that Justin Adams kissed his bride before the wedding and almost never made it to the chapel at all.

* * * * *

THE UNCLAIMED BABY

Chapter One

Sleet slashed through the bitter cold February night. A few hours from now it was expected to turn to snow, layering over ice in a way that would leave the roads treacherous. Sharon Lynn stood in the doorway at Dolan's Drugstore and shivered, even though it was plenty warm inside. It was Friday night at eight, an hour when the store should have been closed, but she'd taken to keeping it open later and later. It meant she didn't have to go home to an empty house, didn't have to go to sleep and face the nightmares.

Even though months had passed, the images came back whenever she closed her eyes. The bright headlights glaring into her eyes, weaving across the center line of the quiet country road. The screaming crunch of metal against metal, then just the screaming. Her own and Kyle's.

And then just her own.

That summer night had been clear, with a vibrant sprinkling of stars and a glorious full moon. No danger on the road then, except for a man who'd had too much to drink.

She had been married for little more than a split second when the tragedy struck. It had been their wedding night, a night she had been anticipating and dreaming about for years, it seemed. She was finally Mrs. Kyle Mason and the rest of their lives was spread out ahead of them, a storybook future with a houseful of kids and her wonderful family nearby. In the Adams clan, family meant everything and she'd been waiting a long time to start her own.

Then, in the blink of an eye, her marriage was over and she was alone again. Worse, she had been driving the car, and even though the accident was another driver's fault, Sharon Lynn had been consumed with guilt and grief ever since, wondering if there hadn't been something—*anything*—she could have done to prevent it. For weeks it had taken every bit of strength she had just to propel herself out of bed.

Buying Dolan's, where she had worked for years and where her mother had worked during her tumultuous relationship with Sharon Lynn's daddy before their wedding, had given her a reason for getting up in the morning, but it had done nothing to heal her broken heart.

She had been in love with Kyle Mason forever. An honest, decent man, he had bought a ranch that neighbored the family spread at White Pines. Then he had quietly and persistently courted Sharon Lynn, consuming enough milk shakes at Dolan's that it was a wonder he'd been able to stand the sight of them. Once he'd caught her attention, there had been no turning back.

But when it came to getting to the altar, one thing after another had delayed their vows until that fateful night.

After waiting patiently for marriage, only to have it snatched away from her in a heartbeat, Sharon Lynn had finally concluded that she was not destined for either romance or the family she had always dreamed of. She had resigned herself to a quiet, lonely existence—if it was possible to be lonely with an entire clan of Adamses on her doorstep daily with one feeble excuse or another. Cheering up grief-stricken Sharon Lynn had become the family's mission. All the attention was wearing her out.

She wasn't the one deserving of pity, though. It was Kyle, barely thirty when he'd been killed. She shuddered and forced the memory of that night aside. The guilt, however, wouldn't budge, despite what everyone had said. The official sheriff's report had exonerated her completely. Her cousin Justin, who'd been on the scene in the horrible aftermath of the collision, was a by-the-book kind of deputy. If there'd been any question of her guilt, though he would have hated laying the blame on her doorstep, he would have done it. Knowing that, she should have been able to rest easy, but she couldn't.

Even all these long months later and despite her best intentions, the images crowded back, refusing to be ignored. She'd still been wearing her wedding dress, her beautiful silk-and-lace gown, but by then it had been torn and spattered with blood. Her husband's blood. When her cousins had wanted to get rid of it, she'd refused to let them. It was packed away in the attic as a grim reminder of what might have been. Someday she would have to let it—and the memories—go.

"Oh, God," she murmured as tears streaked down her cheeks. When were the memories going to blur? When would this unbearable, soul-sick pain stop?

Blinded to everything except her own internal misery, it took a blast of icy air from the unexpected opening of the door to snap her out of it. She hadn't even seen the man approaching, hadn't expected anyone to be out on such a cold and furious night. She glanced up to meet worried brown eyes flecked with gold.

"What's a pretty lady like you doing all alone on a Friday night?" he asked in the easy way of a man to whom flirting was second nature. The words were barely out of his mouth when the crooked smile faded from his lips and worry creased his brow. He stepped closer and skimmed a knuckle down her cheek. "Tears? Darlin', are you okay?"

There was a gentleness to his voice that soothed, even as alarm flared at the startling way that touch awakened her senses. She looked him over—from the curling black hair damp with rain to the soaked sheepskin jacket, rain-streaked jeans and well-worn boots. Despite the kindness in his voice, there was a hardness to him, not just to his lean body, but in his eyes. It was an intriguing combination, a dangerous one. That must be why her pulse was ricocheting all over the place.

Was he a would-be robber, checking to make sure she was all alone before seizing every penny in the cash register? Her imagination roared off down a frightening path.

Let him try, she thought fiercely, thinking of the gun that Justin had insisted she keep in the store if she was determined to hang around here alone until all hours of the night. She was a better shot than most of the family and not a one of them missed what they aimed for. Of course, there wasn't much cash worth killing over. She'd taken most of it to the night-drop at the bank just before the new pharmacist had left for the evening.

She scowled up at the man, saw then the exhaustion in his eyes, the stubble on his cheeks, the sensuality of a mouth beginning another slow curve into a disarming smile that softened the harsh angles of his face. What she missed was any hint of a real threat. Whatever this man's story, it seemed evident to her that he meant her no harm. His concern struck her as genuine, as impulsive and automatic as his smile.

Satisfied, she met his grin with one of her own and briskly wiped away the last traces of her tears with an impatient swipe.

"I was just debating whether to close up," she said, turning back inside and heading for the lunch counter, which was her domain even though she owned the whole place now. A few months back she'd hired a pharmacist and a teenager to work the rest of the store once Doc Dolan had retired and headed off to the Gulf Coast of Texas. "I didn't expect anyone to be out on a night like this. You startled me."

"Sorry. I've been on the road all day. When I saw the sign and the lights on, I was thinking more about my empty stomach than I was about whether I might scare you to death. If you need to close up, I can go somewhere else."

Sharon Lynn heard the underlying thread of disappointment in his voice and watched his gaze settling on the stale doughnuts left over from morning. She could toss those in a bag, give them to him with a takeout cup of coffee and he'd be on his way. The idea held no appeal, not when it would mean empty, lonely hours ahead. These days she was eager to snatch a few moments of companionship wherever she could find it.

"I'm in no rush," she said quickly. "I still have some soup that's hot and I can rustle up a hamburger or a grilled cheese and fries. I doubt you'd find anyplace else in town open on a night like this. Los Piños tends to shut down early when the weather's bad. Nobody likes driving on the icy roads."

"What about you?"

"I don't drive," she said and left it at that. She hadn't been behind the wheel of a car since the night of the accident. In fact, she'd moved into her cousin Dani's old house in town, just so she could walk to work. When she wanted to go out to visit the family at White Pines, there was always one relative or another around who could take her. There was no place else she needed to go.

She ladled up a bowl of homemade vegetable soup and set it on the counter in front of him. "Now, what else can I get for you?"

"A couple of cheeseburgers and fries, if you're sure you don't mind."

Mind? Not if it would keep her here a few minutes longer, provide a welcome distraction from her grim memories. Her inability to shake them earlier indicated tonight they were going to be worse than usual.

"Coming right up," she told him. Her innate curiosity and friendliness kicked in. "What brings you to Los Piños?"

"A job," he said. "My name's Cord Branson. I've heard there's an opening on a ranch around here. It's a place called White Pines. Maybe you know the owners."

Sharon Lynn grinned and relaxed, the last of her fears vanishing. "I ought to. White Pines belongs to my grandfather, Harlan Adams. My father—his name's Cody Adams—and my brother, Harlan Patrick, run it." She held out her hand. "I'm Sharon Lynn."

"Well, I'll be a son of a gun," he said, grasping her hand in his and holding it just a shade longer than necessary, long enough to remind her of that earlier tingle of awareness.

"First I meet a beautiful lady and then I find out she's related to the folks I hope to work for," he said. "Looks like this is my lucky night, after all. Do you mind telling me about the place?"

"Of course not." She described the ranch with the affection of someone who'd grown up roaming its vast acreage. "You'll never see any place more beautiful, if you don't mind land that's a little rugged. Grandpa Harlan inherited it when the house was crumbling and the herd of cattle had dwindled down to almost nothing. His daddy wasn't meant to be a rancher, I suppose. At any rate, now it's one of the biggest operations in the state."

"But you don't live out there?"

"No, I stay right here in town now to be close to the store."

"Don't you miss it?"

Sharon Lynn grinned. "There's hardly time for that. There's always something going on out at White Pines. I'm back there practically every weekend for one celebration or another or just for an old-fashioned barbecue if granddaddy starts getting lonely for a little commotion."

She caught the faintly wistful expression on his face. "What about you? Did you grow up on a ranch?"

"If you could call it that. It was probably every bit as bad as you say White Pines was way back when, but every time my daddy had a chance to make a real go of it, he squandered the money on booze. After he was gone, I sold the place to get a stake so I could move on to someplace where I could learn how a real ranch was run. I drifted a bit through Montana and Wyoming before heading south. Once I crossed into Texas, I kept hearing about your granddaddy and White Pines."

"Well, you picked the right place. Nobody knows more about ranching than Grandpa Harlan and my daddy, or Harlan Patrick, to hear him tell it."

She caught herself. "Just listen to me. I'm going on and on. Maybe you'd like to finish your meal in peace. I've got things I could do in the back."

"No, indeed. Don't even think of it. I've been on the road for days now. I'm glad of the company and the conversation, especially when the company's as pretty as you and the conversation's fascinating."

The words were all glib charm, but as he met her gaze and smiled slowly, Sharon Lynn felt another of those quick little quivers in the pit of her stomach. Cord Branson was a very disconcerting man, more direct than most she'd met, outside of her brother and her cousins. He was certainly less subtle than Kyle, who had tended toward shyness.

She gazed into those devilish eyes with their golden sparks and something told her that she was in more danger now than she would have been if the only thing he'd wanted was to rob the place.

Cord wolfed down two of the best hamburgers he'd had in ages and tried to remember what it was that had brought him to Los Piños. He knew better than most that a man didn't get anywhere in life, if he let himself get distracted.

And yet, he couldn't help thinking that Sharon Lynn Adams would be a damned fine distraction. He'd never seen a woman with more sorrow written all over a face that was meant for angels. He had watched with amusement as she'd run the gamut of emotions when he'd first walked through the door. He'd seen the tiny flicker of fear, the fierce resolve and then the quiet, ingrained compassion that made her take him in and feed him despite the probable inconvenience. He thought he'd also noted a hint of relief in her expression, but, unable to imagine the origin of that, he'd dismissed it.

He pegged her age at late twenties and, after glancing at her ringless fingers, wondered why no man had snapped her up. Even in the past few minutes he'd seen that she was easy to get along with and even easier on the eye. To say nothing of being an Adams. From everything he'd heard, that counted for something in these parts. Maybe for too many men that was *all* that counted and she'd simply gotten used to warily fending them off.

He enjoyed watching her work, the quick efficient movements, the sway of hips a little on the generous side. Even more, he liked the ready rise of color in her cheeks when he teased and the way her laughter sounded when he finally managed to coax it out of her with one of the worst jokes either of them had ever heard. He'd found himself lingering long after he'd finished his meal, drinking more caffeine than his body needed if he was to get any rest at all tonight. Still, the coffee had been an excuse. He wasn't looking forward to going back out into the cold night or to leaving her.

"Do you have a place to stay?" she asked eventually, when a glance at the clock and the discovery that it was after ten clearly startled her. "There's a motel outside of town, but on a night like this it's probably full and I'm not sure you ought to risk driving that far on the icy roads."

"No problem. Unless you think the local law enforcement will object, I'll just find a place to pull my truck off on the side of the road and sleep in back," he said. "I've got a nice warm sleeping bag and I'm used to roughing it."

Even as he said it, she was shaking her head. "No way. I won't have your freezing to death on my conscience. If you truly don't mind roughing it, you can sleep in the back room here. The floor's hard as a rock, but the sleeping bag ought to help and at least you'll have heat."

"I couldn't."

"Of course you could."

He frowned at her. As generous as it was, the offer filled him with concern. He didn't like thinking of her taking that kind of risk with other strangers. "You know," he chided, "it's possible that you're entirely too trusting."

She shrugged off the suggestion. "That's the way folks around here are. First impressions count for a lot, and I can see you're a decent man."

Cord regarded her with blatant amusement. "I thought you said first impressions counted?"

"They do."

"Your first impression of me was that I was here to rob you."

A guilty flush confirmed his guess.

"Okay, yes," she admitted, "just for a second, I did wonder. Most people would have been inside on a night like this, unless they were up to no good."

"But you don't wonder anymore?"

Her gaze met his, blue eyes the exact shade of wildflowers searching his face. "Not anymore," she said at last, giving his hand a brief, reassuring pat.

He told himself later that it wasn't the way his pulse leapt when her fingers grazed his that mattered. It wasn't the unexpected yearning that came over him looking into her eyes. It was the fact that she said those two simple words with such quiet confidence that made him fall in love with her. It had been a very long time since anyone on earth had believed in Cord Branson.

Before he could get lost in the wonder of that, a heavy thump against the back door startled them both. Sharon Lynn whirled in that direction, but Cord was faster. "You stay put. I'll check it out." He gestured toward the back room. "Where's the door? Through there?"

She nodded. "It was probably just a dog bumping into a trash can or the wind knocking something over," she said, right on his heels.

Cord glanced over his shoulder. "I thought I told you to stay put."

She shot him a defiant look. "It's my store. Besides, I have a gun right here." She snatched a very deadly look-ing rifle out of its hiding place. "I can look after myself."

He grinned at the fierce response and the determined jut of her jaw. "Yes, I can see that. Okay, but would you stay behind me at least and keep that gun pointed at something other than my backside?"

She regarded him with a faint glimmer of amusement, then shrugged. "I suppose I could do that."

"I do love an amenable woman," he said as he began twisting locks. When he'd unlatched the last one, he slowly turned the knob, shot Sharon Lynn one last warning look, then eased outside. What he found stunned him almost as bad as confronting a thief would have.

"Holy Mother of God," he murmured as he bent down over the basket.

"What is it?" Sharon Lynn asked, nudging against him.

The quick bump of her hip was surprisingly provocative. She was so close he could smell her perfume, something light and innocent, maybe little more than scented hand lo-tion. It set off a surge of pure lust just the same. There was no time for that now, though.

"A baby," he replied, his voice hushed as he scooped the tiny child up into his arms. "Some damned fool left a baby out here in this weather. If we hadn't been here, it would have been dead before morning." Just the thought of that filled him with cold fury.

"Let me see," she demanded, scooting around him. At the sight of the tiny infant, her eyes went wide with a mix of shock and indignation every bit as violent as his own.

"Oh, sweetie," she whispered, reaching at once for the

baby. "Let me. Maybe they knew we were inside and knew we'd find the baby before any harm came to it."

"Maybe," Cord said, because the notion seemed to console her. The basket had been left a little too close to the trash Dumpster for his liking, though. And the way the snow was coming down now, in no time at all, the basket and its contents would have been shrouded in a way that might have made it blend in with the bags of trash heaped nearby. He suspected that thump they'd heard had been an accident, not a deliberate attempt to catch their attention. No, this had been a cruel and heartless attempt to leave a child to die. He'd stake his life on that.

"Whoever did this can't have gotten far," Sharon Lynn said. "See if there's any sign of him or her."

"Him," Cord said grimly.

"How do you know that?"

"The boot prints. There's just enough snow on the ground to see the size of the shoe. It's too big for a woman's."

Cord knew there was no point in following the trail. Whoever had done this despicable thing was long gone by now, but he went to the end of the alley just to satisfy Sharon Lynn. The footprints ended at the curb around the corner. A melted patch in the midst of all the snow indicated someone had left an engine running for a few minutes at least. Skid marks in the fresh snow suggested that whoever had driven away had probably heard the store's back door open and left in a hurry.

By the time Cord got back inside, Sharon Lynn was holding a squalling, wide-awake baby in her arms as naturally as if this were something she did every day. The look of awe and concern on her face was enough to take his breath away. For one wild and improbable second, he imagined that she was his, the baby theirs. In that instant, with a certainty that stunned him, he knew that whatever it took, somehow he would make it happen.

Over the years he had seen too many of life's most valuable treasures slip through his daddy's fingers. Hawk Branson had lost his wife—Cord's mama—to another man. He'd lost a fortune and most of the payments on the family ranch to the bottle. There'd been pitifully little left for Cord, once all the debts had been settled. Watching Hawk's downfall had made Cord an impatient man.

When he spotted something he wanted, he went after it with a no-holds-barred vengeance. He had come here intending to claim a place for himself at the famed White Pines ranch, vowing to work harder and longer than any other hand.

He could have stayed in Montana and tried to save his daddy's spread. The local bankers trusted him. They knew he wasn't anything like his daddy. But there were too many defeats and bad memories associated with the place. He'd wanted a fresh start, not just as a hand at a truly successful ranch where he could learn everything there was to know about running a decent herd of cattle, but someplace where he could earn enough to buy his own land, acre by acre if he had to. Ownership and self-respect were all tied up together in his head.

Instinctively he'd aimed for Texas and its sprawling cattle ranches. He'd hung out in a bar in Fort Worth and asked questions. He'd gone to a couple of cattle auctions and asked more questions. White Pines and its owners had come up time and again, always accompanied by respectful anecdotes.

The last time he'd stopped, about a hundred miles from Los Piños, he'd asked pointedly about the ranch and learned that not only was White Pines taking on new help, but there was a neighboring ranch that might be for sale. The owner had died in a tragic accident and the widow wanted no part of it. The story had piqued his interest. He'd wasted no time in getting to Los Piños.

He'd been prepared to do whatever he had to to get the job he was after and to lay claim to that ranch, if the widow was willing to wait to make a sale. What he hadn't been prepared for at all was spotting a woman like Sharon Lynn on his first night in town. She was the missing piece of his dream. Gut instinct told him that destiny had brought him into Dolan's on this icy, miserable night.

He glanced down at her head, which was bent low as she soothed the fussing baby in her arms. The baby's fat little fist held a thick strand of silken hair and was tugging mightily. Sharon Lynn smiled, even as she tried to disengage that tiny hand. Watching her, Cord felt a swirl of powerful emotions that rocked him on his heels. Just like that, he knew that what he was feeling was love. Impossible, unexpected, but love, just the same. The lightning bolt kind that changed a man's life when he least expected it.

Slow down, he warned himself. He might be bold and impetuous and ready to believe in fate, but he doubted this woman or any other would be quite so ready to throw caution to the wind and jump into a relationship with a stranger.

He felt a smile tugging at the corners of his mouth, just the same. For once in a life filled with nasty twists and turns, it appeared that fate had finally dealt him a winning hand.

Chapter Two

Cord spent a restless night in the back room at Dolan's. For every pleasant dream he had about a beautiful, mysterious woman sharing his bed, there was a counterpoint—the nightmare of a baby's whispered cries fading into silence. He awoke bathed in a cold sweat more times than he could count.

Finally just before dawn, unable to face the torment of another nightmare, he'd crawled out of his sleeping bag, rolled it into a neat bundle, then tried to repair the night's ravages to his face. Eyedrops and a shave took care of the worst of it. A microwaved cup of last night's leftover coffee gave him a much-needed jolt of caffeine and a couple of stale doughnuts gave him a sugar rush that would last him through the morning. By six he was feeling almost human and ready to face the day.

But he still couldn't shake his worry about the baby he and Sharon Lynn had rescued from the frigid night. Had she been out there long enough to catch her death of cold? What if she were spiking a fever? Would Sharon Lynn know what to do? Probably every bit as well as he would, he conceded.

The temptation to go by her place to see how the pair of them were doing was tremendous. It was also a distraction, one he'd vowed not to allow, especially since he couldn't be sure that concern for the baby was the only reason he wanted to drop in. He was determined that the previous night's incidents weren't going to take his mind off of what he had to do today.

Right after his discovery the day before that White Pines was hiring, he'd made a call to the ranch. He was scheduled for a 7:00 a.m. meeting with Cody Adams and nothing on God's earth was going to keep him from being on time for it. Allowing for the condition of the roads, it was going to take every second he had allowed to drive to White Pines. He figured showing up on schedule despite the adverse conditions would be a point in his favor.

His tight timetable and grim determination not to allow any distractions might not permit a visit, but he could detour past Sharon Lynn's house. That might not be nearly as satisfying as getting a peek at the two of them, but it would be enough to reassure himself that they were nice and cozy inside on this miserable morning. Then he could go on to his job interview with a clear conscience.

"That's a plan," he concluded, slamming the door on his pickup and easing out onto a road covered with snow and a treacherous undersheet of ice. The drive was going to be a picnic, all right, he thought as the tires skidded, then finally held.

The sun was just beginning to sneak over the horizon as he eased cautiously down Main Street. He caught a glimpse of the huge orange ball in his rearview mirror as he crept down the block, then turned the corner to drive past Sharon Lynn's.

The small, neat house, which also doubled as a veterinary clinic, had surprised him when they'd arrived there the night before. He'd been expecting something bigger, fancier, but once he'd walked through the front door he'd had the feeling that the house suited Sharon Lynn. It was homey and warm, a welcoming kind of place with its cheery yellows and mellowing blues. And she'd explained that the veterinary practice belonged to her cousin, who actually owned the property and, she added with a grin, most of the cats and kittens who were scrambling around their ankles the instant they'd walked through the door.

"Dani's always taking in strays, me included," Sharon Lynn had told him. She indicated the baby in her arms. "This would be a little over the top even for her."

"But not for you," he'd guessed. "You're a natural mother."

The comment had brought on a too-quick denial…and tears she hadn't been quick enough to hide. There were emotions there he couldn't begin to fathom and she hadn't given him time to try.

With a briskness that had amused him, she'd thanked him for walking her home, for helping with all the baby supplies she'd taken from the store, and hustled him out the door before he could blink. Before he knew it, he was outside looking in, just as he had been all his life. The woman was a self-sufficient whirlwind, all right. It was an irritating trait, especially to a man who had hoped to be needed.

She wouldn't go on brushing him off, he'd promised himself as he left. Soon he would be part of her life, but only after he was settled, only when he had something to offer. He wasn't long on patience, so he'd just have to make sure he had steady work by the end of the day. That would give him confidence and resources, so he could begin phase one of his campaign to win Sharon Lynn's heart.

As his pickup idled, he gave the house a quick survey

in the pale morning light. There was a light on—in the kitchen, he thought, recalling the layout of the house from his brief stay the night before. He pictured Sharon Lynn, her hair tousled from sleep, her cheeks flushed, maybe wearing nothing more than a robe, heating a baby bottle or maybe making coffee. It was like gazing into his heart and seeing what he'd longed for all his life—someone to come home to, someone who cared. And a baby they'd created together, one who would never know the kind of abandonment he'd felt when his mama had run off.

He imagined he heard a baby's whimper, though it would have been impossible at this distance with windows closed and the wind howling. Just thinking of that tiny baby brought on a smile, one that lasted until he thought of the son of a bitch who'd left her in the alley. Heaven help the man if Cord ever came across him. Or if Sharon Lynn did, he thought, grinning at the memory of her outrage and the flash of temper that had accompanied it.

Satisfied that short of going inside to check in person, he'd made sure that all was well, he sighed deeply and drove on. He was more determined than ever to get to White Pines in time to get that job. Though he didn't like thinking that his goals had shifted and had gotten all twisted up with staying close to a woman and a baby, he couldn't help conceding he had more reasons than ever for wanting to settle down in this little corner of west Texas.

By Saturday morning Sharon Lynn was exhausted. The baby hadn't settled down for more than a minute all night. Fortunately the drugstore had had all the supplies she'd needed to keep the baby comfortable and fed. Cord Branson had walked her home carrying all the packages. Even though she'd said she could manage, he'd given her one of those impatient, superior male looks, picked up the supplies and waited for her to lead the way. It hadn't seemed worth arguing about. And it had been reassuring to have someone to cling to each time her feet had slipped on the icy sidewalks. She was forced to admit it wouldn't have been easy to avoid a tumble without him. For her own sake and the baby's, she'd been grateful that he'd insisted.

At the house, though, she'd been eager to have him leave. Other than family, she hadn't had any male company since she'd moved in and Cord was the kind of man who made his presence felt the instant he walked through the door. All that potent masculinity was an unnecessary distraction when she wanted to concentrate on the baby.

Cord had offered to stick around and help, to bunk on the sofa, but she'd figured she was going to have enough explaining to do about the baby without having to come up with explanations for letting a total stranger—a very masculine stranger—spend the night in her house. It was a very logical excuse for ridding herself of a man who made her nervous for reasons she wasn't quite ready to explore.

The minute she'd hustled him out the door, the baby had begun to cry as if she'd felt abandoned all over again. Sharon Lynn had begun her night of pacing. Even after the baby had fallen into a restless sleep, she'd been unable to fall asleep herself. There were too many decisions to be made, too many unanswerable questions to consider.

By morning she'd reached only one conclusion. She knew she was going to have to call someone, Justin maybe, and report the baby turning up. She probably should have done it at once, but the instant Cord had placed the child in her arms, she had known she couldn't let go until she could come up with a plan to keep the baby safe from whomever had abandoned it on her doorstep. Protecting the child was all that mattered.

She wanted to believe it was someone who'd chosen her store because he or she had known that Sharon Lynn would care for the baby. She tried to envision a mother desperate enough to let her child go but concerned enough to assure that the baby was in good hands.

But even as she tried to put the best possible spin on things, she couldn't help thinking that the baby could have died, could have been left in that alley all alone, undiscovered, until it was too late. She knew that was what Cord thought had happened. He hadn't believed for an instant that the baby was meant to be found. Skepticism had been written all over his face when she'd suggested it. The possibility that he could be right infuriated her.

How could anyone be so heartless? How could any mother do that? she wondered fiercely.

Then she recalled what Cord had deduced. The person doing the leaving had been a man. The baby's father, perhaps? A man who couldn't cope with his own responsibility for a newborn? Somehow that was even worse. She prayed for the chance to see that man rot in jail for his crime against the precious baby now sleeping in her room.

It hadn't required a lot of detective work last night to determine that the baby was a girl. One diaper change had answered that question. The baby wasn't a newborn. That question had been answered as well. The umbilical cord had healed. She had to be a few weeks old at least. That meant that the mother had held her and fed her and comforted her—and then let her go.

Which brought Sharon Lynn right back to the question that had been tormenting her all night long. How could any mother give up her baby, especially in such a cruel and heartless manner? Had an unwilling father or a new boyfriend been the one to take the baby and leave it in the alley? Why would any woman choose a sick man capable of doing that over her own precious baby?

Those were all questions for the authorities, but as the night had worn on, Sharon Lynn hadn't been able to imagine letting them take the baby away while they searched for answers. There had to be some way she could become the child's temporary guardian, if only to assure that the baby wouldn't become just another statistic in the overburdened foster care system. She'd read too many horror stories about slipups, about babies sent home only to wind up beaten or dead within days or weeks. It wouldn't happen to this child, not if she had anything at all to say about it.

At dawn she called her part-time employee, Patsy Driscoll, and asked her to open up at Dolan's. Two hours later with the baby fed and her own breakfast churning acid in her stomach, she drew in a deep breath and forced herself to dial the sheriff's office. To her dismay her cousin wasn't in yet, but the new dispatcher clucked sympathetically at Sharon Lynn's explanation for needing Justin and promised to track him down and get him to her house on the double.

"I can try him at home," Sharon Lynn protested.

"No, indeed. You just take care of that child," Maribel Hawkins insisted. "I'll find the sheriff for you. With the roads a mess, people skidding into ditches and every deputy out on calls, there's no telling where Justin might be. He hasn't checked in with me yet, but that doesn't mean he's not on duty. He has a way of forgetting that it helps if I know where to find him."

Sharon Lynn grinned at the touch of indignation in Maribel's voice. She'd taken over while the regular dispatcher was out on maternity leave and her oft-stated goal was to change Justin's lackadaisical ways. Obviously she was relishing this latest chance to chide him for not following the rules about reporting in at the start of the day. Maribel wasn't the least bit intimidated by the fact that as the town's newly elected sheriff, Justin was the one who made the rules.

"Don't forget he could be at Dolan's having breakfast," Sharon Lynn said.

"Believe me, honey, I know all the man's hiding places. He'll be over there in a heartbeat."

True to Maribel's promise, Justin arrived within minutes, looking disheveled and cranky. Apparently the dispatcher had dragged him out of bed on what had turned out to be his first day off in two weeks. A newlywed, he was none too pleased about that or about the reason for it.

"Maybe I was still half asleep, maybe I didn't hear dispatch right," he said as he came in the front door without bothering to knock. "Maribel said somebody left a baby on your doorstep last night."

There was enough censure and disbelief in his tone to have Sharon Lynn scowling at him defiantly. "That's correct."

His voice climbed. "And the reason you didn't notify me before now would be?"

"Because it was late and I figured there wouldn't be a thing you could do before morning, anyway. Cord and I had things under control here."

His scowl deepened. "Cord?"

"Another story," she said dismissively. If Justin was this worked up over the baby, she could just imagine what he'd have to say about the stranger who'd been a big part of the night's events. Thankfully he let the mention of Cord pass.

He glanced around the living room. "Where's the baby?" he asked.

"Sleeping, or at least she was until you came in here bellowing." Hands on hips, she faced him belligerently. "Tone it down, or you can leave right now."

"I don't think so."

They scowled at each other for a full minute, before she finally relented and led the way to her bedroom. The baby was squarely in the middle of her bed, surrounded by pillows. She was so tiny, so precious, with her halo of soft blond curls and rosy cheeks. Her solemn, watchful eyes seemed to fix on Sharon Lynn. Just looking at her was enough to fill Sharon Lynn's heart with joy. With her gaze immediately drawn to the sleeping child, she moved to the edge of the bed and skimmed a finger across a pudgy cheek.

"Isn't she beautiful?" she whispered.

"Oh, no," Justin said, his gaze locked on her and not the baby.

Sharon Lynn blinked at his fierce tone, then glanced up at him. "What?"

"You can't keep her, Sharon Lynn."

She had known that, of course, but something in Justin's voice riled her. Her stubborn streak kicked in. She lifted her chin. "Why not?"

"You know perfectly well why not. She's not yours."

"Well, obviously the mother doesn't want her."

"Unless she was kidnapped," he suggested.

Sharon Lynn swallowed hard. It was one explanation she had never even considered. Kidnapped babies were held for ransom. They weren't abandoned. Were they?

"You don't seriously think…"

He raked a hand through his hair and snapped impatiently, "I don't know what to think. I would have known a hell of a lot more by now if you'd told me about her last night, if I'd been able to check out the alley behind the store for any evidence, and if I'd had time to check all the faxes about missing kids."

"Do that now," she said reasonably. "Whatever evidence was in that alley hasn't gone anywhere. As for the faxes, I've seen your desk. They haven't gone anywhere, either."

"I'll do all that right after I take her to the hospital to be thoroughly checked out and call social services," he said. "They're going to love being hauled out on a Saturday after a blizzard."

Sharon Lynn instinctively moved between her cousin and the baby. "My point exactly. If it's going to be such a bother, then don't call them."

His expression turned sympathetic. "Sweetie, there are procedures in cases like this. You know this is what has to be done."

"She'll just end up in foster care, unless you locate the mom, right?"

"I suppose."

"Then let her stay with me. I'll call Grandpa Harlan. He can pull a few strings and get me temporary approval as a foster parent. It's not as if I'm an unfit candidate for it. We can call Lizzy to come check her out medically, if that will make you happy. She's practically a full-fledged doctor. She's doing her residency in Garden City, while granddaddy builds that clinic he promised her here in town. It'll be by the book." She beamed at him, then shrugged at his intractable scowl. "More or less."

"Sharon Lynn—"

"Justin, this is the way it's going to be," she said fiercely, ready to fight him on this if she had to. "That baby would have died last night if Cord and I hadn't found her. I'm not letting her out of my sight until I know she's going to be safe. Whoever left her there doesn't deserve to live, much less have the baby given back to them."

"Well, of course not, but—"

"No buts. You know I'm right. You know she's better off with me, at least for the time being. I feel like I owe her that much."

She watched his face intently, saw the worry, the indecision and prayed he'd go along with her on this. Justin had a powerful sense of right and wrong, a fierce dedication to playing by the rules. She knew she was probably asking him to break a million of them.

"Please," she begged. "Just think of what's best for the baby. Think of all the trauma she's already been through. She's here now, she's warm and safe. Don't start dragging her around again now, just so you can cross all the *t*'s and dot all the *i*'s on your paperwork."

He sighed heavily. "Okay," he relented finally. "But this is temporary. You understand that, right?"

"Of course."

He regarded her skeptically. "You're sure?"

"Justin, I understand."

"All right, then. Hopefully Lizzy's not on duty over at Garden City. Call her and get her over here. If she gives the baby a clean bill of health, that'll do for now. Meantime, I'll go check out all the reports on missing kids to see if there's a match."

"Thank you," she said softly.

"Don't thank me," he said curtly. "Something tells me I'm setting you up for heartbreak."

Chapter Three

"Tell me again how you wound up with a baby," Lizzy said when she arrived an hour later.

She looked every bit the doctor with her little black bag and white lab coat over a silk blouse. She'd even coiled her long, black hair into a tidy topknot. Sharon Lynn still hadn't gotten used to her professional demeanor. To her way of thinking, Lizzy was still first and foremost a rambunctious, anything-for-a-lark cowgirl. Her medical degree from the University of Texas said otherwise.

As Sharon Lynn repeated the same story she'd told Justin, Lizzy's eyes widened. Her mouth narrowed into a thin, disapproving line before she muttered a stream of expletives that would have blistered the ears of the person who'd abandoned the baby. Sharon Lynn said only, "My sentiments exactly."

"How long was she outside, then?"

"Probably not more than a minute or two. We heard a thump, went to investigate and there she was."

"So her body temperature was warm enough when you brought her inside?"

Sharon Lynn nodded. "She was pretty well bundled up.

She felt fine to me. Cord thought so, too. I took her temperature and it was normal."

Just as Justin had, Lizzy seized on the mention of the unfamiliar name. "Cord?"

"The customer who was there when it happened. He was actually the one who found her."

"Interesting," Lizzy said, studying her face. "Is this Cord person handsome, sexy and single?"

"I have no idea," she claimed. At Lizzy's skeptical look, she conceded, "Not about the single part, anyway."

Lizzy grinned. "Then he is handsome and sexy?"

"I suppose. I hardly noticed."

"If he'd turned up *after* you found the baby, I might believe that, but he'd been there how long? A couple of hours? That's a long time to hang around a drugstore during a blizzard, unless the man had something besides food on his mind."

"Are you here to check out the baby or to cross-examine me?" Sharon Lynn grumbled.

Lizzy patted her cheek. "Not to worry. I have time to do both. Come on, let's see the baby. We'll get back to this Cord person later."

Without waiting for Sharon Lynn, she headed to the bedroom and bent over the baby, who was wide-awake and waving her tiny fists in the air. Lizzy sighed. "She's a cute one, all right. And obviously someone has been taking good care of her. Looks to me as if her weight's normal and her color is good. Just look at those rosy little cheeks."

She began examining her with practiced fingers, pausing to tickle a laughing response from her every now and again. When she was finished, she plucked her up off the bed and cradled her in her arms. "You are a little doll."

Sharon Lynn watched her aunt, who was actually

younger than she was, and had an almost overwhelming desire to yank the baby out of her arms. Even *she* recognized that as a bad sign. If she was this possessive after less than twenty-four hours, what was going to happen when the time came to give the baby up? Maybe Justin had been right to worry. Maybe this wasn't going to be as easy as she'd thought.

"Don't go getting any ideas," she told Lizzy. "You've got one of your own and I don't see Hank letting you bring another one home for him to take care of while you finish your residency."

"Are you kidding? Hank's in seventh heaven playing full-time daddy. If he could figure out some way to convince me to stay pregnant and have another kid every nine or ten months, he'd be a happy man. He loves ranching, but parenthood is his true calling. I'm not sure which one of us was more surprised by that. For a long time making a go of his ranch was all that mattered to him. Now he just leaves most of that to Pete and the hands. I come home and he has a zillion and one stories about Jamey for me."

"And how do you feel about expanding your family?"

"I wouldn't give up Jamey for anything, but it is way too soon to be thinking of having another one. It's easier now that med school is over and I'm here all the time, but doing my residency over in Garden City is no picnic. The hours are a killer and, despite what Hank says, I can't put all the burden of taking care of Jamey on him. Besides, I don't want to miss these early years. Things change too fast. He's walking and talking a blue streak. To hear Hank and Daddy tell it, he'll be ready to run the ranch by the time he's five."

"Well, obviously Grandpa Harlan would think any child of his precious baby daughter's would be a genius," Sharon Lynn teased. "As for Hank, he's totally and thoroughly be-

sotted with you. It was a given that any child you two con-
ceived would be brighter and cuter than any other baby on
earth, at least in his eyes."

She reached for this baby and took her from Lizzy's
arms. "Of course, this one could give little Jamey a run
for his money in the looks department."

"You sound an awful lot like a proud mama," Lizzy said,
regarding her worriedly. "Sweetie, you aren't getting any
ideas about trying to keep her, are you?"

"Of course not," Sharon Lynn denied a little too emphatically. "This is just temporary until Justin can find out who
abandoned her and whether there's any family to take her."

"Then why did you bring home enough diapers and formula for months, rather than days?"

She could feel the color flooding her cheeks. "I just
grabbed stuff last night. I wasn't counting. Neither was
Cord. We just accidentally doubled up on some stuff."

As soon as the last was out of her mouth, she realized
her mistake. The repeat mention of Cord's name was like
waving a red flag in front of Lizzy.

"Okay, into the kitchen," Lizzy ordered in the imperi-
ous manner of a woman used to having her demands taken
seriously. "You can feed the baby and I'll pour the coffee.
I want to hear all about this Cord person."

"Don't you have to get back to your own family?" Sharon Lynn asked hopefully.

"You are my family," Lizzy reminded her. "I'm the aunt.
I get to be nosy."

"You're younger than I am."

"Doesn't matter. In the family pecking order, I have
rank. Ask Daddy."

"It would be a waste of time asking Grandpa Harlan,"
Sharon Lynn conceded. "Precious Lizzy has ruled the roost

since the day she was born. After all those impossible sons of his, to say nothing of Jenny who was a fourteen-year-old troublemaker when he married your mom, you were his darling angel. Little did he know that you'd turn out to be the most stubborn and impossible of all of them."

"None of which has a thing to do with the topic," Lizzy reminded her, oblivious to the familiar teasing.

"Which is?"

"Cord. Tell me about him."

Sharon Lynn forced a casual, disinterested shrug. "He's a nice guy. He came into Dolan's last night, right off the road in the middle of that storm. He'd been traveling from Montana. He's here looking for a job."

"What kind of job?"

"Actually he has an interview at White Pines today."

"Oh, boy," Lizzy said, chuckling. "And you think *I'm* subjecting you to an inquisition. Just wait till Daddy gets wind of the fact that you and Cord rescued a baby from a blizzard."

That was precisely what Sharon Lynn was most afraid of. Her grandfather was notorious for his matchmaking schemes. She gave Lizzy a pointed look. "Then hopefully he won't find out about it."

"You have to be dreaming. Daddy has a sixth sense for this sort of thing. Not to mention the fact that Justin and I already know about it. I had to tell Hank I was coming here on my way to work at the hospital. Who knows how many people Justin has spoken to? And Cord is at this very moment out at White Pines meeting with whom?"

"Daddy, more than likely."

Lizzy grinned. "Oh, yes, indeed, Uncle Cody is definitely known for his discretion. Add it up, sweetie, and you're in big trouble."

"Cord is being interviewed by my father," Sharon Lynn reiterated. "Not Grandpa Harlan."

Lizzy chuckled. "And you think that's an improvement?"

Sharon Lynn sighed. "Okay, maybe not much of one. Maybe Cord won't mention having met me."

"Did you swear him to secrecy?"

"No."

"If you were hoping to get hired on by the biggest rancher in the state, wouldn't you use the fact that you happen to know his daughter?"

"Okay, maybe, but it's not like we're old friends or anything. We just met."

"And rescued a baby together. It's a bond, sweetie, the kind that will set off all sorts of wild speculation around White Pines. There's no getting around it."

It was a bond, Sharon Lynn thought with a sigh. Cord's tenderness with the baby had touched her heart. His outrage and indignation had been every bit a match for her own. Beyond that? She refused to look beyond that. She wasn't remotely interested in allowing a new man into her life, especially not a charming stranger who might be all too capable of slipping past her defenses. She'd lived amidst charming rogues and scoundrels all her life. She wasn't interested in dating one. That's why Kyle, the polar opposite of the men in her family, had held such strong appeal for her. Judging from Lizzy's expression, she hadn't yet made herself clear enough. She tried again.

"Lizzy, for a woman with a practical, scientific mind, you're talking like the ultimate romantic. Get a grip. Cord Branson is a total stranger."

"He might have been when he walked into Dolan's last night, but something tells me he isn't now."

"You're imagining things."

"We'll see," Lizzy predicted. "If there's one thing I've learned the last couple of years, it's that fate has a sneaky way of turning life upside down when you least expect it. Jamey is proof enough of that."

Sharon Lynn could certainly testify to that, too, but her experience with fate wasn't something she had any intention of repeating. She was in total control of her life these days and she intended to stay that way. She said as much to Lizzy.

"And this time yesterday were you cuddling a baby in your arms and trying to figure out how you were going to juggle your schedule at Dolan's and care for her?"

"No, but—"

Lizzy grinned. "I rest my case." She slipped on her coat, then leaned down to brush a kiss across Sharon Lynn's cheek. "See you, sweetie. Call if you need any help. If I'm not around, talk to Hank. He's the baby expert, anyway. He'll probably insist you bring this little princess out to the ranch to play with Jamey."

Sharon Lynn grinned. "I think this one might be a little young for play-dates, don't you?"

"I do, but Hank won't. Promise you'll call if you need anything."

"Thanks. I'm sure we'll be fine."

Lizzy's expression sobered then. She picked up Sharon Lynn's hand and pressed it against her cheek. "Don't get too attached, okay? It would be easy to do. Nobody could blame you, but—"

"I know," Sharon Lynn responded bleakly. "It can only end in heartbreak. I've been there, done that. One more time won't matter."

"It would matter," Lizzy said fiercely. "You're strong,

Sharon Lynn. We all know that. But even you have a breaking point."

Sharon Lynn forced a smile. "Then I can't let myself get too attached, can I?"

When Lizzy was gone, she glanced down at the now-sleeping baby in her arms and sighed. She had a terrible feeling it was already too late.

The interview had gone well enough. Cody Adams had asked tough questions, questions that might have put Cord on the defensive, but he'd asked them in a way that had encouraged Cord to give straight answers about his past, as well as his ambitions.

"In other words, we can't count on you sticking around here as a hand until your dying breath," Cody summarized after the questions were done and they'd spent some time touring the ranch. "You scrape up enough money, find some land you want and you'll leave?"

"To be perfectly honest, yes," Cord admitted. "But until I do, I'll work longer and harder than any other man you've got."

"Why White Pines?"

"Because everybody says you're the best."

"Who is everybody?"

Cord mentioned all the places he'd stopped and asked questions. "The Adams name kept coming up."

Cody nodded, his expression thoughtful. "I like a man who does his homework. I also like a man who doesn't make promises he doesn't intend to keep. Depending on how good you are at tucking away your pay and not squandering it on poker games and such, I suppose I can count on you being with us for a while, long enough for it to be worth my while to break you in."

Cord thought of another reason for staying right here, not just in the short term, but forever. She had the most incredible blue eyes he'd ever seen. He doubted Cody would want to know about his intentions in that regard just yet. Instead he said only, "Yes, sir, I think you can count on me being here that long."

"Then the job's yours. When can you start?"

Cord barely managed to contain a whoop of triumph. "When do you need me?"

"Today would be good. I'll settle for tomorrow. I'm short one man and I've got two more down with the flu. I'm running in circles trying to keep up. My brother-in-law's been pitching in, but he's got his own spread to worry about, plus a kid who's just learning to walk and is running both him and his housekeeper ragged."

"Just tell me what needs doing and I'll get started," Cord told him, pushing aside his regret that there wouldn't be time to head back into town to see Sharon Lynn and the baby until later that night or early the next week.

Before Cody could reply, the phone in his office rang. He grabbed it up, listened intently, then glanced at Cord with renewed curiosity.

"Sure thing, Daddy. I'll send him over to the house. Don't be taking up too much of his time, though. I've got chores for him to do." He grinned. "Yes, I recall that it is still your ranch and you do have some say about what goes on around here. Even if I should forget, you take great pleasure in reminding me every chance you get."

He hung up and turned back to regard Cord speculatively. "You didn't mention that you'd met my daughter."

"Sharon Lynn?" he asked, impressed by the speed of the family grapevine.

Cody nodded. "How'd that come about?"

Cord debated just how much he should say, finally settling on the bare minimum. "I stopped in town last night for a bite to eat. Dolan's was the only place open."

"I see. Anything else interesting happen while you were there?"

Cord chuckled at the careful probing. Apparently he was wasting his time being discreet. "Obviously you've heard about the baby that was dropped off on the doorstep."

"Daddy told me just now. He wants to hear the whole story. So do I, but in my case it'll have to wait for another time. You go on up to the main house and fill him in, then come back here when you're done."

Cord stood up and started for the door, but Cody stopped him.

"You know, if you'd mentioned what happened, I'd have given you the job without asking a million and one questions. The fact that you helped out my daughter and that poor little abandoned baby would have been enough."

Cord nodded. "I suspected as much, sir. I wanted to get the job on my own."

Cody regarded him with approval. "An admirable decision. I think you're going to work out just fine. Now get on up to the house before Daddy comes looking for you. Once he's here, he won't be able to resist telling me how to do things."

"I imagine that would be time-consuming, sir."

Cody grinned. "You have no idea."

Cord had seen the main house in the distance when he'd driven up to White Pines a few hours earlier. It reminded him of a Southern plantation. Cody had explained that was exactly what it was, almost a replica of the burned-to-the-ground home that his ancestors had left behind when they'd fled the South after the Civil War.

He parked in front of the house and climbed the steps, which had already been cleared of snow. Before he could ring the bell, the door swung wide and an older version of Cody with white hair and stooped shoulders held out a hand.

"You must be Cord. Come on in. I've heard all about the goings-on in town last night."

"I gather Los Piños has an active grapevine."

"I can't swear for the town, but this family does," Harlan Adams said with pride. "There's not much that goes on that I don't know about." He started down the hall and beckoned for Cord to follow. "Let's go in the kitchen if you don't mind. If I'm right there, I have half a chance of getting a decent cup of coffee, instead of that pitiful decaf everybody's been insisting I drink the last few months."

In the huge kitchen, Harlan Adams glanced around, poked his head into what was apparently a large walk-in pantry and gave a nod of satisfaction. "Good, the housekeeper's gone. If you'll grab a couple of cups from that cupboard over there, I'll pour."

Cord found two large mugs and put them on the table, hiding his amusement that one of the most powerful men in Texas was having to sneak a cup of real coffee in his own home.

"Are you sure you ought to be drinking this?" he asked.

"Of course not. My daughter, the one who's got a fancy medical degree now, got a notion that the real stuff is bad for my heart. I'm way past eighty now. It's my opinion that if I want a cup of coffee, then by God, I ought to have one. Age should have some privileges."

"Just don't keel over on my watch," Cord said.

The old man's blue eyes twinkled merrily. "I'll guarantee that, if you'll keep my little secret."

"Done."

"So tell me about this baby you and Sharon Lynn found."

"What have you heard?"

"Pitifully little. I tried to wheedle more information out of my grandson, but he's the sheriff and as tight-lipped as an old maid when it comes to an investigation. All I know for sure is that Sharon Lynn talked him into leaving the baby with her for the time being. I've called a judge to make it official that she can provide temporary guardianship for the child, while Justin does his poking around."

Cord gave a little nod of satisfaction. "She'll take good care of her."

"Well, of course she will. The girl has a heart as big as Texas. Trouble is, she's mighty vulnerable these days. I just pray she doesn't get hurt. I know Justin thinks she's making a big mistake. Giving up foster care babies isn't always easy, not even on folks who do it all the time."

"I'll admit I don't know your granddaughter all that well, but she struck me as being a pretty sensible woman. She didn't waste a lot of time getting emotional last night. The instant we found that baby, she just took charge."

"That's her way, but it's been a terrible year for her. Take my word for that."

Cord had the feeling that was all Harlan Adams intended to say on the subject, but his measured words only confirmed what Cord had read in her eyes. Something tragic had filled her with sorrow. It reminded him that he needed to move slowly, even though his every instinct was to pursue her without pause until he swept her off her feet.

"You a single man, Cord?"

The question took him by surprise, especially in the context of the conversation they'd just been having and his own thoughts.

"Yes, sir."

"I see," Harlan Adams said, surveying him speculatively.

Cord tried not to flinch under the intense scrutiny. Finally he met the old man's gaze evenly and asked, "How do I measure up, sir?"

Harlan threw back his head and laughed. "Oh, you'll do well enough, I imagine."

"Are we talking about ranching now or something else?"

Before he could reply, a woman with black hair threaded with silver and the angled cheekbones of Native American ancestry swept into the kitchen, snatched the mug from in front of Harlan Adams and poured the contents into the sink, even as she gave Cord a smile.

Despite the look of longing he cast at the emptied mug, Harlan Adams's gaze softened as he looked at the woman. "Cord, this is my wife, Janet. She has a sixth sense about when I'm straying from the straight and narrow. It's a damned nuisance."

Janet Adams smiled at Cord and touched her husband's cheek. "I don't intend to lose you, old man, not if I have to spy on you twenty-four hours a day."

The affection between the two of them stirred a yearning inside Cord. He wanted what they had. He wanted to have someone in his life who cared enough about his well-being to defy him when it mattered, someone who would treasure every minute they managed to snatch as they grew old together.

Once more an image of Sharon Lynn came to mind. Judging from her grandfather and father, the years would be kind to her. He could envision sharing them with her. The prospect had taken him by surprise the night before, but it was growing on him now. It seemed as natural as breathing, as inevitable as the sunrise.

"I'd best be getting back to Cody now," he said. "He has chores for me."

Harlan barely pulled his gaze from his wife, but he said, "Welcome to White Pines. We'll be seeing a lot more of you around here, son."

As he headed back to Cody's office, Cord kept hearing the echo of that one word—*son*. He supposed Harlan Adams referred to a lot of men in that same easy, casual way. He couldn't possibly have guessed how much it would mean to Cord to be accepted so readily.

Or how soon Cord intended to make the ties between them real and deep by marrying his granddaughter. Then, again, he recalled the expression on Harlan Adams's face earlier when they'd been talking about Sharon Lynn. He was a wise man. Maybe he'd already been able to read what was in Cord's heart.

Chapter Four

Sharon Lynn was falling in love. With every hour that passed, she grew more and more enchanted with the baby she and Cord had discovered in the alley behind Dolan's. The little angel rarely fussed and had a smile that could light up the world.

Because of the weather, she'd had the baby to herself the rest of Saturday and all day Sunday. It had been surprisingly easy to fall into the baby's rhythm, frightening to realize how easily her heart could be stolen.

In a few short hours, it began to seem totally natural to have a child tucked into the crook of her arm as she went about her other chores. Old lullabies she hadn't thought of in years came back to her as she held the baby and rocked her to sleep.

As the time flew by, she began to dread the ringing of the phone. Each time she answered, she expected it to be Justin with word on the baby's family, with an announcement that someone was coming to claim the child. She couldn't help wondering how she would cope with that inevitable end.

On Friday night, the baby had needed Sharon Lynn to survive. By Sunday, she worried that maybe it was turning the other way around. Finding the baby on her doorstep was giving her, at long last, a reason to live.

But such a tenuous reason, she warned herself, one that could be snatched from her at any moment. Yet how could any woman defend herself against loving a beautiful, helpless child?

There were limits, though. Even she could see that. It was one reason she resisted the temptation to name the baby. Surely the child already had a name. She had to. It wasn't Sharon Lynn's place to choose another, even if it meant calling her nothing more than *sweetie* or *little one*. It was awkward and frustrating at times, but it was the way it had to be.

When the phone rang at nine o'clock on Sunday night, she jumped. At the sound of Justin's voice, her heart slowed to a dull thud.

"Everything okay over there?" he asked.

"Of course. Have you found out anything?"

"Nothing. Still no reports of a missing baby. It's as if she appeared out of nowhere."

"Maybe she's just a gift from heaven," Sharon Lynn said quietly, unable to hide the wistfulness. "Maybe this was meant to be."

"Don't go there," Justin warned. "Please don't go there. Not yet. We're just in the early stages of the investigation. Anything could happen."

She sighed. "I know."

"What do you intend to do about work tomorrow?"

"I'm taking her with me, of course."

It was Justin's turn to sigh heavily. "I figured as much. Lizzy called. She says she has a portable crib and a carrier out at her place that you can use. I'll pick them up first thing in the morning and drop them off at Dolan's."

"Thanks, Justin. You're an angel."

"I hope you still feel that way when this is all over."

"No matter what happens, I won't blame you. I promise."

"I'll see you in the morning."

After she'd hung up, Sharon Lynn went in to check on the baby and stood for a long time just watching her sleep. She was so innocent and trusting and yet already in her young life, she had been betrayed in the cruelest way of all. Was she aware of that on some level? Would it affect her for the rest of her life? Or did she only know that there was someone now keeping her warm and fed and safe? She certainly seemed to be sleeping peacefully enough.

As the night wore on, Sharon Lynn envied her that. She tossed and turned, knowing that the day ahead would be chaotic, that it would be filled with unanswerable questions and maybe with heartwrenching loss. The weather had saved her from the visitors and the questions all weekend, but she wouldn't be so lucky come morning. It wasn't in the Adams genes to let something like this pass unnoticed.

Sure enough, not only was Justin on the doorstep when she arrived at Dolan's, but her mother and grandmother were there right on his heels. Her aunts and her cousins followed at a head-spinning clip.

Thanks to Lizzy's contributions, the baby was settled into a portable crib behind the lunch counter where every single Adams could ooh and aah over her, along with half the town. By noon Sharon Lynn was so sick of advice, so tired of warnings about getting attached that she was ready to scream. She would have thrown everyone out and locked the doors, but Dolan's was a business and the novelty of an abandoned baby on the premises had the lunch counter busier than it had been in weeks.

By two, things had finally settled down again. Patsy

Driscoll had gone home after pocketing more tips than she usually did in a week. Sharon Lynn finally had a chance to hold the baby herself.

"You charmed the socks off of them," she informed the gurgling child. "Little wonder. You're every bit as cute as any Adams baby I've ever seen and, believe me, there are a lot of them."

"Hey, are you maligning my descendants?" Grandpa Harlan inquired as he slid onto a stool next to her, his gaze locked on the baby.

Sharon Lynn sighed. "I should have known you wouldn't be able to resist coming into town to see her for yourself."

"Why should I be the only one left out?" he inquired.

"Because she's a baby, not a circus sideshow."

"You upset because everyone's interested or because they're all offering up advice you don't want to hear?"

Of course, he would see that, she thought. Her grandfather was the wisest man she knew. She gazed into his bright blue eyes and saw the concern there.

"I know what I'm letting myself in for," she assured him.

"I'm sure you do," he agreed. "Doesn't mean we can't worry about you."

"Do you intend to add in your two cents?"

He grinned. "Not if you'll let me hold her, while you go pour me a cup of real coffee."

Amused by his eagerness, Sharon Lynn relinquished the baby gladly enough, but she poured decaf into the cup she handed him. Her grandfather scowled.

"You, too?"

"I take my marching orders from a higher authority."

"Who's that?" he demanded indignantly.

"Janet."

"Whatever happened to the days when an old man was respected?"

"We do respect you and we love you. That's why we want you to stick around. Now, drink the decaf. It tastes just as good as the high-octane stuff."

"If taste were all that mattered, there wouldn't be two kinds. I want a little kick."

"Well, you won't get it here and that's that."

"Stubborn brat."

"Stubborn old man."

He grinned. "If you're calling me names, I guess your spunk is back. Might's well go along home and find something else to worry about."

"Might's well," she agreed. "I really am okay, Grandpa Harlan."

He lifted the baby above his head until she giggled, then brought her down for a kiss before handing her back to Sharon Lynn. He headed for the door, then turned back.

"By the way, Cord's working out real good at White Pines. Your daddy's kept him hopping and from what I hear, Cord is up to it."

"He got the job, then? I'd wondered."

Surprise registered on his face. "You haven't talked to him?"

"Not since Friday night."

"Interesting," he said thoughtfully. "Well, something tells me he'll be coming around first chance he gets."

Her gaze narrowed at the vague innuendo in his tone. "What is that supposed to mean? You haven't been meddling again, have you?"

"I asked a few questions, that's all. We were hiring the man. What would you have me do?"

"I thought Daddy interviewed him."

"He did. I just came along behind him and picked up a few more details, tidied up some loose ends, you might say."

"Such as?"

"Oh, this and that."

"Grandpa!"

"You take care, darlin' girl. Bring that baby out to the ranch this weekend, if she's still staying with you. Nothing I love more than fussing over a new baby."

He was gone before she could reply, but not before the casual invitation stirred up all of her worst fears. Would the baby be with her by the weekend? Would she even be with her tomorrow? The uncertainty was difficult now. How much worse would it get as time passed? What would her impulsive decision to become the child's foster mother lead to? What would it cost her?

"It doesn't matter," she murmured, settling the baby into the carrier so she could clean up the lunch counter and grill from the day's onslaught of customers. *She* didn't matter. The baby's well-being was all that counted, and for now she was in a position to see that nobody ever hurt that precious child again.

Another round of curious neighbors and family members dropped in around four. By nightfall, she was sick of being subjected to concerned glances and of listening to all the warnings. She was ready to close up on the dot of six, if only to prevent any more lectures from well-meaning relatives. Just as she was about to lock the door and breathe a sigh of relief, Cord appeared. Given the hints her grandfather had dropped earlier, she wasn't sure just how welcome she ought to make him.

"Too late to get dinner?" he asked, his expression hopeful.

She regarded him warily. "That depends."

"On?"

"Whether you intend to offer advice."

He grinned. "I gather your family's been calling on you today. I assumed as much from the ruckus going on out at the ranch all day. Every time one of the women came back with a report, all the men gathered around to hear it. I got the feeling your brother and your father were just itching to sneak into town and take a look for themselves. I wouldn't be a bit surprised if they showed up tonight."

"They'll probably hold out till tomorrow. Grandpa Harlan came in their place."

"I'm not surprised. He probably would have been here Saturday right after he talked to me, if the roads hadn't been so bad. He had more questions than a reporter sniffing out a hot scoop."

"I'll bet. Watch your step around him or you won't have a secret left."

Cord met her gaze evenly. "I'm not all that big on secrets, not with the people who matter to me. I'm a cards-on-the-table kind of guy. What about you?"

"I don't know. In my family, it's virtually impossible to keep any," she said a little wistfully. "It might be nice to try sometime. I've always wanted to be mysterious. That's hard to pull off when you've lived in the same town all your life and your life's an open book. Do you know how difficult it is to get any privacy at all with relatives looking over your shoulder every time you turn around?"

"Think about the flip side. You could be like me and not have anyone to share things with at all. Believe me, darlin', you're better off."

"I suppose," she said, but after a day like today she had a really hard time relating to his perspective. "Sometimes I wonder if I shouldn't have done what you did, just

taken off and gotten a fresh start someplace totally new."
She thought of her uncle Luke and her cousin Angela. "Of
course, others in my family have tried it and wound up
right back here again. Only one moved far enough away to
get some peace and quiet, but she's back with her family
at the drop of a hat. All she has to do is hint and Grandpa
sends Uncle Jordan flying up to bring them all down."

Cord listened thoughtfully, but his expression was skeptical. "Why would you leave all you have here, a family, a
business, your home?"

"It might have been easier," she said quietly, thinking
of the days after Kyle's death, when she'd faced reminders
everywhere she turned. That would have been the time to
go. Instead she'd bought Dolan's and pretty much ensured
that she'd be here forever.

"Easier?" Cord repeated. "I don't understand."

She forced a smile. "No, I don't suppose you do." She
shrugged. "It doesn't matter."

"I'm not sure I believe that." His gaze searched hers.
"Something tells me it matters very much. Are you going
to tell me the whole story?"

"Maybe," she said. "One of these days."

He tilted his head "Now, you see, you do know how to
keep secrets, after all."

She could feel a slow grin spreading across her face.
"You're right. I guess I do. Does that make me a woman
of mystery?"

"It does to me."

She gave a little nod of satisfaction. "Well, then, that's
something." She flashed him a brilliant smile. "So, tell me,
what are you doing here? I'm surprised you're not eating in
the bunkhouse out at White Pines. The food's better there
than anything I could throw together for you."

He winked at her. "But the company's a whole lot more fascinating around here."

Sharon Lynn flushed under his warm gaze, but before she could warn him off, before she could make it clear that she wasn't interested in pursuing anything more than conversation—or maybe just a hint of flirting to see if she was still any good at it—he turned away and scanned the drugstore.

"Where's my girl?" he demanded. "I've spent the whole weekend wondering how she was getting along. Everybody at the ranch was offering up opinions, but I couldn't wait to see for myself."

So that was why he'd come, she thought, feeling oddly disgruntled by the discovery that this visit was all about the baby. Apparently he'd just been making idle, small talk with her, biding his time.

Before she could reply, Cord spotted the portable crib and headed straight for it. Sharon Lynn watched as he scooped the baby up and held her in the air. The baby gurgled with delight as she had earlier for Grandpa Harlan. Sharon Lynn wanted to haul the baby into her arms and explain that girls shouldn't go trusting a man whose attentions were so fickle. Then again, maybe she was the one who needed that advice. She'd realized when Cord walked through the door that she'd been half watching for him all weekend long.

"You've made a conquest, I see." She couldn't seem to help the testy note in her voice. Fortunately Cord seemed oblivious to it.

"I've always been a big hit with ladies under two."

Sharon Lynn was willing to wager he'd been a huge success with women of any age. Aside from his looks, there was that quick wit and easygoing charm about him that could weave a spell in the blink of an eye. If she'd been a lot less wary of men and relationships, she might have been taken with him herself. As it was, she could view the ingrained flirting with tolerant amusement. Or so she reassured herself.

"Have you ever been married?" she asked.

He took the out-of-the-blue question in stride. "No, why?"

It was as if the words had just popped out of her head. She couldn't have explained if her life depended on it. She swallowed hard and managed to improvise. "You're so good with the baby. It's as if you're used to this. I thought maybe you'd had a wife and kids."

He shrugged. "Nope. Just second nature, I suppose. I like kids, but I've never had any of my own. Guess I always thought kids deserved two parents who loved each other and intended to stick together through thick and thin. There's never been a woman I felt that way about."

"Lots of brothers and sisters, nieces and nephews?"

He shook his head. "No, an only child. Maybe that's why I gravitate toward big families with lots of kids underfoot."

"Then you're at the right place at White Pines. As you've seen already, the ranch is crawling with family."

He settled the baby against his shoulder, then turned his penetrating gaze on Sharon Lynn. "Ever heard the expression about being all alone in a crowd? Sometimes when what you want most in the world seems almost within reach, it's harder than ever to accept that you don't really have it."

As his words sank in, Sharon Lynn's gaze sought out the baby. It was true. For the past two days, she had been caught up in a game of make-believe. She had held a child in her arms and despite all the disclaimers she had voiced to her family, she had pretended that the baby was hers to keep. She had longed for it to be so.

Knowing that it wasn't, accepting that it might never be,

brought the salty sting of tears to her eyes. Before she was aware he'd even moved, Cord had placed the baby back in the carrier and was drawing her into his arms. To her surprise, not only did she not resist, but she went willingly.

"I'm sorry," he whispered.

He tucked her head beneath his chin, where she could feel the beat of his heart and smell the clean, masculine scent of him. The comfort was her undoing. Tears, never far from the surface these days, spilled down her cheeks and soaked the soft chambray of his shirt.

"I'm sorry," he said again. "I never meant to make you cry. What was it I said?"

"It's not you," she managed to choke out. "I've been a regular waterworks for months now. It doesn't take much to set me off."

He tipped her chin up with a finger, then swiped gently at her tears with his thumb. The tender gesture left her trembling.

"Want to tell me why?" he asked.

"Not really." She regarded him with a watery glance. "Do you mind?"

"I mind that you're sad, but I don't mind that you're not ready to share the reason for it with me. After all, we're little more than strangers."

Right now, though, Cord Branson didn't feel like a stranger. He felt like a trusted, undemanding friend, someone she—and the baby—could rely on. Everyone in her family was certainly reliable, but at the first sign of tears, they worried. They plagued her with solicitous invitations or plunked themselves down in her living room and tried to cheer her up. Adamses wanted to fix things for her. Cord seemed willing to just be there.

"Thank you," she whispered against his chest.

"No need to thank me," he insisted. "One of these days I'll pry the secret out of you and then I'll go after whoever hurt you."

"I appreciate the thought, but heroics aren't needed." She rested her head against the solid wall of his chest again, unwilling to leave the warmth and comfort of his embrace, even though she knew it would be the wise thing to do. Her life had gotten complicated enough in the past few days without dragging him into the middle of the storm of emotions that the baby had unleashed inside her.

Finally she sighed and pulled away. When she glanced up, it was into twinkling eyes.

"No need to move on my account," he said lightly. "I was just beginning to enjoy myself."

She shot him a wry grin. "That's what I was afraid of."

His expression sobered at once. "You don't have to be afraid with me, darlin'. Not ever."

"I'm not afraid of you."

He touched a finger to her lips. "That's not what I said. I said you don't have to be afraid *with* me. Nothing will ever hurt you when I'm around. That's a guarantee."

For reasons every bit as mysterious and every bit as certain as those that had led her to keep the abandoned baby with her, rather than turning her over to foster care, Sharon Lynn believed him.

Because she trusted him so implicitly, she glanced around Dolan's to be sure everything that needed to be done before closing had been done, then met his gaze.

"Why don't you come to my place for dinner? You can put the baby to bed, while I make spaghetti and a salad."

"Throw in a beer and you're on."

Sharon Lynn froze at the mention of beer. Ever since the accident, she hadn't wanted to be near anyone who was drinking, not even a single beer. Sensitive to the circumstances, everyone in the family had been careful to avoid alcohol around her. But, of course, Cord couldn't possibly know that.

"I'm sorry. There's none in the house."

The words came out more stiffly than she'd intended. In the awkward silence that followed, she waited for him to suggest stopping off to pick up a six-pack, but after an intent study of her face, he merely shrugged.

"Soda will do, with coffee for a chaser," he said easily.

"Now that I can accommodate," she said, relieved that he hadn't pushed, either for the beer or an explanation.

"Then let's get out of here. Something tells me our little buddy here is going to be starving herself pretty soon and we'd better be ready to swing into action. She's not nearly as patient as I am."

Nothing about Cord Branson suggested he was the least bit patient, but Sharon Lynn let that pass. He'd allowed an awkward moment slide by without comment and that was all she cared about. A man who could ignore hints and innuendoes, who could detect a puzzle and let it rest until the solution was offered voluntarily was a rarity. After months of people poking and prying into her feelings, she was more grateful than he would ever know.

"Let me grab another package of formula and we're set."

"I'll get that. You bundle up the little darlin'."

When everyone was wrapped snugly in enough layers to withstand the bitter cold, they walked briskly to her place. She couldn't help thinking that on a night just like this one a week ago, the cold had cut through her and left a chill not only throughout her body, but in her heart. What a difference a few days—and the presence of this man and this baby—had made. What would happen to her when—not if, but *when*—they were gone?

Chapter Five

Cord had never spent a more frustrating few minutes in his life. First the unexpected flood of tears from a woman who seemed so strong, then the admission of secrets and the shuttered expression at the mention of beer. There was a story there, but he had a feeling it was a whole lot more complicated than anything he could imagine.

It would be simple enough to get at the truth out at White Pines. Sharon Lynn had said it herself—she had no secrets from her family. Fortunately he was wise enough to know that the answers had to come from her. He wanted her to trust him enough to share them with him, to let him into her life totally and completely. That kind of trust didn't happen overnight and it surely wouldn't happen if he started prying. Obviously this was going to be just one more test of his patience.

In the meantime, though, his imagination was working overtime. To silence all the wild speculation going on in his head, he focused on the baby. Every time he held her, he was more awestruck. She was so tiny, so perfect. Powerful, amazing emotions swept through him, made him vow to protect her with his life if it ever came to that. The emotions were all the more astonishing because he had no idea where they'd come from. His own pitiful parents had never set such an example.

"Have you ever in your life seen a kid this size eat this much?" he asked as she sucked lustily on her bottle, her little hands gripping it tightly as if she feared he might take it from her. "You don't suppose she was half starved when we found her?"

"Lizzy says her weight appeared to be normal and that she wasn't showing any signs of being malnourished." Her expression darkened. "Have you thought about the mother at all?"

"I've tried not to. It's too infuriating. What about you?"

"I can't help thinking that she must have been truly desperate."

"Maybe the mother wasn't in any position to care for a child."

"You mean financially?"

"I mean maybe she was sick herself, maybe she even died after the baby was born and the baby's father couldn't cope."

Her expression shifted from anger to sympathy. "Oh, God, I hadn't even considered that." She came to stand close and brushed gentle fingers over the baby's head. "Poor little thing."

Cord glanced up at her. "Not so poor. She landed with you, didn't she? She's warm and safe."

"But all alone."

"She has you. She has me," he said fiercely.

Sharon Lynn grinned. "She certainly does seem to have you wrapped around her little finger."

He snuggled the weight of her a little closer, laughed when her face screwed up as the bottle's nipple slipped from her mouth. "Are you still hungry?" he murmured incredulously, even as he offered her more. He glanced over at Sharon Lynn, who had gone back to stirring spaghetti sauce, filling the kitchen with an enticing aroma. "Have you given any thought to giving her a name?"

Her hand stilled. "I don't think I should. It's not my place."

"We can't just go on referring to her as the baby. It sounds like she's interchangeable with every other kid." He studied the baby intently, then said, "I think we should call her Ashley."

"Ashley? Why Ashley?"

"I don't know. I like it."

Sharon Lynn hesitated for a full minute, her expression troubled. "I don't know…"

"Then you pick."

"I meant I don't know if we should do this."

"Why not?"

She drew in a deep breath and met his gaze. "It makes it too much like we think she's going to stay."

"She is staying, for a time, anyway. While she's here, she deserves a name," he insisted. "She shouldn't be anonymous, even for a short time."

After a moment, Sharon Lynn smiled. "How about Cordelia, then? After the man who found her."

He laughed, even though something deep inside him yearned to say yes. It would give him a lasting connection to this baby no matter what happened, but *Cordelia*? No way. He shook his head. "She'd never forgive us."

"If she goes back to her family, she'd probably never even know. It would just be between us," Sharon Lynn said pointedly.

He grinned. "You hankering for another secret?"

"Maybe."

"No. I still vote for Ashley. That's got some class to it. I can see her growing up to run a whole cattle empire one day."

Sharon Lynn faced him, her expression troubled. "Don't," she whispered, the word barely more than a broken cry.

Startled by the reaction, he stared. "Don't what?"

"Don't make plans for the future. Don't look too far ahead. She could be gone tomorrow."

Instinctively he held the baby a little tighter as if to prevent her going. "That's the advice you've been hearing all day, isn't it? That's what had you so upset when I turned up tonight?"

She nodded. "It's good advice. It really is. I can't think beyond the moment."

Cord sighed at the well-meaning logic. "You're right, of course. I'm sorry. It's easy to get caught up in the fantasy."

Her expression turned sympathetic. "I know. Believe me, I know."

He glanced down at the baby and saw that she had finally fallen asleep. He lowered his voice to a whisper. "I'll put her down for the night. Do you want her on your bed again?"

"I think the portable crib tonight. You can set it up in my room, next to the bed. I'll get a blanket to put in the bottom."

She followed him down the hall, then held the baby while he set up the portable crib they'd brought with them from Dolan's. Cord caught a glimpse of her face for just an instant before she realized he was looking. There was a raw yearning there every bit as deep as his own. Gently he took the baby and placed her in the crib, then reached out to brush a stray curl from Sharon Lynn's cheek. She trembled at his touch, then gazed at him with an anguished expression.

This time he was the one who whispered, "Don't. Don't look ahead. She's with us now."

She gave him a wavery smile. "Yes, she is. She's with us now."

When they returned to the kitchen and dinner was on the table, neither of them seemed to have much of an appetite. Though it was the last thing in the world he wanted, Cord drew in a deep breath and said, "Maybe your family is right. Maybe this isn't such a good thing."

She stared at him with obvious shock. "What are you saying?"

"There are professionals, people who deal with this kind of case all the time."

"She's not a *case*," Sharon Lynn protested vehemently. "She's a baby. She needs me."

"And you need her," he suggested cautiously, recognizing that his own needs ran just as deep and were just as troubling. "That's the real danger, isn't it?"

"Okay, yes," she said, her eyes glittering with defiance. "But she's all that matters. Until we know more, she's staying with me and that's final."

"I just don't want to see you hurt."

"People get hurt all the time. They live with it," she said flatly.

"Some pain can be avoided, though."

"She's staying, Cord. If it turns out there's family to take her, somebody who can care for her properly, give her the love she deserves, I'll deal with it."

She said it with the strength and conviction of someone who'd survived other losses. Cord wondered if he could say it as readily. He'd spent even less time with the baby— Ashley—and already he was ready to fight to hold on to her. It was a totally irrational response, one based on emotions, not logic, but that was pretty much how he'd lived his life. His gut instincts hadn't steered him wrong yet.

"We'll wait and see, then," he said finally.

"*We?* I'm the one responsible for her," Sharon Lynn protested. "When did you get a say in what happens?"

Cord's jaw tightened at the attempt to dismiss him. "Friday night, when I found her in the snow."

"If you hadn't been there, I would have heard the thump. I would have found her."

"But I was there," he reminded her quietly. "If there's a decision to be made, we talk it over, understood? We're in this together, darlin'. Get used to it."

Sharon Lynn didn't know what to make of a man like Cord Branson. How many men would assume responsibility for an abandoned baby? How many would insist on being a part of any decisions that were made? The men in her family would have, even worrywart, by-the-book Justin, but Adams men were a breed apart. She hadn't met many others like them.

Of course, as a practical matter, Cord was at White Pines. The baby was here in town with her. She was responsible for the day-to-day care, the middle-of-the-night feedings, the diaper changes, juggling the baby and work. How often was Cord likely to pop in for a few minutes of cuddling the baby, maybe a feeding? How long would it be before he tired of making the long drive? How long before the novelty of make-believe parenting wore off?

Quite a while, she finally concluded at the end of the week, when Cord had turned up every single evening promptly at six and insisted on taking over Ashley's care.

"You've had her all day. I'll pitch in now," he told her emphatically on Tuesday and every night after.

She'd never seen a man so taken with a child. On the one hand, knowing how precious little time they might have, she begrudged him every second he spent with the baby. It was time lost to her. On the other hand, it was amazing and wonderful to see just how tender and patient he was. Ashley responded to him with gurgles of delight. No matter how fussy she'd been, she quieted at once in his arms. He had a magic touch, all right. Sharon Lynn envied him that.

"Why the disgruntled expression, darlin'?" he inquired from his perch on a stool at the counter. Ashley was settled in his arms with a pacifier in her mouth.

"Sorry," she said, forcing a smile.

"Better, but I don't believe it. What's on your mind?"

She slapped down the rag she'd been using to wipe the counter. "Okay, here it is. I just don't get it. She's been cranky all afternoon. You walk in, pick her up and *bam*, she's peaceful as a little lamb."

He grinned. "Seems to me you're the cranky one, darlin'. You want to slip up here in my lap and see if I can settle you down, too?"

She scowled. "That is not what I meant."

"No, what you meant is that you're doing all the hard work and then I waltz in and get duty that's a snap. You get the tears. I get the smiles."

He'd hit the nail on the head, but it seemed selfish and mean-spirited to admit it. "You don't have to help out at all," she told him stiffly. "I can manage."

"I thought we'd settled that. I'm going to do my share, at least as much as I can, given our circumstances. Now, come on. Finish up here and I'll take you out to dinner. Then you can go home and get a decent night's sleep. I'll bunk on the sofa and take the 2:00 a.m. feeding. I don't have to work in the morning. Your brother's taking over for me."

Sharon Lynn regarded him skeptically. "Harlan Patrick volunteered for extra duty? Why?"

"I didn't ask questions. I just grabbed at the chance to relieve you."

"I suppose this was Daddy's bright idea," she muttered under her breath. "Or Grandpa Harlan's."

"Does it really matter? I thought you'd be grateful."

"Oh, I am," she said, thinking longingly of getting an uninterrupted night's sleep for a change. But she had a feeling that whoever had dreamed up the notion had been more interested in throwing her and Cord together overnight. Fortunately he seemed oblivious to that particular motive.

When she'd put the last of the cleaning supplies away, she glanced up and saw Cord watching her.

"On second thought," he suggested, "why don't we go to your place? You can prop your feet up, put on a little music, relax and I'll cook."

"You cook?"

"Well enough. Tempted?"

"Oh, yes," she said fervently. "It sounds like heaven. Maybe I could even take a nice long bubble bath, while you're in the kitchen."

"If you'd like," he agreed, though his voice suddenly sounded a little husky.

Sharon Lynn discovered that she was enjoying the reaction just a little too much to let it pass. "That wouldn't bother you, would it?" she asked innocently.

"Bother me?" he echoed irritably. "Why would it bother me?"

"I can't imagine," she said. "I mean, it's just a bubble bath. There's nothing provocative about that."

He scowled at her as he led the way out of Dolan's and

waited while she locked up. When she glanced up there was a wicked glint in his eyes.

"Don't push your luck, darlin', or I'll be sharing that bubble bath with you," he warned.

Now there was an interesting idea, she thought before she could stop herself. Dear heaven, what was happening to her? She didn't want to seduce Cord Branson.

Or did she? Was that why she'd been so frustrated and edgy all week? Was she more attracted to him than she'd wanted to admit? Was she actually jealous of the amount of attention he was devoting to the baby, rather than to her?

No, she told herself firmly. Of course not. Flirting was just that. Teasing. Setting off a few sparks. Part of nature's male-female game. It didn't have to imply anything more. It never had to go beyond taunts.

But there was no mistaking the slow reawakening of her senses the past few days. Maybe that was just indicative of the healing process and nothing more. Maybe it didn't have a thing in the world to do with Cord, per se. Yeah, right.

So, the bubble bath was out, but a long, quiet evening stretched out ahead of them. Cord was going to fix her dinner. Behind that offer was a surprising sensitivity to her exhaustion.

When was the last time anyone outside of a few family members had seen through the facade she'd been putting on since shortly after Kyle's death? Everyone was constantly talking about how brave she was, how strong. Cord instinctively seemed to know better. Somehow that kind of intuitive understanding was scarier than the stirrings of desire he'd sparked in her.

Moreover, he'd just announced that he was going to stay the night. A sexy, virile man was going to be sleeping under her roof, albeit for the most innocent of reasons. Even so, that certainly hadn't happened in a very long time.

Anticipation, something she hadn't felt in months, stirred deep inside her. She was actually looking forward to going home, looking forward to the evening stretching out ahead of her. It felt a lot like a miracle. Her steps, which normally slowed as she neared that empty, lonely house, picked up a little.

She glanced at Cord as they walked up the front walk. He turned toward her and smiled, that easy, crooked smile that could charm a saint.

It would be so easy—too easy—to get used to this, she warned herself. This, too, was temporary. The baby was their link. When she was gone, the bond would be broken. The realization was a harsh reminder not to let herself care too much for either of them, to bask in the warmth of having a thoughtful, attentive man beside her, to seize tonight and look for nothing more.

Ashley had fallen asleep on the walk. Cord put her into the portable crib, then turned to Sharon Lynn.

"Go take your bath. I'll see what I can rustle up in the kitchen."

"I'll help," she said automatically.

He shook his head and turned her toward her bedroom. "Go, before I have to strip you out of those clothes myself."

She tilted her head and studied him consideringly. "You'd do it, too, wouldn't you?"

He grinned. "With pleasure."

"Maybe a quick shower," she decided.

"It won't be the same."

This time she grinned. "For you or me? I have a feeling your imagination's been working overtime conjuring up images of that bubble bath."

"That's exactly right," he admitted, surveying her boldly. "Give me something here. Take the bubble bath."

He sounded as if the images alone would be enough to torment him. That was enough to convince her. It had been a long time since she'd stirred a man's fantasies. "Maybe I will."

She left him staring after her, felt his intense gaze following her. In the bathroom, she stripped off her clothes as the water ran into the tub, turning it into a froth of lilac-scented bubbles. When it was filled almost to overflowing, she stepped in and sank down to her chin. It was sheer bliss.

She rested her head against the back of the tub and closed her eyes, as the warm water lapped gently over her.

It was the last thing she remembered, until she felt herself being scooped out of the water, the air cold against her damp skin.

"Cord?" she murmured sleepily.

"Yes, darlin'."

"What happened?"

"You fell asleep in your bath," he said as he briskly toweled her dry and tucked her robe around her.

She was too out of it to feel embarrassment, though something told her she should. Instead she just snuggled against him and let him pick her up and carry her into the bedroom. He'd already turned down the sheet and spread. He set her gently on the bed, then pulled the covers over her, his movements quick and decisive.

"Weren't we going to have dinner?" she murmured, struggling to sit up.

He pushed her right back down. "You need sleep more. If you wake up and you're hungry, call me. I'll bring you a tray."

"Okay."

"Sleep tight, darlin'," he whispered and then he turned out the light.

He didn't leave the room at once, though. She sensed him standing over her. It was odd, she thought groggily. She hadn't felt this cared for, this cherished in years. Not even with Kyle.

On that thought, she fell into a deep and dreamless sleep.

It was daylight before she awoke. The pale, wintry sun was filtering into the room. She hadn't felt this rested in ages, she thought, stretching languidly. No nightmares about the accident. Not a one.

She was still indulging in the wonder of that when she remembered. "Oh, my God, the baby."

Ashley must be starving by now. As Sharon Lynn tightened the belt on her robe, she listened intently for Ashley's cries, but there was only silence.

Then the rest of the memories flooded back—falling asleep in the tub, Cord rescuing her and putting her to bed. The thought of him touching her made her skin tingle. Blast, she thought with a touch of regret. She'd had a man's hands all over her last night and she barely recalled a second of it. What a waste!

She crept into the living room, then came to an abrupt stop, the beginnings of a smile on her lips.

Cord was sprawled awkwardly on the sofa, one arm outflung, the other curved tightly around the baby resting stomach-down on his chest. They were both sound asleep.

Now there was an image to steal a woman's heart, she thought, watching them.

Even as Sharon Lynn stared, Ashley began to squirm. Sharon Lynn reached down to pick her up, but before she could, Cord snagged her wrist with his free hand.

"Why don't you come on down here and join us?" he inquired lazily.

She pulled away. "I thought you were asleep."

"Just resting my eyes."

"Yeah, sure."

"I was. How much sleep do you think I could get with this little one demanding food every fifteen seconds?"

"She's not that bad."

"Seemed like it. No wonder you fell asleep during your bath last night."

The mention of that brought color flooding into her cheeks. She could feel the heat of it. "About that…"

He grinned, obviously enjoying her discomfort. "You gonna thank me for saving you from drowning?"

"How long was I actually in there?"

"Long enough for the water and dinner to get cold. I finally got scared that you'd slipped in, so I tapped on the door. When you didn't answer, I decided it was time to invade your privacy."

"The water was cold?"

"Like ice."

"Any bubbles left?" she inquired hopefully.

His grin broadened. "Not a one."

"Oh," she said faintly.

"Not to worry, darlin'. I would have seen all there was to see when I scooped you out of there, anyway. Besides, it was purely a professional rescue operation." He solemnly sketched a cross across his heart. "You were just a lady in distress."

"Uh-huh," she murmured, amused by the vehement defense. "Somehow it sounds like you're protesting a little too much."

"Would you rather I tell you that I thoroughly enjoyed myself?"

She told herself to let it drop, to let the incident rest, but she couldn't seem to do it. "Did you?"

"Not half as much as I would have if you'd been awake and willing."

Her face burned at that. Okay, she'd asked for it and now she knew. The man had wanted her. That should terrify her, right? But it didn't. For the first time in ages, she felt like a whole woman again.

She felt alive.

Chapter Six

"What's on the agenda for today?" Cord asked as he flipped pancakes, while Sharon Lynn sat at the kitchen table feeding the baby.

"I haven't even thought about it," she admitted. "It's too cold to do anything outdoors. I suppose we'll just stick close to home."

He was shaking his head even as she spoke. "I don't think so. We're going shopping."

She stared at him in astonishment. Men hated to shop. She knew. With the possible exception of her uncle Jordan, who always dressed impeccably, not a single Adams male ever set foot in a store unless he had to. Then they bought jeans, underwear, socks and shirts by the dozens, so they wouldn't have to repeat the traumatic experience for another year. When it came to gifts, they were top-of-the-line catalog shoppers.

"Shopping for what?" she asked.

"Baby supplies."

"We have plenty of formula and diapers," she argued. "Lizzy and Justin's wife have passed along some hand-me-down baby clothes."

"They're all blue," he noted. "That's all wrong for our girl. She needs, I don't know, maybe something pink and frilly."

Unwilling to admit just how tempted she was, Sharon Lynn regarded him with amusement. "You want to go shopping for pink and frilly girl clothes?"

He turned and scowled as if she'd questioned his manhood. "You have a problem with that?"

She swallowed the laugh that was threatening to bubble up and shook her head. "I'm just surprised, that's all."

"I thought women loved to shop," he grumbled.

"We do. It's men who get all antsy at the mention of spending more than ten minutes in anything other than a sporting goods store."

"Where's the nearest mall?" he asked, as if the question alone were proof that he wasn't like other men.

"Garden City."

"How far?"

"Thirty miles."

"Close enough." He shoved a plate piled high with pancakes in front of her. "You game?"

He sounded so grimly determined to challenge her, she couldn't help nodding her acquiescence. "Sure." She hesitated, then added, "We can't go overboard."

"I'm not talking about buying out the stores, just getting a few things she really needs."

"Okay, then."

By four o'clock, with the baby ensconced in her new top-of-the-line stroller and Cord weighed down with more packages than Santa's sleigh on Christmas Eve, Sharon Lynn insisted enough was enough.

"I have to rest. There is not a single store left in this

mall that we haven't been in," she complained. "I need something to drink. I need food. I need to get off my feet."

Cord grinned at her. "Can't take it, huh?"

"The only person I know who shops with more enthusiasm and endurance is my aunt Jenny, but she got her start as a kid in New York. Bloomingdale's was her idea of a corner market. That was before she and her mom moved here and Janet married Grandpa Harlan. Jenny could keep up with you. I can't."

"Next time, maybe I'll invite her."

He sounded serious enough that Sharon Lynn felt a sharp pang of jealousy, before reminding herself that Jenny was happily married and therefore completely unavailable for anything more than shopping with Cord Branson. She glanced over to find Cord grinning broadly as if he'd read her mind.

"Don't even go there," she muttered.

"Go where?" he inquired innocently. "I thought we were going to the food court."

She weighed another sharp retort, then wisely swallowed it. Cord followed along as she steered the stroller to the cluster of fast-food outlets where she collapsed into the first available chair. Cord deposited the packages beside her.

"Okay, sweetheart, what can I get you to put some color back in your cheeks and wipe that scowl off your face?"

"A transfusion, maybe."

"Sorry, this place is a little short on those. How about a burger, fries and a soda?"

"Sounds too much like what I could fix for myself at Dolan's. I think maybe a dozen tacos, some guacamole, the hottest salsa they have and a chocolate milk shake."

Cord stared at her and shuddered. "Mexican food and a milk shake?"

"I don't see why not."

"It's your call. You serious about that dozen tacos?"

She considered the question, then said, "I suppose two would do for a start. We'll see how I feel after that."

When he was gone, she glanced into the stroller and grinned at the baby, who was wearing her new frilly pink bonnet that was about as practical on a cold winter day as sandals would be. Her little fists clutched the brim as if she couldn't quite decide whether to tug it on tighter or rip it off.

Every single passerby gazed into the stroller and grinned at the sight. More than a few stopped to comment on her beautiful baby girl. Rather than correct them, Sharon Lynn merely murmured her thanks, but her reaction was worrisome. She felt a maternal stirring of pride, along with a deepening of the wistfulness that was constantly with her these days.

When Cord came back with the food, he studied her intently. "Something wrong? I mean something other than low blood sugar?"

"No, not really."

Just then another woman bent down to smile at Ashley, then turned to Cord. "Your daughter is just precious. My granddaughter's just about the same age. She's in Oklahoma. Oh, how I miss her."

Cord flashed a sympathetic look of understanding at Sharon Lynn, then smiled at the woman. "I can just imagine."

"You two count your lucky stars. You've been given one of God's greatest blessings," the woman said, then turned and walked on.

Cord sighed as she left. "That happen a lot while I was gone?"

Sharon Lynn nodded.

He reached over and took her hand in his. "I know it's hard, darlin', but she is our blessing for now."

"But what happens when…" She couldn't even say the words.

"When she has to go?" Cord finished for her. "We'll get by. We'll have to."

Sharon Lynn didn't think that was going to be nearly as easy as he was pretending. Not for either one of them. One thing was clear to her now, Cord was every bit as caught up in this world of make-believe parenting as she was. She might not totally understand his motives, but she knew they were as deep and sincere as her own.

She reached for a taco and bit into it, but her appetite had vanished. She put it back on the tray and gazed bleakly at Cord.

"I'm ready to go if you are."

"Not yet. Finish your food. You'll feel better. There's not much that can't be fixed with the kick of a little salsa." He picked up the taco and held it for her. "One more bite."

She dutifully took that bite and then, with his gaze locked on hers, she took one more. Before she knew it, she'd finished one taco and was reaching for the second.

"Better?" he asked.

"Okay, yes. You're a very wise man."

"I do have my moments," he agreed with a twinkle in his eyes.

"So, smarty, tell me again why a baby who's not yet one needs a saddle."

His cheeks flushed a dull red. "Okay, maybe that was going a little overboard, but she'll be able to ride a rocking horse soon. After that she'll graduate to the real thing."

"Do you realize how long that will be?" she protested.

His expression sobered. "I know."

A tear escaped and began to slide slowly down her cheek. He reached over and brushed it away with a gentle caress.

"Don't think about that, Sharon Lynn. Concentrate on the here and now. It's all any of us ever have, anyway."

Cord was getting to be a mighty fast talker. He managed to convince Sharon Lynn to let him spend another night on her sofa so he could take the middle-of-the-night feedings. He made it sound like a generous and unselfish gesture, but he knew it was anything but that. As long as he was in that house, spending time with Sharon Lynn and the baby, he could pretend that that was the way it would always be. A fine one he was to be telling her to concentrate on the present and not to look too far ahead, when he was already gazing years into the future.

Sunday morning he awoke to see a vision standing over him. Used to seeing Sharon Lynn in jeans and cotton blouses or sweaters, he was stunned to see her all dressed up in a dress made of soft blue wool in a shade the exact color of her eyes. She'd let her hair fall to her shoulders and had brushed it to a shine.

"Going someplace?"

"I thought I'd go to church, if you don't mind staying here with Ashley a little longer. Do you need to get back to White Pines?"

"Not right away."

He thought he knew why she was so anxious to go to Sunday services. There were prayers she needed to say in a place where she'd be sure God would hear her. He wouldn't mind offering up a few of those prayers himself.

"We could bundle up the baby and go together," he suggested.

She shook her head. "That's okay. I'm running late as it is."

"Then go," he said. Something told him her words would be heard more readily than his own, anyway. There were a few sins he probably needed to acknowledge before the Almighty would be interested in much else he had to say. He could start off with lust, which seemed to be slamming through him on a regular basis lately.

"We'll be right here when you get back," he promised.

Sharon Lynn turned away, then hesitated before turning back. "If you don't have any plans for the rest of the day, Grandpa Harlan wants me to bring the baby to White Pines for Sunday dinner. You're welcome to join us."

Much as he wanted to go along, Cord was hesitant. "Are you sure that's such a good idea? I'm a hired hand out there."

A smile flickered then faded as she said wryly, "Believe me, no one will be happier to see you with us than Grandpa Harlan."

"Am I supposed to understand what you mean by that?"

"Not yet, but when you figure it out, you might want to run like hell."

He thought he was beginning to get the picture. It was definitely one that could work to his advantage. "Not to worry. I know how to hold my own with a man like your granddaddy." Especially when he suspected they had very similar goals in mind. It might be helpful to have an ally like Harlan Adams pushing Sharon Lynn his way.

"Well, just consider yourself warned."

"Duly noted. Now scoot or you'll be late. The little one and I have to get all spiffed up for our debut at White Pines. She'll charm the socks off of them."

"So will you," Sharon Lynn murmured under her breath.

"What was that?" Cord asked, hoping she'd repeat it. His ego could use a few more encouraging slips of the tongue like that. Most of the time she kept a friendly, but frustratingly impersonal distance between them.

"Nothing," she said and hurried off before he could pursue the point.

When Sharon Lynn returned a little over an hour later, she looked more at peace. Cord wished his own faith were strong enough to see him through whatever lay ahead. His had been tested a time or two too many with things turning out badly on each and every occasion.

Then, again, he reminded himself, the last time had led him to Texas and eventually to Sharon Lynn. Maybe he ought to be rethinking to whom he owed a debt of gratitude.

"So, do the kid and I pass muster?" he asked, holding up Ashley. She was wearing one of her new outfits, a snuggly little yellow romper with lace trim and colorful ducks embroidered across the front. "She picked it out herself."

"Oh, really? How did she do that?"

"I held up everything we bought until I got a smile out of her. This was the clear winner."

"I see. Did you all discuss anything else while I was gone?"

"Just that we hoped that worried crease in your brow would be gone when you got back. It is."

"I do feel better," she conceded. "I'm certain everything is going to turn out the way it's supposed to."

It had been days since they'd heard anything from her cousin about the investigation. Maybe today they would get more answers. "Will Justin be at dinner?" he asked.

"Everyone will be at dinner, except maybe my uncle Luke and Jessie. It's a long way from their place and they don't always make the trip. Then, again, I doubt Jessie will miss the chance to get a look at the baby. She's called every single day to ask about her."

"All your cousins will be there, too?"

"Except for Angela, Luke and Jessie's daughter. She's living in Montana with her family. They get back for holidays or whenever a whim strikes her. Other than that, Sunday dinners are pretty well jam-packed with relatives. Don't panic, though. You've already met quite a few people. You know my dad and Harlan Patrick and Grandpa Harlan. You're working with them, so that'll be a high enough recommendation for everybody else. You don't have a thing to be nervous about."

But he was. He hadn't been this edgy going on his first date ever. Facing parental inquisitions had been nerve-racking then, but they hadn't really mattered in the long run. Though Sharon Lynn couldn't possibly realize it, this family gathering did matter. It was vital that he make a good impression. He needed the whole slew of Adamses on his side. Without that, he had a feeling he'd never win over Sharon Lynn.

"Let's do it, then," he said finally.

"You sound like you're going to an execution," she noted with amusement.

"Feels a lot like it, too." He ran a finger around the inside of his collar, which felt as if it was cutting off breath. He scowled at her. "Don't you dare laugh."

"Never," she promised, though she looked as if she were having to fight doing just that. "You might try thinking about the fact that I'm walking into that house with a stranger beside me and a baby in my arms. You won't even be the center of attention. I'll be plagued with more questions than a politician caught up in the middle of a sex scandal."

"You really do know how to bring a man back down to earth."

"I was trying to reassure you."

Cord wasn't reassured, but he pushed aside his own uneasiness to concentrate on hers. When they walked up to the front door at White Pines, he gave her arm a reassuring squeeze. "Ready?"

She shot him a brave little smile. "Hey, it's only dinner, right? How bad can it be?"

Of course, dinner was the least of it. From the instant they walked through the door, they were being subjected to a mix of speculative glances and, in his case, downright penetrating glares. He was relieved when he finally spotted a familiar, friendly face.

"Cord, I'm so glad you could come along with Sharon Lynn," Harlan Adams said, wrapping an arm around his shoulder and guiding him over to speak to his wife. "Janet, you remember Cord, don't you?"

She gave him a warm smile and shook his hand. "Of course. I'm so delighted Sharon Lynn brought you along today."

"Thank you for including me."

She shot an amused glance toward her husband. "Trust me, Harlan couldn't wait to have you over. He's already thinking of you as family."

"Hush, Janet. Do you want to scare the man to death?"

"Just giving him fair warning."

Cord grinned at her. "Not necessary. I think your husband and I understand each other completely."

He wasn't sure who was more surprised by his statement, but Harlan Adams recovered first. With a hoot of laughter, he slapped Cord on the back. "You need any help, son, you just come to me. I still have a little influence with my grandchildren, no matter how old and independent they think they are."

"If you don't mind, sir, I think I'll just take it from here on my own."

"Confidence, I like that," Harlan Adams enthused. His expression sobered. "Just remember what I told you when you first came around. Sharon Lynn's had a rough time of it. You'll have to take things nice and easy."

Cord wanted to grumble that if he took them much more slowly, he'd be standing still, but he simply nodded. "I've gentled a lot of skittish horses in my time. I figure a woman who's been hurt is a lot like that."

Harlan grinned. "I'm not sure Sharon Lynn would appreciate the analogy, but you've definitely got the right idea. Now you come with me. I want to get another peek at that baby you two have been looking after."

"She's the prettiest little girl I've ever seen," Cord told him as they worked their way through the crowd surrounding Sharon Lynn. "Smart, too."

"You sound a lot like a proud papa."

Cord didn't even bother trying to deny it. "Yes, I suppose I do."

Sharon Lynn glanced up just then and met his gaze. A smile lit her eyes for just an instant and then she was distracted by the arrival of yet another relative.

"Justin," she murmured in a tone that held both welcome and panic.

"Hey, Sharon Lynn," he said, giving her a subtle shake of his head, even as he stroked a finger lightly down the baby's cheek. "Hey, beautiful," he whispered.

Cord moved closer. As if there had been some signal, the others slipped away, leaving Justin alone with Sharon Lynn, Cord and the baby.

"There's no news, then?" Sharon Lynn asked after she'd introduced him to her cousin.

"Nothing concrete," Justin said.

Cord thought he heard an unspoken warning in his voice. "But you expect to have something soon, don't you?"

"It's possible we're getting close," Justin said with a worried look at Sharon Lynn.

She swallowed hard, but she didn't crumple at the news. "How close?" she asked in a breathless whisper.

"I'm meeting with someone in Garden City tomorrow who may know who the mother is."

The color washed out of her cheeks. She turned suddenly and shoved the baby into Cord's arms, then fled from the room. Startled by the abrupt move, Ashley began to cry. Justin met Cord's gaze evenly.

"Here, let me take her. You go see how Sharon Lynn's doing. Right now, I'm probably the last person she wants around."

Cord handed over the baby, then went in search of Sharon Lynn. He found her in what was apparently her grandfather's office, standing at the window, staring off into the distance. He doubted she even saw the beautiful rugged scenery. He stepped up behind her and rested his hands on her shoulders. She trembled at his touch.

"Don't panic, darlin'. We've known all along this could happen."

"That doesn't make it any easier."

Cord sighed heavily. "No," he agreed. "It doesn't make it any easier."

Whether it was the evidence that he understood or sheer need, she turned and wrapped her arms around his waist and buried her face against his chest and wept. Cord had to fight the sting of his own tears as he held her and let her cry.

When she was all cried out, he tucked a finger under her chin and tilted her head up until their eyes met.

"It's not over yet," he reminded her gently. "This could be a false alarm. Or the mother could be incapable of caring for the child. We don't know yet what this means."

"I know but—"

He touched a finger to her lips. "No *buts*. Right now we need to get back out there and see how our girl is doing. It's the here and now that counts, remember?"

He watched as panic flared when she realized for the first time that he hadn't brought Ashley with him.

"Who has her?" she asked.

"I left her with Justin. He seemed capable enough."

"He'd better be," she said dryly. "He and Patsy have a little boy from her first marriage and one of their own on the way. Nobody's better qualified to be a daddy than Justin, though. He's totally unflappable. It's ironic, really. His father—you met Jordan—was absolutely panicked at the idea of becoming a father when he married Kelly and adopted her daughter. That's Dani."

"The veterinarian whose house you're living in?"

"Exactly. Anyway, Jordan thought he was totally unsuited for parenthood. Turned out he was a natural."

"Seems to me as if all the Adamses are naturals when it comes to parenthood. I've never met a group of people more taken with babies than your family."

"I know. It's one of my biggest regrets—" she cut off the potentially revealing statement before its conclusion.

"What is?" Cord prompted.

"That I'll never have a family of my own."

"Why on earth would you say that?" Cord demanded. "You're a young woman. If ever anyone was suited to marriage and kids, it's you."

She refused to meet his gaze. "I had my chance and lost it," she said bleakly.

Before he could respond to that, she turned and walked away.

How? Cord wondered. How had she lost her chance and why was she so convinced that she would never have another one? If ever they were to have a chance, he had to know the explanation behind that despairing remark. How much longer would it be before she trusted him enough to tell him? At the moment, he was deeply regretting his promise to himself not to seek the answers wherever he could find them.

Chapter Seven

On Monday, still panicked by Justin's announcement of a lead on the baby's mother, Sharon Lynn refused to let Ashley out of her sight. Barely was the baby ever out of her arms, even as she worked at Dolan's. She felt as if time were slipping away from her, as if she might turn around at any second and discover that the baby had vanished as quickly and miraculously as she had appeared.

Despite her best intentions, despite all the warnings everyone had given her, she had gone and fallen in love with the child for whom she'd been caring the past couple of weeks. Holding her, loving her, had been like a gift from God, a second chance to have the family she'd dreamed of.

How ironic that another woman had held the child—had given birth to her—and had still somehow managed to let her go. Had it been a sacrifice, an act of desperation, or had the mother been relieved by the very act that so terrified Sharon Lynn—letting go?

Even though she'd known from the beginning that her claim on the baby was tenuous, known that it could end at any moment, with every day that passed without a lead, hope had taken root and started to grow.

By Saturday when she and Cord had indulged in that
totally impetuous shopping spree, she had begun to envision a future, one that included all three of them, because
somehow she couldn't think of the baby without thinking
of Cord, too. As impossible as it seemed, it fit. It all fit.

And it was all make-believe. Justin's words had been
the proof of that. Ashley had a real mother out there somewhere, a woman who was entitled to her daughter.

No, Sharon Lynn thought fiercely. A woman who abandoned her baby in the middle of a blizzard had no rights.
None. She closed her eyes and tried to shut out the thousand and one voices telling her that until she knew all the
facts, she shouldn't be making judgments. It was a lesson
her grandfather had instilled in all of them.

"Wait until you know the facts," he would say when one
or another of them claimed some slight.

Sharon Lynn reminded herself of that now. All that really mattered, she told herself, all that *could* matter was
that the baby remained safe, that she had a good life. If her
family could give her that, then so be it.

It hurt, though. It hurt to think she might never see Ashley again, might never hold her or comfort her or watch
her grow. She'd never imagined how difficult it would be.

"Are you okay?"

Cord's quiet question startled her. She'd thought she was
alone behind the counter at Dolan's. The morning rush was
over and it was another hour before the lunch crowd would
begin straggling in. The last person she'd expected to see in
the middle of a busy ranch workday was Cord, especially
when he was so committed to making a good impression
on his new job. One glance at his haggard expression told
her that he'd slept no better than she had the night before,

even if he had been back in his own bed out at White Pines, rather than on her sofa.

"What brings you into town? Shouldn't you be working?"

"My mind wasn't on my work," he admitted. "Your father finally took pity on me and sent me on some errands before I could make a costly mistake. I'm pretty sure he intended that I wind up here. He said your mother didn't like the way you sounded on the phone this morning."

Sharon Lynn smiled ruefully. "Which explains why she was here an hour ago, claiming she had to pick up a few little things, even though she left without buying anything more than a cup of coffee."

"I guess everyone heard the news yesterday, then. Once Justin said it, everything else going on out there pretty much faded into the background for me."

"Believe me, that little tidbit spread like wildfire," Sharon Lynn acknowledged. "Though everyone was very careful not to mention it around me."

"I know they're worried about how you'll take losing Ashley if you have to give her up, but I got the distinct impression there was more to it than that," Cord said, regarding her cautiously. "Is there something else they're worried about?"

Sharon Lynn sighed. She knew he was fishing for an explanation for all the hints and innuendo people had no doubt been dropping ever since his arrival. Maybe it was time she simply told him why everyone tended to walk on eggshells around her. Why they stared at her sometimes as if she might crack like a delicate bit of old porcelain.

"I suppose there's no reason for you not to know," she said eventually. "Everyone else does."

She hesitated, wondering if she could get the words out.

For a long time now, she'd thought if she didn't talk about the accident, never mentioned Kyle at all, the pain would go away. Of course, it hadn't.

While she debated what to say, Cord remained silent, watching her patiently. She found that reassuring.

"I was engaged for a very long time." She began slowly, then went on in a rush. "Last summer we finally got married."

His eyes widened with unmistakable shock and, perhaps, something more, something that could even be regret. But his voice was steady, "You're married? But where…?"

"I'm getting to that," she said, her gaze pleading with him for patience. She drew in a deep breath before going on. "That night, leaving the reception, we were hit by a drunk driver. My husband was killed."

She managed to get the words out in a matter-of-fact way, despite the raw emotions that were churning inside her. She avoided looking directly at Cord, fearful of what she might read on his face. She wasn't sure whether to expect disgust or dismay or pity. She wasn't prepared to deal with any of them.

"The damned fool!"

His sharp, angry words startled her into looking up. He reached for her hand and enveloped it in his. There was genuine warmth and comfort in his touch, but it was his obvious outrage on her behalf that meant the most.

"I'm sorry. I'm sorry you had to go through that." His gaze narrowed as a thought apparently occurred to him. "You're not blaming yourself, are you?"

"I was driving."

"What the hell difference does that make? The other driver was drunk. He was responsible, not you. There ought to be a special place in hell for people like that."

She was stunned by his fierce tone. It was more than sympathy for her tragedy. That much was clear, but she didn't know exactly what to make of it.

"Cord?" she whispered.

He blinked as if he'd been someplace very far away and had been suddenly drawn back by the sound of her voice.

"What is it?" she asked.

"I was just thinking about my father," he said with stunning bitterness. "He was picked up more times than I can recall for drinking and driving. Around where we lived, everyone knew him. The sheriff's deputies would pull him over, load him into their car and haul him on home. Maybe if they'd arrested him, thrown his sorry butt in jail, he would have sobered up, instead of wasting his whole life on booze."

He glanced at her, then sighed. "Sorry. I didn't mean to get off on that. We were talking about what happened to you. I just couldn't help thinking that but for the grace of God, my father could have killed someone and left someone like you to grieve and blame themselves."

"But he didn't," she reminded him. "That's something to be thankful for, isn't it?"

Cord sighed. "Yes." He studied her. "That's why you don't drink, isn't it?"

She nodded. "Just seeing a beer in someone's hand is enough to upset me."

"I should have guessed that night you told me you never kept alcohol in your house."

"How could you? It could have been anything."

"There are people who drink responsibly," he reminded her. "A glass of wine with dinner, a beer while they're working in the hot sun."

"I know that, but I find myself watching everyone like

a hawk, worrying that the next drink will be the one that makes them a menace on the road." She gave a rueful shrug. "I guess I'm not likely to be the life of the party ever again, am I? In fact, I'm sure there are those in my family who blame me for putting a damper on all our gatherings."

"I'm sure your family understands exactly where you're coming from. How could they help it?" He regarded her intently. "Maybe sometime you'll tell me more about your husband."

Sharon Lynn was startled by the suggestion. "You want to hear about Kyle? Why?"

"Because he was important to you. Why is that so shocking?"

"Because no one else even mentions his name anymore."

"Maybe they're afraid of bringing up bad memories."

"I suppose, but it makes it lonelier, you know? As if he never even existed."

Cord held out his hand, waited until she'd put hers into it again. "We'll make a deal then. Anytime you feel like talking about him, you come to me and I'll listen."

"You won't mind?"

"I'd only mind if you thought there was anything you couldn't share with me."

She stared at him in amazement. He meant it, too. What a remarkable man Cord Branson was! It wasn't the first time she'd thought that, but it made her wonder how many more surprises her relationship with him was likely to hold. Just knowing that he understood her feelings about possibly losing Ashley, knowing that he shared those feelings, was a small comfort. Knowing that he would listen if she needed to talk about Kyle or the accident made her feel doubly blessed. His offer had been a generous one.

"Thank you."

He gave her a quizzical look. "For?"

"Listening to me go on and on."

"Now, darlin', that was my pleasure. It gave me a reason to stay right here with my two favorite girls."

Ashley gave him a toothless smile as if she'd understood exactly what he was saying. Sharon Lynn's smile was more restrained. There was a huge lump in her throat that wouldn't quite go away. How much longer would either of them have their baby girl to hold and fuss over and love?

She turned away so he wouldn't see her tears. "I hate this," she murmured. "I hate this endless waiting."

"Me, too," he said quietly. "Maybe you should call Justin and see what he's learned. Get it over with."

"I don't know if I dare. I'm not sure I want to know the answer."

"It's the not-knowing that's a killer. Once we know, we can deal with the rest."

She sighed heavily. "I suppose you're right." She reached for the phone at the end of the counter and dialed the sheriff's office. She was surprised to find the old dispatcher back on the job.

"Hey, Becky, is Justin around?"

"No. He's gone over to Garden City. Is it urgent? I can get him on the radio and tell him to call you."

"That's okay. Just tell him when he gets back. That's soon enough."

"Will do."

"How's the baby, Becky? I thought you had another week of maternity leave coming?"

"I did, but Justin started growling around here and the temp just up and quit on Friday, so here I am."

"I know he's glad to have you back."

"That's what he says today. By tomorrow my return

will be old news and he'll be jumping down my throat like always."

"Yes, but you know how to growl right back," Sharon Lynn reminded her with a laugh. "Justin has never intimidated you."

"That's because we've known each other since kindergarten. I know all his dirty little secrets. Whoops, I've got another call coming in. You take care now."

"Bye, Becky." She hung up the phone slowly.

"No news?" Cord asked.

"Justin's in Garden City. He'll call when he gets back."

"Do you think he's over there checking out the lead?"

"The dispatcher didn't say."

"But you think that's what he's gone over there for, don't you?"

She nodded. "Garden City's not his jurisdiction. I don't think he'd be over there otherwise."

"Then we wait."

"Don't you need to get back out to White Pines?"

"Not until we know something," he said.

"But Daddy—"

"Your father will understand." He gave her a look suggesting she might as well stop arguing. "Now how about heating up a bottle for our girl? She's beginning to get fussy."

"I'll take her," Sharon Lynn offered.

"No, you won't. She's just fine right here with me, aren't you, sweet thing?"

The baby reached up and looked for all the world as if she were patting his cheek in agreement. Cord had a silly, enchanted grin on his face that almost broke Sharon Lynn's heart. He might not have said the words, he might be taking this wait with stoic patience, but he had every bit as much at stake on the outcome of Justin's investigation as she did.

When she had the bottle warm, she came out from behind the counter and stood beside Cord as he fed the baby. When Ashley was sucking lustily, he glanced at Sharon Lynn, then reached over and slid his arm around her waist, drawing her closer. It was an intimate gesture, one that reminded her all too vividly of how thoroughly, solidly masculine he was, but there was nothing sexual about the loose embrace.

So why was she suddenly imagining the sweep of his hand from her waist to her hip, the slow caress of her breast? Why was she tingling in a totally unexpected and purely feminine way? Why in the midst of panic, with the threat of losing Ashley imminent, why was she feeling so totally and thoroughly alive again? She wasn't at all sure she wanted to know the answer to that.

They were still close together when the first of the customers came in wanting lunch. She left his embrace with reluctance, stepped away from him and the baby. It was only a few feet, with merely a narrow span of Formica separating them, but suddenly she felt colder and more alone than she could remember feeling at any time since Kyle's death.

After making a call to Cody to explain the delay, Cord lingered at Dolan's for the rest of the afternoon. He couldn't bear to leave Sharon Lynn to face the wait alone. Truthfully he wasn't sure he could have endured the wait any better out at White Pines, even if Cody had tried working him to death.

The truth was he was stunned by the speed and depth of his feelings for Sharon Lynn and the baby he'd refused to put down all afternoon. Every time he was with them that initial tug of yearning he'd felt to turn them into a family grew into something more and more powerful. As impossible as it seemed, the bond between him and Sharon Lynn was already deep and lasting, every bit as strong as if they'd been husband and wife and shared the birth of this child.

For the first time in his life, he wasn't afraid to admit that he was gut-deep scared. Not of the emotions. They'd felt right to him from the beginning. But of losing it all, everything he'd found here in Los Piños. Justin Adams had the power to take it all away from him, if he came back from Garden City with news that the baby's mother wanted her back. He feared that losing Ashley would break the bond between him and Sharon Lynn, that she would shut him out and face her grief all alone, as she'd apparently done after losing her husband.

At the thought of Kyle Mason, he realized what he should have guessed sooner. Mason was the man he'd heard about whose ranch might be up for sale. Sharon Lynn was the widow he'd been told might be anxious to sell. Oddly enough, none of that mattered now. He had far more important things on his mind.

By closing time, there still had been no word from Justin. Sharon Lynn was a basket case and even the baby seemed to have picked up on their uneasiness. She'd been fussing for an hour and nothing they tried seemed to soothe her.

"Why don't we all go out to dinner?" Cord suggested. "The wait will be easier if we're not just sitting around staring at each other."

"Do you honestly believe there is anything that will make this easier?" she asked skeptically. "Besides, Ashley's not settling down. We'll just be on edge the whole time we're at the restaurant."

They were still debating the issue when her cousin Dani came in. She honed straight in on the crying baby.

"What's the matter, sweetie?" she said to Ashley, lifting her out of Cord's arms. She frowned at the two of them. "Judging from the expression on your faces, it's little wonder she's crying. What's up?"

"We're waiting to hear from Justin," Sharon Lynn said.

"Ah, I see. I thought that might be it." She glanced from Sharon Lynn to Cord and back again. "Why don't I take the baby back over to the house and put her to bed? You two go have a quiet, relaxing dinner and stop worrying."

"But what about Justin?" Sharon Lynn protested.

"I'll send him to the restaurant if he gets back before you do," Dani said.

"Don't you need to get home to your own kids?" Sharon Lynn asked.

"Hey, what's the matter? Don't you trust me with the little one?"

"Of course, but—"

Cord snagged Sharon Lynn's hand. "Let's take Dani up on her offer. We won't stay out long, but we both need the distraction."

Her glance went from him to the baby. "I don't know," she said fearfully.

"Well, I do," he said.

"Me, too," Dani chimed in. "Go. This little peanut and I will be just fine."

"You'll send Justin to the restaurant?" Sharon Lynn asked worriedly.

"I told you I would," Dani reassured her, already bundling the baby up in her snowsuit and blankets for the walk home.

Sharon Lynn continued to look uneasy, but Dani gave

her a quick hug and headed for the door. Cord watched with amusement as she brushed off Sharon Lynn's last-second concerns, then gave him a wink.

"Try to make her eat," Dani called back to him. "A little lasagna will put some color back into her cheeks."

As soon as she was out of sight, Sharon Lynn sighed heavily. "I suppose we might as well get on with it."

"Having a nice dinner, making a little conversation is not supposed to be torture," Cord reminded her.

"Sorry. It's just that—"

"It's just that you're worried. Well, so am I, but I am also starved, so take pity on me and let's get going." He grabbed her coat and purse from the back room, then guided her toward the door.

Even as she allowed him to help her into her coat, she grumbled, "How could you possibly be starved? You wolfed down two cheeseburgers and a large order of fries not three hours ago."

He grinned. "I had no idea you were keeping such close track of my diet."

"I just worry about seeing your arteries clog before my very eyes."

"Next time I'll order a salad," he promised as he took the key from her hand and locked up. "Italian okay with you?"

"Whatever."

Despite her lack of interest, he noticed that once they walked in the door of the restaurant, she seemed to perk up a little. The aroma of garlic and tomato sauce tended to do that for some people.

"Lasagna?" he asked when they'd been seated. "I gather from what Dani said that it's your favorite."

"Yes, but I'll never be able to eat it," she insisted.

"Eat what you can and we'll take the rest home."

"You're every bit as pushy and annoying as my cousin, do you realize that?"

"If you'd give me just a little cooperation here, there would be no reason for me to be pushy and annoying."

She almost smiled at that. Her lips began a slow curve, then snapped into a tight line. "I don't know. Something tells me that's just your nature."

He teased and tormented her all the way through dinner. She ate most of her lasagna, probably without even realizing that she was lifting the fork to her mouth between barbs. To Cord's amusement, when her plate was almost empty, she stared at it as if a thief had snuck in and stolen her meal.

"Hungrier than you thought, I guess," he observed mildly.

"I had no idea," she murmured.

"Turns out I'm a halfway decent distraction."

She met his gaze evenly and this time the smile built slowly and stayed in place. "You're a miracle worker."

"I'll put that on my résumé when I'm out of a job again."

"You were the one who said my father would understand about you being here in town with me."

He shrugged. "I might have stretched the truth just the teensiest bit. I told him I'd try to get back for evening chores."

"Cord, what on earth were you thinking?"

"I was thinking that you needed me more than your daddy did."

"But this job was so important to you. I'll call him. I'll explain."

"You'll do no such thing. I'll talk to your father. If he wants to fire me over this, there will be other jobs." Hopefully right here in Los Piños, but if not, well, he'd worry about that when the time came. He was pretty sure Cody was a reasonable man and that his concern for his daughter would make him lenient with Cord under the circumstances.

He glanced across the table and saw that Sharon Lynn was gathering up her things.

"Hey, darlin', where's the fire?"

"We're going home right this second. You can drop me off and then go on out to White Pines and try to straighten things out with my father."

"I'm not leaving until we've heard from Justin and that's that."

"But—"

He met her gaze evenly. "No buts, Sharon Lynn. That's final."

She regarded him with amusement. "Are you sure you don't have Adams blood in you?"

"Meaning?"

"You're as stubborn and single-minded as anybody in my family. Believe me, that is not a compliment."

He grinned at her disgruntled tone. "You'd do well to remember it, though. I always, *always* get what I'm after."

Chapter Eight

Sharon Lynn was shivering by the time they reached her house, though Cord couldn't tell whether it was from the bitter cold temperature outside or from anxiety. It was plain that she dreaded walking in to find Justin waiting for them, but as it turned out Dani was alone, flipping through veterinary medicine journals as the baby slept in her portable crib in the bedroom.

She glanced up at their entrance, surveyed Sharon Lynn closely, then gave a little nod of approval. "Much better. I don't know if it was the food or the fresh air that did it, but you look a hundred percent better than you did a couple of hours ago."

"Any word from Justin?" Sharon Lynn demanded without even acknowledging Dani's observation.

"Not a peep." At Sharon Lynn's crestfallen expression, she added, "Maybe that's a good sign. Maybe the lead he thought he had didn't pan out."

For an instant there was a spark of hope in Sharon Lynn's eyes. "Do you think that could be it?"

"Of course it could be," Dani assured her.

Cord wanted to believe that as desperately as Sharon

Lynn obviously did, but he wondered. What if Justin's being out of contact all day meant that the lead had actually panned out and taken him in a new direction? What if he'd been gone so long, because he was following it straight to the mother's doorway?

Dani continued to study her cousin closely. "Are you going to be okay?" she asked worriedly. "Want me to stick around?"

Sharon Lynn didn't answer. Her gaze kept straying toward the bedroom.

"I'll be here," Cord said finally. "She won't be alone."

Dani grinned at him. "Then I'd say you're in good hands," she told Sharon Lynn as if her cousin was actually paying attention, which she hadn't been since they'd walked in. Her focus was totally on the baby down the hall.

"I'll pop into Dolan's in the morning before I open up the clinic to see if there's been any news," Dani added. "If you need me in the meantime, call."

Sharon Lynn nodded absently, then wandered off, leaving Cord to thank Dani for looking after the baby.

"If they take the baby away, she's going to take it hard," Dani said, staring after her worriedly.

"We both will," Cord replied grimly. "She's strong, though. She'll do okay."

"And you?" Dani inquired, regarding him thoughtfully. "How will you do?"

"If I'm going to be any good to Sharon Lynn, I'll have to do okay."

"For someone who just arrived in town, you've been very kind to her."

He had the feeling there was both concern and surprise behind the statement. "She matters to me," he said simply.

Dani's eyes widened a bit. "You really mean that, don't you? It's not all about the baby, is it?"

He shook his head. "No, it's not all about the baby."

She smiled slowly. "Life's funny, isn't it? Sometimes love smacks us between the eyes when we least expect it." She stood on tiptoe and brushed a kiss across his cheek. "You'll be good for her, I think. Good luck. You're going to need it. It won't be easy convincing her to take another chance with her heart, especially not if she's lost the baby, too."

"Easy doesn't matter. It's the result that counts."

She laughed. "You'll do just fine, Cord Branson. No wonder Grandpa Harlan's already given you his stamp of approval. With that, you don't need to worry much about the rest of us. We usually fall into line eventually. As for Sharon Lynn, she desperately needs someone like you in her life, whether she's ready to acknowledge that yet or not."

After Dani had gone, Cord drew in a deep breath, then forced himself to walk into the bedroom to check on Sharon Lynn. She was standing beside the portable crib, gazing down at the sleeping baby with tears tracking down her cheeks. He moved up behind her and wrapped his arms around her waist. She leaned back against him with a sigh.

There was no need for words. They were both thinking the same thing, terrified by the same fear. When the knock came on the front door, she trembled violently, then turned to gaze at him with wide, vulnerable eyes.

"It'll be Justin," she said.

He paused and brushed away her tears, fought against the sting of his own, then took her hand. "Then let's go see what he has to say."

The knocking turned into a pounding before they could move.

"I suppose there's no choice," she said ruefully. "He's

not going to go away, not with lights blazing all over the house to tell him I'm here."

When they reached the living room, Cord suggested she go and make a pot of coffee while he got the door. "Something tells me it's going to be a long night."

As if he'd given her a much-wanted reprieve, she fled toward the kitchen. He opened the door and faced Justin's scowling expression.

"What the hell took so long?" he demanded, brushing past Cord. "Where's Sharon Lynn?"

His attitude was every bit as suspicious now as it had been on Sunday. Harlan Adams, Dani and a few others might be willing to trust Cord's motives, but Justin was a sheriff through and through. He obviously wanted a lot more information before he fully trusted Cord.

Cord gave him a wry smile. "I haven't locked her away in the attic. She's in the kitchen making coffee. I wanted a minute alone with you." He searched the other man's expression. "Is it bad news?"

Justin's temper seemed to ease at the question. "Depends on your point of view."

"Dammit, man, don't play games with something like this. A baby's life is at stake."

Justin brushed his hand over his short-cropped hair, then sighed. "I'm not here to take her away," he said at last. "That's all I can promise for now."

Cord saw that Justin was every bit as tormented by the circumstances as they were. "Then we'll have to be grateful for that for the moment."

Sharon Lynn stepped to the kitchen doorway. "Justin?"

"I'm here, sweetie. I hear you've got coffee brewing. I could sure use a cup. It's been a long day."

Cord followed him through the dining room and into the

kitchen. Sharon Lynn cast a quick look at him, searching for answers. He gave her what he hoped was a quick, reassuring nod. That sent her gaze straight back to her cousin.

"Justin?"

"Have a seat," he said as he grabbed a mug from the cupboard and filled it with coffee. "Cord, can I pour you a cup?"

"Sure."

"Sharon Lynn?"

"Justin, please," she pleaded. "I don't care about the blasted coffee. I need to know what you found out."

Justin still took his own sweet time getting to it. He handed Cord his coffee, then sat down opposite Sharon Lynn. Cord stood just behind him, his back braced against the counter where he could keep a close watch on Sharon Lynn's face.

"Where have you been?" Sharon Lynn demanded. "Did you find the mother?"

"Okay, now, hear me out before you get too upset."

"Oh, sweet heaven," she murmured. "You've found her, haven't you?"

"We're pretty sure we know her name," Justin said. "She's an eighteen-year-old from Garden City. Vicki Murdock. Her friends say she was pregnant, that the baby was due a few weeks ago, but that she suddenly dropped out of sight. Her friends said her boyfriend was a real creep, that he didn't want the baby, wouldn't let her see a doctor. She was totally under his spell. None of them would be surprised if she had the baby, abandoned her, then went off with the boyfriend. I'd like it better if there were hospital records, but I had Lizzy check. Vicki Murdock didn't give birth there. Even so, everything points to this being the woman we're looking for."

Sharon Lynn struggled visibly to keep her composure. "You said she'd gone off with the boyfriend. Were you able to find her?"

Justin slowly shook his head. "The two of them have just vanished. They've dropped out of sight."

Hope flared in Sharon Lynn's eyes. "They're gone? What does that mean? Can the baby stay here?"

Justin nodded. "For now."

"Oh, God," she murmured, covering her face with her hands as sobs shook her shoulders. "Thank you. Thank you."

Cord studied Justin's grim expression and guessed there was more. He crossed the room and put his hands on Sharon Lynn's shoulders, waited until her sobs ended.

"That's not the end of it, is it?" he asked eventually.

Justin drew in a deep breath, closed his eyes, then shook his head. "No. There's more."

Sharon Lynn stilled beneath his touch. "What?" she asked in a voice barely above a whisper.

"In the process of identifying the mother, we talked to a woman who may be the baby's grandmother. We'd have to do blood work to confirm all this, but, like I said, all the pieces seem to fit."

"But you could be wrong," Sharon Lynn insisted. "It might be a mistake."

"Let him finish, darlin'," Cord said, stroking a soothing hand over her hair.

"The grandmother, what was she like?" Sharon Lynn asked. "Was she kind?"

Justin shot a very revealing look toward Cord. "Far from it," he said tersely.

"Tell me," Sharon Lynn demanded. "What kind of a woman was she?"

"Naturally she was taken aback when I showed up to talk to her. She confirmed everything the friends had said about the pregnancy and the boyfriend. She said she'd thrown her out of the house when she'd found out. She said she hadn't seen her daughter in months, that the girl was a tramp and a troublemaker and if she was gone, good riddance."

Sharon Lynn looked shocked. Even Cord was stunned by the woman's reaction. Was it any wonder that an eighteen-year-old had abandoned her child after being raised by a judgmental, unforgiving mother like that?

"She cursed a blue streak when I told her we were looking for her daughter because we thought she'd abandoned the baby. Then she said by God, she'd do her duty by the child, if no one else would."

"But I will," Sharon Lynn protested.

Justin patted her hand. "I know you would, sweetie. That's why I told her the baby was in good hands for now, that she had nothing to worry about. I assured her that as soon as we could verify that the baby indeed belonged to her daughter, we'd be back in touch. I've stalled her for now. She let us call in a doctor to get blood tests done, so we'll see if they're genetically compatible. She was quite a martyr about it, said she would do what was right, take on this burden, even if no one ever thanked her for it."

Cord tried to envision turning little Ashley over to a woman like that. Could Sharon Lynn do it? Could he? Could they fight her right to become the child's legal guardian? Should they? Or would that only delay the inevitable heartache?

"Don't panic, you two. Let's just wait and see what happens," Justin said, clearly intending to soothe Sharon Lynn, but settling Cord's temper as well. "Something tells me this woman's not all that anxious to take on a brand-new baby, despite what she said. Once she's thought it over, she may decide the baby's better off right where she is. After what I've seen, that would certainly be my opinion, not that it counts for much."

"But she may decide to fight for her granddaughter," Sharon Lynn said bleakly. "That's certainly what I would do."

She gazed up at Cord and the expression in her eyes would haunt him for days. "What do we do if she doesn't change her mind?"

"Justin's right, darlin'. We'll cross that bridge when we come to it." He squeezed her shoulder reassuringly. "For now, let's just be grateful that Ashley's still right here with us where we can keep her safe." He glanced at Justin. "How long are we talking about on those blood tests?"

"We'll have to get Lizzy over here to draw some blood tomorrow for a comparison. As I understand it, if the blood types are a clear mismatch, that'll be the end of it and we'll be back to square one. If the typing matches, then they'll run DNA tests. Allow a week or two for that. Could be longer."

"No court would turn the baby over to her without clear evidence of a match, though?" he asked.

"Absolutely not," Justin agreed. "We'll take our time on this one and make absolutely sure we get it right. Social services will want to do a whole slew of checks as well. Believe me, Hazel Murdock's life will be put under a microscope before she gets the baby. It might be different if the natural mother were trying to get custody, but so far we've had no luck at all locating her. As long as it's the grandmother we're dealing with, I'd say the baby could wind up right here." He regarded Sharon Lynn intently. "If that's the way you really want it."

"It is," she said emphatically.

Cord couldn't have asked for anything more, but one look at Sharon Lynn's still-shattered expression made him question how she would survive the delay, especially if the result was losing Ashley.

"Thanks, Justin. We appreciate your help," Cord said. "I know it was above and beyond the call of duty."

Justin's worried gaze never left Sharon Lynn. "This isn't about duty. It's about family."

"I'm going in to be with the baby," Sharon Lynn murmured and slipped past them.

Justin watched her go, his expression uneasy. "You planning to stay here with her tonight?"

Cord nodded. He was surprised when Justin nodded his approval.

"Good. She's taking this hard."

"Does that surprise you?"

"Of course not. Sharon Lynn's always had a tender heart. That's why she was so accepting when Kyle came up with a million and one excuses for delaying their wedding. She always understood. She always waited. That's why it rocked her so badly when she lost him on their wedding night. It wasn't just feeling guilty about being the driver. It was all those regrets for the years they lost."

Justin sighed. "Despite that hope I held out about the baby staying here in the end, I can't help wondering if it wouldn't be easier on Sharon Lynn if we just made other arrangements for foster care now."

"The same thought crossed my mind a minute ago," Cord admitted. "But we can't. For one thing, she'd never hear of it. For another, something in my gut tells me this is going to turn out all right in the end."

Justin clasped his hand. "I hope you're right. I really do.

I'll see to it that Lizzy gets by here in the morning to get the blood for the lab and I'll call the minute I know anything."

"Thanks."

At the door Justin hesitated again. Cord grinned at his obvious reluctance to go. "It's okay, you know. I won't take advantage of the situation."

Justin gave him a rueful grin. "Was I that obvious?"

"Let's just say you're not a man who should try bluffing at poker."

Justin laughed. "No wonder I keep losing in those games out at White Pines." His expression sobered. "I'm counting on the fact that you're being straight with me. I'm trusting you with my cousin."

"I won't do anything to make you regret it. I swear it."

Justin nodded. "Then that's good enough for me. I'll be in touch."

After he'd gone, Cord remained standing where he was, trying to work up the courage to join Sharon Lynn in the bedroom. Seeing her there, with that big old brass bed of hers dominating the space, was going to make keeping his promise to Justin downright maddening.

But keep it, he would. For a man known for his impatience, Sharon Lynn surely was becoming the test of a lifetime.

Sharon Lynn couldn't seem to draw her gaze away from the baby, not even when she heard Cord walk into the bedroom. Her grip on the edge of the crib was white-knuckle tight.

"You doing okay, darlin'?"

"Sure." She glanced over her shoulder at him. "You don't have to stay. I know you need to be back at White Pines tomorrow."

"I'm not going anywhere."

She was relieved by the refusal. She wasn't entirely sure she could bear to get through the night alone. "Thank you."

"No need to thank me." He reached around her and loosened her fingers from the crib, then slowly turned her to face him. He tucked a knuckle under her chin. "You need to get some sleep."

Sharon Lynn folded her arms around her middle and shivered. "I don't think I can."

Cord drew her against him and held her. "You have to," he repeated, rubbing her back gently. "Take another one of those bubble baths, if that'll relax you."

He grinned at her. "Then I'll come back and tuck you in."

"Will you stay with me?"

"I've already said I would."

"I mean in here. Will you sleep beside me?" She searched his expression. "I know it's asking a lot."

"Do you really think you'll sleep better if I'm next to you?"

She almost grinned at his doubtful tone. "I will."

"Then that's the way it will be," he said.

He said it so grimly that this time she did grin. "If it'll be too hard on you…"

"Hush. I'll manage. Get ready for bed. I'll go turn out the lights and be back in a flash."

As soon as he left the room, she pulled out a long T-shirt and slipped into it. She had a feeling the sexy nightie she might have preferred was a very bad idea under the circumstances. There was no mistaking the fact that she was already asking too much of Cord's restraint.

She had slipped under the covers by the time he returned. He flipped off the bedroom light, then sank down on the side of the bed and removed his boots. She found herself holding her breath, waiting for him to shed the rest of his clothes.

Instead, with a heavy sigh, he stretched out beside her, on top of the bedspread.

"Cord?"

"Yes, darlin'?"

"You don't have to sleep in your clothes."

"Oh, yes, I do," he said fervently.

She had no difficulty at all interpreting his meaning. That made her next request all the more dangerous.

"Cord?"

"Yes?"

"Would you mind very much holding me?"

She thought she heard him groan softly, but he dutifully rolled toward her and gathered her close. She sighed with pleasure at the reassuring feel of his arms around her. Then, surrounded by his warmth and his strength, she finally closed her eyes and slept.

Chapter Nine

After taking one last, longing look at the woman beside him, Cord slipped out of bed at dawn, grateful that he'd made it through the night without violating Sharon Lynn's trust. Holding her had been sheer torture. He'd wanted to make love to her, to make her forget all about the heartache that might lay ahead of them, to give her hope in the future. Their hope.

But there'd been a million and one reasons why he couldn't, why his arms had curved loosely around her, why his hands had remained still, why his lips hadn't brushed hers. The baby had been right there in the same room, for one thing. For another, he would have been taking advantage of her vulnerability. His promise to Justin, his own sense of honor prevented that.

Still, he thought with some regret, it would have been so easy to seduce her. She was scared and needy. She had turned to him for reassurance, for comfort, maybe even for a distraction, which he could have provided with pleasure. But she wasn't prepared for the consequences of reaching out to him, not for *those* consequences, anyway.

So, he'd done the honorable thing. He'd counted sheep.

He'd focused on anything and everything *but* the woman in his arms. Even so, he was pretty sure he'd never get the light, flowery scent of her out of his head, never forget the silkiness of her skin or the curve of her hip. He wanted the tenderness and warmth she gave so readily to their abandoned baby directed his way. He needed her to want him as desperately as he was beginning to want her.

Since that was out of the question for now, he moved quietly to the bathroom across the hall, cleaned up, then went back to check on the baby. She was wide-awake and about ready to cry. He plucked her out of the crib, made soothing little noises as he carried her into the living room, then changed her.

"You hungry, angel?"

She gave him a beaming smile that convinced him she understood exactly what he was saying. For an infant who'd endured what she had, she was astonishingly happy. Cord felt a silly grin spreading across his own face in response.

"You were a good girl last night," he praised. "You didn't wake up once. Sharon Lynn's gonna be real grateful that you're starting to sleep through the night."

With Ashley tucked into the crook of his arm, he popped a cup of last night's coffee into the microwave, then heated her bottle. When both were ready, he sat at the kitchen table and fed her, while sipping the coffee.

A glance at the clock told him he'd better make a call to White Pines. Work would be getting underway and Cody was bound to wonder where he was. He reached for the phone and dialed.

"White Pines," Cody growled.

Obviously not a good morning, Cord concluded.

"Cody, this is Cord."

"Where the hell are you?"

"In town with your daughter and the baby."

That was greeted by a long, telling silence. "I see," he said finally, though he sounded as if the opposite were true. "Mind telling me when you intend to get back to work?"

"Look, it was a rough night last night," Cord explained. "Justin thinks he's found the baby's grandmother. Sharon Lynn was taking it hard. I couldn't leave her here alone."

Cody muttered a harsh expletive, then added, "No, I suppose not. Is she okay?"

"She's sleeping now. She's due at Dolan's within the hour. As soon as she's up and on her way, I'll be out there. Leave my assignment with Harlan Patrick or one of the other men."

"Just see me when you get here," Cody said and hung up abruptly.

"Oh, boy," Cord murmured, grazing a knuckle over the baby's cheek. "Looks like I'm in for it." She regarded him with wide, solemn eyes. "Not to worry your pretty little head, though. I'll handle it."

"Handle what?" Sharon Lynn murmured groggily, wandering into the kitchen just then.

She was clad in a thick, terry-cloth robe, but she was still sexily tousled, reminding him all too vividly of the night and the bed they'd shared. No woman had the right to be that seductive at the crack of dawn, not when there was nothing to be done about it.

"Nothing," he replied in a choked voice, regretting that he couldn't snag her wrist and haul her down for a long, slow kiss that would wake them both thoroughly.

She seemed to accept the response at face value. "You should have gotten me up," she complained with a yawn. "I could have fed the baby, so you could get to work. Daddy's probably fit to be tied."

"He's a reasonable man," Cord said, despite recent evidence to the contrary. "He'll understand."

"Are we talking about my father?" she inquired dryly. She reached for the baby. "Go. Don't jeopardize your job."

After his conversation with Cody, Cord knew she was right. He relinquished the baby reluctantly, then finished the last of his coffee. He was almost to the door, when she stopped him.

"Cord?"

Shrugging into his coat, he turned back. "Yes?"

"Thank you for staying last night. Thanks for…" She seemed at a loss for words. "Thanks for everything."

He grinned at the all-encompassing word. "Anytime. I'll see you two later."

"It's not necessary."

He frowned. "You keep saying that, darlin', I'll get the feeling you don't care about me. Besides, I thought we were past that. I'll be back."

She nodded, a smile barely perceptible on her lips. "I'm glad."

He resisted the urge to go back and kiss her. He'd been hard and aching all night long. He knew he could never pull off a quick, chaste brush of his lips over hers. If he touched her now, it would be a go-for-broke kiss and it would lead them down a path she wasn't anywhere near ready to take. He had to keep reminding himself of that—over and over, if that's what it took.

"See you," he promised again and left before he could change his mind.

At White Pines, he found Cody in his office, clearly waiting impatiently for his arrival. He leaned back in his chair and scowled at Cord's entrance.

"Finally."

Clearly his boss was spoiling for a fight. Cord tried to placate him. "I got here as quickly as I could. What is it you need me to do today?"

"We'll get to that. First I think you and I need to have a talk." He gestured toward a chair. "Sit."

Cord had a feeling this talk wasn't going to be about ranching, that it was going to be about matters he'd just as soon not get into with Sharon Lynn's daddy, but he dutifully sat just the same.

"What exactly is going on between you and my daughter?" Cody began bluntly.

Cord bristled at the question, even though he understood Cody's need to ask it.

"With all due respect, sir, she's a grown woman. I think that's between Sharon Lynn and me."

Cody rose halfway out of his chair, a scowl on his face. "Now, listen here, you impertinent son of a gun."

Cord held up a hand in a quieting gesture. "Sir, I know where you're coming from. You're worried about her. What I can tell you is that I will never do anything to hurt her. Circumstances, fate, call it what you will, threw us together and brought that innocent little baby into our lives. There's a bond between us because of that. It may lead to something more. It may not. For myself, I hope it does. That's as honest as I can be."

Apparently it wasn't quite enough to satisfy his boss. Cody's gaze remained suspicious. "And this has nothing at all to do with the fact that she owns a ranch of her own?"

Cord went absolutely still, caught between shock and fury. He should have anticipated the question. Somehow, though, he'd pushed his discovery that Sharon Lynn was the widowed owner of a nearby ranch from his mind. He should have seen that Cody would add up his plan to buy his own place and his growing friendship with Sharon Lynn and come up with a devious scheme. In Cody's place, he might have done the same. Still, the question rankled.

"What are you asking me?" he demanded quietly.

"I'd say it's plain enough. I'm asking if your interest in my daughter has anything at all to do with the fact that she has some property. You told me yourself that it's your goal to move on as soon as you can get enough money for some land. I can't help thinking that courting Sharon Lynn would be a quicker way to go about it, wouldn't it?"

Cord was on his feet before the words were out of Cody's mouth. Because he was older, because he was Sharon Lynn's father, he cut him more slack than he would any other man asking the same questions, making the same rotten accusation. He braced his hands on the desk between them and leaned across.

"You listen to me and listen good," he said tightly. "I've gotten nothing in life that I haven't worked for. I sure as hell don't intend to start now. Until she told me the story of her marriage, I didn't even know Sharon Lynn was related to the man who had owned that property nearby. She's not using his name. She's not living there. I had no idea she was the widow folks had told me might be interested in selling."

"Why should I believe you?"

"Because I don't lie," Cord said emphatically.

Cody still wasn't through. "But now that you do know," he began, his expression hard, "that's all the more reason for staying in contact with her, isn't it?"

"I am with Sharon Lynn because of the baby and because I've grown to care deeply for her. For you to say otherwise is a disservice to her and an insult to me." He met Cody's harsh glare with one of his own. "Maybe you'd like it better if I move on. I can be out of here in an hour."

"And leave Sharon Lynn after telling me how devoted you are to her?" Cody asked with an edge of sarcasm.

"I didn't say I'd be leaving her or Los Piños, but I will leave White Pines this morning, if that's what you want."

Harlan Adams stepped into the office just then and stared from Cody to Cord and back again. "What the hell is going on in here? You two are making enough ruckus to scare the horses clear down to the barn."

"Just a little disagreement, Daddy," Cody said in a milder tone.

Harlan turned a skeptical gaze on Cord. "Is that the way you see it, too?"

Cord nodded, despite the anger churning inside him.

"Then what was that crazy talk I heard about you leaving?" Harlan asked.

"I was just asking if that's what Cody wanted."

"Well, why the hell would he?" Harlan retorted, gazing at his son. "Right, Cody?"

Cody flushed a dull red. "Daddy, you don't know all the facts."

"What facts? I know this man knows ranching. I know he's a hard worker."

"Couldn't prove that by me," Cody muttered.

"Excuse me?" his father said.

"Nothing."

Harlan nodded. "That's better. I also know that he's been a real godsend to Sharon Lynn in this crisis. Dani and Justin have both told me how he stuck by her all day yesterday, when she was jittery as a June bug waiting for news about that baby's mama."

"He should have been working," Cody repeated defiantly.

His father frowned. "Since when is work more important

to us than family? I'd think you'd be grateful he was there for your girl when she needed somebody to stand by her."

"If that's all it was," Cody said, "I would be grateful."

"You have any reason to believe otherwise?" Harlan asked. "I'm talking hard, cold facts, not crazy suppositions."

"No, but—"

"Until you do, then, I'd suggest we all settle down and get back to work."

Cody sighed heavily. "Yeah, fine."

Cord couldn't let the matter rest so easily. He met Cody's gaze evenly. "You sure that's what you want?"

"Yes," Cody said with obvious reluctance.

Harlan Adams beamed. "There, now. Isn't that better?"

"Yeah, right," Cody said. "I just pray we don't all live to regret it."

"You won't," Cord assured him quietly. "I guarantee it."

His temper still hadn't cooled. He doubted Cody's had, either. The truce between them wasn't likely to last. But it had bought him some time.

Time to prove his intentions were honorable. Time to convince Sharon Lynn that they had a future and that that property of hers had nothing to do with it.

When her brother slid onto a stool at Dolan's late that afternoon, Sharon Lynn was surprised. Usually Harlan Patrick headed out to be with Laurie Jensen the minute his work was done. She automatically filled a glass with ice and his favorite soda, then put it down on the counter in front of him.

"I haven't seen much of you around here lately," she commented. "What brings you by?"

"I just felt like it. Is that a problem?"

She frowned at his tone. Normally he was the most affable man in the world. "What's wrong?"

"Nothing, dammit."

"Well, you don't have to bite my head off," she snapped right back. "You came in here. I didn't chase after you just to pester you."

He raked a hand through his sun-streaked hair and mumbled an apology.

"What was that?"

"I said I'm sorry, blast it all. Can't you hear, either?"

She slapped down the rag she'd been using to wipe the counter and walked out from behind it. She grabbed his elbow and spun him around until they were face-to-face.

"Listen here, you big jerk. If you and Laurie had a fight, you don't get to come in here and take it out on me."

"Who says I had a fight with Laurie?"

"I can't think of another thing that would send you running in here behaving like a bear with a thorn stuck in his paw. Am I right? Did you two argue?"

"You could say that, though it's hard to argue with a woman who won't listen to a damn thing you have to say."

She saw the flash of genuine hurt in his eyes and said more soothingly, "You two fight all the time. Is there some reason this time is different?"

"She's left," he said succinctly.

Sharon Lynn stared at him in shock. "Left? To go where?"

"Nashville."

"She actually left?" she repeated incredulously. "She didn't just threaten to go?"

"I said she left, didn't I?"

"Okay, okay. I just can't believe she finally did it."

"Neither can I," he said in a bemused, betrayed tone that came close to breaking her heart.

For all of his jovial, devil-may-care attitude, Harlan Patrick had loved Laurie Jensen deeply. Always had. Probably always would. But her desire for a singing career had stood between them for a very long time. Harlan Patrick had never taken it seriously enough. Everyone in the family had warned him about that, but he'd been so sure Laurie would give up singing for a life with him.

Sharon Lynn sat down on the stool next to him. "You know she loves you," she reminded him.

"Just not enough to stay here and marry me."

"She'll be back. Country music is a tough business. Stand by her, be there for her. There's no guarantee she'll make it. Let her take her best shot. That's the only way to get it out of her system."

He regarded her bleakly. "She's good, though. Really good," he admitted. "What if she makes it? What if she becomes this huge success and never comes back? What if someone else comes along and makes her forget all about the cowboy she left behind in Texas?"

"Don't you think you're selling yourself short? You're every bit as handsome and sexy as any man she's likely to meet."

Harlan Patrick gave her a lopsided grin. "And you're biased as hell, but, thanks, anyway. Even so, you know what they say about out of sight, out of mind."

"You could have gone with her," Sharon Lynn reminded him. "That was always an option. You've got that business degree Daddy insisted on. The two of you could have learned the music business together."

"I might have a business degree, but the ranch is all I care about. It always has been."

"Is it more important than Laurie?"

"No, of course not, but—"

"But you've always gotten your own way and you can't believe it didn't work out the way you wanted this time, too."

"Hey, whose side are you on?"

"Yours, but you are stubborn, just like all the rest of us. Maybe one of us should learn to bend once in a while."

Harlan Patrick gave an exaggerated shudder as if the very idea of compromise were repugnant to him. Sharon Lynn grinned. "Not an option, huh?"

"Not this time." His gaze met hers. "Let's change the subject. This one's depressing. How are things with you and the cowboy?"

"Cord?"

"You know any other cowboys?"

"A whole slew of them," she reminded him.

"Okay, smart-aleck. Yes, Cord."

"You've probably seen him more recently than I have. You tell me."

Harlan Patrick grinned. "Let's just say he survived his first big-time run-in with Daddy."

"He fought with Daddy? Because he was late this morning?"

"I don't think that was it."

"What, then?"

Her brother looked vaguely uneasy. "I wasn't there."

"But you heard. The men out there are worse than a bunch of old ladies when it comes to gossip."

"Daddy seemed to disapprove of the amount of time he's been spending with you. He apparently asked straight-out if it had anything to do with Cord trying to get his hands on Kyle's ranch."

Sharon Lynn stared at him in shock. A queasy sensation began in the pit of her stomach. "Daddy asked him that?"

"That's what I heard." He gave her a penetrating look. "Is that what he's after, sis?"

"No, of course not," she said indignantly. "The subject of Kyle's ranch has never even come up. I don't even know if he's aware that I own it."

"If he wasn't, he is now. Could be that Daddy has succeeded in planting the idea in his head. It would be mighty convenient for him if he could take it off your hands for a pittance of what it's worth."

She scowled at him. "That's insulting, to me and to Cord, especially since you know perfectly well that I made a deal with the foreman out there."

Harlan Patrick grinned. "That's pretty much what he told Daddy, too. He threatened to quit."

"He didn't do it, though, did he?" The idea of Cord leaving the area bothered her more than it should have. Whether he went or stayed shouldn't matter, but it did. The prospect of him leaving a place he'd wanted so badly to work was all the more troubling if he was being virtually forced to go by her overly protective father. "Harlan Patrick, tell me exactly what was said out there."

"You sound worried, sis? Would it really bother you if he did leave?"

She ignored the question. "Did he go through with it or not?" she persisted.

Harlan Patrick's smirk indicated he found her response telling enough. "No," he reassured her. "Granddaddy busted in on them and saved the day. They're operating under a cease-fire for the moment."

Sharon Lynn barely contained a sigh of relief. She would step in, too. Smooth things over.

Harlan Patrick regarded her knowingly. "Don't even think about getting into the middle of this, sis."

"Why not?"

"It'll only convince Daddy he's right to worry and it'll be a slap at Cord's pride. He doesn't need you fighting his battles for him."

"Amen to that," Cord said, joining them. He gave Harlan Patrick a curt nod. "You've told her?"

"I thought she should know," her brother said defensively.

"You're right, she should," Cord agreed, "if only so she can make up her own mind whether or not to trust me."

"But I do," Sharon Lynn insisted.

Cord smiled. "Thanks, darlin'."

"As for the ranch—"

"I don't want to discuss the ranch," Cord retorted grimly. "Not ever. I've heard about as much about that ranch today as I care to. I won't have it getting in between us."

She was pretty sure she saw a new level of respect in Harlan Patrick's eyes as he gave Cord a nod, then kissed her goodbye.

"Later, sis. See you in the morning, Cord."

"Harlan Patrick?" she called after him.

"Yes?"

"Things will work out with Laurie. They always have before."

"I hope you're right, but something in my gut tells me this time is different. She's never put quite so much distance between us before."

"Uncle Jordan's plane can cover a piddly little distance like that in no time."

His expression brightened for the first time since his arrival. "So it can," he murmured thoughtfully. "And it just so happens, I have a pilot's license."

"See there. There's always hope."

He walked out whistling, looking a whole lot happier than he had when he'd come in an hour before.

"His mood's improved," Cord noted. "You must have a magic touch."

"Not really. Used to be I had a tendency to always look for the silver lining in all the clouds. For a while now I'd forgotten how."

Cord grinned. "But it's coming back to you."

She gazed straight into his eyes and nodded. "Yes, lately it's been coming back to me."

Chapter Ten

Even though he'd told Harlan Adams he would put it behind him, the fight with Cody kept gnawing at Cord. He was silent through most of the evening with Sharon Lynn, pitching in to help her with dinner, sitting across the table from her, but unable to make himself say what was on his mind. She kept casting worried glances his way, but she didn't try to pry.

"Did Lizzy come by today to draw the baby's blood?" he asked eventually, just to fill the silence.

She gave a little nod, clearly no more eager to talk about that than he was to bring up the fight with her father. "How long will the typing take?" he asked, anyway.

"She should be calling any minute," Sharon Lynn said with a nervous glance toward the phone. "She promised to check with the lab before she left the hospital."

Knowing that only added to the strain already filling the air. The tension was thick enough to turn a sun-baked rattler jittery. They fell silent and stayed that way.

After dinner, with the baby already asleep, Cord knew it was time to either go or stay. And, if he stayed, he was going to have to get into the substance of his argument with

Cody. Sharon Lynn had already heard just enough from her brother to deserve a complete explanation from him.

As she put the last dish away in the cupboard, she turned to face him. "We've been avoiding it all evening and it hasn't worked. You might as well tell me exactly what happened out at White Pines today," she said. "I've heard some from Harlan Patrick. I'm going to hear the rest eventually, anyway."

He didn't even bother trying to pretend that he misunderstood. "Just how much did Harlan Patrick tell you?"

"That Daddy's afraid you might be after Kyle's land," she said bluntly. "Just so you know, I meant what I said earlier. I don't believe it for a minute."

Well, that was certainly to the point, Cord thought ruefully. "That's about it. I don't know what else I can say."

"I don't understand how he could even accuse you of such a thing. You didn't even know that property belonged to me." She hesitated, her gaze fixed on his face. "Did you?"

He thought he heard a tiny hint of uncertainty in her voice. It made him angrier than ever at Cody for indirectly giving her a reason to distrust him.

"No," he said flatly. "I'm curious about something, though. Why didn't you tell me about it yourself? Maybe if you had, we could have gotten the issue out in the open a long time ago."

"To tell you the truth, it never even occurred to me," she confessed with a sigh. "That property means nothing to me. I hardly even think of it as mine. Kyle had changed his will the morning of the wedding. Even if he hadn't, I probably would have inherited it because as of that night I was his wife, his only family."

Cord had been so caught up with Sharon Lynn, the baby and his new job, that he hadn't even checked into the ranch.

What would have been the point? He didn't have the money to buy a bag of dirt at the moment, much less a ranch.

"Have you kept it up and running?" he asked.

She nodded. "Kyle had a good foreman out there and plenty of hired hands. I saw no reason to close it down. I let the foreman and his family move into the main house. I told him we'd keep it going for a year and see how it went. I even promised him a chance to buy me out, if he decided he wanted to."

"So that land's spoken for, anyway, right?" Cord hoped his disappointment wasn't obvious. It was for the best that it wasn't available, not when its very existence could have put a huge stumbling block between them.

"We didn't put it in writing, if that's what you mean, but we made a verbal agreement. In my book, that's binding enough." She studied his face. "Does that disappoint you?"

He forced a smile. "Darlin', I've never pretended I didn't want a ranch of my own someday. And it's true that I'd heard there was one nearby that a widow might be willing to sell. I swear to you, though, that I had no idea you were that widow, not until you told me about the accident and Kyle. Then it all added up."

"But you didn't say anything," she said pointedly.

"Because I'm a very long way from being able to buy so much as an acre of land, from you or anyone else, and until I can, what's the point of talking about it? If your land is all but sold, it's for the best. I don't want it coming between us. I don't want you to ever have any reason not to trust me. When the time comes, I'll buy my own land and I'll pay a fair price for it."

She regarded him with obvious regret. "If only I'd known—"

"Stop that," he said, cutting her off. "Even if you had

known I was going to turn up, the foreman out there has more right to your husband's ranch than I would have. What you've done is exactly the right thing." He grinned. "Maybe it'll even get your father off my back, once he knows."

"I'll tell him," she said, her expression brightening. "That ought to put an end to it. I won't have him making any more ridiculous accusations where you're concerned, not when you've been so kind to me."

"I'll tell him, but don't blame him for any of this. He's your father," Cord said, surprised to find himself defending Cody's behaviour. "He has every right to look out for your best interests. Much as I hate to admit it, that's exactly what I would have done if our positions had been reversed."

Sharon Lynn seemed amused by his passionate declaration. "Did you tell him that when you two were fighting?"

"You can laugh if you want to, but yes. In so many words, that's exactly what I told him."

She looked surprised. "You did?"

"Haven't you noticed, darlin'? I'm a reasonable man. I can see more than one side to things, even when a man's all but accusing me of trying to use his daughter to get what I want in life."

"I had no idea men were capable of a thing like that," she said dryly. "Or are you just a remarkable man?"

"Maybe I'll just let you go on thinking that I'm unique. It'll work in my favor in the end."

She directed a look his way that was oddly shy. "You don't need any extra brownie points with me. You've already earned enough to last a lifetime."

He could feel his smile spreading slowly across his face. "In that case, maybe I'll cash one in."

"Oh?"

"Come here, darlin'."

He knew it was reckless, knew it was more than a little dangerous, but still he beckoned her over to where he was sitting on the sofa, then patted the space right next to him. She hesitated, seemed to consider the request, then moved slowly across the room. After another hesitation, another quick search of his face, she sat.

"Closer," he urged.

Her gaze narrowed. "What are you up to?"

"I told you. I'm cashing in one of those brownie points."

"I'm not sure it works that way," she protested.

"We can make it work any way we want it to," he countered. "This is between you and me. We set the rules, right?"

"I suppose."

He pointed to a spot on his cheek, right where he'd been told often enough that there was an intriguing dimple. "Now, how about a little kiss right here?"

She went absolutely still at the request. There was a fleeting instant of panic in her eyes before it gave way first to resignation and then to what he interpreted as bold anticipation. She reached over and touched the same spot on his cheek with the tip of her finger.

"Right there, correct?"

His pulse had begun to race at the slight caress. He nodded, rather than trying to force an answer past the sudden lump in his throat.

She leaned forward ever so slowly, deliberately taunting him. Cord clenched his fists at his sides to keep from reaching for her, claiming her. The brush of her lips, when it finally came, was as light and feathery soft and rapid as the touch of a bird's wings. He had a feeling her heart was racing just as quickly.

"Nice," he murmured. He glanced sideways in her direction. "How many of those points did you say I'd accumulated?"

She grinned. "Enough."

"Then let's try that again."

This time just as her lips neared his cheek, he turned so that the kiss landed squarely on his mouth. After the first startled instant, the first flaring of panic in her eyes, she sighed softly and stayed right where she was, her lips teasing his.

Cord's hands came up to cup her face. His fingers threaded through her hair. Another sigh shuddered through her and as it did, he deepened the kiss, tasting her, dipping into the mysterious, honeyed sweetness of her mouth.

The kiss lasted forever…but not nearly long enough. He was the one who pulled away, though he didn't release her face. He studied the bright patches of color on her cheeks, the confusion in her eyes.

"Was that a mistake?" he asked quietly.

She swallowed hard, then returned his gaze bravely. "No," she said in a whisper. "Not a mistake. Just a surprise."

He grinned at that. "You didn't see it coming? Haven't expected it since the day we met?"

"Okay, yes, maybe." The confusion was back. "Do we have to talk about it?"

"Only if it's a problem."

She shrugged helplessly. "I don't know if it is or not. Cord, I can't make promises. I can't look ahead. You need to know that."

He pressed a finger to her lips. "*Shh.* It was a kiss. Not a commitment."

In time, though, in time he wanted more from her. Much more.

The phone rang then, jarring them both out of their rev-

eries. Sharon Lynn's hand trembled visibly as she reached
for it. After she'd answered, she turned to him and mouthed,
"It's Lizzy."

Her expression darkened at whatever Lizzy was telling
her. "I see," she said finally. "What happens next?"

Cord could see from her bleak expression that the news
wasn't good. He reached for her as she hung up, pulled her
closer so that her back was resting against his chest.

"The blood type's a match," she said, her voice thick
with choked-back sobs. "They'll have to do more testing."

Cord held back his own dismay. "She could still be ruled
out as the baby's grandmother," he reminded her. "Millions
of people have the same blood type."

"I know. It's just that…"

"It's just that you wanted it to be over, at least for now."
He felt her barely perceptible nod against his shoulder. "The
testing won't take forever. We have to be absolutely sure."

"I know," she said.

Her utter stillness, the sadness in her voice, combined
to touch him in a way that Lizzy's report hadn't. It galva-
nized him into plotting his own strategy for handling things
from here on out. Let the police and medical experts do
their thing, he thought. There were other kinds of evidence
that would be needed if there was to be a court battle, other
ways to gather proof. He didn't have a lot of money left and
it had been meant as a stake toward buying his own ranch,
but this was a better use for it.

"I'll hire a private investigator tomorrow," he promised
her. "By the time he's done, we'll know everything there
is to know about Hazel and Victoria Murdock."

She turned to face him. "Private investigators cost
money," she protested. "You're supposed to be saving every
cent toward a down payment on a ranch."

"That can wait. This can't."

"I have some money."

"No. This is something I need to do." He met her gaze. "Let me, Sharon Lynn. Let me do this for you." He hesitated, gazed directly into her eyes and added quietly, "For us."

Maybe it was his imagination, but it seemed to him that she visibly relaxed. A halfhearted grin came and went.

"You're just after more brownie points, aren't you?" she teased.

He laughed at that. "Okay, you've got me. That is something I am surely counting on."

First thing in the morning Cord sought out Sharon Lynn's father. He wanted to settle the matter of the land with him and he wanted to see if Cody could recommend a private investigator to look into the background of the Murdocks.

Cody glanced up from his paperwork when Cord walked into his office. Despite the truce, his eyes were still filled with distrust.

"I'm delighted you decided to show up this morning," he said sourly.

Cord let the comment pass. He knew he needed to prove that he was a responsible employee. He hadn't demonstrated it up until now, even if his reasons were sound.

"Do you have a minute?" he asked.

Cody put down his pen and gestured toward the chair. "Have a seat."

"It's about Sharon Lynn and that land of hers."

"I'm not sure we ought to be getting into that," Cody said. "We're likely to come to blows. Daddy'll pitch a fit if I injure the man he's all but handpicked for my daughter."

Cord grinned. "You're assuming you'd actually manage to lay a hand on me."

Cody scowled for an instant, then sighed. "I may be out of practice, but I can still hold my own in a brawl," he muttered. "And I'm just itching to prove it."

"Yeah, I'm sure. I just don't think it'll be necessary after you hear what I have to say."

"Go on then."

Cord told him what he and Sharon Lynn had discussed the night before. "So, you see, that land isn't available. She's made an agreement with the foreman and she's sticking by it, just as she should. And I'm going to go right on working here and saving my money. I'll have my own spread one day, but it won't be that one." He gave Cody a wry look. "Satisfied?"

The older man looked relieved. "To be truthful, yes. Despite what happened yesterday, I like you, Cord. I didn't want to believe that your motives where Sharon Lynn were concerned were anything but honorable, but I had to say something. I couldn't just let my suspicions pass."

"I know that, sir. I didn't like what you had to say, but I could understand your need to say it. I told Sharon Lynn that myself when she wanted to come out here herself and tear a strip out of your hide."

Cody chuckled. "She would have, too. That girl's got the Adams's temper and spunk, even if it has been in short supply the last few months. I'm glad to hear it's coming back and relieved to learn it won't be directed at me."

"There's one more thing," Cord told him. "It looks as if there's a good chance that woman Justin found over in Garden City is the baby's grandmother. They're running another set of tests to confirm it. I wasn't crazy about what Justin had to say about her and I'm not sure he didn't leave some of it out. I was thinking it might be a good idea to hire a private investigator to do some checking. I wondered if you knew of anyone."

Cody's gaze narrowed. "It sounds as if you and Sharon Lynn are thinking of fighting the woman's claim to the baby, if it turns out she has one. Is she that attached to the child?"

"We both are, but we'll fight only if it seems like the right thing to do," Cord insisted.

Cody stood up and began to pace. "I don't like it," he said. "Sharon Lynn's getting too involved with that child. Now you're talking about a private investigator." He shook his head. "It's going to get messy. She doesn't need that."

"Believe me, I understand where you're coming from," Cord assured him. "Like it or not, we are involved. Whoever left that baby on Sharon Lynn's doorstep saw to that. I just want to be sure whoever winds up with custody has the baby's best interests at heart."

"And you think this woman who might be the grandmother won't care about that?"

"It's just a feeling I got from what Justin said and what he didn't say. He's got a responsibility to go by the law. I understand that. He may not be in a position to dig deep enough into this woman's life to make sure she's the right person to care for that baby."

"What about social services?"

"I'm sure they'll do their jobs. I'd just feel better if we had all the facts, too. I know Sharon Lynn feels the same way."

The mention of his daughter did the trick. Cody nodded. "Let me call Justin and see what he thinks. If he agrees, I know just the man for the job. Lizzy's husband and I hired him a while back when we were having some problems around our ranches. He was fast and he was thorough."

Cord could see that was the only concession he was going to get for now. Maybe Cody's caution was justified. It wouldn't hurt to wait a few more hours. He stood up.

"I'll be waiting to hear from you, then."

"By the way, who's paying this private eye, if you hire one?"

Cord frowned at the question. "I am."

"With the money you've been saving to buy a ranch?"

Cord nodded.

"Why?"

"Because what happens to that baby matters to Sharon Lynn," he said readily. "And to me."

Cody regarded him with approval. "That tells me everything I need to know about you, Cord Branson."

"Then you don't object to me spending time with your daughter?"

"It hasn't mattered to you up until now whether I did or I didn't, has it?"

"Truthfully, no," Cord responded with a grin. "But it would be nice to know I have your blessing."

Cody walked over to where Cord stood and held out his hand. "You have my blessing, son." Then he grinned. "Not that it'll matter a whit to Sharon Lynn one way or the other. The woman has a mind of her own."

Cord laughed at the warning. "Yeah, but it can't hurt to have one more Adams on my side."

"Son, I may be her daddy, but it's Grandpa Harlan who does the matchmaking around here, and he's been on your side from the get-go. Now, go on and get to work. I'll be in touch about the private eye before the end of the day."

Cord nodded and went to find Harlan Patrick. The last

time he'd seen him he was nursing a hangover and a broken heart. What they both needed was some good hard work to take their minds off their troubles.

Unfortunately an entire day in the bitter cold checking for downed fences didn't do anything except come close to freezing their butts off. When they rode back in just before dusk, they found Justin waiting.

"Hey, cousin, you here to take me out to drown my sorrows again?" Harlan Patrick inquired hopefully.

"From what I've heard you did that last night," Justin said. "Seems to me like a good night's sleep is called for tonight."

"I think I had every right to have a couple of drinks," Harlan Patrick grumbled. "When did you turn so judgmental? Oh, wait, it was when you put on that uniform, wasn't it?"

Cord watched Justin's expression. He remained perfectly cool in the face of the taunt, though his eyes were unreadable behind his reflective sunglasses.

"Picking a fight with me won't solve your problem," Justin said mildly. "Besides, I'm here to see Cord."

That brought Harlan Patrick up short. He stared at Cord. "You in some kind of trouble?"

"None that I know of," Cord said, his gaze locked on Justin. "I suspect this is about a matter I discussed with your father this morning."

Justin gave an imperceptible nod. "Can we go someplace and talk? Cody said his office would be empty."

"Fine," Cord agreed.

"I'm coming along," Harlan Patrick said at once.

"No need," Cord said.

"It's not your concern," Justin added.

"If it's about that baby," he began, then nodded when he

caught their expressions. "I thought so. Then it concerns Sharon Lynn and that concerns me. Hell, it concerns all of us."

Cord couldn't argue with a brother wanting to look out for his sister. "Come on, then."

In Cody's office he and Harlan Patrick settled into chairs, while Justin stood behind his uncle's desk. He slowly removed his sunglasses as if to assure that they got a good look at the glint in his eyes.

"The last thing we need is a private investigator poking around in this," he declared.

Cord froze at his warning. "Why is that? You have a need to protect your turf?"

"No, dammit. I'm just afraid it'll look to the court as if we're using Adams money and influence to try to get this poor woman and steal her grandbaby from her."

When Cord started to protest, Justin held up his hand. "Look, I know how you feel. Believe me, I was not impressed with this woman or with her sincerity. She's the last person I'd want raising a kid of mine, but that's gut instinct, not law."

"What you're saying is we need facts," Cord said. "How else are we going to get those, if not by hiring a private investigator?"

"You seem to be forgetting that I'm a sheriff. I'm already investigating this case, because abandoning that child was a crime. I'll get all the evidence we need if there's going to be a fight for custody."

Harlan Patrick fixed a hard gaze on his cousin, then seemed to reach a conclusion. "Maybe Justin is right, Cord. He won't let Sharon Lynn down."

Cord could see both men were sincere, but it wasn't enough to reassure him. "I'd just feel better if we had an objective outsider doing the digging into this family's background."

"I'm telling you, it's the wrong tactic," Justin declared. "You haven't met this woman. I have. If she realizes somebody's out there poking around in her life, it'll get her back up. She'll fight just to prove a point. If we handle her right, I say she'll just walk away from the baby without a backward glance."

"I'm sorry," Cord said. "I can't take that chance. If a P.I. is a bad idea, then I'll do some checking on my own."

"You'll be like a bull in a china shop," Justin protested. "There's no way she won't know what you're up to."

"It's me or a P.I.," Cord insisted stubbornly.

Justin threw up his hands in defeat. "Do what you have to do, but I don't want to know about it." He caught Cord's gaze and held it. "Hazel Murdock better not know about it, either."

"She'll never guess a thing," Cord promised. He stood up and headed for the door.

"Where are you going?" Harlan Patrick asked.

"I thought I'd take a ride over to Garden City and buy myself a drink."

Harlan Patrick's expression brightened "Mind some company?"

Justin groaned. "Heaven protect me from amateurs," he muttered.

"We're not amateurs," Harlan Patrick protested. "We're just a couple of guys out on the town."

"See that one of you stays sober to drive home," Justin said.

They were almost out the door when he called out to them. "You might try the End of the Road Saloon. I understand it's where Hazel Murdock likes to spend her evenings."

Harlan Patrick went back and gave his cousin an exuberant pinch on the cheek. "You sweet thing," he taunted. "I just knew there was a little bit of that old hell-raiser left in you."

"Just forget where you got the information," Justin pleaded.

Cord grinned at him. "Hell, we don't even know your name."

"I wish," Justin grumbled. "Try to stay out of trouble, okay? It would be really embarrassing if I had to come over there and bail the two of you out of jail."

"But just think of how long you could hold it over our heads," Harlan Patrick responded with a grin.

Justin brightened. "Now that is something to look forward to."

Chapter Eleven

The End of the Road Saloon was aptly named. It was at the end of a long, dusty road that led to nowhere Cord could see. He was surprised by the fact that Harlan Patrick seemed to know the way without bothering to check on the address or ask for directions.

"I take it you've been here before," he said as they pulled into a parking space outside the huge barn of a building.

He shrugged indifferently. "Laurie Jensen used to sing here once in a while."

Cord recognized the name and the woman's connection to Harlan Patrick. "Laurie's the one who just took off for Nashville, right?"

Harlan Patrick's expression fell. "Yep. That's the one."

Cord glanced around at the old wooden building, which hadn't seen a coat of paint in years, at the half-empty parking lot and neon beer sign with most of the letters burnt out. "I'm surprised she'd want to leave a golden opportunity like singing here," he observed wryly.

Harlan Patrick scowled at him. "Okay, maybe it's not the Grand Ole Opry, but she drew a big enough crowd here.

The place was always hopping when she sang. People drove in from all over west Texas."

"But she wants more?"

"More?" he repeated scathingly. "She wants it all. She wants a recording contract, concert tours, the whole nine yards." He made no attempt to hide his bitterness. "She couldn't wait to leave me in her dust. Well, good riddance." He frowned. "Can we drop the subject?"

"Fine by me," Cord agreed, aware that he didn't know enough about the pair's history to offer either advice or consolation. "Let's go see what we can find out about this Murdock woman."

"Let me ask around," Harlan Patrick suggested when they were inside. "I've been here enough that some people know me. It won't seem as if a stranger's poking around."

Cord could see the sense in that. He followed Harlan Patrick's lead and took a seat at the bar.

The interior of the place was one step up from the exterior. The bar itself was an elaborately carved relic from another era and the mirrored wall behind it was lined with liquor bottles that went from the rot-gut stuff to the priciest labels on the market. Apparently people from all walks of life in Garden City reached the End of the Road sooner or later.

There were a dozen or so people scattered around the large room. One group of four, all men, were tipping beers and arguing about politics. A man at the end of the bar was staring with a glassy gaze at the TV, which had been tuned to a sitcom rerun. There were couples in a few of the booths. Every one of them had a thick hamburger and a mound of crispy onion rings in front of them. That was recommendation enough for Cord, whose mouth watered at the sight of them.

When the bartender finally approached, he greeted Harlan Patrick by name.

"I hear Laurie's on her way to Nashville," he said, obviously unaware of what a sore subject it was. "I'm guessing she'll have herself a recording contract by springtime. That little gal's got talent. I'll bet you're close to busting with pride."

Harlan Patrick gave a grim nod. "She's got what it takes, all right. Bring me a beer, Jack."

Cord ordered a hamburger and onion rings. "I'll have a beer now, then coffee after."

When the bartender had gone, Harlan Patrick grinned at Cord. "Guess that makes you the designated driver."

"Okay by me." He glanced around the room. "You see anybody here who could be our potential grandmother?"

Harlan Patrick whirled his stool around and looked out over the scattering of people. "No one here who looks a day over forty to me."

"I was thinking the same thing."

"Maybe she's just not here yet."

Cord's gaze fell on a woman tucked into the shadows of a nearby booth with what looked like a double whiskey in front of her. "Then again, maybe she's just a young grandma," he said thoughtfully, nodding in the direction of the booth. It was hard to tell too much about the woman, because of the way she'd huddled in a corner of the darkened booth, but she didn't look like any grandmother he'd ever seen. For some reason he'd been envisioning a white-haired old lady. This woman had hair the color of straw and an outfit meant for someone half her size.

Harlan Patrick followed his gaze. "Could be. She can't be much more than forty, but it looks as if she's been around the block a time or two. I'll check it out when Jack comes back."

Another flurry of customers arrived and it was a half hour before the bartender brought their food and had time enough to chat.

"Who's the lady who's all alone over there?" Harlan Patrick asked. "I don't think I've ever seen her in here before."

Jack followed the direction of his gesture. "Hazel? Oh, she's one of the regulars. She's here by five. Never leaves before closing. I'm not surprised you haven't noticed her. She stays to herself, doesn't say much. The lady's into serious drinking. Can't say I've ever heard her story. All I know for sure is that she pays her check, she's never rowdy and she gets home under her own steam. Lives a couple of blocks from here and walks. I offered her a ride one night when it was raining cats and dogs, but she refused. Said she didn't mind getting wet."

"Is she friendly with any of the other regulars?" Cord asked.

"You asking if she picks up men?" the bartender asked. "Not that I've ever noticed. Like I said, she concentrates on her whiskey and the music, if we have anybody performing."

He glanced up then, spotted a customer beckoning from the other end of the bar and went off to get the man another drink.

"Looks like that's the lady," Harlan Patrick said. "What do we do now?"

Cord was at a loss. Obviously they couldn't go and pump her for information. "Watch her, I guess. From what your buddy said, it doesn't sound as if she'd appreciate the company of a couple of strangers."

"Isn't this going to be a little bit like watching grass

grow?" Harlan Patrick grumbled. "Doesn't look to me as if we're going to see a lot of action."

"You sound disappointed," Cord said, regarding him with amusement. "What exactly were you hoping for?"

Harlan Patrick shrugged. "I don't know. Something dangerous, I guess."

"Seems to me you ought to be grateful you were wrong. Now you can get down to the serious business of drowning your sorrows, while I keep an eye on our friend over there."

Harlan Patrick swirled his beer around in the glass, took another sip, then pushed the glass aside with an expression of distaste. "To tell you the honest truth, I think I had enough of that last night. It didn't stop me from thinking about Laurie and I woke up with a splitting headache and a queasy stomach. What's the point?"

Cord barely contained his desire to laugh at Harlan Patrick's despondent tone. Growing up was surely hell. "Is that a pool table I see over there? We could play a little to pass the time."

"Now you're talking," Harlan Patrick said eagerly. "There's nothing I like better than taking a man's money from him over a friendly little game of pool."

"Just don't forget to keep one eye on our lady-friend, in case she decides to slip out before closing."

Maybe it was because he was still distracted over his girlfriend's defection, but Harlan Patrick's mind was definitely not on pool. A few hours later, Cord was a hundred bucks richer and not feeling one bit guilty about it. The betting had been Harlan Patrick's idea, after all.

"How'd you do that?" Harlan Patrick grumbled as they returned to the bar just in time for last call.

"Concentration and skill," Cord said simply, pocketing his winnings.

"All in all, the night has been a total bust."

"Not really," Cord said. "It looks as if our friend is about to head home."

"And you want to do what? Follow her? What good will that do? Justin already knows where she lives."

"But firsthand information is always best. Are you coming or not?"

Harlan Patrick eyed his beer with renewed longing, then shrugged. "I'm coming."

They climbed into Cord's truck. He turned on the engine, but not the headlights and waited until Hazel Murdock was halfway down the block before pulling to the edge of the lot and waiting again.

"I thought you were going to follow her."

"I am, but as long as we can see her from here, why pull out?" Cord said. "As slow as she's walking, we'd just end up passing her and having to circle the block. She'd get suspicious for sure."

"You've got a point," Harlan Patrick admitted. "What happens when she gets to her house? You're not proposing to spend the night outside, are you?"

"No," Cord said to Harlan Patrick's obvious relief. "But once we know where it is, we can come back tomorrow while she's at the bar and take a closer look."

Harlan Patrick's eyes widened as the implications of that sank in. "Oh, no," he protested. "Tell me you're not thinking of breaking in."

"Who said anything about breaking in?" Cord asked innocently. "Besides, you were the one hoping to do something dangerous."

"I really do not want to land in jail."

"Not even to help your sister and that sweet little baby?"

Harlan Patrick moaned. "You heard what Justin said.

He's going to be ticked as hell if we get ourselves arrested, to say nothing of what Daddy and Grandpa Harlan will have to say about it."

Cord regarded him with grim determination. "Then we'll just have to be sure not to get caught, won't we?"

Blast Hazel Murdock, Cord thought the next night as he and Harlan Patrick crept up to her house. He'd been hoping that she'd go off and leave lights blazing so the two of them could do their snooping from outside. For all of his bravado the night before, he wasn't any more thrilled with the idea of getting arrested than Harlan Patrick was. It would definitely be counterproductive to any custody battle, if he had a very recent breaking and entering charge on his record.

Unfortunately old Hazel apparently saved money on electricity so she could afford her booze. The little two-story bungalow was as dark as a tomb when they drove up in front of it after making sure that Hazel was, indeed, settled in at the bar for the evening.

"Now what?" Harlan Patrick asked, sounding resigned.

"We hope she's the type of woman to leave her front door unlocked," Cord said. "If not, we start looking for open windows."

"It's twenty degrees out here. How many windows do you expect to find open?"

"It only takes one. And it only needs to be unlocked, not pushed up."

"Why do I think I'm going to regret this?" Harlan Patrick grumbled, but he followed Cord up the walk and reached for the door handle.

"Wait!" Cord said, grabbing his arm. "You're not wearing gloves. I am."

"Sorry. Apparently I'm a little rusty at breaking and entering."

"If the door's unlocked, it's only entering," Cord replied.

"I want to be there when you try that explanation out on the judge."

"No doubt you will be, if it comes to that," Cord stated as the door eased open on the first try. "Bingo."

He slipped inside and pulled the flashlight he'd brought along from his pocket.

"Mind telling me exactly what we're looking for?" Harlan Patrick said.

"Evidence."

"Evidence of what?"

"That Hazel Murdock wouldn't be fit to raise that baby."

"Her evenings at the End of the Road ought to take care of that."

"I want more." He flashed the low beam of the light around the room, which was decorated with framed religious pictures and not one single snapshot of her daughter as far as Cord could tell.

"So far all I see is evidence of a God-fearing, churchgoing woman," Harlan Patrick commented, holding up a stack of programs from Sunday services at the church down the block. "I don't think that's going to go against her."

Cord was forced to admit that the house was well maintained, if not lavishly furnished. There wasn't a speck of dust on anything and in the kitchen not even a coffee cup had been left in the sink.

He opened the refrigerator and peered inside. There was a six-pack of beer on the top shelf, a half-used stick of butter and a package of stale cheese slices that had darkened around the edges. Apparently Hazel wasn't much of a cook.

The cabinets weren't much of an improvement. He found

a loaf of bread, some peanut butter and a tin of coffee. There wasn't even a canned vegetable or box of cereal in sight. Under the counter, though, he did find several bottles of whiskey. It was obvious she didn't confine her drinking to the saloon down the street. It made him wonder how she managed to stay upright on those walks home at night.

Still, would that be enough to keep her from getting custody? Especially if she worked hard, went to church Sundays, and stayed to herself. Who would testify that she was anything other than a responsible woman, who was willing to take on the burden of raising her grandchild? There were plenty of folks who would probably sing her praises for the sacrifice she was willing to make to care for her daughter's baby.

"This place is giving me the creeps," Harlan Patrick murmured, coming up behind him. "Can we get out of here?"

"Might's well," Cord agreed.

When they were back in the car and on their way back to Los Piños, Harlan Patrick asked, "Did you find what you were looking for?"

"Aside from the booze, I'm not sure if there was anything at all there to suggest she couldn't care for the baby," he admitted, not even trying to hide his disappointment. "Who knows, though, maybe her drinking will be all it takes? Or maybe when she's had time to think about it, she'll decide that she doesn't want a baby messing up her dull little routine."

"I sure as hell hope so, for Sharon Lynn's sake and for the baby's." Harlan Patrick shuddered. "I know I wouldn't want to grow up in that house. Reminded me too much of a monk's cell. Is it any wonder that her daughter didn't think she could go home with the baby? Dear old mama would probably have bombarded her with a diatribe about her sins. I counted four Bibles in the place."

"There's nothing wrong with owning more than one Bible. Some would see that as a sign that she's a pious woman," Cord replied.

"Maybe," Harlan Patrick said. "But I'll lay you odds, the words in the Bible weren't used with love in that house. I'll bet they were used as weapons."

"Unfortunately, unless Vicki reappears, we won't be able to prove that, and the last thing we want is the natural mother coming back to claim the baby."

"Yeah, I suppose you're right."

Cord glanced over at Harlan Patrick. "Thanks for coming with me. I know you had your doubts about the wisdom of going in there tonight."

"Somebody had to go along. Besides, you were doing it for my sister."

"I just wish we'd accomplished more. I wish I could go back there and tell Sharon Lynn that there's no chance a court would award custody of Ashley to that woman."

"You've warned her. We all have," Harlan Patrick reminded him. "Once she held that baby, there was no way that Sharon Lynn was going to do anything except see this through, even if she got hurt in the process. You get a lot of credit from all of us for sticking by her."

"I had no choice, either."

Harlan Patrick turned a suddenly serious look on him. "Are you planning on being there for her, no matter how this turns out?"

Cord knew what he was asking in his roundabout way. "If she'll let me, I'm in this for the duration."

"If I haven't said it before, I'll say it now. It was lucky for her you walked into Dolan's that night."

"No," Cord said softly. "I'm the lucky one." Now all he had to do was figure out how to put a positive spin on all of this for Sharon Lynn.

Waiting and wondering when the grandmother would appear and snatch the baby out of her arms was driving Sharon Lynn a little crazy. It hadn't helped matters that Cord had suddenly vanished. She hadn't seen him for two days now. Nor had he called. It made her realize just how much she had come to depend on his presence.

On the second day she finally broke down and called her mother.

"Darling, how are you?" Melissa asked. "I've been so worried about you. How's the baby?"

"The baby's fine. I'm fine."

"You don't sound all that terrific. What's really going on?"

"Actually I was just wondering if you'd seen Cord around the ranch the last couple of days."

"I haven't, but then I rarely see any of the men outside of your brother. Let me ask your father."

"No, don't," Sharon Lynn protested, only to realize she was talking to dead air. She could hear her mother calling out to her father as she walked through the house.

Since there was no way to prevent her mother from asking, she concluded she might as well stay on the line until she had an answer. It was several minutes before the phone was picked up again, but this time it was her father on the line.

"I hear you're looking for Cord," he said. "What's up? Is there a problem? Do you need one of us to come into town?"

"Of course not. Everything's fine here. I was just wondering about out there. Cord hasn't come down with the flu or something, has he?" She couldn't bring herself to voice her greatest fear, that he might have taken off.

"He's not sick. He's been at work right on time the past couple of days. I've got to admit he's damned good at it, too," he said grudgingly.

Sharon Lynn grinned at his disgruntled tone. "Were you hoping he'd be lousy, so you could fire him? Especially since you didn't manage to get him to quit."

"How'd you hear about that? Isn't there anything that happens on this ranch that the whole world doesn't know about?"

"Not when you've never learned to lower your voice," she teased. "That's why the whole town always knew exactly what was going on with you and Mom, even though you dragged her into the back room at Dolan's to have your battles."

"Okay, smarty, that's about enough out of you," her father grumbled, but he was chuckling. "As for Cord, I have no idea where he is, but I'm pretty sure he's with your brother. They've been thick as thieves the past couple of days."

That was the last thing Sharon Lynn expected him to say. What on earth were the two of them up to? Probably no good, given Harlan Patrick's current state of mind.

"Should I tell Cord you were looking for him?" her father asked.

"No, I'm sure I'll catch up with him sooner or later." She was about to hang up, when another thought occurred to her. "Dad, how is Harlan Patrick handling Laurie's leaving?"

"You mean after he got over the shock that she actually left?"

"Yes, though I still don't know why that caught him off guard. She'd been telling him for years she was going."

"His ego wouldn't let him believe she'd walk away from what they had."

"And his pride won't let him go after her," Sharon Lynn added.

"Why should he?" her father demanded. "She made her choice plain enough. I say good riddance."

"Dad, you don't mean that. You always liked Laurie. We all did."

"I don't like anyone who hurts one of my kids."

She grinned at his fierce tone. "Yeah, we do tend to stick together, don't we? Heck, I might even take a poke at Laurie myself if she turned up again. Ever think we might intimidate the daylights out of anyone who tries to break into our tight-knit circle?"

"Not the good ones," he retorted. "Nothing intimidates the ones worth having." He paused, then added thoughtfully, "Could be your Cord's one of those."

She was surprised at the praise, but found herself denying the relationship. "He's not my Cord."

"Uh-huh."

"He's not."

"Whatever you say, baby. You need anything, you let me know, okay?"

"Thanks, Daddy." As always, after talking with her father, Sharon Lynn felt safer, more reassured that all was right with her world. Despite her fierce protest to her father, she felt the same way with Cord around.

So where the devil was he? She didn't believe for an instant that he and Harlan Patrick were off on some male bonding ritual. Her brother had plenty of drinking buddies, if that's all he needed. No, this had something to do with the baby. She would stake her life on it.

She wandered into the bedroom to check on Ashley, then lingered just to watch her sleep. She couldn't resist trailing a finger over the soft curve of her cheek.

"Oh, sweetie, what's going to happen to you?" she murmured. "And what will happen to me, if you have to go?"

When she heard the knock on the front door, she jolted, then brushed away the tear that had been tracking down her cheek. When she finally got to the door, she found Cord waiting on the porch, his hands jammed into the pockets of his sheepskin-lined coat, his cheeks ruddy from the cold.

"Sorry to come by so late. Mind if I come in?"

"Of course not." She stepped aside, hoping he couldn't tell how relieved she was to see him. "Can I get you a cup of coffee? You look half-frozen."

He nodded. "Coffee would be great."

He followed her into the kitchen, but instead of sitting, he leaned back against the counter and watched her. Feeling his gaze following her made her movements jerky. She splashed the water as she poured it into the coffeemaker, then scattered coffee grounds every which way.

"Something wrong?" he asked finally, amusement threading through his voice.

"You're staring," she admitted. "It's making me nervous." She turned to scowl at him, only to catch a smile hovering on his lips. "You don't have to look so blasted pleased about it."

"Why not? I figure it has to be a coup to rattle your supreme self-confidence."

She stared at him. "Me?"

"Yes, you. You're unflappable. Didn't even let finding a baby on your doorstep cause you to miss a beat."

"Maybe I just don't let it show."

He seemed skeptical. "You pride yourself on your acting skills, darlin'?"

"No, of course not."

"Good, because you didn't manage to hide the fact that you'd been crying when I turned up here. What was that about?"

"Nothing."

"Our girl's okay?"

"Ashley's fine."

"Nothing new from Justin?"

"Nothing," she agreed.

"Then why the tears?"

"Something in my eye."

"Now, sweetheart, that's not acting," he chided. "That's outright lying."

"You don't have to know everything, you know."

"When it comes to you or Ashley, I do," he said matter-of-factly.

She decided enough was enough. It was time to turn the tables. "Does that work both ways?"

He suddenly looked uneasy and evaded her direct gaze. "I don't know what you mean."

"I mean do I have a right to know what's going on with you, if it has something to do with Ashley?"

"Of course."

"Then why don't you tell me what you and my brother have been up to the last couple of days?"

He grinned. "You missed me."

He said it with an irritating touch of triumph. "No more than I would a stray cat who'd been coming around and then suddenly vanished," she retorted.

"Is that right?"

"Do you intend to answer me or not?"

"Maybe. In time. Right now, I'll take some of that coffee, if it's ready."

Sharon Lynn chafed at the delay, but she poured the coffee, then plunked herself down at the kitchen table. "Talk to me, Cord Branson."

He pulled out a chair, turned it backward and straddled it. "It'll be my pleasure. Any particular topic you're interested in?"

"Cord!"

"Okay, okay. Your brother and I were over in Garden City doing a little nosing around about Hazel Murdock."

Her heartbeat seemed to thud dully. "And?"

"To tell you the truth, we didn't find out much."

"Is she coming after the baby or not?" she asked, unable to keep the frantic note out of her voice.

"I don't know. I purposely avoided talking directly to her."

Sharon Lynn buried her face in her hands. "Oh, God, she is. I just know it."

"You don't know any such thing. Be grateful that it's taking her so long to make up her mind."

"Why?"

"Because the longer it takes, the less likely the courts will view her as being the best person to raise the baby. They'll have to wonder why she waited, if she was so concerned about the baby's well-being."

Sharon Lynn sighed. It was something she hadn't even considered, but it made sense. "You're probably right. Why do you suppose she's waiting?"

"Having second thoughts would be my guess. From appearances, she's had a tough life. I can't imagine she's any too eager to disrupt her current routine to care for a baby."

"Why? What's her routine?"

"Let's just say she likes her afternoon toddy a little too much. There's a bartender in Garden City who says not a day passes that she's not in his establishment from sundown until he closes up."

His description was enough to solidify her resolve. She couldn't turn Ashley over to a woman like that. Somehow, some way, she would protect the baby. *Her* baby.

Oh, God, she thought as she realized what she'd been thinking. Her hand shook as she reached for her own cup of coffee. It had happened, just as everyone had warned it would.

That innocent little baby wasn't hers, she reminded herself sternly.

But that wasn't how it felt. In every way that counted, she felt as if she were Ashley's mother.

Chapter Twelve

It had been a stressful day from beginning to end. The baby had awakened fussy and remained that way. Advice had been offered from every single customer who'd passed through Dolan's. Sharon Lynn was ready to scream.

"She's teething," one person said.

"Too young," another had scoffed. "Probably colic."

"Maybe a little winter cold," suggested another.

When Cord walked in just after five, she glowered at him. "Don't you start."

Rather than asking what the devil was wrong with her, he bypassed her completely and went to pluck the miserable baby from the portable crib. Only when he was pacing up and down with the baby gazing at him adoringly—and without a single tear—did he turn to Sharon Lynn.

"Rough day?"

"Oh, go to blazes," she muttered, uncertain whether the remark was directed at him or the traitorous child in his arms. He did have a way with the baby that was enviable.

He grinned and tickled Ashley, who gurgled delightedly. "Guess so," he concluded, then gazed at the child in his arms. "Were you the cause of that?"

The baby responded with a series of incomprehensible sounds. Cord nodded as if he'd understood every word. "Guess what she needs is a night on the town," he concluded. "What do you think, little angel? Should we take her out to dinner?"

"I'm not going out to dinner," Sharon Lynn grumbled. "I'm going to go home and crawl into bed and pretend I've never met either one of you."

Cord gave her a look that would have singed steel. "Works for me. The crawling into bed part, anyway."

"You're not invited," she shot back, then sighed. "Sorry. I shouldn't be taking this out on you."

"I can take it," he said easily.

She sank down onto a stool at the counter and regarded him wistfully. "I just don't get it. I have done everything I know how to do all day long and I could not get her to settle down. You walk in here and, bingo, she's smiling and babbling."

"You know, darlin', there are just some females who respond to a man's touch. If you'd like, I can hold you and see if you won't feel better, too."

Ah, the power of suggestion. She instantly thought of what it would be like to have those powerful arms of his folded tightly around her, of how reassuring it would be to rest her head against his chest, to listen to the beat of his heart. She imagined being surrounded by the clean, soap-and-water, all-male scent of him. It was tempting, all right. A little too tempting. And he, blast him, clearly knew exactly how easily he could get to her.

Up until now, she had been very careful not to cross the line with Cord, not to let him think for even a second, that there would ever be anything between the two of them. Okay, there had been a kiss or two, but kisses happened all the time. Chaste kisses. Experimental kisses. Even the kind of breath-stealing kisses she'd shared with Cord didn't have to foreshadow a relationship.

She owed it to herself and to him not to muddy the waters now, just because she was exhausted and desperately in need of a hug. If she intended to spend the rest of her life single, she couldn't start leaning on someone else the minute things got a little rough.

"I think I'll pass," she said eventually, but even she could hear that her voice sounded choked and thick with longing.

"You sure about that, darlin'?"

"Oh, yes," she whispered fervently.

"You wouldn't be scared now, would you? We were just talking about a little old hug, maybe an innocent little massage to get rid of the tension in those shoulders." His gaze was as innocent as a lamb's. "What's the harm in that?"

There was absolutely nothing wrong with a hug—if it came from a friend and not a man whose touches were beginning to worry her. She couldn't pinpoint precisely when the effect of a casual caress had turned alarmingly dangerous, but it had happened, all right. Her pulse was zinging around right now like an Indy 500 leader in the final lap.

There was certainly nothing inappropriate about a massage, either—especially one administered by a professional and not by a man whose intentions were not entirely honorable, if that gleam in his eyes was anything to judge by.

"No harm," she told him finally. "But I'll pass just the same."

He gave the baby a sorrowful look. "Angel pie, I don't know what we're going to do about her," he lamented. "She's a very uptight lady."

Sharon Lynn didn't especially like the label. "Well, you'd

be uptight, too, if you were worried night and day that Ashley was going to be snatched away from you."

His expression sobered at once. "Now that's where you're wrong," he said, clearly insulted by the criticism. "I am worried half to death about what the future holds when it comes to this baby girl. She means as much to me as she does to you. I don't want you ever thinking otherwise."

She winced at his tone, which was a mix of anger and hurt. "I'm sorry. I know you care about her. I just figured it wouldn't be the same for you."

"Well, it is," he retorted. "Why the hell do you think Harlan Patrick and I went poking around over in Garden City? I don't want this baby to wind up in the custody of the wrong person any more than you do."

"I'm sorry," she said again.

As if she sensed the tension suddenly brewing in the air between the adults, the baby began to whimper. At once, Cord's expression softened. "*Shh*, sweetie. It's okay. We're just having a little discussion. Sometimes grown-ups don't agree about things. It's a fact of life."

Sharon Lynn couldn't help smiling as the baby stared at him quizzically. "You talk to her as if she can understand every word."

"Maybe she does," he countered. "Ashley's a smart one. After all, who knows better than she does that all it really takes to be happy is a full tummy and someone to love her? Maybe we'd all be better off if we were wise enough to stick with those priorities."

She sensed yet another implied criticism in his words. "And I'm not wise enough to take you up on your offer, is that it? Do you honestly think you can make everything all right by taking me to dinner and giving me a shoulder to lean on?"

He shrugged. "Seems to me it's worth a try."

Maybe he was right. Maybe she was being uptight and skittish over nothing. Maybe he only intended kindness and she was reading way too much into it.

"Okay, okay, I'll go to dinner."

"Now there's a gracious acceptance, if ever I've heard one."

"Take it or leave it."

"Oh, I'll take it," he said, then inquired innocently, "Want the hug before or after?"

"We'll discuss it after," she said. Maybe in a couple of months, she thought. Better yet, a couple of years, when she could get a sharper grip on this tug of longing that kept sneaking up on her when she was around him.

"Your friend here is not very spontaneous," he told the baby, then regarded Sharon Lynn with amusement. "But I can work with that."

That was exactly what she was afraid of. If she let her guard down with Cord Branson for even an instant, things were going to get so spontaneous, so deliciously wicked, she might be thrown permanently off-kilter. She might even start to care. And that, she had vowed on the night Kyle was killed, was never going to happen again. She reminded herself that it was essential that no one—not that precious little baby and certainly not Cord—ever mean that much to her again.

She gazed at Ashley then, felt a lump forming in her throat and realized yet again that it was too late. The vow was already broken. Ashley had breached all of her defenses and Cord was very much on the verge of doing the same.

The realization left her feeling shaken. Though Cord did his best to cheer her up over a spaghetti dinner, she barely touched her food. Only because the baby was content in her carrier on the seat beside her did she manage to resist the urge to sweep her up and cling to her.

"You're a tough audience," Cord grumbled when yet another of his attempts to coax a smile from her fell flat.

"Sorry," she apologized halfheartedly. "I'm not very good company."

"Maybe I'm just not enough of a distraction."

The rueful comment did exactly as he'd apparently intended. Her gaze met his for the first time all evening. As their gazes clashed, she realized that Cord could be a very fine distraction if only she'd let him. There was an unmistakable sizzle between them, though she'd done everything in her power to ignore it.

"Don't sell yourself short," she muttered. "You could distract a saint."

He grinned. "Now that's a promising remark. Are you actually flirting with me, Sharon Lynn?"

"Absolutely not," she insisted as if horrified, though she had to swallow a laugh at his blatant enthusiasm for the idea. There were some things about which Cord Branson was totally transparent...and others about which he was totally inscrutable.

He looked disappointed now. "I wish you would do a little flirting now and again. It might be good for you."

"For me?" She all but hooted at that, then asked, "What's the matter. Can't you take being resistible?"

"I can take it. I'm just not crazy about it." His expression sobered. "At least not where you're concerned."

"Don't," she protested, when it seemed the conversation had taken too serious a turn.

"Don't what?"

"Don't go there," she scolded. "And don't pretend you don't know what I mean."

He seemed duly chastened by that. "Okay, then, no more teasing, even if it does make you smile."

"Other things can make me smile."

"Name one. I've been telling jokes all evening and nothing."

She grinned. "Maybe that should tell you something about the quality of your jokes."

He shook his head. "Now you're resorting to insults. I'm crushed."

"It would take a bulldozer to crush your ego."

He reached across the table and took her hand in his. Before she could blink, he'd lifted it to his lips and brushed a kiss across her knuckles. Her knees actually went weak at that. She'd always thought that was just a romantic notion that never actually happened. Now she knew better.

"You're wrong about that," he insisted. "You can do it with a word."

Something in his voice told Sharon Lynn he was telling the raw, unvarnished truth, that she had the power to shatter him with nothing more than a word. It was a power she didn't want and yet, on some level, somewhere deep inside, the knowledge filled her with a kind of satisfaction.

"Cord…" she began, but didn't know how to go on.

"It's okay, darlin'. There's nothing to be said about the truth. It just is."

The only thing he might have said that would have troubled her more was that he loved her. Gazing into his eyes, she had to wonder if that admission might not be right around the corner. What worried her even more was the awareness that a part of her yearned for the moment when he'd say it.

Over the next few days Cord did his best to keep Sharon Lynn distracted while they waited for the blood test results or the appearance of Hazel Murdock. He wasn't sure which he dreaded more. The blood test could confirm the woman's claim to the baby, but her appearance in Los Piños would mean that she was serious about taking Ashley home with her. How would he be able to bear it? How would Sharon Lynn?

She would be devastated. She was already as jittery as the proverbial cat on a hot tin roof. He'd seen her startled expression every time a female stranger had walked into Dolan's. There was no mistaking the flare of panic in her eyes when a middle-aged woman she didn't know offered to hold the baby while Sharon Lynn prepared her meal.

"She's fine in her crib," Cord overheard Sharon Lynn saying emphatically as he walked in.

"Oh, but I don't mind at all," the woman insisted, starting around the counter to pick up the baby.

"No!"

Sharon Lynn's voice was so harsh that the woman instantly looked affronted and Ashley began to wail. Cord stepped in to smooth things over. He scooped the baby up and was rewarded with a dazzling smile. He turned and winked at the woman.

"Don't mind Sharon Lynn. You know how protective new mamas are." He figured it was a stretch of the truth that was called for under the circumstances.

"Yes, I'm sorry," Sharon Lynn apologized at once, apparently somewhat reassured by Cord's friendly intervention that this woman wasn't Hazel Murdock.

"Of course," the woman said. "I shouldn't have pushed. It's just that I miss my own grandchildren so much. I'm on the way home after visiting with my sons and their families and all of a sudden I'm aching to hold a baby again. After your own kids are grown, you forget what it's like. Then when you're reminded of it, you miss it."

Cord shot a quick look at Sharon Lynn, judged her expression to be one of understanding and compassion, then turned and offered the baby to the woman. "Here you go. I'll take her back as soon as your meal's ready."

Cord watched with amusement as Sharon Lynn prepared the woman's dinner with lightning quick speed. She served it with a warm smile, but there was no mistaking the relief on her face when Cord took the baby back and settled her on his lap. He had a feeling if more customers hadn't come in just then, Sharon Lynn would have insisted on taking the baby herself.

After everyone had left, he regarded her worriedly. "This can't go on," he said quietly. "You can't be in such a state that you're a wreck every time a stranger walks through the door. If you keep on snapping at the customers, it won't be long before you don't have any."

"Can you blame me? I never know when this Murdock woman will show up."

"Or if she will," he reminded her gently. "Maybe she's waiting for an official confirmation from Justin. When are the blood test results due?"

"I called Lizzy earlier. She checked with the lab. They should be back any day now." She gave Cord a haunted look. "I don't know if I want to know the results or not."

"Of course you do," he said at once. "We have to know, darlin', one way or another. The sooner the better, if you ask me."

"I didn't ask you," she snapped, slapping her dishrag onto the counter and walking away.

Cord waited right where he was, knowing that pretty soon she would collect herself and come back filled with regret. He also knew that she was as close as anyone could be to the breaking point.

Maybe he should consider taking Sharon Lynn to Garden City so she could see Hazel Murdock for herself. At least that would stop these panicky moments around the customers. She would have a face to go with the name of the woman she obviously considered to be her mortal enemy.

Or maybe it was time he put in a call to Lizzy himself and pleaded with her to put a rush on getting those results. That, at least, was something he could do right now.

He was about to reach for the phone when Sharon Lynn came back, picked up the dishcloth and began methodically wiping the counter again. For several minutes she avoided his gaze and he let her.

"Your quarrel's not with me," he reminded her finally.

She lifted her chin and regarded him with tear-filled eyes. "I know," she whispered. "I'm just so scared."

He beckoned to her. "Come here."

She came to stand directly in front of him, with the counter still squarely between them. He held back the urge to grin at the obvious distancing. Instead he shook his head and beckoned again.

"Around here."

She hesitated, then finally circled the end of the counter and came closer. He tucked the baby securely on one side and opened his other arm. "Come on, darlin'."

A smile quivered on her lips. "Another hug?"

He nodded. "That's right. Grin and bear it."

She stepped into his embrace eagerly enough then and rested her head on his shoulder. He felt a sigh shudder through her, felt tears dampen his shirt. He had to force himself not to think beyond that. He couldn't allow the awareness of her scent, of her warmth, of her curves to sweep him beyond giving comfort and on to wanting.

Even though holding her was sheer torture, he knew

that not holding her, seeing her suffering all alone would be worse torment. Whether she knew it or not, she needed him, and for now that had to be enough.

When she was calmer, when her tears had dried and her shoulders were resolutely squared again, she stepped back and gave him a wobbly smile.

"I seem to be doing that a lot lately."

"What?"

"Crying on your shoulder."

"I offered."

"But it's not fair. I need to handle things on my own, not be relying on you."

"You are handling things on your own," he commented. "You've taken on the care of a new baby without even having a moment to prepare for it. You've fit her in with your life with no promise that she'll stay and the very real danger that she'll go. That's an enormous amount of stress to be under. Seems to me it only makes good sense to share a little of it with whoever's handy and willing."

She regarded him with curiosity. "You really don't mind, do you?"

He decided on a little dose of straightforward honesty. "To tell you the truth, it feels good to be needed. Being an independent loner has its merits, of course, but it's always seemed to me that the good Lord put us on this earth to go through life two-by-two so there'd be someone to count on when times got tough."

"I can't let that happen," she protested. "I can't count on you."

"Why not? I'm here. I'm not going anywhere."

"You can't guarantee that. No one can."

She was thinking of Kyle Mason, of course, the man who'd promised to love, honor and cherish her all the days of their lives, only to leave her in fewer than twenty-four hours. How could any woman allow herself to have faith in the future after that?

"No," he agreed at last. "I can't guarantee that, but I can swear that as long as it's in my power to be here for you, I will be. No human being can do more."

"That's just it," she said wearily. "It's not you I don't trust. It's fate."

Her bleak, worn-down expression was almost more than Cord could bear, but she was right. He didn't have an argument to counter that. Only time would prove to her that he meant what he said and even a dozen tomorrows or a thousand wouldn't be enough, when the day after that remained uncertain. That required a huge leap of faith and she wasn't yet ready to take it.

It was possible, he admitted with regret, that she would never be able to take such a leap. But he would wait, he promised himself and her, just in case the time came when she could.

Chapter Thirteen

Sharon Lynn had fallen asleep the instant she got home from work on Friday. She was awakened by the sound of raised voices on her front porch. Familiar voices. Lizzy's, Justin's, Dani's and then Cord's. There could only be one topic that would have stirred them all to such a frenzy. Panic whipped through her, followed by a whispered cry of denial. Finally she forced herself to cross the room and fling open the front door.

"If this has anything to do with me, don't you think you should bring it inside?" she inquired politely.

Four startled, guilt-stricken faces turned her way.

"I thought you were going to take a nap when you got home from work," Cord muttered, coming to stand beside her in what struck her as an almost symbolic show of unity.

"I did, but all the chattering out here woke me up."

"Sorry," Justin said. "We'll come back." He looked all too eager to make a break for it.

She latched on to his arm. "Oh, no. You're not getting away that easily. Inside, now! All of you," she added when it looked as if Dani might creep right on back to her veterinary clinic via the entrance on the opposite side of the house.

Everyone dutifully trooped inside.

"Sit down," Cord encouraged, guiding her toward the sofa.

Sharon Lynn sat and was promptly surrounded. Cord sat on her right, Dani on her left. Lizzy took up guard behind her. That left Justin as the outcast.

"I need coffee," he grumbled and headed for the kitchen.

"I thought he'd be better at breaking bad news by now," Sharon Lynn observed wryly. "That is what has you all in a tizzy, right? The blood test results came back?"

Lizzy nodded. "It's a match, at least enough of a match to take into court. Hazel Murdock is Ashley's grandma."

Sharon Lynn had been telling herself she was prepared for this, but she'd been lying. She felt as if she'd just taken a blow to her midsection. She swallowed hard against the bile rising in her throat.

"What happens now?" she asked, folding her hands together tightly in her lap. Cord reached over and covered them with his own hand. To her surprise, his touch helped. She felt, if not reassured, at least a little stronger because of it.

"Justin says…" Lizzy began, only to have Justin finally emerge from the kitchen and interrupt her.

"I'll tell her. It means that I have to go to Garden City and talk to Hazel Murdock again and pass along the good news," he said with a wry grimace.

"And then?"

"And then, since there's still no sign of her daughter, the ball's in her court."

"She could decide to let matters rest, then?" Cord asked.

"She could. If that's her choice, then Sharon Lynn could ask the court to let Ashley remain with her."

Hope stirred inside her. "Could I adopt her?"

"In time, once the court is satisfied that every effort's been made to find the real mother."

She took a deep breath and forced herself to ask the question that had been plaguing her day and night. "Could Hazel Murdock just walk into Dolan's one day, say she wants the baby and walk out with her?"

Justin shook his head. "No, she'll have to petition the court. The judge has jurisdiction in this matter, since he's already put her in foster care with you."

"Then if Mrs. Murdock isn't capable..." Her voice cracked. "If she's awful..." She met Cord's gaze, found reassurance there, then turned back to Justin. "Then I could fight her?"

"You might not win, but you could. If there are real grounds, then you could."

"There are grounds," Cord muttered darkly.

Justin's gaze zeroed in on him. "Now how would you know that?"

"I just know, that's all," Cord retorted defiantly.

"Dammit, I knew it," Justin exploded. "You hired that private eye, didn't you?"

"No."

Justin's gaze narrowed. "Then you and Harlan Patrick did the sleuthing yourselves, the way you'd threatened to."

When Cord remained stubbornly silent, Justin shook his head. "Dammit, I should have seen that coming. I should have pushed when Harlan Patrick evaded all my questions."

"The point is, there is evidence that she's unfit to care for a baby. Any social worker on the planet would have to see that," Cord said violently.

"Look, I can't argue with you about that," Justin soothed. "I'm on your side here. All I'm trying to say is that blood ties hold weight with the court. Plus Sharon Lynn would be a single mom."

"And Mrs. Murdock wouldn't be?" Sharon Lynn retorted. "Or have I missed something about the presence of a Mr. Murdock?"

Justin rubbed his forehead as if trying to fend off a throbbing headache. "No, there's no Mr. Murdock. I'm just trying to point out that it won't be cut-and-dried. It won't be easy. Sweetie, this could get downright ugly."

"I don't care about easy or ugly," Sharon Lynn insisted. "All I care about is keeping that baby away from a woman who can't care for her properly. If she could…" She swallowed hard. "If she could, as difficult as it would be, I wouldn't fight her."

Cord gave her hands a squeeze. "It's okay, darlin'. We're getting a little ahead of ourselves here. There's no guarantee she's going to try to take the baby. We'll know more after Justin sees her, right, Justin?"

Her cousin nodded.

"When will that be?" Cord asked.

"The sooner the better," Sharon Lynn said. "I'm not sure how much more of this I can take."

Justin came over to hunker down in front of her. When his gaze was level with hers, he regarded her sympathetically.

"No time like the present," he told her. "Try not to worry. I'll do everything I can to make sure Ashley winds up where she'll get the best possible care."

"I know you will." Tears welled up in her eyes and spilled down her cheeks just the same as she watched him leave. Then she turned instinctively toward Cord, who opened his arms and enfolded her in them.

"Don't cry, sweetheart," he murmured. "Please don't cry."

She felt Lizzy reach down and give her shoulder a squeeze. Dani pressed a kiss against her cheek and then they were gone and she was alone with Cord. She drew on his strength. Despite the turmoil of the past few minutes, despite the fear that was ricocheting through her, she felt surprisingly calm in his embrace. She had spent her entire life surrounded by strong men, but none were any more steadfast than this man who had been a stranger only a few short weeks ago. Whatever happened in the future, she would always be grateful to him for that.

As he held her, she regretted more than ever that she couldn't repay his kindness by giving him the ranch he'd always dreamed of owning, land she had no need for herself. And yet, she knew that even if she hadn't already promised that ranch to another man, Cord wouldn't have accepted it. He wasn't here for her now because he expected payment. He was here because he cared, for her and for Ashley. He was here, because that was the kind of sweet, generous man he was, though she had a feeling he would have hated either label.

"I wish…" she began, the words a muffled whisper against his chest.

"What do you wish?" he asked, smoothing a hand over her hair.

"That there was some way I could thank you, some way to show you how grateful I am for what you've done the past few weeks."

"No thanks are necessary."

She was struck by a sudden idea. "I could talk to Daddy

and Grandpa Harlan. Part of White Pines will be mine one day. I could sign that over to you."

Cord released her as if she were suddenly too hot to hold. "Forget it," he said.

"But it's a wonderful idea," she said, warming to it. "Kyle's land is promised, but I certainly don't need my share of White Pines."

He regarded her with a wry expression. "I can just imagine how your father and grandfather would react to this. If your father blew a gasket over the possibility that I might be after your late husband's land, just what do you think he'd have to say if you presented him with this crazy idea? White Pines belongs to your family, Sharon Lynn. Someday it will be your children's heritage. You can't just go giving that away."

"But Daddy would have to listen to me," she argued. "I owe you."

"You owe me nothing," he insisted. "When will you get that through your head?"

"But…"

He shook his head. "I can see there's no reasoning with you, so I'll just have to come up with another way to shut you up," he said grimly, bending down and sealing her mouth shut with a kiss.

Sharon Lynn's senses reeled. At first she blamed that as much on the afternoon's emotional upheaval as Cord's skill, but when her skin began to heat, when her heartbeat accelerated to a brisk pace and her breath caught in her throat, she had to admit it was more than that.

In fact, she couldn't seem to recall exactly how the kiss had begun or what they'd been discussing that was so all-fired important. All she knew was that his lips on hers were magic. The touch of his tongue inflamed. His hands, tentatively at first and then with more certainty, stroked and caressed until her body responded in ways that shocked her. No man's touch had ever been so deft, so arousing. She was trembling with the kind of longing, the kind of desperate urgency that she'd been convinced she would never feel again.

It would be so easy to let this exquisite tension escalate until it was out of control. It would feel so good to welcome Cord inside her, to give in to desire and forget everything else. She would welcome that momentary oblivion, that ecstatic release.

Just when she was on the verge of making a conscious decision to let Cord make love to her, he uttered a harsh groan and pulled away. She blinked in surprise at the sudden absence of heat, the sudden withdrawal of his weight.

When she dared to open her eyes, she found him seated beside her, a careful few inches away, raking a hand through his hair and looking as distraught as she'd ever seen him.

"Cord?"

"I'm sorry."

She swallowed hard against a tide of disappointment. Apparently there would be no quick and urgent release. "Sorry?" she repeated, her voice heavy with her own regrets.

"That should never have happened, not now, not when you're so vulnerable."

There it was again, that deeply ingrained sense of honor, that evidence of the type of man he was. At some other time in her life, she would have regretted that there was no room in her heart for a man like that. Now, determined that there would be *no* man in her life ever again, she regretted only the immediate loss of his nearness, of the comfort he'd been offering before passion had intruded.

She reached out a hand, but he shied away from it.

"I'd better go," he said.

"Why?" she demanded, though the answer was obvious.

"Because if I stay, I can't swear that I'll stay away from you. Not tonight."

"But you'll be back?"

The expression on his face turned rueful. "Oh, yeah. I'll be back. If there's one thing that's become crystal clear to me since I met you, it's that I'll never be able to stay away. You can count on it."

She pulled herself together. She drew her knees up to her chest and wrapped her arms around them as he headed for the door. "Then that's what I'll do," she said. He turned at her softly spoken words and her gaze locked with his as she added, "I'll count on it."

She didn't stop to analyze where it would lead, this counting on Cord. All she knew was that at this moment, with so much uncertainty in her life, relying on him was as natural as breathing.

What the hell was wrong with him? Cord wondered as he sought out a place to get a drink and a grip on his rampaging hormones. He had almost made a costly mistake. He had almost seduced Sharon Lynn into making love with him. For a few incredible moments, he had known what it was like to caress her skin, to feel her tremble in his arms. As lost as they'd both been on a sea of sensations, it wouldn't have taken much to carry them the rest of the way. She'd wanted it, too, wanted it every bit as badly as he had. He'd seen that much in her crushed expression when he'd pulled away.

But it would have been wrong, he reminded himself, a temporary bliss at best. She would never have forgiven him or herself.

No, when he finally—and inevitably—made love to Sharon Lynn, it would be when she wasn't feeling so lost and alone that she reached for him in despair. It would be when she wanted him and him alone, beyond reason, and because she could no longer be without him. He had to reassure himself over and over that that time would come. Otherwise, he truly would have cursed tonight's lost opportunity.

He gravitated toward the Italian restaurant, where he could order a pizza and a beer and hope that the two combined would satiate at least one of his hungers. The other was a lost cause, at least for now.

He was halfway through his beer and about to take his first bite of pizza, when Harlan Patrick turned up, looking every bit as down in the mouth as Cord felt.

Cord gestured toward the opposite side of the booth. "Have a seat."

Harlan Patrick managed a halfhearted grin and slid in. "I'm surprised to find you in here."

"Why is that?"

"The family hotline is burning up with the news about Hazel Murdock being Ashley's grandma. I figured you'd be with Sharon Lynn."

"I was."

Harlan Patrick regarded him speculatively. "She throw you out?"

Cord grinned. "No. Sorry to disappoint you."

"Then that brings us right back to where we started. What are you doing here?"

"Taking a time-out."

The response drew a knowing chuckle. "Being honorable is the pits, isn't it? I used to follow that path with Laurie and look where it got me."

"It sure as hell doesn't keep you warm at night, that's for sure," Cord acknowledged.

"Of course," Harlan Patrick added thoughtfully, "in this case, it can also prevent you being run down by a whole slew of gun-toting Adams men."

"Something I never considered," Cord confessed.

"Really?"

"Not even once."

"Then this was all about doing what's best for Sharon Lynn?"

Cord shrugged. "Could be."

"Fascinating." He shook his head and gave Cord a sympathetic look. "You're a goner, man."

"Could be."

Before Harlan Patrick could explore that, which he certainly seemed eager to do, Justin strolled in looking every bit as glum as the two of them. He nudged his cousin over and slid in beside him.

"Well, that was fun," he said, ordering his own beer.

"How'd Hazel Murdock take the news?" Cord asked.

"About like you'd expect. She grumbled about her tramp of a daughter, moaned a little about fate, then vowed to do her duty by the poor little tyke."

"Do you think she'll turn up?"

"Oh, yeah," Justin said. "Especially now that she's aware that her precious grandbaby is living with an Adams. Big mistake on my part."

Cord's pulse began to thud dully. "What do you mean?"

"I mean that I made the tactical error of mentioning who was caring for the baby," Justin admitted. "I was hoping to show her that she could rest easy if she decided to leave the baby right where she is."

Even Harlan Patrick groaned at that.

"How did she respond?" Cord asked.

"Well, obviously that little tidbit fascinated her. It wouldn't surprise me at all if she came over here, raised a ruckus, turned Sharon Lynn's life upside down, then allowed herself to be persuaded to disappear from the baby's life for a hefty settlement."

"She'd sell the kid?" Harlan Patrick asked, looking as disgusted as Cord felt.

"Like I said, it wouldn't surprise me if she tried," Justin replied.

"But that would play right into our hands," Cord said. "That would prove to the court that she shouldn't have custody, that she's nothing more than an opportunist."

Justin nodded. "I agree, but you're forgetting one thing. In the meantime, she'll terrify Sharon Lynn into thinking that she's going to lose the baby. She'll be willing to pay her off, just to make sure she goes away."

"We'll just have to see that doesn't happen," Harlan Patrick said. "Cord, you can get through to Sharon Lynn, can't you? You can make her see that it'll be for the best to go through all the legal hoops, right?"

"I can try." He paused as something Justin had said earlier in the day came back to him. It had been nagging him for hours. "Do you think Sharon Lynn could have difficulty getting permanent custody because she's single?"

"I don't really know," Justin admitted. "I brought it up because it's a possibility, especially with long lists of couples waiting to adopt."

"But she's the one who's been taking care of the baby all along," Cord protested. "She's the one who saved her. If anyone has a right to that child, it's your cousin."

"The two of you did that," Justin stated. "And I agree with you. I'm just telling you that Sharon Lynn got temporary custody because of the circumstances and because Grandpa Harlan interceded on her behalf. When it comes to outright adoption, the rules may not be the same at all."

"She'll have Janet on her side," Harlan Patrick reminded them. "There's not a better attorney in the state than grand-daddy's wife. And she'll have the Adams name going for her."

"She'd better be careful how she uses that," Justin warned. "It's a double-edged sword. Yes, the name is highly respected, but the last thing she needs is for people to get the idea that it's being used to bypass the system. She could wind up caught in some sort of public backlash if the media latches on to the story. I'm just grateful that there's been nothing at all in the local paper about this from the very beginning."

"That was probably Grandpa Harlan's doing," Harlan Patrick said. "Janet probably put a bug in his ear about the long-range implications of getting the media involved and he probably asked Mort over at the *Journal* to lay off the story."

Cord nodded. "I'd wondered why there hadn't been a mention of it. It's got all the ingredients of a big story. Abandoned baby rescued from a blizzard, the Adams name, et-cetera. It wasn't like anybody tried to keep it a secret. The local paper had to know every detail."

"Which proves my point," Harlan Patrick said. "I detect Grandpa Harlan's hand in it with Janet nudging him."

Cord glanced at Justin. "What do we do now?"

"We wait."

That wasn't the advice he'd wanted to hear. If there was one thing Cord was downright lousy at doing, it was waiting. Especially when an alternative plan had been nagging him for the past half hour.

He pulled some money from his wallet and tossed the bills on the table. "I'm out of here."

Two pairs of eyes regarded him suspiciously.

"To go where?" Justin demanded.

"Home, of course," he replied innocently.

"Whose home?"

"Oh, for heaven's sakes," Harlan Patrick muttered. "Stop being a cop, Justin. It's none of our business whose home he's going to."

"It sure as hell is, if it's Sharon Lynn's," Justin retorted, his gaze lethal.

"Settle down," Cord soothed. "Not that it's any of your business, but I'm going to the bunkhouse at White Pines. I've got some thinking to do."

And if he reached the same conclusion overnight that he'd reached just now, he'd have a plan that just might solve all their problems.

Chapter Fourteen

A restless night of tossing and turning and mulling over the idea he'd had while talking to Harlan Patrick and Justin left Cord in desperate need of coffee first thing in the morning. He was about to pour himself a cup, when he looked up and saw Harlan Adams coming through the bunkhouse door. He looked like a man on a mission.

His eyes lit up when he saw the pot in Cord's hand. "You got another cup around this place? I wouldn't mind some decent coffee for a change."

"I can find the cup, but I wouldn't call this decent. It's yesterday's mud."

"It has caffeine, doesn't it? Believe me, that's all that matters."

The comment reminded Cord that caffeine was a clear violation of the older man's diet. He turned and dumped everything left in the pot into the sink before he could be tempted into caving in.

"Now why'd you go and do a durn fool thing like that?" Harlan Adams demanded with an indignant expression.

"To save us both a lot of aggravation."

With a sigh of resignation, Harlan sank into a chair. "I

suppose it was the smart thing to do, from your point of view," he conceded.

"Yours, too. From what I hear, your wife has her spies everywhere."

The older man chuckled. "You're right about that, especially around here."

Cord sat down opposite him. "What brings you by here this early? Is there something I can help you with?"

"That depends."

"On?"

"Just how involved you are with my granddaughter."

Uh-oh, Cord thought. "Involved?" he repeated cautiously.

"You're a smart man. Do I have to spell it out for you?"

"I think maybe you do."

"Are you in love with her? I know what my eyes tell me, but I want to hear it from you."

"Don't you think that's something I should be discussing with her, not you?"

His expression turned impatient at the evasion. "Oh, stop beating around the bush, boy. Any fool can see you care about Sharon Lynn. I'm just asking if it's walking-down-the-aisle serious."

Cord gave up the pretense. "Okay, yes. I'm serious. But it's way too soon for her to believe that. There's her past, for one thing. And the timing. It hasn't been all that long since I turned up here."

Harlan gave an approving nod. "Good, you can see that, too. I knew you had a head on your shoulders. Trouble is, there's no time to waste."

Cord stared. "Excuse me?"

"I've been mulling over this mess with little Ashley," Harlan explained. "It seems to me like the only sensible thing to do would be for the two of you to get married and adopt that child yourselves. Any judge would see that the two of you'd be better parents for her than that drunken old crone over in Garden City."

Maybe if he hadn't reached the exact same conclusion himself, Cord would have been shocked by the suggestion. As it was, it was just more proof that his thinking hadn't been clouded by pure lust or his powerful longing for family. He glanced up and saw that the older man was watching him expectantly.

"Well, what do you think?" Harlan demanded. "Will you do it?"

"With all due respect, sir, I'm not the problem. It's Sharon Lynn who's going to require some convincing. In case you haven't noticed, the woman has a mind of her own."

"Family curse," Harlan conceded. "We're all stubborn as the day is long, but I've thought about that. I'll talk to her. She'll listen to me. Always has. She trusts me to say what's what."

Cord held up his hand. "I appreciate the offer, but not this time. If there's any proposing to be done, I'll do it myself."

To Cord's relief, Harlan didn't put up a fuss about being left out. He just gave Cord a measured look and advised, "Well, you'd best get a move on then. Once that old hag shows up and starts making waves, there won't be a second to waste."

The warning made perfect sense, but it wasn't going to be that simple. "I understand what you're saying," Cord agreed, "but tactically, it seems to me the only way it's going to work is for your granddaughter to be desperate. I think I have to wait until Hazel Murdock puts in an appearance."

Harlan nodded slowly, his expression thoughtful. "You could be right. Sharon Lynn has dug in her heels when it comes to love. After that tragedy with Kyle, she's made up her mind never to marry. She won't say yes just like that, no matter how much she might want to."

"Could I ask you a question?" Cord ventured.

"Of course you can."

"Doesn't it bother you just the teensiest bit that you're all but pushing your granddaughter into marriage to a man she hasn't even said she loved?"

Harlan Adams laughed at that. "Like I said, she's stubborn. She won't be pushed, unless it's what she wants deep down. I happen to think it is. I've seen the way she looks at you, the way you look at her. More important, I've seen the way you treat her. When a man treats a woman with that much respect, that much caring, the love is there. All it needs is a little time and nurturing. I'm just trying to make sure it gets the jump-start required."

"Maybe the time and nurturing ought to come before we've said our vows," Cord suggested. It was a worrisome idea that had plagued him all night long. He was hoping Harlan Adams would have something to say that would reassure him.

"If the circumstances allowed for that, maybe so," Harlan agreed. "But we don't have that luxury. Even if there weren't little Ashley to consider, there's me. I'm an old man. Ever since Kyle died, Sharon Lynn's been fixated on this notion that she's not cut out for marriage. I'm not sure I'll last long enough for her to figure out for herself that she's all wrong."

He gave Cord a conspiratorial grin. "I'm counting on you to move this along."

"I'll do my best, sir, but you'll have to leave the timing to me," Cord insisted.

This time Harlan looked vaguely disgruntled at being

forced out of the driver's seat, but he finally grumbled his assent. "Just get the job done. That's all I care about."

It was all that mattered to Cord, too. But something told him it was going to be a whole lot trickier than sidling up to Sharon Lynn, going down on one knee and popping the question. The woman was going to have to be desperate for it to work. That might not do a lot for his ego, but at this point he'd be grateful for just about any state of mind that allowed him to get past those rock-solid defenses of hers.

For the next week, Cord bided his time. Knowing that Harlan Adams was anxiously awaiting signs of progress didn't ease the pressure any. He expected to be summoned for progress reports on a daily basis, but the old man restricted himself to dropping by every day or two instead. He was clearly growing dissatisfied with the lack of an engagement announcement.

The time Cord spent with Sharon Lynn and Ashley left him restless and uneasy. He was tempted more than once to announce his plan and let the chips fall where they may, but there was too much riding on the outcome for him to speak out that impulsively. Once more, his patience was being tested to the limits. Maybe all this waiting around was building character, but it felt a whole lot more like torment.

It was another week after that before Hazel Murdock finally staggered into Dolan's late one afternoon to see her precious grandbaby. It was the first time he'd gotten a decent up-close look at her and what he saw wasn't reassuring. Though he guessed her age to be under fifty, the deep lines in her face, the perpetual frown and hair that was more gray than bottle-blond suggested she'd paid a heavy price for every year she'd lived. There wasn't a speck of joy in her expression, not even when she got a first look at her granddaughter.

As Cord had predicted, she was drunk and her language was coarse, but one thing was clear. She was grimly determined to take the baby home with her—or so she claimed. There was a wily gleam in her eye when she looked at Sharon Lynn that suggested otherwise.

Sharon Lynn clung protectively to the baby and cast a desperate look at Cord. He gave her shoulder a reassuring squeeze, then latched on to Mrs. Murdock's elbow and guided her to a place at the counter. She perched on the stool, squared her shoulders and clung to her worn purse as if she feared it might be snatched at any second. There was something a little sad and pathetic about her, but he couldn't afford to feel any sympathy, not when her sole purpose in being here was to take little Ashley away from them.

"How about a cup of coffee?" he said, as much to give Sharon Lynn something concrete to do as to sober the old lady up.

"Coffee'd be good," Mrs. Murdock agreed, her gaze following Sharon Lynn and the baby she still held in her arms.

"Mrs. Murdock, have you really thought this through?" Cord asked carefully. "You've already raised your daughter on your own. Are you sure you want to take on the burden of another child, a brand-new baby, at this stage of your life? That's an eighteen-year commitment, minimum."

"God never gives us burdens we can't handle," she said self-righteously.

She cast another look toward the baby and, for just an instant, something in her eyes softened. "She's a pretty one, isn't she?" she asked and this time there was nothing cagey in her voice.

"She's beautiful," Sharon Lynn agreed fervently. "She's a wonderful baby. She deserves the best possible future."

Hazel Murdock's gaze narrowed. "Are you saying I wouldn't do right by my own blood?"

"Of course not," Cord soothed. "It's just that it's a lot of responsibility to take on."

"Who'll do it, if I don't?"

"She could stay with me," Sharon Lynn blurted, before Cord could warn her not to.

"You've fallen for her, haven't you?" the old woman said. Despite Sharon Lynn's silence, she reached her own conclusion and nodded. "Yes, I can see that you have. Maybe we could come to some sort of an arrangement, just between the two of us."

Before Sharon Lynn could speak, Cord asked, "What kind of an arrangement, Mrs. Murdock?"

Her gaze darted nervously from him to Sharon Lynn and back again.

"A little money, maybe, just to help out with my expenses," she said at last. "Like you said, I'm getting up in years. My pension won't be much."

"You would sell your granddaughter?" Cord asked, his tone deadly. Even though Justin had warned him to anticipate something exactly like this, he was appalled.

She clearly heard the disgust in his voice and backpedaled. "Sell her? I never said such a thing."

"That's what it sounded like to me. What did it sound like to you, Sharon Lynn?"

Sharon Lynn was too near tears to answer.

"I don't think we have anything more to discuss, Mrs. Murdock," Cord said emphatically, propelling her toward the door. "If you want your granddaughter, file the appropriate papers with the court."

"I don't have money to hire a fancy lawyer," she whined. "You know that, too, don't you? I'll go to a reporter. I'll tell him you're trying to take away an old lady's only blood relation. You'll regret this. I'll see to it."

Cord let her rant, then said quietly, "You'll take Ashley over my dead body, Mrs. Murdock."

He gave her a curt nod, then shut the door and locked it behind her. He flipped the sign on the door to Closed and went back to Sharon Lynn, who was trembling so badly he took the whimpering baby from her, then circled an arm around her waist and drew her in tight, too.

"I can't give her up to a woman like that," Sharon Lynn whispered. "I just can't. Cord, she was drunk. She was here to see her grandbaby for the first time and she was so drunk she could hardly stand up. What if she took the baby in a car with her like that?"

He heard the horror in her voice and knew that it was her two greatest fears all wrapped up into one terrifying threat. "She won't take the baby," he insisted. "No matter what, she won't take Ashley away from us."

"How can we be sure?"

Here it was then, the moment he'd been waiting for. A part of him hated having to resort to using her quiet desperation to get what he wanted most in this world. Only the firm belief that she needed a family—needed *him*—every bit as much as he needed her permitted him to go through with the plan already supported by her grandfather.

"Come over here and sit down," he urged. "I have an idea."

Sharon Lynn was dazed. The whole time that horrible woman had been there, she had felt as if all the life were being sucked out of her. Only the weight of the baby in her arms had felt real. That and Cord's unwavering presence. He had been so angry, so fiercely furious she had been astonished that Hazel Murdock hadn't understood that and kept that awful offer to sell the baby to herself.

His anger had died now, but it had been replaced by a firm resolve. Gazing into his eyes in the gathering darkness, she saw that resolve, and her own fears were quieted. It no longer seemed to matter that she couldn't imagine what they could possibly do to guarantee that Ashley would remain safely with them. It was enough that Cord seemed convinced that there was something that would give them a chance.

"Do you think she'll go to court?" she asked, voicing her most immediate fear.

"I doubt it, not unless there's money in it for her," he said scathingly.

"But what if she does?"

"Then we'll offer the court a better alternative, one no judge could possibly resist if he has the best interests of the baby at heart."

She considered the all-too-scanty list of possibilities, but there was only one that made sense to her, only one she could live with.

"I could offer to keep the baby myself. I could adopt her," she said tentatively, then went on with more enthusiasm. "Why not? I'm responsible. I have my own business. I could give her a good home." Her conviction wavered ever so slightly. "It shouldn't matter that I'm not married, should it?"

His gaze caught hers as he slowly shook his head. "To be honest, it could."

There were a zillion single moms in the world. "But—"

He cut off her protest. "Just wait. I have a better plan. You and I will ask for custody."

"Together? But how…?" Her voice trailed off as understanding dawned. "You and I…" She couldn't seem to make herself complete the thought.

Cord had no such hesitation. "We'll get married," he said as if it were no more than a date for coffee. "We'll show the court that we can offer Ashley the kind of stable, two-parent home she deserves. It's the perfect solution."

She waited for the shock of the outrageous suggestion to sink in, waited for her stomach to rebel at the mere thought of taking another risk on marriage, at going through another ceremony that could end in tragedy, but it didn't happen. This wasn't a real marriage he was proposing, after all. It was a strategic alliance, a way to prevent Ashley from going home with that awful woman. And this was Cord, a man she'd come to trust. Her heart wouldn't be on the line, nor would his.

As she heard herself ticking off rationalizations, she realized that she was going to consider saying yes. If it could keep the baby safe, she would consider it.

She knew what it would mean to her, what it could mean to Ashley to agree to such a marriage, but Cord's motives were less certain and that troubled her. Of course, he cared about the baby. There wasn't any doubt about that, but this was a huge step to take to protect a child who wasn't even his own.

She studied him intently, but his expression was unreadable as he awaited her answer. "Why would you agree to something like that?" she asked eventually.

He grinned. "You seem to forget I'm not agreeing to it. I'm suggesting it."

She shrugged off the distinction. "Why, though?"

"Because I've thought long and hard about this and it's the only thing that makes sense. It would be the right thing for the baby, to keep her with you." He shrugged and admitted, "And with me. I've fallen for her, too, you know. I want to go on being a part of her life. I want to be a dad, a different kind of dad from the one I had, different from the one biologically responsible for Ashley."

He cupped her cheek in his palm and the graze of his fingers sent heat flaring through her.

"You're a strong woman, Sharon Lynn. I have no doubt a court would take your petition for custody seriously, but weighed against a willing blood relation, I don't know. It could go either way. Even Justin concedes that. Together, though, we'd be an indomitable force to reckon with."

He made the case passionately. Convincingly. Sharon Lynn's hand shook as she reached for her cup of coffee to buy herself some time to think it through, to analyze the pitfalls.

There were a million of them, most of them for Cord. She would be getting what she wanted most in this world, a chance to be a mother to a little girl she had already come to think of as her own.

She tried to look at the proposal from Cord's perspective. He claimed that a chance to be a father would be enough for him, but would it, really? Could any man be satisfied with so little in a marriage, even a temporary one?

"For how long?" she asked eventually. She swallowed hard, then cleared her throat. "How long exactly would we have to stay married?"

For once he couldn't seem to look directly at her and he hesitated for a very long time before answering. Finally he lifted his eyes to fix a steady gaze on her. "As long as it takes."

"And you would make that kind of a commitment, just like that?"

He nodded slowly. "I already have."

She believed him. How could she not? He was willing to put months, maybe even years of his life on the line for her and Ashley. How many men would do that and ask nothing in return? That was what he was saying, wasn't it? She faced him squarely, determined to get every detail spelled out, no matter how embarrassing.

"This would be a marriage in name only, right? That is what you're suggesting."

He stirred uneasily at that, but then his gaze locked with hers, held it until the blood seemed to pool low in her body, sending waves of warmth flooding through her. The sensation—the pull—was strong enough to make her wonder if *she* could live with that.

"If that's the way you honestly want it," he said.

Did she? Did she want nothing more than a marriage of convenience? She thought of all the kisses they'd shared, of the one time when it had almost gone beyond that. She would have to be a fool or a liar to say that there wasn't a powerful attraction between them. If they married, if they were living in close proximity day after day, would it be possible not to act on that attraction? Would willpower and resolve be enough to keep things from getting wildly complicated?

"Sleeping together would be dangerous," she said in a choked whisper.

He gave her a knowing look. "Make it harder to walk away when the time came? Is that what you mean?"

She nodded.

Cord regarded her with a rueful grin. "Would that be so awful then?"

"What?"

"To not walk away. To make it a real marriage." Before she could reply, he pressed a finger to her lips. "Don't answer that. It's not something we need to decide right now. We can take this one step at a time. Go as slow..." He grinned. "Or as fast, as you want."

The gentle teasing should have reminded her of how easily he was capable of setting off sparks in the pit of her stomach, but instead she found it oddly reassuring. If they could talk like this—and joke—wouldn't they be able to get through anything? Wouldn't they be able to make this work for as long as they needed to?

Her hands felt icy. She picked up her mug of coffee again and clung to it for the warmth it provided. She felt steadier then, as well, and filled with resolve. She lifted her gaze and met Cord's anxious glance.

"I'll do it," she said quietly. "For the baby."

"For the baby," he agreed softly.

The air around them seemed suddenly charged with electricity. There was a new awareness, a new, but thrilling tension between them.

"So, what do we do next?" she asked at last.

For an instant, he seemed stymied. She found that oddly reassuring, too, for some reason. Even though he'd had longer to consider this option, he obviously hadn't taken her reply for granted. He'd known there were doubts and uncertainties she would have to overcome.

"Buy an engagement ring," he suggested finally. "Tell your family."

"Oh, boy," she murmured as she thought of the chaos likely to ensue. "Maybe I should break the news first, by myself."

"No way, darlin'. From this moment on, we're in this

together. I'm going to be right there by your side, every bit the proud fiancé."

"Cord, we won't…we don't have to tell them about the arrangement, do we?"

"Absolutely not. That's why we need a ring. We're going to do this by the book."

She thought of another wedding not even a year before. She couldn't go through another fancy ceremony, another lavish reception. Besides, there was no time for that.

"Couldn't we just elope?" she asked wistfully.

He tucked a finger under her chin and turned her head until they were facing each other. "I promised I won't ask more of you than you're ready to give, but I will ask this. We are not going to slip away as if we're doing something wrong. I'll agree to a quiet ceremony with just family there, because there's not time for more, but we want this to be believable. We don't want anyone thinking for an instant that we're not ecstatic about this marriage. It wouldn't look good to the judge."

She considered that. "Yes, I see what you mean." She could also see that to do otherwise would hurt his pride. He might not say it, but no man would want the world thinking that he was marrying for anything other than love. Come to think of it, she didn't want that, either.

He held out a hand, waited until she'd placed hers in it, then said, "Let's go jewelry shopping."

"Here? In Los Piños?"

"Why not?"

"You realize everyone in town will know before night-fall."

An irrepressible grin spread across his face. "Then that'll pretty much solve our other problem, won't it? It ought to bring the whole darn family running to us."

For the first time in hours, she actually laughed. "You know, this could be fun. It's been a long time since I've done anything to shock that crowd."

"Then I'd say it's way past time."

They bundled up the baby, closed Dolan's for the night and walked down the block to the jewelry store. It wasn't big or fancy, but it did have a nice collection of expensive rings. Faced with the selection and the curious glances of Michael Trent, who owned the place, Sharon Lynn told herself it was perfectly natural that she felt jittery. Surely it wasn't actual anticipation, not when this was all essentially make-believe.

Cord gestured toward a modest, but elegantly set solitaire diamond. "That one," he said.

Sharon Lynn didn't know a lot about jewels, but she knew that the one he'd chosen would be way too expensive given the circumstances. She smiled at Michael Trent.

"Excuse us a minute, would you?" She tugged Cord away from the counter for privacy. "You can't spend that kind of money on a ring."

He faced her defiantly. "Why can't I?"

"You can't use the money you've been saving for a ranch like this."

"Darlin', if we're going to make this believable, then you have to have a ring that's suitable. Now stop arguing and tell me if you like that one I picked out."

"It's beautiful, but—"

He gestured to the owner. "She'll try that one."

"Cord, simple wedding bands would do."

"No," he said succinctly and took the ring from Michael Trent. "Hold out your hand." When she did, he slid the ring on her finger, then smiled, looking inordinately pleased. "Perfect fit. It was made for you."

"Cord—"

Her protest was lost as he turned his back on her, chose matching wedding bands and concluded the transaction, practically before she could blink.

Outside, she scowled at him. "It's a very good thing this marriage isn't for real, Cord Branson."

"Why is that, darlin'?"

"You don't listen."

"Not when you're talking foolishness," he agreed easily. "Let's go buy some nonalcoholic champagne so we can celebrate when your family starts turning up."

"You're a blasted bulldozer, you know that, don't you?"

He grinned. "If you say so, dear."

"Agreeing with me now won't get you off the hook. I'm going to remember the past few minutes for a very long time and I am going to make you pay."

He actually had the audacity to laugh at that. "I'll look forward to it."

For the first time since this incredible turn of events had begun, Sharon Lynn wondered if she had any idea at all of exactly what she was letting herself in for. Shaking Cord Branson when the time came just might not turn out to be the breeze she'd been anticipating.

Chapter Fifteen

Cord had to work very hard not to appear triumphant as
he and Sharon Lynn put together an assortment of appe-
tizers for the visitors he had no doubt would be popping
in before the evening was out. He had a hunch that rather
than stuffed celery and carrot sticks, they could both use a
couple of vitamin-enriched milk shakes and a thick, juicy
steak for fortitude if they were going to withstand the intense scrutiny of her family.

"Want to take bets on who'll show up first?" he inquired
to try to coax a smile from her. She'd been looking a little
panicky for the past half hour.

She sighed and sank onto a chair at the kitchen table.
"Does it really matter?" She regarded him worriedly. "What
am I going to tell them?"

"The truth, that you and I are going to get married just
as soon as the necessary paperwork can be taken care of."

"You know what they're going to think, don't you?"

"That it's a shotgun wedding," he guessed. He wasn't
about to tell her that her grandfather already knew otherwise. Harlan Adams might be proud of his matchmaking

skills, but Cord knew for a fact that Sharon Lynn would rebel if she thought they'd conspired in any way.

He gave her hand a quick, reassuring squeeze. "Well, in a manner of speaking, it is. When it's over we're going to have a baby—Ashley." When she didn't seem persuaded, he hunkered down in front of her and rested his hands on her thighs. "You're going to have to look happier about this. We need them to buy the idea that we're desperately in love."

"How do you suggest we convince them of that?"

"Oh, I have a few ideas. Just try not to bolt for the door when I put them into action."

If anything, she looked more worried than ever. "Cord, I don't think—"

Fortunately she was cut off by the ringing of the doorbell. "I'll get it," he said, anxious to escape before she started analyzing their plan to death. "You try to muster up one of those zillion-kilowatt smiles."

"Yeah, right," she muttered as if she had nothing in the world to smile about.

"Remember to show off your ring." He shook his head as she glanced down at her hand as if she'd never noticed the ring before.

"Oh, dear God," she murmured.

He bent low and planted a kiss on her that brought the color back into her cheeks. He nodded with satisfaction. "Better. You're starting to look like a woman who's been in the kitchen messing around with her fiancé."

Leaving her looking as if she'd been poleaxed, he went off to answer the door. He found Dani on the porch, her expression vaguely troubled. The frown lines deepened at the sight of him.

"You're here," she said as if that confirmed her worst fears.

"Come on in. I figured you'd be the first one on the scene

once the word started spreading. All you had to do was walk around the corner of the house. Come to think of it, I'm surprised you didn't bolt straight through the connecting doorway."

She did not seem to find his remarks amusing. "Is it true?" she demanded, clearly prepared to defend her cousin's honor if necessary.

Cord regarded her innocently. "Is what true?"

"Did you buy my cousin an engagement ring earlier today?"

Interesting that she chose that, rather than the implications of the ring to focus on. "Is that some sort of a crime?"

She scowled at him. "Did you?"

"Why don't you go in the kitchen and ask Sharon Lynn that? I'll pour you a glass of champagne. You look as if you could use it."

She hesitated, her concern shifting quickly to shock. "Champagne?"

"Nonalcoholic, of course."

She waved off his explanation. "No, I meant it sounded as if you were celebrating. Am I interrupting?"

"Dani, something tells me you're just the point man. I pretty much figure the entire clan will be here before the night's out. We're just prepared, that's all."

"Yes, I can see why you would be." She walked past him and went into the kitchen, her eyes widening at the sight of all the food on the table. Dismissing it, her gaze went at once to Sharon Lynn who was standing by the sink with her hands behind her back.

"I hear you've had an interesting day," Dani said lightly. "Anything unusual happen?"

Sharon Lynn's gaze wavered, sought his, then she drew in a deep breath and held out her hand.

"Oh, my," Dani murmured, taking her hand to examine the ring. "Then it's true? You two are engaged?"

As if she still couldn't quite manage to say the words aloud, Sharon Lynn merely nodded.

"This is a little fast, isn't it? Are you sure you're ready to take a step like this?" Dani asked, then turned to Cord. "No offense to you."

He offered a wry smile. "None taken."

"Sharon Lynn," Dani persisted. "Are you sure?"

"I'm sure," she said at last.

Her cousin seemed to accept that. "Well, of course, this is only an engagement ring," she said thoughtfully. "You haven't set a date for the wedding yet, have you?"

"As soon as we can take care of the paperwork," Cord told her, giving her a look that dared her to argue with the plan. He crossed the room to stand beside Sharon Lynn, sliding an arm around her waist. "We're anxious to get on with it, aren't we, darlin'?"

Dani looked shell-shocked. So did Sharon Lynn, if the truth were told. He figured another kiss ought to get that color back into her cheeks again. With a wink for Dani, he slowly lowered his head to touch his lips to Sharon Lynn's. The kiss lasted no more than an instant, but he knew if he had to put on the same display for every member of the family, the total—and the effects—were going to add up. He wasn't at all sure his poor body could take it.

"Aren't you going to congratulate us?" he asked quietly, forcing himself to focus on their guest. Maybe if they could convince her this was a love-match, she'd help with the others.

"Well, of course, I'm happy for you both," Dani said, though it was evident from the semimechanical tone of her voice that her heart wasn't entirely in it. She kept searching Sharon Lynn's face as if looking for answers.

The rest of the family began turning up then, one right after another, until the whole house was packed with Adamses and their spouses. Kids were racing around underfoot. They were the only ones who didn't seem to be giving the matter of this sudden engagement much thought. Doubts and confusion were evident with everyone else, though some were more polite than others about expressing it.

Cord would be forever grateful to Harlan Patrick, who gave his sister a fierce hug and said in Cord's hearing. "I knew it, sis. You picked a winner this time."

She seemed startled by the statement. Even Cord wondered at the choice of words, until Harlan Patrick clarified them himself. "Cord's not the kind of man who'll let anything stand in the way of getting what he wants, and it's been obvious to me he's wanted you since the day he rode into town."

The implied criticism of Kyle Mason's endless delays surprised Cord. He'd always been under the impression that everyone in the family had looked favorably on that union. It appeared that at least one Adams hadn't. He'd worried for some time now about competing with a saintly ghost, but perhaps Kyle had been only human, after all. Of course, it wasn't Harlan Patrick's impression of the man that counted. It was Sharon Lynn's memories.

There was no time to think that through, though, because Justin came roaring in just then, still in uniform and looking as if he were anxious to put Cord under arrest for trying to steal his cousin.

"I don't know what you're up to, Branson, but I don't like this," he muttered after drawing Cord away from the others.

Cord kept a tight rein on his temper. This was exactly what he'd expected from Justin. The man was totally honorable and fiercely loyal. Cord wanted Justin on his side.

"I love your cousin," he said quietly. "She's agreed to marry me. That's all you need to know."

"If you hurt her, you'll answer to me."

Cord met his defiant glare evenly. "Fair enough," he agreed. "But I have no intention of hurting her. My goal is to see to it that all her dreams come true."

It was easy enough to make the vow sound convincing because he meant every word. The marriage might be a sham on Sharon Lynn's part, but on Cord's, it was the answer to a prayer.

The engagement party was a fiasco. Sharon Lynn sensed that every single person crowded into her house—with the possible exception of her brother and her grandfather—suspected that this was not a love-match. Why Grandpa Harlan and Harlan Patrick thought otherwise was beyond her.

Of course, her grandfather was a dyed-in-the-wool romantic. That would explain his quiet, beaming acceptance of her announcement. But Harlan Patrick had every reason in the world to have no faith in love at all these days, yet even he seemed to be overjoyed by her news. Maybe he and Cord had bonded in some totally male way on those trips they'd made to Garden City.

As the night wore on with its unceasing questions, her head began to throb. She was no good at this deception stuff. If anyone had thought to sit her down and cross-examine her, she would have cracked like an egg. As it was, despite the overt skepticism, everyone seemed to be going along with the claim that the two of them had fallen madly in love practically overnight. Each time someone actually tried to corner her, Cord stepped in with a kiss and moral support to lend credence to their impression and put an end to their questions.

Only Justin made no pretense of being convinced. He'd been scowling since he'd walked through the door. He'd hauled Cord off to a corner for a few obviously intense moments. Whatever Cord had said in response hadn't exactly reassured her cousin, but it had quieted him down. She could tell, though, that he was just biding his time until he could get a moment alone with her. She did everything in her power to preclude that from happening.

Unfortunately Justin was both patient and clever. He snared her coming out of the kitchen, whirled her around and half dragged her back inside. He all but pushed her into a chair and stood over her as if she were the chief suspect in a major crime and he were the bad-cop interrogator.

"Are you out of your mind?" he demanded.

She frowned at his tone and his attitude, but she knew better than to start a shouting match that would draw the whole family into the kitchen. "I don't think so," she said blandly.

Justin looked incredulous. "Are you telling me you're in love with him?"

The point-blank question startled her. If she was at least half in love with Cord, it hadn't had time to register yet. Still, she raised her eyes to level a look at her cousin. "Why else would I be marrying him, if I weren't?"

"What about Kyle?"

She knew the question wasn't asked out of any deep-seated loyalty to her late husband. But Justin knew how devastated she'd been by Kyle's death. He'd been on the scene the night of the accident and there for her afterward. She supposed it was natural for him to wonder at her sudden leap into the arms of another man. Compared to Kyle's courtship, Cord's had set a stunning, record pace.

"Kyle is dead," she reminded Justin quietly. "I can't change that."

"But that relationship built up over time. The two of you didn't rush into marriage."

"I'll say," she murmured. She forced a smile. "Justin, Kyle and I waited and waited and waited to get married. Look at all the time we wasted."

"So that's it? You're rushing into this because you've suddenly concluded that life's too short and you have to grab on to it while you can?"

"Something like that."

"Bull. That's not who you are."

She regarded him with a touch of defiance. "Maybe it's not who I was, but maybe it's who I am now."

"I don't believe it," he insisted stubbornly.

"Whether you choose to accept it or not, I am marrying Cord. The sooner the better."

"There's more to it. There has to be."

"Such as?"

"I don't know, but I'll figure it out. I'm a cop and every instinct tells me this isn't the stars-in-your-eyes love-match you two are pretending it is." Suddenly he looked as if he'd been struck by a bolt of lightning. "The baby. Of course. That's it, isn't it? This is about the baby."

He searched her face, then moaned. "I knew it. Cord as much as asked me if you'd have a better chance at keeping her if you were married. Oh, sweetie, don't do it."

She saw no point in trying to deny it, not when the truth was likely written all over her face. She reached up and touched his cheek. "I have to, Justin. It's the only way. In fact, you were the first one to mention that it would make a difference if I were married. Cord just picked up on that."

"Dammit, Sharon Lynn. Use your head. It's not the only

way. Grandpa Harlan has influence around here. He'll use it if he has to."

She sighed heavily. "I know he would, but that's not what I'm going to do. Cord and I are in this together. He loves that little girl as much as I do. This marriage is what we want to do, Justin. Leave it be, please. Don't tell another soul. Promise me."

He looked torn by her plea. "You're certain? You're absolutely, positively certain you're willing to take such a drastic step?"

She was anything but. Still, she managed a smile. "Absolutely."

She had no choice. She had to believe that this crazy, impulsive marriage plan could work. Whatever Cord's motivations, it had to work. She couldn't bear to think of losing the baby she had come to think of as her own. She didn't allow herself to think about what marrying Cord and living with him would mean at all, because that would have stirred up too many things she wasn't prepared to deal with.

After their talk Justin appeared somewhat reconciled to her engagement, but that left at least one more major hurdle to get past: her mother.

Even more so than Sharon Lynn's father, Melissa Adams was capable of probing beneath the surface to get at the truth of things. Where her father blustered, ranted and raved, her mother was more subtle. But she was a more than even match for any Adams when it came to being stubborn. She'd resisted Sharon Lynn's father for a very long time, even though Sharon Lynn had already been born and, in a thoroughly untimely twist, Harlan Patrick had been on the way.

Oh, yes, Melissa Adams was a tough cookie and she was still there when most of the others had left. How she'd gotten Sharon Lynn's father to leave her behind was an enigma, but it was testament to her determination to get the answers she wanted from her only daughter.

"Sit," her mother ordered, after all but hauling her into the kitchen. "Now, my darling girl, why don't you tell me what this is all about?"

Sharon Lynn cast a look of longing toward the door, wishing Cord would appear, but she suspected her mother's fierce warning look had been enough to keep him out. "I'm engaged to be married. What more can I tell you?"

Her mother reached across the table and gently brushed a wayward curl from Sharon Lynn's face. "You could start with telling me why. Not that I don't happen to think Cord is a hunk."

"Mother!"

"Well, he is. He's also a decent guy from all accounts."

"Yes, he is."

"And that's why you're marrying him," her mother concluded.

Sharon Lynn heard the trap. There'd been no mention of love. Her mother was waiting to see if she'd add that into the mix.

"That and all the other usual reasons," Sharon Lynn said carefully, avoiding her mother's penetrating gaze. She couldn't bring herself to lie outright, not to her mother.

"That's utter nonsense," her mother exclaimed impatiently. "This isn't your father you're talking to or even your brother, who seems to have turned into Cord Branson's best buddy. This is me and I want the truth."

"Cord asked me to marry him. I said yes. I don't know what else there is to say," Sharon Lynn said, clinging tenaciously to her story.

"Sweetheart, you can't do something like this," her

mother said, clearly unconvinced. "It's all wrong. You're not an impulsive woman. You take your time and think things through."

"I took my time with Kyle and look at how that turned out," she shot back, refusing to explain that this had nothing to do with marrying Cord Branson and everything to do with keeping the baby. Her mother simply didn't need to know that.

Though she still looked troubled, her mother said, "You're happy then? Truly?"

"Very happy," she insisted, keeping her gaze level and unblinking. It was the hardest deception she'd ever had to pull off and, she found, only a tiny white lie. She might not be deliriously happy, but she was far from miserable about the prospect of being Cord's wife.

"This is exactly what I want," she added for emphasis.

Her mother regarded her worriedly for several minutes, then finally nodded, her expression resigned. "Then we'll get together tomorrow and start planning the wedding."

Sharon Lynn shook her head. "We don't want a big wedding. As soon as we get the paperwork out of the way, we'll have a quiet ceremony with just the family there."

"Absolutely not," her mother said, sounding appalled. "If there's going to be a wedding, it will be done right."

Sharon Lynn laid a silencing hand on her mother's arm. "Mom, I've had my fancy church wedding and a huge reception. I don't want that again. It will be too painful."

Nothing else she could have said would have been more effective. Tears sprang into her mother's eyes. "Of course. I'm sorry. It's just that you're my girl. I want the day to be lovely, something you'll remember."

"Mom, I'm marrying Cord. How will it be anything but memorable?" Oddly, even as she said the words to reassure her mother, she knew somewhere deep inside that it was true. Marrying Cord, whatever the reasons for it, would be one of the most unforgettable moments of her life.

Sharon Lynn wasn't one bit surprised when her grandfather came into Dolan's the next morning. Since he hadn't weighed in with his own opinion the night before, she'd been fairly certain it wouldn't be long before he did. Because he had impeccable timing, he arrived just as the last of the breakfast customers left.

"Hand over that baby," he said, peering behind the counter toward the portable crib. "I never got so much as a peek at her last night."

Sharon Lynn lifted Ashley up and boosted her across the counter into her grandfather's waiting arms. The baby beamed for him, just as she did for Cord. Obviously they had a little flirt on their hands.

"Do you want a cup of decaf or did you just come in to play with the baby?" Sharon Lynn inquired.

"I came to talk to you. Holding this cute little one is just a bonus."

"I knew it was too good to be true," Sharon Lynn murmured.

Her grandfather scowled. "Don't you go getting sassy on me, young lady. You can pour me a cup of real coffee to make up for it."

She grinned. "I don't think so."

He shrugged. "Oh, well, it was worth a try." He bounced Ashley on his knee, then said casually, "This is a mighty big step you're thinking of taking."

"You're not going to start on me, too, are you? Between Mama and Justin, I already feel as if I've gone ten rounds with a world-champion prosecutor."

"No," he said at once. "I happen to think Cord Branson

is a fine man. He'll be a good husband." He gave her a sly look. "I also happen to think he's in love with you."

Her head shot up at that. "In love with me?" she repeated incredulously. "Don't be ridiculous. He barely knows me." Despite the denial, she couldn't seem to help the little thrill that came over her at her grandfather's claim.

Grandpa Harlan didn't seem to be impressed by her vehement protest. "Sometimes it doesn't take but a heartbeat for a man to recognize the one woman on earth who's right for him. In Cord's eyes, you're that woman. I've never been more sure of anything in my life."

"But..."

"Can you say the same about him?" he asked. "Or is this all about holding on to that precious baby?"

Sharon Lynn sighed.

Her grandfather nodded. "I thought so. I'm not telling you not to go through with it, darlin' girl. I happen to think it's a strong match."

"Then what are you saying?"

"Maybe Cord loves enough for both of you, but I wanted you to go into this with your eyes wide-open. Whatever he may have told you, I'd stake my life that he's not looking for a marriage in name only. You'll owe it to him to make a real stab at making it work. Can you do that?"

Sharon Lynn fought her way through panic and an unexpected burst of anticipation to meet her grandfather's gaze evenly. "I'll have to, won't I?"

"If you'll listen to a few words of wisdom from an old man who loves you, what Cord is doing to protect you and that baby is a noble and decent gesture not many men would make. A man like that is worth holding on to."

"I know that," she told him quietly. It was a fact that had crept into her heart when she'd least expected it.

Chapter Sixteen

Cord figured Cody must approve of his relationship with Sharon Lynn. He gave him time off to get blood tests and paperwork done without so much as a grumbling comment. If he'd had to describe his boss's mood, he would have called it resigned. Obviously Cody was a man who had given up fighting the inevitable, at least when it came to his willful daughter.

Their earlier dispute over the designs he suspected Cord had on Sharon Lynn's property seemed to have been put behind them. Cord had a hunch he had Harlan Adams or Harlan Patrick to thank for that. Or maybe the fact that Kyle Mason's ranch had been promised to someone else. Thank heaven, he'd talked Sharon Lynn out of giving him her share of White Pines. He could just imagine what Cody would think about that. Cord doubted he would live to walk down the aisle.

All in all, the wedding plans were moving along without a hitch and with them, Cord's optimism was escalating. He was all but certain Sharon Lynn wouldn't duck out on him at the last second, if only because she was clinging to this marriage as the only way to protect Ashley from Hazel Murdock.

He'd been stunned by the strength she'd demonstrated as she'd withstood her family's doubts and skepticism. She'd almost had him believing by the end of their impromptu party that she was marrying him out of love. He promised himself that none of them would ever learn from him that nothing could be further from the truth, at least from her perspective.

Less than twenty-four hours from now, she would be Mrs. Cord Branson. Even though his confidence was strong, he couldn't seem to keep himself from dropping by Dolan's on his way to the bachelor party Harlan Patrick had insisted on planning. He wanted to make sure she hadn't panicked and changed her mind. He wondered if there'd ever come a day when he could be as sure of her love for him as he was of his own for her.

"Aren't you supposed to be hanging out with the guys tonight?" Sharon Lynn inquired when he settled into his usual place at the counter.

"In an hour."

"So you thought you'd spend it in here checking up on me?"

"Now, darlin', why would I need to check up on you?"

"To make sure I haven't bolted." She gave him a knowing look. "That is what you're afraid of, isn't it?"

"It's true," he conceded lightly. "I am afraid you might wake up and notice you're not getting a great bargain."

Her expression softened and she reached for his hand, one of the few times she had ever initiated any contact between them. Her touch was gentle, but it was enough to make his blood roar.

"You're wrong about that," she told him, her tone fierce.

"I think I'm doing okay for myself. I just hope you won't live to regret it."

"Can't happen," he assured her. "Now tell me what your plans are for tonight. I understand all you ladies intend to go out and kick up your heels."

She blushed slightly. "We're not going out, but I am told that someone has hired a male stripper for the occasion."

Cord stared. "Excuse me?"

"Hey, it wasn't my idea." A grin tugged at the corners of her lips. "Of course, it might be interesting in a purely educational sort of way."

"Darlin', any education you require along those lines, you can get from me."

She tilted her head and regarded him impishly. "You almost sound jealous. Is that possible?"

"Not jealous," he insisted, then searched for a different spin to put on the emotions choking him. He finally settled for describing them as protective.

She gave him a mocking, skeptical look. "I am a grown-up. This won't be a complete shock to me."

His gaze narrowed. "Exactly how many male bodies are you familiar with?" he asked testily.

"You mean in the intimate sense?"

"Yes, I mean in the intimate sense," he snapped.

She chuckled. "You should see your expression."

"What is wrong with my damned expression?"

"It's so very…male," she said finally.

Cord studied her intently. "You were teasing me, weren't you?"

A full-fledged grin spread across her face. "It was more like a test."

"To see how far you could push me?"

"To see if there was a double standard at work here."

"Double standard?"

"Harlan Patrick says he hired a stripper for your bachelor party. It just seemed to me as if turnabout was fair play."

"Couldn't you have just asked how I'd feel about it?"

She shook her head. "This was definitely better. I got the pure, unvarnished truth."

"Maybe we should just skip this whole prewedding ritual and go home and spend a quiet evening with Ashley," he suggested. He wasn't entirely kidding. Tonight was just something he had to get through before beginning what would be the rest of his life.

Sharon Lynn regarded him as if he'd suggested sunbathing nude at high noon on Main Street. "And disappoint the whole family? I don't think so. Not when they've had to give in about the wedding. Mother is still seething over the fact that we're having the ceremony in a judge's chambers, instead of a church."

"There wasn't a choice, given the timetable."

"I know that. I'm perfectly happy that we're doing it this way. I'm not sure I could have coped with all the hoopla a second time."

Cord went absolutely still at her words. He took them to mean that the first marriage had been a real one, that this one was only a mockery, that she didn't want anyone confusing the two. He finally met her gaze and saw that she was regarding him with a perplexed frown.

"What did you think I meant?" she asked.

"Nothing."

"Don't start evading the truth with me now. I can see in your eyes that what I said hurt you. Why?" At his continued silence, she muttered a harsh expletive he'd never heard her use before. "Cord, surely you aren't thinking that my comment was meant to imply that that ceremony was more important than this one."

"Well, it was, wasn't it? You were marrying the man you loved and you were doing it for real."

"And I lost him just hours after the ceremony. The two events will be forever linked in my mind," she said. "Do you think I want a repeat?"

He winced at the explanation. "No, of course not. I didn't think…"

She sighed. "No. Why should you? It's not as if you're supposed to be able to read my mind."

But, oh, how he wished he could. He would give anything to know if there was some tiny little part of her that was glad they were getting married tomorrow, not just to protect the baby, but because of the feelings and chemistry between them, feelings she had thus far refused to acknowledge.

Don't, he warned himself. Don't start wishing for things that weren't part of the bargain. If he did and Sharon Lynn could never live up to his expectations, if she could never let herself love him the way he loved her, then their marriage—however long it lasted—would be hell.

No, he had to take this one day at a time, just as he'd vowed to her he would. And every day he'd have to pray just a little harder that she'd learn to love him as deeply as he loved her. Perhaps then he'd finally be able to tell her that for him their marriage had never been just about the baby.

Sharon Lynn awoke on her wedding day with sunlight streaming in through her bedroom window and the aroma of cinnamon buns coming from the kitchen. She and the baby had spent the night at her parents' house at White Pines, just as she had on the night before her wedding to Kyle.

She closed her eyes and leaned back against the mound

of pillows, trying to remember how she'd felt that day. It was funny, though. The memories hadn't faded, but the sharp, bittersweet feelings had. Cord was responsible for that. He was giving her a whole slew of new and tangled emotions to deal with, starting with this odd little flutter of anticipation deep in her belly.

She glanced over toward Ashley's crib and was surprised to find her gone. Obviously her mother had slipped into the room and taken her downstairs to feed her in order to give Sharon Lynn more time to prepare for her wedding.

The ceremony was scheduled for eleven. It was barely eight now and she had the luxury of rolling over and going back to sleep if she chose.

Or so she'd thought. Pounding on her bedroom door suggested otherwise.

"Wake up, sleepyhead," Lizzy and Jenny called out as they opened the door. Dani was right on their heels.

"Shouldn't you all be home with your husbands?" she grumbled as they surrounded her on the bed and waved a freshly baked cinnamon roll under her nose.

"That's a fine welcome, when we've come bearing gifts," Dani retorted, turning over not only the pastry, but a small, flat package that weighed next to nothing.

"I thought we'd agreed there would be no presents," Sharon Lynn said, even as she regarded the gift with curiosity.

"These aren't presents, exactly," Lizzy explained, dropping her own offering into Sharon Lynn's lap. "They're tradition. Something old, something new, etcetera."

"Don't open them yet," Jenny warned. "Not till your mom gets up here. She's finishing up with the baby. That child does like to eat."

"She has a perfectly normal, healthy appetite," Sharon Lynn said defensively.

"Oh, don't mind her," Lizzy retorted. "She's just trying to stir up trouble. It's second nature to her. You would have thought marriage and a couple of kids would have settled her down, but it hasn't happened. If you ask me, Chance hasn't done nearly enough to tame her."

"You should talk," Jenny shot back. "Hank spoils you rotten, just the way Daddy did."

"Ladies, ladies," Dani soothed, in her traditional role of peacemaker between the sisters. "Let's not forget what day this is. We shouldn't be upstaging the bride with all this petty bickering."

Just then her mother rushed into the bedroom, looking harried, with Ashley already sound asleep in her arms. "Have I missed anything?"

"We waited," Dani told her. She gestured toward the package she'd put in Sharon Lynn's lap. "Open that one first. It's something blue."

Sharon Lynn dutifully shook the box, then took her time about removing the fancy white paper and neatly tied bow.

"Oh, for goodness' sake, hurry up," Jenny urged. "We don't have all day."

"This is her party," Lizzy reminded her.

Sharon Lynn removed the top from the box, lifted the tissue paper and gasped. The bikini panties inside were indeed blue. They were scraps of lace and not much else. She flushed with embarrassment, even as she had a vivid image of Cord's likely reaction to them. To bad he wasn't going to see them, she thought with genuine regret.

"Cord ought to love those," Jenny proclaimed as if she'd read Sharon Lynn's mind.

"Any red-blooded male would love those," Lizzy agreed. "And Cord is all that."

"Girls, there is a mother present," Melissa Adams reminded them, reaching for the panties. "Hmm, I wonder if your father…"

Sharon Lynn stared at her in shock. "Mom!"

"All right, Melissa," Jenny enthused. "No wonder Cody never takes his eyes off of you, even after all these years. Girls, there's a lesson to be learned here."

Sharon Lynn snatched back the panties. "Get your own," she advised her mother. "Just be sure Daddy has his heart checked first."

"Okay, enough," Jenny said, pointing to another box. "That one next. It's something new."

After the shock of the last gift, Sharon Lynn was even more cautious about opening this one, especially given Jenny's daring. Sure enough, inside she found a couple of scraps of lace purporting to be a bra that matched those dangerously wicked panties.

"Are you sure any of this is for me?" she demanded. "Seems to me as if you all had Cord on your mind when you shopped."

"Not me," Lizzy said. "I'm the practical, down-to-earth one." She handed over her gift to hoots of laughter. "Quiet, all of you. Now, Sharon Lynn, this is borrowed and don't you forget it. Hank gave it to me on my wedding day and I want it back."

Inside the box was a gorgeous heart-shaped diamond pendant on a gold chain. As far as she knew, Lizzy never went anywhere without it. Because Lizzy washed her hands so often at the hospital, she often left her wedding and engagement rings safely at home, but she always wore the necklace. Her fingers strayed to it again and again, as if it were a talisman. Sharon Lynn was deeply touched that Lizzy would loan it to her, even for a day.

"It's for luck," Lizzy said, reaching for her hand and

squeezing it. "That's what it's brought me every single day since I married Hank. I just wanted you to get off to a good start this time."

Tears welled up in Sharon Lynn's eyes. "Thank you," she said in a choked whisper. Lizzy couldn't possibly know just how desperately she needed a little luck these days, not just for the next few hours but in all the days to come when she and Cord would be battling to keep Ashley.

"I guess that leaves me," her mother said, pulling out the box she'd tucked into the baby's blanket. "These were your grandmother Mary's. Your grandfather asked that I give them to you today with his love."

Diamond stud earrings were inside the jeweler's box. They weren't the largest she'd ever seen, but they were the most beautiful—perfectly cut and shooting off sparks of blue fire.

"He gave them to her on their first anniversary," her mother explained. "They didn't have much money then, because he was trying to make a go of White Pines. In later years, he gave her fancier jewelry, but these were always her favorites. I remember her wearing them on every important family occasion. Now you can wear them on the day you start your own most memorable dates with Cord."

Sharon Lynn couldn't prevent another flood of tears. Would they have been so kind, so generous if they knew the truth? she wondered. Probably so, because they loved her and whatever her reasons for marrying Cord, they wished her well.

"I love you all," she whispered.

"Be happy, darling," her mother said, hugging her fiercely.

"I'm going to be," she said, surprised to discover that she actually believed it.

"Oh, my, look at the time," Dani said. "We'd better get this show on the road. You can't be late. Harlan Patrick says

Cord's nervous enough without being left to pace outside the judge's chambers."

The next few hours passed in a blur. The ceremony was little more than perfunctory with its hastily spoken vows and cursory kiss at the end. She and Cord had given in on having a small reception for the family, but not at White Pines where it had been last time. Sharon Lynn had put her foot down about that. She would have been terrified to get in a car and leave when it was over. Obviously understanding why she was being so adamant, Justin and his wife had organized it at their place in town.

"Let me make up for giving you such a rough time," he had pleaded and she had agreed.

He and Patsy had spared nothing. Grandpa Harlan's housekeeper had cooked a feast and the bakery in town had prepared a small but spectacular wedding cake. Sharon Lynn gazed into Cord's eyes as he fed her the traditional bite of cake and almost gasped at the longing she saw in his gaze.

So, she thought, her grandfather had been right. Cord did love her. Please, she prayed silently, don't let me let him down. Don't ever let me hurt him.

Because there was no honeymoon to rush off to, the family lingered at Justin's. Only when they could postpone their leaving no longer did Cord approach her.

"If we don't get out of here soon," he said, leaning down to whisper the words in her ear as if they were a loving secret, "they're going to start to wonder if we're dreading being alone together."

In truth, this *was* the moment she had been dreading. Walking out of here as Cord's wife, surrounded by good wishes and taunted by broad innuendoes about the night ahead, she knew she was going to feel like the world's worst fraud.

"Buck up, darlin'. Let's give 'em the show they're expecting," he said with a devilish glint in his eyes.

"What—?"

The word was barely out of her mouth, when he tucked his arm behind her knees and scooped her up against his chest. The short skirt of the white wool suit she'd worn for the occasion rode up her thighs. With an exaggerated survey of her bared legs and a wink at her family, he said, "If nobody objects, I'm taking my bride home now."

"It's about time," Grandpa Harlan taunted.

"Cord, put me down this instant," Sharon Lynn demanded, only to be tucked more firmly against the broad expanse of his chest.

"And spoil their fun? I don't think so."

He left the house at a pace that left no doubt that he was an anxious new husband. When they turned the corner out of view, Sharon Lynn once again pleaded with him to put her down. "There's no need now. They can't see us."

"Doesn't matter. I kind of like having you cuddled up here next to me." He gave her a wry look. "Could be the last time I get this close to you tonight."

Sharon Lynn sighed. The remark had been made in jest, but there was a longing behind it that touched her soul. "I'm sorry," she said, the words a soft whisper against his neck.

"Don't be sorry, darlin'. This is what I bargained for."

"It's still not fair. This is your wedding night."

"It's our wedding night," he stated. "You said those vows, same as me."

"You know what I mean."

"Don't worry about it," he insisted. "Nothing will change this being our wedding night. The rest will come when it comes."

"You aren't disappointed?"

He paused on the steps to the front door and his gaze locked with hers. "Disappointed? Yes. I won't lie to you about that. I want you so badly I ache with it," he told her with brutal honesty. "But I respect the deal that we made. I won't push for more."

For just an instant she wished things were different, but then he was crossing the threshold and lowering her to her feet so he could pay Patsy Driscoll, who had baby-sat Ashley all afternoon.

When the teenager was gone, Sharon Lynn took Cord's hand in hers. "Let's go in and see the baby. Everytime I'm away from her, I'm scared to death she'll be gone when I get back."

Cord gave her a look of complete understanding and walked with her to the bedroom. There, in the gathering dusk, they stood over the baby's crib and stared down at her. She was sleeping peacefully on her tummy, her little bottom poked into the air. She looked so precious, so innocent to have been caught up in such a tempest.

Gazing at her, tears ran down Sharon Lynn's cheeks. She was thinking not just of Ashley then, but of Kyle, and of another tragic wedding night. When Cord saw the tears, he gathered her close.

"It's going to be okay," he promised. "All of it, darlin'. It's all going to be okay."

There, with his arms around her, his heart beating sure and true, she could almost believe it.

The next morning they were served with court papers indicating that Hazel Murdock had formally filed for legal custody of her granddaughter.

Chapter Seventeen

On the day set for the custody hearing—April 1, of all days—Sharon Lynn felt as if her world were being torn apart. She couldn't even look at the baby without tearing up. She couldn't touch a bite of the breakfast Cord had insisted on making for her, hadn't been able to eat much since the papers had been delivered the day after their wedding two weeks earlier.

Those two weeks had been consumed with preparations for the court date. Janet had taken on the case eagerly and no one was more fierce in a courtroom battle. Sharon Lynn should have found comfort in that, but right now nothing short of a positive custody ruling in their favor would calm her.

Cord had been wonderful. Though he'd continued to work at White Pines every day, he'd spent every spare second with her. He'd tried valiantly to anticipate her needs, to offer reassurance when she needed it most and a shoulder to cry on whenever she was overcome with panic. No man could have been more devoted. She would owe him for the rest of her life for standing by her as he had.

"You need something in your stomach," Cord said now,

watching with a disapproving scowl as she toyed with the oatmeal in her bowl. "Can't you eat just a little?"

"I'm sorry. I don't think I could keep it down." She regarded him fearfully. "Cord, what if…?"

He touched a silencing finger to her lips. "Don't. Whatever happens, we'll deal with it."

"I can't let her go with that woman," she whispered. "She won't be safe."

"The judge will see that," he promised, moving behind her to massage her shoulders. His touch was like magic, soothing away tension.

"Do we dare take a chance that she won't?" she asked, unable to shake her sense of dread. "Maybe we should just pack everything up and leave Los Piños."

His hands stilled on her shoulders. She could feel the tension that was now radiating from him.

"You don't mean that," he chided. "We can't spend the rest of our lives on the run. What kind of home could we make for Ashley, if we did that? What kind of example would we be setting? And more than that, what kind of man would I be if I encouraged you to leave the family you love?"

"But Ashley would be safe. That's all that matters."

"She will be safe," he insisted. "The judge will leave her with us. I believe that with all my heart."

"Then why do we have to take the baby with us to court?" she asked reasonably. From the moment she'd learned of that demand, there had been a terrible knot of dread in the pit of her stomach. "I'll tell you why. It's because the judge might decide to take her from us right then and there."

Cord sighed heavily. "She could, yes, but, darlin', I don't believe that's going to happen, not with the evidence we have about Hazel Murdock's fitness, not with your family there to testify to the care we've given the baby. We have to have faith."

Sharon Lynn had plenty of faith. She believed that God had guided Vicki Murdock's boyfriend to her door that icy winter night. He'd been protecting the baby then. She just wished she could be as sure that the judge would be guided by God's wisdom. It had been her experience that humans sometimes made terrible mistakes with tragic consequences.

"Come on, darlin'. It's time to go," Cord said quietly. "I'll get Ashley."

"No. I will." She needed to hold on to the baby as long as she could, especially since it might be the last chance she ever had.

Cord regarded her with understanding. Before she could rush from the room to get the baby, he placed his hands on her shoulders and forced her to meet his gaze.

"Darlin', I believe with every part of me that this will turn out all right."

"I want to believe that," she whispered. "I really do."

"Whenever your faith starts to waver, put your hand in mine and hold on tight."

She reached up and touched his cheek. "Thank you. I don't know if I could have faced this without you." She wished she could say more, wished she could say the words she knew he wanted to hear, but she was afraid to, terrified to admit that she had come to love him for fear he would somehow be lost to her, too.

"You could have faced it, because you're an Adams. You come from a long line of strong people," he said, his gaze warm and steady and reassuring. "But I'm glad we're in this together. Ashley needs us both."

She drew herself up, squared her shoulders and smiled bravely. "Yes, she does, and we're going to see to it that the judge recognizes that."

Cord grinned. "That's the spirit."

At the courthouse a few minutes later they were instantly surrounded by a whole slew of Adamses. Even Sharon Lynn had to admit that united, they presented a formidable force to be reckoned with. She was also reassured that the judge was an old friend of her grandfather's, a woman known for her fierce protection of the rights of children. Surely that would work in their favor.

Janet presented their case for retaining custody. Calling first Cord, then Sharon Lynn, she led them through testimony about the brutally cold night on which they'd found the baby abandoned in the alley behind Dolan's.

"What did you think when you saw her there?" Janet asked Cord.

"That she'd been left there to die," he said angrily.

"Not that she'd been dropped off in the hope that she'd be found by someone who'd love and care for her?" Janet persisted.

"No," he said flatly.

"Do you agree with your husband's impression?" Janet asked Sharon Lynn when her turn came.

"I do," Sharon Lynn said softly. "I didn't want to believe any mother could allow that, but there was no other way to look at it. The baby was left too far from the door."

Tears welled up as she remembered. "The snow was coming down so hard by then. In a few more minutes, an hour at most, she would have been under a cold blanket of snow. She would have…" She choked back a sob, then drew in a breath and faced the judge, who seemed shaken by the testimony. "She would have died."

When Sharon Lynn left the stand, Janet called witness after witness who could talk about the love and care Cord and Sharon Lynn had given to the baby in all the weeks since that terrible night, about the love they'd discovered in the process that had led them to marry.

And finally Janet called on witnesses who could describe Hazel Murdock's life-style.

"Your honor, I ask, is that the kind of situation in which you wish to see an innocent baby raised?" Janet asked passionately when the evidence had been presented. "I mean this as no disrespect to Mrs. Murdock. She has raised a daughter with little or no help from the child's father. But that daughter—this baby's mother—has vanished. Can Mrs. Murdock be expected at her age to raise yet another baby, this one her grandchild, with so few emotional and financial resources, especially when there are others capable and willing to give the child a warm, loving home?"

By contrast to Janet's well-organized and passionately stated presentation, the attorney handling Mrs. Murdock's case had little to offer the court in defense of his client. Even Mrs. Murdock herself seemed to be going through the motions on the stand, repeatedly citing her duty to rear the child, not her love for the baby she'd visited only once and never even asked to hold.

The judge listened to her intently, then interrupted her attorney's questioning.

"Mrs. Murdock, do you truly want to take on the job of rearing this child?" the judge demanded.

"I've said so, haven't I?" the older woman retorted with a defiant lift of her chin. "She's my kin." She gestured across the courtroom. "They have no claim on her."

"Other than love," the judge replied quietly. She uttered a sigh. "I wish I could end this matter right now, but there are any number of moral issues to be considered. Normally I would not rule against blood ties. And then there is the fact that the biological mother's whereabouts are not known. She could turn up here tomorrow wanting her baby back. Or she might never be heard from again."

She glanced at Sharon Lynn, who had been holding the baby cradled in her arms ever since she'd left the witness stand. Cord was snugly by her side, his hand resting reassuringly on her shoulder. A smile seemed to touch the judge's lips for just an instant at the picture of a loving family that they presented.

"I think time is what's needed here," she said. "Time for me to consider all the facts, time for the police to complete their search for Victoria Murdock and her boyfriend." She gave a pointed look toward the woman fighting them for custody. "Time for Mrs. Murdock to consider thoroughly what is truly best for her granddaughter."

Sharon Lynn's heart was in her throat as she waited for the judge's ruling. Cord folded her hand in his and squeezed.

"Therefore I am granting temporary custody to Mr. and Mrs. Branson. We will come back here on July first with any additional evidence that becomes available. At that time I will be prepared to rule on permanent custody."

Sharon Lynn released the breath she'd been holding. Three months. They had three more months with Ashley at least. She would be teething in earnest by then, crawling, maybe even trying to pull herself up to a standing position.

They had three more months for her to steal their hearts.

"I say we go celebrate," Grandpa Harlan said, when the gavel had fallen and they'd left the courtroom.

"No," Sharon Lynn said, casting a pleading look toward Cord. "I want to take her home. Just the two of us." She turned to the rest of the family. "You don't really mind, do you?"

"Of course not," her mother said.

Cord grinned. "Then that's what we'll do, darlin'. You all will excuse us, won't you?"

Despite everyone else's agreement, her grandfather regarded them with a troubled expression, but Janet stepped in and touched his hand. To Sharon Lynn's relief, that was all it took to silence him.

Cord turned to Janet and took her hand in his. "Thank you. You were terrific in there today. The legal profession lost a real treasure when you decided to retire. We owe you."

"You don't owe me a thing," Janet protested. "The past few months, we've all come to love that little baby and to think of her as one of us. She deserves the life and the love the two of you could give her."

Sharon Lynn could hardly wait to get away from all the worried looks. She knew that everyone was wondering how she would have taken it if things had gone differently in the courtroom. Truthfully she didn't know what she would have done if she hadn't been walking home with the baby in her arms and Cord at her side. The sun broke through as they walked, as if God were giving them His blessing on today's outcome. For now that would have to be enough. If she looked too far into the future, she'd never leave the house. She'd stay right there where she could keep a close eye on the baby hour after hour, savoring every memory in case it turned out to be all she had.

As soon as they were home, she put the baby down for her nap, then wandered into the kitchen to find Cord staring out the window, a cup of coffee cooling in his hand. He jumped when she whispered his name.

"Sorry, darlin'," he said, turning to her and putting the cup on the table to reach for her. "I was at least a million miles away."

"I could see that," she said, hesitating for only a heartbeat before stepping into his embrace. "Where'd you go?"

"I guess I moved ahead in time, rather than going to a different place."

"To July?"

He nodded. "It will only be harder if the decision goes the other way, then."

"It won't," Sharon Lynn insisted, struggling against tears. "It can't."

"If I were a betting man, I'd say you're right, but it's the outside chance that worries me."

"We can't think about that. I won't believe for a single instant that we're not going to get custody of Ashley."

"But what if we don't?" he persisted. "Will you be able to live with that?"

"I don't know what I'll do," she confessed candidly, then searched his bleak expression. "But that's not all that's troubling you, is it?"

He gave her a weary, halfhearted smile. "When did you start reading my mind?"

"I don't know about reading your mind, but your face is transparent. Sometimes I look into your eyes and it almost breaks my heart."

"Why is that?"

She drew in a deep breath and confronted the issue that they occasionally alluded to, but never discussed. "I know you love me. You've shown it in a thousand different ways. And you're scared to death that if the baby is taken away, our marriage will be over."

He shot her a rueful look. "On the nose. That baby is what brought us together, what's keeping us together."

It was time—way past time, probably—for her to own up to the feelings that had been growing for so long now, time to risk putting her heart on the line again. But could she do it?

"Ashley's not the only thing," she insisted.

"What then?"

She searched her heart and came up with an answer that was as honest as she could make it, but in the end she settled for a safer half-truth.

"I care about you, Cord. How could I not? Look at all you've done for me. Look at how much you love Ashley, the way you are with her. You're a wonderful man, as decent and kind as anyone I've ever known."

"High praise, considering the quality of the men in your family." He sighed. "But you still can't say it, though, can you?"

"Say what?"

"You still can't say you love me."

Her silence was answer enough. She could see that. The irony, of course, was that she was falling in love with Cord. With each day that passed, the feelings grew stronger, his hold on her deepened.

She was just terrified of admitting it. She had loved Kyle and he had died. She loved Ashley and the baby could be ripped away from her at any second. How could she admit to loving Cord, when loss always seemed to follow such an admission?

Cord was absolutely certain that Sharon Lynn loved him. It was in every heated glance, in every lingering caress. Until she could recognize the emotion for something more than gratitude, though, their marriage was tied totally to Ashley's fate. It was a terrible burden to put on a tiny baby, who, in the end, had no control over her own destiny, much less theirs.

Somehow he had to get Sharon Lynn to acknowledge her feelings, to accept their marriage as a real one before July, before a judge's ruling either cemented their relationship or tore it apart.

Being with Sharon Lynn day in and day out, living with her, sharing everything except her bed was the sweetest kind of torment imaginable. Every time her hand brushed his, every time he dared to steal a kiss, his blood sizzled. He'd used so little hot water in his showers, the water heater could have gone on the fritz and he wouldn't have known it.

But icy showers weren't cutting it. He wanted her, wanted to make her his wife in every sense of the word. But how? They had established the ground rules on the day she'd agreed to marry him. What would she do if he tried to change them now? What would she do, if he swept her into his arms, carried her into the bedroom, kicked the door shut and tried to seduce her? Would she give in, but hate him afterward? Or would she finally be able to admit that she wanted him as desperately as he wanted her?

His whole life he'd been a man of action. He made quick, impetuous decisions and lived with the consequences. Now he was suddenly questioning his own instincts, twisting and turning every plan this way and that until he was dizzy with all the thinking and frustrated by the lack of action.

He'd spent the entire day at White Pines riding hard and doing every backbreaking task Cody could come up with just to keep from thinking, but it hadn't worked. He was exhausted, but his mind was still going a mile a minute and his pulse kicked up every single time an image of Sharon Lynn came to mind.

What this marriage needed, he concluded, what it had suffered from from the outset was the lack of a honeymoon. There'd been plenty of logical reasons not to suggest one at the outset. There were probably a million more reasons why it was a bad idea now. She might panic at the very mention of the word.

But, he thought with growing enthusiasm, she couldn't possibly say no to the notion of a little vacation. A trip all three of them could take, somewhere far from Los Piños, where lazy days on a beach would turn into romantic nights under the stars. A trip away from their cares, away from the threat of impromptu visits from Hazel Murdock. He grinned just thinking about the potential.

When he got back to the ranch office, it was already dusk. Even so, Cody was still in the office, doing whatever it was he did on that fancy computer of his that Harlan was always making a fuss about.

"I'm surprised to see you still here," Cody said. "Lately you seem to take off the minute your work is done."

"Newlywed syndrome," Cord said. He drew in a deep breath. "Mind if I ask a favor?"

Cody regarded him uneasily. "I don't mind you asking, as long as you don't mind if I say no."

"I think when you hear what I have to say, you'll agree it's important."

Cody gestured for him to go ahead.

"I want to take Sharon Lynn and the baby on a trip, not a long one, just a few days to get away from all the pressures around her. I think she deserves it."

Cody grinned. "Right button to push with a concerned

father. I couldn't agree more. And the two of you never did get a proper honeymoon. What did you have in mind?"

"Maybe a weekend at the beach," he suggested, not wanting to ask for too much when Cody had already been more than generous about his work schedule.

"Son, let me give you a piece of advice. If you're hoping to put the sparkle back in Sharon Lynn's eyes, you're going to have to do better than that. Now, here's the plan I'd suggest. You call up a travel agent, get yourselves booked at a fancy hotel on a Caribbean island and don't even think about Los Piños or anything else for at least a week."

His grin broadened. "Now I'm not suggesting you take him along, but I've seen Harlan Patrick moping around here for the past few weeks. Seems to me he could use a break, too. He could take Jordan's plane, fly you all wherever you want to go, spend a few days on the beach and bring you all back."

Cord chuckled at Cody's suggestion. He was acting far more like an indulgent daddy than a boss. And the idea itself was perfect. "You wouldn't mind?"

"Hell, no, not if it means I could get some real work out of the two of you when you get back. You're both so distracted I'm surprised we have any cattle left. I've got half the men in the crew chasing around behind you to make sure the gates are closed."

Cord winced. "It's that bad?"

"Well, I've got to say you're better than my son. Since Laurie took off, his head's in Nashville whether he'll admit to it or not. Might's well go on up there, for all the good he's doing me." He regarded Cord intently. "So, is it a deal? Should I talk to Jordan about the plane and get Harlan Patrick ready to take off, say, tomorrow?"

"Make it the day after and we're on." He figured it was

going to take him at least that long to convince Sharon Lynn to go along with this and to pick a destination she'd always dreamed of visiting. He met Cody's gaze. "Just one thing."

"What's that?"

"You're not expecting Harlan Patrick to move into the same hotel we do, are you?"

Cody chuckled. "No, if I were in your shoes, I'd probably insist her baby brother go on to another island."

"Another hotel would probably do," Cord said, then grinned. "That way he'll be close enough to baby-sit."

"You know something, son? This could turn out to be the damnedest honeymoon anyone in the family's ever taken," Cody said approvingly. "Daddy's going to be real disappointed he's not the one who thought of it."

Chapter Eighteen

"**Y**ou want to go where?" Sharon Lynn demanded, staring at Cord incredulously.

"To the Caribbean," Cord explained patiently.

"Now?"

"Why *not* now?"

"You have a job. I have Dolan's. There's the custody battle. How can you possibly suggest going away?"

"Because we need a break. We need time alone with the baby to catch our breath, to just be a family."

Her gaze narrowed. "A family?" she repeated, regarding him warily. "Cord, we're not a family, not really."

"Who says we're not?" he retorted heatedly. "In the eyes of the law, we are. In the eyes of your family, we are. It's only the two of us who set down a bunch of silly ground rules we don't know how to change."

Those silly ground rules were the only reason she'd been able to accept the idea of this marriage in the first place and now he wanted to change them? She should have seen this coming, should have known he'd want more from her than she could give, that his patience would wear thin. Her grandfather had warned her of that.

Before she could refuse this idiotic offer of an expensive vacation, he reached for her hand. He seemed to know that she couldn't think straight when he was touching her.

"Cord," she protested, but not nearly vehemently enough.

He met her gaze evenly. "We need this, darlin'. We surely do. What could be so terrible about taking a trip? We'll spend a few days sitting by a pool or swimming in the warm Caribbean waters. Maybe go out dancing. Eat some exotic food. Take a moonlit walk on the beach."

He painted an idyllic picture. "It does sound tempting," she admitted. So tempting that her already weakening resolve to keep Cord at arm's length was likely to fly out the window by the end of the first romantic day. Though he'd never once mentioned the word, it sounded an awful lot like a honeymoon. The very idea made her tremble.

"Then let's do it," Cord urged. "Harlan Patrick's agreed to fly us down, hang out nearby to serve as doting uncle and baby-sitter. If you don't want to do it for yourself, just think what this will do for him. He's pining for Laurie. He needs a change of scenery to think things through."

Her brother would be with them? She was supposed to think of this as something they were doing for his benefit? That didn't sound much like a honeymoon. She should have found that reassuring. Instead she found it irritating. As much as she adored Harlan Patrick, she wasn't sure she wanted him along on her honey… Whoops, she'd almost done it herself. She didn't want him along on their vacation.

Then, again, she reasoned, he could prove valuable. He could take Ashley while she and Cord spent time alone. She owed Cord that much, if only to thank him for all he'd done for her. Maybe she even owed herself a chance to discover if these feelings she'd been trampling on out of fear would blossom into the real thing, something strong enough to withstand whatever curves life tossed them. Was she brave enough to take that final, giant leap of faith?

She met Cord's gaze, caught the hopeful expression on his face and her heart flipped over. This trip could be a turning point for the two of them.

Suddenly she realized that she desperately wanted it to be. She wanted to stop living in lonely isolation. Even with Cord in the house, that was what she'd been doing, holding him at bay, shrouding her heart in ice so it couldn't be broken again. Maybe it was time to find out if Cord's touches and a fiery tropical sun could melt away the ice and leave her whole again.

"I'll go," she said softly, even as her pulse ricocheted wildly.

Cord scooped her up and whirled around. "Thank you, darlin'. You won't regret it."

Sharon Lynn doubted she would regret the trip. How could she when she was finally going to steal a few days of romance with a man who had proved time and again just how deeply he loved her? It was the heartache that could come after that terrified her.

The breezes in their tropical paradise were sultry and scented with jasmine. The air shimmered with the sound of reggae, a beat that invited the listener to throw away cares and indulge in all life's passions.

Sharon Lynn felt as if she had stepped into another world. She had even put aside her aversion to alcohol and accepted a frothy, icy tropical drink with a sweet taste and an astounding kick. She was pretty sure her inhibitions had vanished a couple of hours ago, right after Harlan Patrick had taken off with Ashley. She hadn't even mounted much of a protest when they'd gone.

When Cord beckoned her onto the tiny, seaside dance floor, she floated into his arms. He smiled down at her.

"Having a good time?"

"I feel like some other person, as if I've fallen into an enchanted fairy tale. How is it possible to step off a plane and turn into somebody else?"

"No one knows you here. You can be anyone you want to be. Back home that's not possible. In Los Piños, there's history and family and a ton of emotional baggage. Here there's just the heat of the sun, the brilliance of the moon, a sky studded with stars." He winked. "And me."

She gazed into his eyes, which were regarding her with amusement. "Do you feel different here?"

"Not so different," he confessed. "I still want you."

Though the words were lightly spoken, the heat in his eyes commanded her to take the statement seriously.

She tightened her arms around his neck and snuggled in closer. The sensations shimmering through her were lazy and seductive. "I think you're a very sneaky man, Cord Branson."

"Why is that?"

"Because you knew I wouldn't be able to resist you here," she murmured, her breath fanning over his chest.

His breath hitched at that. "Is that so?"

"Mm-hmm."

He tucked a finger under her chin and tilted her face up. "This will only go so far, unless it's what you want," he assured her. "You'll have to set the pace."

She took that as an out-and-out invitation to tease. How far could she push him? she wondered.

Could she indulge in an intimate caress? She tried one and heard his gasp. That was enough to embolden her.

Maybe she could sneak a few of those breath-stealing kisses. She tried one and this time she was the one gasping for air when it was over. Still, she was tempted to go on.

Could she slide his shirt off and circle his masculine nipples with her tongue? She wisely held off on that one.

All of these were things she'd been imagining herself doing during the lonely nights when she'd been alone in her own bed while Cord slept just down the hall on the sofa. Was this her chance to experiment with her most wicked fantasies without risking her heart?

She sighed and rested her cheek against his chest, listened to the steady rhythm of his heart. His arms circled her waist. His hands rested low on her backside, tucking her body into intimate contact with his. There was no mistaking the hard length of his arousal beneath his jeans. She found that even more wildly intoxicating than that very dangerous drink she'd had.

This was Cord, she reminded herself. No man on earth was more blatantly masculine. No man she'd ever known could make her knees weak with a glance. No man had ever proved himself as capable of unselfish, generous love.

She felt her skin grow hot, felt the rush of moisture at the apex of her thighs, the pull low in her belly. Surrounded by the heat and the scent of him, she was lost, drawn to become the new woman who had walked off the plane eager for new experiences.

She looked up and met Cord's hooded gaze "Take me back to the room," she whispered. "Now."

He went utterly still. "Are you sure?"

She nodded. "I've never been more sure of anything in my life."

To her amusement, after he'd paid the bill, Cord took her the long way back to the room, along a winding path through scented flowers and twinkling white lights. She supposed he'd done it to give her time to reconsider, but instead the path he'd chosen only added to the magic. She felt as if they were walking through a fairy-tale world, where nothing could ever, ever go wrong.

He cast one last questioning look at her when they stepped inside the room, but at her nod, he moved in close and brushed a kiss across her lips. No butterfly's touch could have been lighter, yet Sharon Lynn felt the impact of that kiss all the way to her toes. It sent her reeling. If he intended to go about this so slowly, so reverently, she was going to shatter into a zillion pieces.

She wanted fast. She wanted mindless. She wanted to be caught up in all-consuming passion. And the only way to make sure of that was to reach for Cord, to strip off his shirt with a scattering of buttons, to startle him with an eager reach for the zipper of his jeans.

After one stunned instant while he assessed her reckless mood, he smiled. He had her out of her own clothes in a matter of seconds, shredding some of them in his impatience.

At last, she cried inwardly as his hands were everywhere, stirring her, arousing her, giving pleasure so intense that she wondered at the foolishness that had prevented her from seeking it before now. He took her to a climax that left her slick with sweat and shuddering with the force of it.

Then and only then did he kneel above her. Gazing into her eyes, he slowly entered her, filled her and took her on another incredible journey to a level of passion she'd only dreamed of.

Stunned by the sensations rippling through in its aftermath, she glanced across the bed to find Cord's steady gaze on her. He reached across and brushed a wayward tendril of damp hair back from her face.

"When you've caught your breath," he suggested softly, "we'll try that again."

Something in his voice hinted at censure. "Cord, what's wrong?"

"The next time I want to make love to you, darlin'. I

don't want to be in a rush just to make sure you won't change your mind."

A chill washed over her. Had he seen through her so clearly, had he guessed that the urgency was borne of panic, the fear that if she allowed herself to make love with him, to truly feel the wild sweep of emotions, she would never be able to let him go?

To her surprise, she must have been crying because Cord brushed away a tear with the pad of his thumb.

"Don't cry, darlin'. Please don't cry. That wasn't meant as a criticism. All I meant was that I've been looking forward to making love with you for what seems like forever. Next time I want to go slow. I want it to be memorable."

"But it was," she protested. That, of course, was the real irony. Even though she had deliberately escalated the pace, done exactly as he had accused and rushed things, she knew she would never forget a single moment of it, could never forget the passion.

"Come here," he said, beckoning until she was resting against his chest. "I know you don't want me to keep on saying this, but I love you, Sharon Lynn. That's a fact. It's not going to go away. I'm not going to disappear on you. The only way you'll ever get rid of me is to end this marriage yourself and kick me out on my butt. Even then, I'll fight you to hold on to what we have."

She blinked and looked into his fierce gaze and knew that he meant it. She wasn't going to shake him ever. And in the last few minutes she'd realized something else: she didn't want to. She wanted desperately to hold on tight to what they'd found, for however long it lasted.

She slid up his body until she could slant her mouth over his. At his look of surprise, she grinned. "Let's try it your way, cowboy, and see which way we like it best."

He made love to her slowly, then, his work-roughened hands gentle on her body and wickedly inventive.

"Interesting," she said, when he had her restless and panting beneath him.

He chuckled at the deliberate taunt. "Sweetheart, it's only going to get better."

There were sly, unexpected kisses in spots she'd had no idea were so sensitive. He made love to her body in a hundred different ways without entering her, teasing her, tormenting her until she thought she'd splinter apart. She would have begged by then, but twinkling, knowing eyes met hers as he slid deeply inside her, then withdrew in a slow, exquisite rhythm that made nothing else in the world matter except Cord's body and hers and the here and now magic between them.

When she was at the edge, when Cord hesitated above her again, he captured her gaze and held it as if to assure himself that she knew precisely who was sparking this magic. His muscles were taut with the tension of holding himself still. His expression was fierce.

"I...love...you," he whispered as he plunged deeply into her one last time, sending them both into spasms of ecstasy.

She felt it all then, not just the sensations of wickedly satisfying sex, but the love. His and, heaven help her, her own. Fresh tears tracked down her cheeks as she touched a finger to his lips, gasped as he drew it into his mouth and sucked gently.

She swallowed hard against a tide of emotions threatening to overwhelm her. "I love you," she confessed in a whisper.

Cord looked as if the words had shattered him. "Again," he pleaded. "Say it again."

"I love you." The words came out stronger the second time.

"Ah, darlin'," he said with a sigh, as he folded his arms around her and held her close. "Now we truly are indomitable."

If Cord thought their idyllic time-out had solved all their problems, he was wrong. Back in Texas, back in the real world, doubts came back, along with renewed fears that they would lose their baby girl. With every day that passed, he could see Sharon Lynn slipping back into old ways, holding him at a distance as if she were once more protecting her heart. When they should have been closest, they were further apart than ever. He'd about run out of ways to change that.

Finally one night when he touched her, only to have her ease away from him, he lost patience.

"Do you want me to go now and get it over with?" he demanded quietly.

Sharon Lynn stared at him in shock. "Go? Why?"

"You're already acting as if I'm not even here. If anything, it's worse than before we went away, because now I know how it can be between us."

She winced at that. "If you want me to sleep with you, I will," she said, but the words sounded stoic, not eager or loving.

"No, dammit, that's not what I want. Sharon Lynn, you're putting your life on hold, our lives on hold, while we wait for the court to decide about Ashley. You have to separate that from the two of us and whether we stay together. I thought we'd worked that out, but apparently we haven't."

"What are you saying?"

"I want a real marriage. Not just for the baby, for us. We're good together and I don't want to lose that. If, God forbid, we lose in court, I don't want that to mean the end of our marriage, too."

She trembled and, for an instant, he felt like a creep for pushing her, but this mattered too much to let it go.

"Decide, darlin'. Once and for all, decide if you're ready to let me in—not just into your bed, but into your heart."

Her lips quivered, but she didn't look away. "I thought you knew," she whispered. "I was sure the trip had proved it. I thought you knew you were already in my heart."

All of Cord's fears, all of his doubts, fled at that softly spoken declaration. It underscored everything she'd said, everything he knew. She hadn't been trying to pretend it wasn't so. She'd just been scared. He could see that now, with her eyes wide at his threat to leave.

"Don't leave me. Don't ever leave me," she begged.

A grin spread across his face at last. "No, darlin', I never will. You can take that promise to the bank."

They made love that night and every night after. In the mornings, too, when Cord could linger in bed. Before long they had a baby of their own on the way. They found out the same day the judge told them that their petition for adoption had been granted, that Hazel Murdock no longer intended to fight them for custody.

As they lingered in the courtroom after the ruling, surrounded by family, Sharon Lynn turned to Cord, saw only him. A smile hovered on her lips.

She reached out to place her palm against his cheek. He was real and he was hers. Forever.

Then the baby in her arms whimpered as if to stake her own right to Sharon Lynn's attention…and her love.

"Oh, my darling," she whispered, gazing down into that beautiful little face. "How does it feel to be Ashley Branson at last?"

"Pretty darned good, I'd wager," her grandfather said.

"Why don't you let me take her for a minute, while you and Cord have a chance to catch your breath?"

Sharon Lynn relinquished the baby and turned to her husband. Cord's expression was serious, far more serious than the occasion called for.

"So," he began quietly, "how does it feel to be a mama for real?"

"Wonderful," she said honestly. "Exhilarating."

"And Mrs. Cord Branson? You still happy about that, too?"

She leaned forward and gave him a kiss that could leave no doubts at all about how she felt about that. "I think I've been waiting for you all my life," she told him honestly. "Even when I didn't trust myself, even when I was scared out of my wits, you never wavered. You just swept me off my feet."

"I intend to keep right on doing that for the rest of our lives," he warned. "Think you're up to it?"

She grinned at him. "I can hardly wait."

Finally, she thought later, as the family gathered to celebrate the day's happy news—not just the adoption, but the baby they were expecting—Cord would have the family he'd always dreamed of and she, well, she would have the only thing in life that mattered, the one thing she'd feared never having again…a heart filled with love.

* * * * *

Read West Texas Nights,
an Adams Dynasty anthology
by #1 New York Times *bestselling author Sherryl Woods.*
Coming soon from MIRA books!